Where Waters Converge

(the second *Song of the Jayhawk*)

Jack Marshall Maness

Wooden Stake Press
Denver, CO

www.woodenstakepress.com
www.jackmarshallmaness.com

ISBN-10: 1-940936-10-1
ISBN-13: 978-1-940936-10-9

Cover Design: Lindsey Runyan
www.coroflot.com/lindseyrunyan

"Behold the monster with the pointed tail,
Who cleaves the hills, and breaketh walls and weapons,
Behold him who infecteth all the world."

-**Inferno**, Canto XVII

Introduction

Things changed quickly in Territorial Kansas. In fact, the 1850s were a dynamic decade in all of the United States and her territories. Bookended by two wars, emotionally charged by social issues related to race, gender, and religion; and punctuated by associated policy concerns, westward expansion and an increasingly international economy, it was a fascinating, exciting, and anxious time to live. Not unlike today, certainly. Wonderful, but also scary and utterly uncertain on nearly every level of life.

Kansans were somewhat at the epicenter of all of this. In the first *Song of the Jayhawk*, the years immediately following the creation of the territory, issues stemming from slavery and violence were pronounced. But something changed after the bloody summer of 1856. A new president was elected, and Washington had had enough. The federal government intervened far more seriously in the West, particularly in Kansas and Utah. In the two or three years that followed 1856, the timeframe of this *Second Song*, parties in these regions began to realize that armed struggle was not necessarily in their best interest at the moment. They began to focus more on controlling not so much the actual "battlefield," such as it was, but the message. And, of special note, the money.

As fall became winter and 1856 became 1857, the U.S. economy began to slump, and later in the year a drastic situation arose that would be termed the "Panic of 1857." A complicated confluence of investment, credit, speculation, and the influence of European markets took hold, and it all had effects throughout the West, including Kansas. Land, commodity, and stock values fell at the same time government lands were auctioned. Exacerbated by the fact that many farms hadn't faired so well due to the bloodshed of the previous growing season, this sometimes meant ordinary families like the Dugans and Hawkinses didn't have enough cash to pre-empt their claims. It was a perfect storm for household finances.

In Atchison, and throughout Kansas, sworn enemies of the previous year became business partners. They sold and bought newspapers and town lots, bank shares and railroad stock, all to keep their interests in the West afloat. This complicated all sorts of social relationships, while a series of political maneuverings unfolded both in Kansas and between Kansas and Washington. In fact, one might see 1857 as a dramatic turn in the city of Atchison: once a Pro Slavery stronghold, it quickly morphed into something else, perhaps most apparent in a truly bizarre moment when control of the new municipal government was decided between the factions by the toss of a coin.

What all this meant for the ordinary farming families that are the protagonists of this trilogy: They faced, yet again, ruination.

None of this is to suggest by any means that money is somehow the penultimate issue. To do so borders dangerously on apologist histories of the Civil War era that seek to distance us from the human cost of slavery, genocide, and repression. Money was certainly of great significance during this period, but it was only one of many drivers affecting human behavior at the time. To some extent we are complicated creatures, existing in any given moment at the intersection of a thousand concerns, those of ourselves, our loved ones, our communities, faiths and ideals. We only pretend we are mono-dimensional, painting faces as we want them to be seen, but behind them often lay depthless strata of being and identity.

All cultures tell timeless stories of conglomerate monsters, their bodies unnaturally yet somehow cohesively made from the parts of different animals and humans. These myths coax out the wondrous metamorphic nature of life on earth, but also remind us how terrifying impermanence really is. We are forever dying and reemerging, reinventing and morphing. Generations past and present and future tumble and boil in this crucible, unsure if we stand at the precipice of transcendence, or the apocalypse.

But when we let go, we somehow find a deeper, ineffable singularity, a path back to one another.

Jack Marshall Maness
Denver, CO, January, 2016.

For my aunts

Where Waters Converge

I

Something told Maria that he would come back for her, but she didn't know if she should listen to it. Joseph James Hawkins had a monster inside of him, and she'd seen it emerge more than once. True, she could feel in the way he'd tied her to the chair that he'd loosened the rope so she could eventually free herself; feel in the way he held her that he loved her more than hated her. But rage often got the better of this man, and there was no reason to believe he would return to her. No reason at all.

And yet, something inside was quite insistent. Like a weed with roots deep and under, around and over, it clung to itself and everything around it and refused to be removed. It told her that he'd survived, that Paddy and Roger had too. It told her that it was time for her to find her husband and her brother in-law, but that he, Joseph, would find her. He was in pain, a pain born not only of the fight, but of the guilt and remorse that arises from the fight. He would come to atone, to let the snow fall upon the fire of his rage. He would come because what he had done to her was wrong, and because he was a good man. She knew this was so.

She sat still at her table, a damp smell and cacophony of insects encroaching into her cabin, heralding a waning year. She sat, listening to the footsteps outside, telling herself it couldn't be so. This man had left her for dead. This man had threatened her family. This man had a dragon inside of him that wouldn't let go. He was evil. But then she rose, picked up the shovel she used to keep the snakes way, and hid behind the door. It was as if generations of Kennys and Farrells were acting for her, controlling her every step. This voice could not be ignored. He was coming. This voice told her so. It didn't even matter if she listened to the voice. It was acting for her now.

When he walked through the door, it told her to hit him in the head with the shovel as hard as she could. And then it told her that the blood of 1856 was washing away with the autumn rains, and that waters must always merge.

***

Joseph James Hawkins knew what he had done was wrong, but decided now was not the time to be realizing it. Maria could still be tied to the chair when he arrived. Withered gardens and a cabin ransacked by raccoons, the body of a woman (one of the best who ever lived) preyed upon by insects and animals—it would be the fitting finale to a bloody summer. And he would probably have to kill himself.

But now, crouched in the brush on a sweltering late-September morning, he could see the Dugan cabin door was closed, the garden watered. Someone had been there and tended to things. It could only mean the Dugan brothers were back, returned from the warfare of summer, and had found their wife and sister dead, tied to a chair and left to starve and rot like an animal. Their next act would surely be to find him and take revenge. A wave of panic rippled through him as he realized his family was back home, unprotected.

It was just like him, he thought. Here they'd finally done well for themselves, moving over the river from Missouri and staking their claim, and he'd gone and gotten them in a terrible mess. Poor Oliver John. Joseph James had gotten poor Oliver John killed in some silly war about niggers. And what did he have to show for it? Nothing. Not a damn thing. Not a goddamn thing. Delilah would never see the brother in-law she'd raised as a son, ever again. George and Sally, as terrible as they were as parents, would never see their son again. And Melissa. Poor little Missy. She'd never know her uncle, the shining little light in the darkest of western cabin nights. Dead. Laying in the corner of the room on a pallet for a bed with a blanket over his face and his feathered hat on his crossed hands. The sweetest little boy you never did see, dead or alive.

Perhaps, he thought of himself, they would all be better off without him. It felt as if all the tonnage of the Missouri River had lifted out of its channel, snaked across the grass, and lay solely on him. He slumped against the trunk of an old oak, and imagined turning the rifle around and sticking the barrel in his mouth. He'd have to take his boots off and pull the trigger with his toe. He'd probably miss, blow his jaw out his skull, and take forever to die. That would be just like him. And then Missy wouldn't have a father, not to mention the other baby that was on its way.

Maria Dugan deserved it, goddamnit. Not only had her husband shot him clean through the shoulder, her brother Roger almost shot his brother Oliver John two summers ago in a hunting "accident." And if that weren't enough to make all the Dugan clan his enemies, Maria herself had helped sneak General James Henry Lane into the territory in the summer, and that had started the whole mess in the first place. Hell, if it weren't for Maria, maybe Oliver John would still be alive. Slamming his rifle in the soft soil of the prairie, he stood.

But then again, if it weren't for the Dugans, Oliver John surely would have died under the tree that fell on him during that storm, nearly two years ago now. If the Irish brothers didn't show up with that Mormon friend of theirs—Clegg and his son Little Joe—and Maria didn't find a way to keep him warm and stop the bleeding that night, he really may have died on the ride either to Atchison, or worse yet, back to Missouri and the old life. The poor life. The life of being a white slave. The Dugans had both saved and taken Joseph James's brother's life from him. They were both friend and enemy.

What a strange and cruel life this is, he thought as he swatted a mosquito on his nose. His shoulder hurt like hell, but he now realized that his soul hurt worse, and what he had done was wrong. It just wasn't the time to realize it. Now was no time for thinking about right and wrong. It was a time to be thinking about living instead of dying. Kansas was still bleeding.

He walked briskly in a crouch across the clearing to the front of the cabin, waving his rifle carefully. At the door, he listened. He sniffed. Nothing. With the stealth of a man who had survived many months of his life solely on what he could hunt and trap, he stepped inside. The cabin was completely orderly, not ransacked as it had been when he left it. No corpse in the kitchen chair, no blood on the floor—the chair was even pushed into the table. The brothers must have returned from the battle, buried Maria, and were in town somewhere. Yes, that was it. The part of Joseph James that felt the Dugans deserved it told him he should burn the cabin down. But the part that had become louder since Oliver John's death, the part that was now a shrill call, like a jay or a hawk or a flock of starlings; the part that told him what he had done was wrong, told him that perhaps he should kneel and pray for forgiveness.

"Stop!" cried a familiar voice from behind him. It sounded like his long-dead grandmother's voice.

Something suddenly pushed his head from behind. At first it felt cold and soft, but then he realized it had hit him, hard. He could feel the blood trickling down behind his ear. Turning, he felt the same on his hand and wrist, and dropped his gun. It would be one of the brothers, surely, the butt of their rifle bloodied. Hopefully they would finish him off quickly and take mercy on Del and Missy.

But she stood in the doorway with the shovel she used to kill snakes. The autumn light streaming in through the door framed her silhouette, her flowing shawl around her head, the red of her hair draped over each shoulder like a tunic, her gown hemmed around her bare feet. It was Maria. She dropped the shovel and both hands to her sides, her palms upturned in the glow of the east, a contemplative smile wisped across her understated chin. A warmth filled Joseph James Hawkins, a warmth he had not expected.

Kansas did things to a man, he thought as he fell to his knees.

And to a woman, for that matter.

***

Earlier that morning, Delilah J. Hawkins woke alone. It was the first time her husband had left the bed since returning from the war, carrying Oliver John's dead bloody mangled body through the front door like the carcass of a deer. She knew her husband was okay. She knew things. Feeling the sheets where he'd laid all these days she knew he'd been gone a while, as they were cold. Now, finally, she would wash them. They were filthy.

Before the baby and the in-laws woke she had the sheets soaking in the wash basin outside, set in the sun to warm the water, hopefully enough to get the blood stains out. She had breakfast ready to cook and the fire ready to cook it. Someday, she thought as she pulled coals out of the flames to the rocks she used to stabilize the pots and pans, I will have a stove in the house. A stove like Maria's, a right and proper stove that doesn't choke me, burn and stain and suck all the water out of my skin. Someday. This is Kansas. A new land. We are land-owners. Anything is possible.

Maria. That is where he went. Yes, that's it. His conscience finally got the better of him, as it always does, and he went to check on her. Del smiled and she rubbed the soot off her palms on her apron and went inside for the eggs and batter. At least Jimmy always made right. At least he knew when he'd done something wrong. It was all you could ask, really. As long as he was safe and didn't get shot by Roger and Patrick, it was the right thing to do.

Her mother in-law, Sarah Sally, was awake with the baby when she returned to the cabin. This no longer surprised her. So much changed that night Oliver John died, even his mother. She had always been such a miserable old woman, but no longer.

"Yer a good baby, Missy," she was saying as Del opened the door. "I'd a-milk ya myself if I could. Never was much good at it, though." She handed the baby to its mother.

"Nurse, mom," said Del. It was the first time she had ever called Sarah Sally her mother. They both paused. Del smiled and sat, donning the shawl she used to hide her breast as she fed Missy. "You milk a cow. You nurse a child."

Sarah Sally laughed, then looked sad. "I never was much for that sorta thing, Del. You know that. But I'm a-learnin'. A merciful God has seen to that." She put her thumbs in the loops in her dress and bit her lip. "Here, let's get rid-a that old man so you can have some privacy." She walked across the room to the pallet where her ex-husband (if you could call him that) George Sherman Hawkins was sleeping and kicked him, swiftly, in the back. "Get up you filthy old disgusting goat. Make yerself useful."

***

Joseph James woke and heard his name. His body hurt all over and he felt his scratchy, unshaven face with his hand. It didn't respond the way it should, and he became aware it was the source of most of the pain in his body.

"Good evening, neighbor!" It was Maria. She was cheerful.

"Maria?" he asked painfully.

"Who else?"

"I thought you were dead . . . I thought..."

"That you'd killed me?" She chuckled, handing him some water. "You should only be so lucky, Joseph James Hawkins." Her tone turned serious, almost angry, and she repeated. "You should only be so lucky."

"You broke my arm."

"And you killed my child."

"You—you were...?"

"Yes, I was."

Joseph James turned his head and looked out the window. The trees were impossibly grey, sunken over as if bowing their heads in grief. "I didn't want to kill anyone." His voice was softer and more childish than it had ever been.

"What!? Men are so stupid." Her voice was the opposite of his—strong and almost lightheartedly triumphant. "And yes, I did break your arm. You're lucky I didn't crack your skull. You'll be even a little stupider now, but you'll mend just fine (heaven help us). I also bandaged your head and wrapped your arm as best I could. It's not set though. You shall have to find someone else to do that. I'll be damned if I fix that arm."

He turned back toward her and was aware of how pathetic and glossy his eyes were. "But . . . how did you escape from the chair?"

"A friend." She turned to leave the room. "Let me just say a friend released me."

"Lane?"

Maria laughed and leaned against the door-jam. "Men are so stupid. Especially Kansas men. Do you really think the general of all Free State forces, in the middle of a war, would have time to do that?"

"You helped him," Joseph James stated in a quizzical melody. When she didn't respond immediately, but held his gaze, he said, "And . . . you're, well, you're Maria."

Studying his gaze a moment longer, as if she understood what he meant, she winced as if she couldn't accept it. "Mother of God, men are so stupid! Don't you see, Joseph, that is how it always is? Women help men, and men take that help and make an utter mess of everything." She crossed her arms on her belly. She still looked pregnant. "Eve may have been the first person to make a mess of things, but the sons of Adam are the ones who have kept it going all these years."

"Then who? "

"A friend, Joseph. A friend who emerged from the woods."

"And where are Paddy and Roger?"

"Why don't you tell me?"

He tried to sit up, but groaned in pain and fell back on the pillow. The same pillow Oliver John had used when recovering from the tree fall. "Ya mean ya don't know? I don't. Patrick did this." He pointed to his still-bandaged shoulder. "He shot me. At Hickory Point."

Maria smiled. Not the contemplative, lip smile, but a full-toothed grin. "And I broke your other arm."

His voice regained is buoyancy and force. "You sure as hell did!"

She stepped forward and pointed at his face. "Don't you *dare* be angry with *me*, Joseph."

He recoiled from her finger. "That is the last I saw of him, I swear. He shot me. I was dragged from the field." He paused. Part of him wanted to use the following to hurt Maria, the other part wanted to protect her from it. "Oliver John is dead."

She straightened her back, dropped her finger, and asked softly, "What?"

"Oliver John. He was killed." Joseph James closed his eyes and took a deep breath. "The night before the battle. A sniper."

Maria looked about, took a staggering step, slowly, tears welling up in her eyes, and picked up her shovel, stomping it into the floorboards. "Men are so stupid!"

***

What George Sherman Hawkins thought as he was jarred awake by a boot in his back was, this is my fault. This is my fault and God has seen to it that I should be reminded of it. Coming here in the middle of the harvest, of crop and of men, with my other life—my lie—hitched in tow like some kind of loot. The pillages of war, the war I wage with myself to be good, to be right, to do what I know a man should do. I really am a good man. But to these boys I am a monster. I have to make it right. If I die tomorrow, I have to die knowing I did what little I could today to make this right.

The night Jimmy carried Oliver John home, Del wailed like only a mother can. She touched him like a mother would (his hair especially), talked to him like one, and worried about him so. And what really told you she was really his mother was how she knew. Delilah J. knew Oliver John had been killed before anyone else, before the last gasp escaped his lips. Everything about that night told you so, the way she paced and lit candles and blew them out and lit them again. Poking the fire, drying the dishes, even readying the laundry for Monday though it was still only the Sabbath. Her hands must have wiped her apron fifty times. No, a hundred.

And Jimmy was his real father. It was clear, the way he laid the body down so gentle-like, the way he combed his hair and pulled the blanket over his face. Jimmy was a father in the way his body slumped in its own blood while the womenfolk tended to the hole in his shoulder—as if it didn't hurt at all, because the bullet wound was as overwhelmed by grief as a mosquito bite in a poison oak rash. Jimmy was a father in the way he comforted his wife, not saying it was okay because it could not be okay, because it was Oliver John. It had to be Oliver John. And Jimmy was a father because his eyes changed that night. Like a star beside the moon, they dimmed.

They buried him the next day. Just out in the little clearing where the old cabin foundation used to be. The proudest moment of George's life was that he had chosen the spot, finding it instinctively like a bloodhound or a dowser, and the family had approved. Rebecca, the love of his life and bane of his family's, kept a respectable distance from the burial for a while. She was a beautiful woman. Tall, a mole that made part of her lip misshapen. From Tennessee to Indian Territory she'd followed him, not her people; and to Sarah Sally and back again, she'd followed him. He knew she followed him for the same reason she kept her distance at Oliver John's services—because she knew things. Rebecca knew things the way Delilah did. At least he and Jimmy had the same taste in smart women.

Just at the right time she came forward. They'd laid the first handfuls of dirt on Oliver John and hadn't really thought much about what was next. They were all in their best clothing, except Jimmy, who had only just been able to stumble out into the pasture for the burial. He could barely stand while he was there, much less find his good jacket and neck-tie and see if they could fit him anymore. Sarah Sally chuckled as he emerged from the cabin, the others knowing why. Oliver John would probably have cried if he ever saw his brother in a tie.

The place was surrounded by cottonwood and some little blackjack oaks, not to mention the big cottonwood that had fallen on Oliver John during that October storm last year and had nearly killed him. George, learning this, had dragged it a few yards out with a horse, leaving a tear in the prairie that would soon heal. Sooner than anyone's hearts, for sure. An owl was just yonder, and as Rebecca came forward, it called out solemnly. Everyone was frozen but as she came around to Joseph James and touched him on the shoulder, they awakened.

Jimmy turned to her as if he knew the truth, responding to her touch and moving to it like an infant, as if he knew nothing else his entire life. He buried himself in Rebecca, a woman he'd never met, simply because she touched him when he most needed touching. Simply because in those two fingers, eternity. In that touch it all disappeared, all the commotion and madness and emptiness, the space between things, the nothingness.

Rebecca touched Joseph James and in an instant they were embracing, just like they should have all those years ago, as if all that time had never passed, as if every sin of neglect could be erased by two fingers being laid upon someone in a prairie.

Rebecca then went to George. They knew. She would leave and he would stay, because it was time that Joseph James knew the truth.

All that night the Hawkinses sat in their little cabin in Kansas touching one another the way Rebecca had taught them before she left. Sarah Sally started it. The matriarch, if you could call her that. She hugged Joseph so tight his hat fell off and he stumbled back, grasping her to hold himself upright. Never had they embraced this way, not even when he was a child. Especially when he was a child. Never had either known they could ballast each other and rock, rippling with pain inside, like four legs on one body. Hands were held, backs were rubbed, and hair was stroked.

Nobody slept. They thought about Oliver John and talked about him until dawn. Sarah Sally told stories about things nobody ever knew, about when he was just a little guy and Joseph and George would be out in the fields (or George was wherever) and they would be left alone. How he'd literally climb the walls, finding foot and finger holds in the planks, until she started letting him outside and he'd climb every tree he could. How he'd lay chicken and squirrel skeletons out on the floor and try to put them back together again. How he'd gather those rocks and sticks and make those big piles out on the stoop. And that only after she made him stop bringing them in the house. Along with the frogs and fish and bugs and such.

Oh, how Oliver John would gather the earth and bring it in the house.

II

Patrick Dugan woke on the morning of September 16th, 1856 to a horrible buzzing sound and a wave of panic. Maria. Roger. Joseph James had said he'd killed Maria. Roger had crawled from the field, shot in the leg. And he'd been arrested, marched to an open field and left to sleep in the open. It was all wrong—he should be with them on the farm, protecting those he loves.

But as he lifted his head the buzz became deafening and was accompanied but sharp, hot pain. Opening his eyes he saw giant wings and legs everywhere, and slowly, through the buzz, heard the laughter of men. As he sat up he also heard the crackling of what sounded like paper at his right ear, and in swiping it off his head—sticky and vibrating—finally came to the realization that he had bedded down in a nest of wasps after the march. They were all over him, and at last the pain became truly alarming. For the next minute or two all he heard was buzzing and laughter as he jumped about, swatting and whirling and spinning, spitting and cussing, thinking he deserved this, all of it. He'd been tricked into war and abandoned what really mattered. Maria.

When he finally rid himself of the wasps he stood panting. "See Irishman," one man called from the other side of the fence, "we got fairies in Missourah too!"

"This is not Missouri," said a prisoner. "This is Kansas."

The other man produced a rifle from a scabbard in his saddle. "It's gonna be the gate to hell if you say that again, you white nigger bastard. All you is white niggers, goddamn Irish and Dutch sonsabitches! I'll shoot you all!" He fired at the ground where several men were still laying down. Patrick stood, his shoulder slumped, and wanted to weep for his wife. If she were dead, he hoped this man would shoot him.

"That's enough!" called a man from horseback in uniform. "These are prisoners of the United States Army. They are not yours to trifle with. If I had my way you would all be on that side of the fence."

"Well, you ain't got your way now, do you, Cap'n?" He pulled a plug of tobacco out of his mouth and snapped it to the ground.

The soldier rode up to the man and dismounted. "Lieutenant, sir."

"Well now, I don't mean no disrespect, Lieutenant. I only mean to say that these here prisoners are the charge of Sam Jones, Sheriff of Douglas County." He cleaned the remaining tobacco out of his cheek with two fingers and rubbed them on his pants.

"You are not only disrespectful, sir, you are treacherous. And so is your sheriff." He mounted and wheeled his horse and addressed all the men in earshot, from thirty or so Free State prisoners on one side of the fence to about a dozen Pro Slavery citizens on the other. "All of you are traitors! Every last one of you! The only reason they are on that side and you are on this is because they were caught inciting civil war and you were not! You are all traitors!"

Another uniformed officer arrived on foot from behind a barn. "That is for the judge to decide, Lieutenant. Stand down."

The lieutenant dismounted again and saluted. "Yes sir, Captain, sir!"

"See to it that poor man is taken to the infirmary," he motioned to Patrick, who began to think perhaps he could escape, find Maria. "And get these men the hell out of my camp. For the time being this land is not Missouri and it is not Kansas. It belongs to the government of the United States and they are trespassing on Federal property."

"Yes sir, Captain! You heard him, get back to your homes!"

The men slowly made their way back to Lecompton and a gate was opened for Patrick. A soldier pointed to a small barn as if to indicate it was where he was being taken, and as he walked toward it he felt his face and head with his hands. It was hot and misshapen, as were his hands and arms. His entire body was vibrating and a shiver and wave of nausea went up and down his spine several times. As he looked down at his hands and saw how badly they were deformed by the stings, his eyes swelled shut and he fell to his knees.

Perhaps he would find Maria in this darkness, her hair full of light.

***

Maria arrived in Lecompton after reading in the Atchison newspaper, the *Squatter Sovereign*, that Free State prisoners from the Battle of Hickory Point had been taken there for trial. She'd tidied up the house and farm the best she could before she left. Many of the chickens were lost, as well as a pig. And the lost opportunities in the ground were enormous. Only a few bushels of corn, a handful of tomatoes, and a lot of carrots were ready, all entangled and constricted by yards upon yards of vine weeds. It was a shame. It would be a hard winter while it could have been bountiful, and they were going to be sick of carrots pretty quickly.

Before leaving she stood at the door several minutes trying to decide whether or not to take her shovel. During her tidying she had imagined herself stomping into the executive headquarters of the territory with it and demanding her family's release. But part of her told her not to do this. That men behaving the way they had been all summer did not take kindly to bossy women. Plus, they would not be afraid of the shovel the way Patrick and Joseph were. They'd never felt its sting the way they imagined they had, having never seen her wield it against snakes or raccoons. They had no idea what she was capable of, and she didn't think it terribly wise to show them. She decided to bring the shotgun.

Oliver John's death was his brother's fault. This thought ran through her head over and over again as she hitched her horse and walked about the little settlement of Lecompton, trying to figure out where the governor's or judge's offices may be. In so many ways it was all his fault, all the way back to last fall when he threatened to kill Patrick and Roger if they didn't move their cabin. Yes, Roger had helped not at all, but somehow that damned Joseph James Hawkins seemed to keep the war going along the Independence, where the Dugan and Hawkins claims lay. They could have left it alone, down south of the Kaw, but no, he had to keep getting involved. Roger was a boy and didn't know any better. But Joseph was supposed to be a man. He was such a stupid, stupid man.

Why, then, she loved him so, Maria could not say. Even as she kicked him out of the cabin with his bloodied head and throbbing wrist, thinking how he deserved so much more pain in exchange for what he had done to her, she couldn't help but smile as she turned away from him. He was a sad, pathetic man, a sad, pathetic and sweet man; the sort of man men fear but women find adorable. A man with a vulnerability so obvious, and a sad way of hiding it from other men that it was even more obvious. And there was a rugged, western-Missouri look about him that was so strong and comforting. He wasn't of the hairy, hunched-shoulder type that other Southern men in Kansas were; he was of the Ulster Irish stock that she remembered seeing from time to time as a girl. Unkempt and unrefined, to be sure, but through and through a breed unto himself. Joseph James Hawkins was an American man, and she loved him for it.

Still, here she was in Lecompton, of all places, searching for her husband and brother in-law. They were dead or captured because of Joseph James Hawkins, and she could not forgive him for it. He was lucky she didn't kill him this morning. She couldn't, not only because she loved him, but because she loved his wife Delilah. Such a sweetheart. Such a strong woman. She deserved a husband, however stupid he may be.

Finally she found what seemed to be the most officious structure in Lecompton, a two-story wooden rectangle painted white and facing east, and walked inside. A man there told her "there ain't no governor here" and sent her back to the river, where she found a six-room log cabin that served as the governor's offices and residence. There she found a man in the dress of a soldier sitting at a desk. A nice desk, no less. Probably the finest desk between St. Louis and San Francisco. She rolled her eyes.

"Ma'am?" a young man—boy, really—seated behind a desk that made him look even younger asked as she let the door slap shut behind her. He glanced at the shotgun. "Can I help you?"

"I've come for my husband."

He looked as if he'd gone from his usual level of nervous to a heighted state.

"Ma'am?"

"Who are you, lad?"

He paused, glanced at the gun again, then repeated without a change in expression.

"Ma'am?"

"Who are you, son? What's your name?" Maria sounded to herself like her own mother now. If she ever gave birth, this is how she'd sound one day.

"Lieutenant Riggs, ma'am. Nelson Riggs." Something in the boy's nervous demeanor relaxed, and he sounded almost confident. "I am adjunctant to the new governor."

"New governor?"

"Yes, ma'am. Governor Geary. He's just arrived."

"Ah yes, Woodson was acting, thank heaven. Where is Geary from?"

"Ma'am?"

"Where is he from, son?" She could barely hold back a smile. This boy was so different than Roger.

"Uh, Kentucky, I believe. I've only been with him a few days."

"Wonderful. The President has found another Southerner. I suppose I should give up on my husband, then."

Something seemed almost prepared about the young Lieutenant's response. "The Governor is neutral in the Kansas Question, ma'am. He's disbanded all militia and stopped another sack of Lawrence the other night. He gave Senator Atchison a good ol' tongue-lashing, too, I might add." Maria smiled, and Riggs's reverted again to more of a boy than a soldier. He began to impersonate the governor. "And you, Senator, one time Vice President of the United States, have fallen so low so as to lead an undisciplined mob against a body of American citizens…"

"Ha! But has he arrested them? As he arrested my brother and husband?" She wasn't smiling any longer. "No, the Southerners go free while Free Staters are tried and executed."

Riggs sat back down. "Ma'am?"

Just then a man appeared from a door to the lieutenant's left. He was tall with an impressive, dark beard, well-dressed, and it was very clear who he was though he appeared only slightly older than his lieutenant.

"Acting Governor Woodson had ordered that militia mustered, ma'am." His voice was deeper than his frame indicated it might be. "My hands were tied. And you, Lieutenant—"

"Yes, sir." Riggs quickly stood, knocking back his chair.

"You should be more careful in mocking a man who once presided over the United States Senate."

"Yes, Governor, but—"

"Just mind your work, son."

"Yes, sir."

"Would you like to join me in my office, Ms.—?"

"Dugan. Mrs. Patrick Dugan. And you have wrongly imprisoned my husband and brother. At least, that is what I pray have become of them."

He opened the door to his office, behind Riggs's desk. "Please, do come inside, though I shall have to ask you leave your bird gun by the door. Lieutenant, fetch our guest some coffee."

"Yes, sir."

"And Lieutenant?" The boy wheeled around, already on his way to the small stove in the corner of the building, and took Maria's gun. "Have a cup yourself if you wish."

"Yes, sir!"

Maria and Geary took their seats in the governor's austere office. Just down the street the large building, housing the legislature and land office, was being completed under the direction of Sheriff Sam Jones, but Geary had decided not to establish the executive office there. And down another street the foundation of a stone building had been laid, intended to support the future capitol building. Geary seemed to prefer this cabin.

"Please, Mrs. Dugan—" He indicated she should explain her accusation.

"You may call me Maria, Governor. Though I must say you seem quite young for such a position." Her expression made her look a foot taller, almost tall enough to fill out the chair in which she sat.

"Ha! Yes." His white teeth shone in his dark beard when he smiled. "I am the youngest governor in the history of Kansas Territory, in fact."

Maria smiled. "Yes, indeed you are. And your tenure here may have outlasted theirs' already." She sat forward. "Perhaps you shall grow old in Kansas, Governor."

"Indeed, it is a challenging office, one I intend to execute fairly, Maria." Governor Geary's smile faded. "I must tell you that I am keenly aware of the situation of the prisoners."

"I am not."

"I see." Riggs entered with the coffee and left, closing the door behind him. "Well, they are being held out of doors just outside town, in conditions that I do not find . . . terribly suitable." He sipped his coffee.

Maria sat hers on his desk. "When will they be released?"

"It is not that simple." Shaking his head, he crossed his legs and pushed his chair back from the desk. "Surely you must understand that."

"Why not? You are the governor, appointed by the President. Order their release." She felt like standing but decided she shouldn't. "They are imprisoned unjustly by men unjustly appointed by other men who were elected fraudulently." She looked out the window. Sometimes it seemed odd that this little corner of the world should so hold the attention of so many. "The entire nation knows that."

Geary appeared to truly consider this point. "That may be true, but the courts are another issue entirely."

"Do you mean Judge Lecompte, Governor?" She could hardly keep from standing and thought of her shovel. "The man who provides arrest warrants to invaders so they may arrest legitimate citizens of his district who wish only to exercise their Constitutional rights?"

"Well, that may also be true, but I must proceed cautiously in that respect. Judge Lecompte has ordered the prisoners held without bail."

"By whom?"

"By Sheriff Jones."

She stood now. "*Jones?*"

Governor Geary smiled, put down his coffee on the rough, hand-hewn pine table, and rose. He turned to the window behind him and gazed out at the Kaw as he spoke. "Are all Kansan women this politically astute?"

She sat back down. She had him. "No, only the Irish ones."

He did not smile, though he did find it witty. Instead he turned back around and sat. "You have many good points, Maria Dugan. But your husband—assuming he is being held and that he was present at the incident in question—broke my executive order. I ordered all militias to disband, but this group was found armed. They took defensive postures against the United States Army, in fact. Hardly a lawful act." He sipped his coffee again. "Hardly something I can allow if I am to be objective in these matters."

"But you will see their Constitutional rights are upheld by the sheriff, I am sure."

The governor smiled again. "Yes. In fact, I shall visit them to ensure that is the case." He paused for dramatic effect. He wanted the following to be received as generosity. "And take you with me."

"Very good then." Maria stood, ready to leave.

Geary smiled broader now than he had thus far in the conversation. In fact, Geary smiled broader now, and more sincerely, than he had in quite some time. "My, it's good to be back in the West," he said.

***

Patrick woke in the barn that served as the Army's infirmary near Lecompton and heard his name.

"Good evening, brother!" It was Roger. He was cheerful.

"Roger?" Relief flooded him.

"That's right," he laughed. "I am glad to see your ears are not as swollen shut as your eyes."

Patrick tried to open his eyes and discovered he could not. He reached up and felt his face with his hands, his hands with his face, and remembered the hornets. "Sweet Mother of Heaven."

"Yes," Roger chuckled. "You should see it from the outside."

"I think I would rather not, so." Patrick's voice quivered along with his skin.

"You always were more wise and cautious." Roger's tone turned into a concerned one. "Are you well? Does it hurt?"

"Of course it hurts. But I'm sure I am better off than you," he said, remembering the last time he had seen Roger he was dragging a limp leg through the dirt in a trail of blood, then put on a cart on its way to Lawrence. "How is your leg?"

"Better. No damage to the bone. I should be walking soon."

"Where are we?"

"Lecompton, brother. The Pro Slavery capital of Kansas. The hornet's nest!"

"Yes, but where?"

"In a barn they call a hospital. We are alone just now but there are several more beds. I suppose they are expecting more wounded, though I don't see why. The fight is over. For now, anyway."

"Why is that?" Patrick could imagine his brother's expressions as he spoke. He knew that now he was animated, wide-eyed and fidgety. He didn't know about Maria.

"Here, have some water, if you can." Roger grabbed Patrick's hand over the space between the beds and helped it find the water he offered. "The new governor ordered the military in Leavenworth to disarm all militias. Of course, they've only disarmed Free Staters."

"Is that why we are here? I thought you had been taken to Lawrence."

"Yes, brother. That is why we are here. I was intercepted late in the night and arrested. You were too. There are about a hundred of us, all told. We are to stand trial for murder and treason."

"Right, so." Patrick stretched the cup of water back across to Roger and he lay back down on the pillow-less bed. "We deserve it, I suppose."

Roger smirked and rolled his eyes at his brother, knowing he could not see it. "Yes, don't we all." Somehow he felt Patrick could feel the glare anyway.

"I deserve it anyway, so." There was a pause. Patrick's throat clenched but he realized he could not shed tears through all the folds of flesh around his eyes. "I killed Joseph, Roger."

"'Twas no sin, brother."

"Yes, it was. Think of Del."

"I would rather not. She is a good woman."

"Exactly. And Oliver John is dead."

"Del is alone."

"Yes."

There was another pause, a longer one. Both Dugan brothers remembered lying next to each other in bed as young boys, talking late into the night until their parents scolded them. "Paddy, if you hadn't killed him he would have killed me. I saw it all. He was going to shoot me as I was crawling away from the blacksmith shop."

Patrick sighed. "Perhaps he would not have."

Roger raised his voice. "Don't be a fool."

"Or, perhaps I should have simply restrained him."

"Paddy—"

"Or shot him in the leg."

"Paddy, you stupid langer!" Roger took a deep breath, sat up on an elbow, and leaned over toward his older brother. Patrick could hear that he was doing and turned his face toward Roger. "Listen," he chuckled upon seeing his brother's grotesque head, "you can't do this to yourself, brother. You decided to fight because it was a just fight. Remember? Pappa is coming, Paddy. Pappa is coming."

"God help us."

"No, God help those who oppose us."

"Roger, I am too old to try and impress my father in such a way."

"He would be proud of you anyway Patrick Dugan!"

"I don't care."

"Yes you do."

"Not as much as you do."

"Perhaps not, so. But you've done nothing wrong, Paddy. Be strong."

"I have, Roger, I have. I've taken the life of another. I've killed a man I know, a man with a wife and child."

"A man who threatened you and your family, Paddy! Have some backbone, man!"

There was another pause in which Patrick wondered if he should say the following, but realized he had no real choice. "He said he killed Maria, Roger."

"What!?"

"He told me he killed Maria before Osawatomie." He paused, found it impossible to swallow, and coughed. "I should have stayed with her. Never." Suddenly he shouted. "Never!" and lowered his voice again, "left her alone."

Roger lay back down on the bed. The word "No" escaped from him, more of a breath than a word, and he swallowed. Something told him it wasn't true. "I don't believe it."

A wave of something—relief and panic, dread and excitement—went through Patrick. His body felt electric, full of pain and regret and hope and venom. "I don't either," said he. Almost as if it was said for him.

"But we can't be sure."

"No." Patrick started to cry. The tears pooled in his eyelids. He had to sit up, face the bed, and open the folds of swollen flesh to let them drain out. "I can't cry like this, brother." He tried to dry inside the swells with his fingers. "I'll drown myself."

"Don't worry, brother. She'll find a way. Maria will find us."

III

What Sarah Sally Hawkins would have thought, just a few weeks ago, was that it was just like the boy. First he comes home with his little brother's dead body in his arms and now he's coming home with his hand dangling from his arm and his head stained in dry blood. How a man can go and somehow get his arm broke and head knocked just hours after burying his little brother, and breaking his wife's and mother's hearts all at the same time, was beyond her. Why can't these Hawkins men just stay home and tend to their families, Sarah Sally would never know. Something's just not right with them.

But what Sarah Sally really thought as her son came in bloody and broken was, this is all my fault. It is my fault that my youngest is dead and oldest is shattered. God has seen to it that I should be punished for my infidelity. All these years I saw Jimmy as a little George, and both my sons as just more Hawkinses, but they are not. They are—were—men unto themselves. And damn good ones at that. Jimmy raised his little brother like the best of men could. He served his country bravely, protected his home like a lion, and treated Del like a queen, which she deserved. And Oliver John was never anything but the perfect little child. But I treated them like they were their father. Such disloyalty and dishonor is always punished.

She couldn't even watch. George Sherman had to pin Joseph James down at the elbow while his own wife pulled his hand out and let it snap back into place with a nauseating sucking and cracking sound. George had to hold his son's head back, rag between his teeth, while Del wrapped the arm from wrist to elbow. Sarah Sally tried to busy little Missy as best she could in the corner, but Missy wasn't as easily entertained as Oliver John always was. A mere stick or rock wouldn't do it with her. She needed lots of eye-contact, attention, and words directed at her. That was hard to do when the girl's father was moaning (trying not to wail) in pain at the table.

Yes, this is all my fault, thought Sarah Sally. I tried to be a good mother all these years, I really did. But it just never took, sort of the way a river otter don't take well to land. Sort of the way a mama cat will shun her runt, or maybe a sow a runt piglet. But more like the otter, she thought. Not so much that I rejected my son. More like I just couldn't take to life as his mother. A mother. Something just didn't sit well about it.

As Jimmy sweated and panted and Del went outside, Sarah Sally sat down in her chair and tried to breathe deeply and not vomit. It wasn't even that she didn't take to mothering. It was that she never took to anything. Anything at all. From the earliest days of her girlhood she felt she was misplaced, some kind of alien, even unto herself. A vague memory of her childhood came to her now and she closed her eyes, turning the memory over and around in her mind like a morsel of food in her mouth. It was something about a plant with a brightly colored flower, and she had dug it up out of a nearby field, potted it, and was trying to keep it alive inside her home. But it wouldn't take. "Won't take," she heard a voice say from somewhere inside the memory like a layer of texture in the morsel, and opened her eyes.

It was her mother. That was all she knew. Her mother's voice, something she had no memory of ever hearing. "Won't take," she heard again, as if the old woman were sitting right next to her in the Kansan cabin. Sarah Sally opened her eyes and began to cry. "Won't take," she said aloud.

George Sherman left his son's side and came over to her. "Yes it will," said he.

***

When it was over Delilah J. Hawkins went quietly outside into the autumn night and vomited in the dying garden.

She wandered out to the well and sat under the stars. The moon was only a couple days past full, and hung above the trees to the east in an eerie, yellow cloud. Delilah drank of the clear water from the well and sat back against a rock. The water in Kansas was better than it was in Missouri. Growing up she'd become accustomed to a silty, flat taste, and didn't know that just across the river the wells would have such a clean taste. She took another mouthful, swished it in her mouth, spat, and drank some more. Behind her she could hear the front door to the cabin open and close. Missy wasn't crying anymore. They'd taken care of her. And they were just checking in on Del, leaving her be. How rare. How wonderful. Not only a moment to herself, but a wholly sanctioned one.

There seemed to be a blackness, a depthlessness, to the night sky that she hadn't seen in many years. The stars were crisp despite the encroaching light of the moon, and between them was a depth of nothingness. Oliver John was in there, she thought, and began to cry. Maybe he was in the stars, too, and the moon and the sun, but he was definitely in that endless abyss. Del thought of her parents, and her aunt, who were there too. She asked them to bless Oliver John. Sitting up, she could see his fresh grave. Lying back down again, she breathed deeply. Oh, Oliver John, of course it was you. It had to be you.

It was so incredibly still, Del thought she could hear the river. It was too far away to be heard, though. It sounded like a breeze in the trees, too, but there was none. She could hear the land, she thought. The growing and decaying of the plants, the breathing of the mammals, the digging of the reptiles and amphibians as they settled in for the coming winter, the shuffling of the insects in the soil and the trees and the water. And then, footsteps.

A man was approaching from the north. He had on the garb of a generation or two past, the raccoon hat, leggings and moccasins of a trapper. He was coming straight for her, decisively but without threat or malice. He emerged from the land as if he hadn't come through it but out of it. He was armed but not against men. Not against anything, from the way he carried his rifle. It was for himself and his family. His gun was a tool, not a weapon.

"You look mighty comfortable a-sittin' there like that, miss!"

"I am, thank you. I should be; this here is my property."

"Oh I know that, ma'am. Mind if I sit? The name's Paschal. Paschal Pensoneau. On my way to my cabin out on the

Grasshopper and a-thought I'd stop in and say hello to a neighbor."

"I'm Delilah Hawkins. You can call me Del."

"Comfortable but concerned, Del?"

"Why, yessir. That's just about right, I figger."

"Well, something in them muscles can teach your brain somethin' if you let it learn. These here are tryin' times, ain't they?"

Del sat up and looked at him. He had sat down next to her on rock as if he had sat there before, and knew exactly which crevasses would hold his hips and elbows and small of his back. "Who are you? Are you a ghost, Mr. Paschal?"

The old Frenchman laughed. "Not yet, missy, not yet. In a manner of speaking, anyway."

Del narrowed her eyes. Paschal smiled back and lit his pipe, waiting. "It's alright, Mr. Pascal. You don't have to play yer games with me. I know what you are."

"Do you now?"

"Yessir." She paused. "And I remember you, too." She held her hand out, asking for the pipe, which he gave to her.

"My, now that is unexpected."

"I don't think so. You came to visit me as a little girl, didn't you?"

"Well, you either remember or you don't. Ain't for me to say."

"I told you you don't have to play yer games with me." She gave the pipe back. "I remember it. I remember you and grandma talkin' to me in the old house back in Cass County."

"Your grandmother was a good woman."

"Yes, she certainly was. Is."

"I suppose she still is, yes. I reckon so, anyway."

The two sat silently in the moonlight as it grew in the trees around them. Del had herself another cup of water. Then she asked, "Is he alright, Mr. Pascal?"

"Who?"

"I said, don't play yer games with me."

"I don't know the answer to that question, Del. You should know that."

"He was so young."

"Yes."

They sat silently another moment and shared the pipe. "Tell me this, then. What was my husband doing over there today? How did he get his arm broke?"

Pascal drew deeply from the pipe and tapped it out on the rock. "He almost killed her, Del. And her husband almost killed yours."

"Stupid men."

"Yes. Indeed. I suppose they know they are stupid, you might say, sometimes anyway. That is why he was there. He's smart enough to know he is stupid. And be careful, Del—you may need the stupidity of a man one day."

"Hell."

"Yes, indeed! Hell!"

"Did she lose her baby?"

Paschal thought a moment, chewing on the stem of his pipe. "I don't think so."

"Me neither. But she's worried she did."

"Yes."

The stars wheeled around in their time and Del fell asleep. When she woke, he was gone, and found her mother in-law had draped a quilt over her in the quiet of the night.

***

By the time Maria arrived Patrick's face had almost returned to normal and Roger was walking with a cane, of sorts—it was really just the straightest branch that could be found outside the barn. Both were going to be released from the infirmary later that day and returned to the open-air prison. It was mid-October now, and the men outside had been rotating through sharing the tents that accommodated only one quarter of them for two weeks. They were tired, hungry, and cold. Maria could not see her husband or brother among them, and didn't know whether she should be happy or scared.

"I don't see them," she told the guard who had been told to help her. "I don't see them!"

"Maybe they escaped. We lost a bunch on the march down and God knows they a-keep tryin' ta 'scape."

"They would have come home then."

"Well, ma'am—"

Another man's approach interrupted the guard. He walked quickly and arrogantly but had an odd swivel to his gait that betrayed some past injury to his back. "Who is this woman? What is she doing here?"

"The governor sent her, Sheriff. I'm a-s'posed to help her find her kin among the prisoners."

"If your kin is among them you are an enemy of the state, Ms—"

"Dugan. Mrs. Patrick Dugan, and I am here under the escort of the governor's office, Sheriff . . . Jones, is it?"

"Yes, ma'am. I'm in charge of these prisoners."

"Yes, I understand. And your treatment of them betrays your bias. Very unbecoming of an officer of the law. You should be ashamed of yourself."

"Watch yer mouth woman." He took another step closer, the swivel being very apparent in that one step. "I ain't in no mood to take lip from some Yankee whore."

"And I am not here to cause any disturbance, Sheriff, you have my word. I only want to find my husband Patrick and brother Roger. Are these the only men you have in your charge?" She motioned to them men, scattered about the prairie in repose, doing what they could to stay comfortable in the partly-cloudy, windy day.

"Mmm," Jones grunted. "I think I know where they are."

"I believe the governor would ask you to show me to them."

"Ain't allowed visitors. They're held without bail under orders from Judge Lecompte."

"Sheriff, I do believe that Governor Geary would ask you to—"

"Alright. Five minutes. Follow me." The two walked around the gated area to the barn on the other side and the sheriff waved aside the guards, who sat playing cards drinking whiskey. He grunted at them as they stood and opened the heavy barn doors. "There're two injured Irishmen in there that seem related, but then again, I never could a-tell any a-them apart. My bet's they's yours." As she crossed the threshold of light Jones grabbed her elbow in a less than friendly manner. "Five minutes." She nodded.

"What happened to your face?" she walked briskly across the hay-strewn dirt floor.

"Maria!?" they both said, sitting up as one.

The light from the October afternoon had somehow stuck to her clothes and skin, following her into the dark barn and leaving a ghostly residue behind her. The Dugan brothers squinted at her, recognizing her only from her voice until their eyes adjusted.

"Who else would come and save the likes of you two in a moment like this?" She was tearful. Patrick and Roger both lept up from their beds and went to her. They embraced. Maria felt both boys with her hands from head to toe, checking tendon and bone and skin in a rapid assessment of their conditions. "Look at the two of you silly goats. Sitting injured in a barn in the middle of nowhere America. And your leg, boy, what's the matter with it?"

"I was shot."

"You stupid, silly man." She clasped his face in her hands and smiled into his eyes. "You'll be the death of me, you boys will. And you—" she turned to Patrick, who drew back just a little. "Your face. Something's not right about it. Are you hiding something from me?"

"No!" he drew back again, took a breath, and gathered his posture back again. "Hornets, Maria, I—"

"He fell asleep on a hornet's nest. He looks fantastic compared to how he did a few days ago."

Maria stared at her husband, who sat perfectly still, waiting for her next expression. He looked as if he were glad she didn't have her shovel. She laughed.

Maria laughed. She sat and leaned back on the mattress of dry leaves and grasses, returned to sitting upright, and gathered her thoughts and mouth to reply. But then she looked at her husband. He stood in the dull light of the barn, dwarfed against its lofty rafters and soaring ceiling like an animal hiding in a cave trying to make itself as small as possible in the corner. One side of his face was still swollen enough for a loved one or loyal dog to notice, and maybe enough in the eye on that side to scare a child.

"And just what are you laughing at?"

She laughed again. And she laughed again after that. Soon Maria was laughing so hard that Roger started to laugh, not so much at his brother but the fact that Maria was laughing at him. He did look funny.

"Oh, my dear Paddy," she said. "I do love you so. Now," she patted the bed. "Tell me about it, boys."

Both started talking at the same time and as she held her hand up and started to shush them the barn door opened. It was Jones.

"Time's up, Dugans." He came to them, silhouetted against and framed by the bright triangle of light from of the askew barn door. He was a hat and boots in shadows. "Dugan," he said almost to himself, his thumbs in his pants, and stopped. "Do I know you? You know sumnthin', I don't think you know the governor at all, Mrs. Patrick Dugan. You know what I think? I think that boy there is the same Dugan I done met on the steps of the Free State Hotel. You all is dedicated Irish abolitionist Yankees. Ain't that right?"

There was a pause, each Dugan wondering which would answer this impossible question. Finally, Patrick turned to Maria.

"You know the governor?"

The barn door opened more and the triangle came across Jones. His face was dirty and strange, his posture crooked. He looked into the broadened shape of light. A voice came from it.

"I see you have found them," it said. "Good." From the light emerged Governor Geary, his beard an extension of the dark uniform in the shadows, his face almost floating above it. "You are not too injured, I hope," he said to Patrick and Roger. There was another pause. "Sheriff, these men have had medical attention, I assume?"

"It's good to finally meet you, Governor."

"And you, Mr. Jones, and you as well. Now, how are your prisoners getting along?"

"These two were to be released from the infirmary, sir. This afternoon."

"Were they now? Free to go?"

"No, sir. Free to leave the barn."

Geary smiled ironically. "And join their comrades in the field?"

"Yes, sir. Their fellow convicts."

"I see. Rather the wrong direction, wouldn't you say?"

"Sir?"

"In terms of movement of prisoners, that is. The wrong direction, don't you think? Much like a fish swimming upstream?"

"I don't follow, sir."

"I mean to say, Sheriff Jones, that moving these two out there to join those eighty men out there is rather the opposite exchange of prisoners, as it were. Do you see?"

Jones hesitated, then smiled. "Are there only eighty now? I a-wondered where the other dozen went. There's murderers on the loose, Governor. In your territory." Geary was stolid, expectant, awaiting the etiquette afforded him. "Sir."

"These prisoners, Sheriff, need shelter. I'm sure you'll see your way to finding how they may make use of this barn. Once these men are recovered, that is."

"That was my plan all along, Governor. You may be assured of that."

"Thank you, Sheriff. My office appreciates that."

"Yes, sir."

"Mrs. Dugan, take your time. A coach is waiting outside the barn once your visit is finished."

"Thank you, Governor."

Geary left and closed the barn door, narrowing the shape of light to a tiny point on the floor that showed only dust moving through the air. Everyone's eyes began adjusting to the darkened barn and they looked around at one another, pausing yet again. At length, Sheriff Samuel J. Jones spoke to Patrick and Roger.

"Don't get too cocky, now. Only thing I hate more 'n a cocky immigrant is a mouthy nigger. 'N ain't neither of em last very long round me. Not in Douglas County, Kansas anyway, not while I'm its sheriff. Law 'n order is all I ask for, and the likes a you ain't none too good for law 'n order. No sir. You're goddamn rebels as far as I know. That's all I see in front a me right bout now. Pope-lovin', nigger-lovin' Paddies. You is in my care as long as the Judge says so," said he. "Ain't nothing the governor can do about it. And this here ain't no hotel, gentlemen." He paused and spat his tobacco toward them. "You'll join your fellow convicts in the yard when she leaves," he said, turned, and left.

IV

At 11:59pm on October 13th, 1856, Patrick Dugan was lying in the mud in east-central Kansas freezing half to death. He was fourth in a line of other men lying in the mud as they slowly slithered, one-by-one, under the fence that had held them captive for nearly a month. It was drizzling, and from directly overhead the light of the full moon soaked through the iron grey clouds. Roger was third in line, and all was going according to plan up to now. A couple dozen men had escaped already, and the worn path in the mud was almost like a cattle chute for their bodies as they found their way under the fence and scuttled off into the night to find their wives, mothers, siblings and children along the slippery roads and trails of the settlers.

Everything had gone right until the man two men in front of Roger found his overcoat snagged on something under the fence. He had been bragging about the overcoat for twenty minutes as he slid along with it toward the fence and freedom. Many had told him to shut it, but he couldn't help but say how lucky and glad he was that he had chosen to take this overcoat along with him back in September as he left his little cabin and marched toward Lecompton to join Lane's Army. Little did he know he'd find Captain Harvey's brigade at Hickory Point, fight in maybe the last battle of "Bleeding Kansas," be taken prisoner, and a month later find that the best thing in the world was that rubber overcoat he'd stuffed into this satchel back when it wasn't even rainin' all that much yet. In the mud, in the rain, rubber was amazing.

But it was loud and tacky. It made an unnatural sound and it stuck to stuff. And now that it was stuck to something on the fence, and stuck this man square in the middle of the hole that stood between several dozen other men and their freedom, the men helping him found that the more they tried to free the rubber of its snag the more squeaking sounds it made, and the more squeaking sounds it made, the more they worried it would alert someone to their presence in the mud in the rain by the fence. Rubber wasn't any good. Rubber was costing them their liberty.

Patrick closed his eyes and rolled over on his back. The rain tickled his eyelids and the glow of the moon still shone when he closed his eyes. This was perfect, just perfect, he thought. It would be his luck for this man to ruin the whole plan right before he and Roger got out. Part of him wanted to stay, along with the handful of men that preferred standing trial just so they could point out the hypocrisy and absurdity of their prosecution to the public, but the other part of him decided he missed Maria too much. Roger may want to get out so he could fight another day—being held hungry and cold and exposed for two weeks had made him angrier than ever at the Pro Slavery parties—but Patrick just wanted to see his lovely little wife again. And his farm. He had to get back.

But no, this man was ruining it all. What a buffoon. What a braggart.

"You idiot!" one man hissed at him. "You've been bragging about this rubber all night and now it's gone and ruined our escape!"

"The hole isn't big enough!" he hissed back.

"Mother of God," Patrick murmured to himself, still on his back. "Will someone get that buffoon out of the hole, please?" he said in a voice that could be heard above all the whispered commotion.

"Shhhh!!!"

"Stop, stop, shutup!" another man's desperate tone rose to the top of everyone's hearing. "I hear something!"

Somewhere between the pattering of the raindrops they all thought they heard something, something like footsteps. They were indeed in the silent spaces among the raindrops, so they were scattered and oddly rhythmic, but they were human footsteps. A human dancing or prancing or something. A different sort of human.

Patrick wasn't surprised when he looked over toward the barn. Some of the sheriff's deputies had tied their horses there and among them stood a man. A man in a fur hat and boots. A man that from ten miles Patrick would recognize. It was Paschal.

A shaft of moonlight found an opening in the clouds and shone upon him. He was smiling an ornery smile right at Patrick. He raised his hand over the haunch of one of the horses. Patrick closed his eyes and sighed in frustration, knowing exactly what was going to happen.

Just as a snap of rubber rang out into the drizzle of the night Paschal slapped the butt of a horse, causing it to whinny and snort, jump about, and cause three other horses to do the same. All the men clambered over Roger and Patrick on their way away from the hole in the fence and the man now scrambling to get out from under it. His rubber coat was making more sound than ever, which agitated the horses even further, until a cacophony of ridiculousness played out in front of the Dugan brothers' eyes. Guards came streaming out into the night from the nearby house.

Roger saw that the man in the rubber overcoat was free of his snag and was just about to get free and make a run for it. He grabbed the man's ankle and slapped his legs.

"What are you doing?" shouted Patrick over the roar of the rain.

"He ruined it for us all!" Roger snorted back. "We can't' let him go!"

"Yes we can! Let him go for the love of God!"

"No!"

"Roger, don't be ridiculous!"

The man was trying to kick Roger off his legs, looked back through the fence as his head was now on the other side, and breathed wildly, "Let me go! Let me go! I'm free! The snag is gone! I'll get away! Let me go!"

"Oh, damnit! Alright! Alright!" Roger let him go and turned over on his back, crossed his fingers on his chest along with his brother, and the two let their heads sink into the mud, sighing. "Damnit!" Roger repeated.

"Yes, I know," Patrick replied. "Goddamnit."

Patrick Dugan had never said such a thing before, and Roger looked at him in shock. Then they both laughed in the rain and the mud and the misery.

***

Another month passed. Patrick realized one day that he had missed what was going to be his first Presidential election as an American citizen. When he thought about it, he realized he had actually never voted before. He had been far too intimidated to vote in any of the territorial elections held over the last two years, and wasn't even sure if he had done all the necessary paperwork. When he thought about that—that he could own land and vote, but found himself owning land so disputed he was threatened not to vote—it depressed him. The world was coming to an end. There was no doubt about it. Such irony doesn't happen every generation.

Or does it? Patrick considered that his father probably felt the same way when he was Patrick's age, maybe still did. Finally standing up to the English and trying to make himself a free man, a land owner, and his sons heirs instead of caretakers, only to find himself in exile. In exile from everything, from his entire life. Not only without land and rights, but now without family, community, language. No wonder his family would think him dead.

Really, it wasn't any different. It never was. Yes, he'd missed his first presidential election (being as he was a prisoner of the United States) but look at who won. James Buchanan. Just how he would differ from Franklin Pierce wasn't ever going to be obvious. Another northern Democrat who would at all costs appease the South; another man who was going to do his best to ignore Kansas, to avoid intervention. Yes, the new Republican Party had made a serious run with a Free Kansas at the heart of its platform. They had run against the "twin relics of barbarism," meaning slavery and polygamy, which made him think of his old friend Harry Clegg, the last Mormon out of Atchison. Patrick remembered the day Pardee Butler was sent down the river on a raft for being a Free Stater, talking with Clegg amid the chimes of hammers and nails and buzz of saws. Kansas was a battleground, the old English convert had told him, but he would one day find his Zion in it. And now Salt Lake was shaping up to be the same sort of battleground. No, no matter how far west you went, the east followed you with the sun. One day the world would run out of West.

Ah, well. It didn't matter. All that mattered was that they had finally issued wool blankets to the prisoners, and Patrick was happy for it. Judge Lecompte had tried almost two dozen of them now. A few had been convicted and sentenced to five years hard labor, but most had been acquitted. Apparently a man by the name of Charles Newhall had been killed in the blacksmith's shop by Old Sacramento, the Mexican cannon captured by Missourians in the Mexican War of the 1840s. Since Governor Geary had already arrived and just hours before issued his proclamation for all militias to disband, this was considered murder by Judge Lecompte. And, apparently, to President Pierce and President-Elect Buchanan as well. Nobody was going to do anything. It didn't seem to matter that Captain Harvey's men at Hickory Point had not received word of the governor's order, nor had the Carolinians, Missourians and Georgians they fought, who, of course, were not arrested.

Maria visited, or tried to visit, often, but the guards under Sheriff Jones would rarely allow her to see them. Patrick could often hear her voice, stern then soft, whatever she thought may sway a young man. But even her charms were often not enough without a higher authority forcing the matter, the way Geary had in September. But he was on a tour of the territory and was of little help. He had done nothing to intervene in Lecompton. Patrick would often stare out at the dull skies and plains, feeling they mirrored his soul. Waiting. Preparing for a dark, cold winter.

Many of the remaining men, including Roger, wanted to stand trial. They wanted to use the courts as a way to expose the inequities of the law. Why weren't the Pro Slavery men there arrested? They were engaged in armed combat, too. Was the military at Leavenworth biased? These men felt there were all sorts of opportunities to uncover the government's prejudice in its prosecution of the prisoners of the Battle of Hickory Point, and all the eastern papers would cover it. The legitimacy of the Free State movement, its territorial government and its constitution, would soon be un-ignorable, even by the likes of men like Pierce and Buchanan. Injustice is like a toothache. It begins as a minor inconvenience but often ends in a bloody mess. But Patrick just wanted out. He wanted to go home.

It was getting cold. Very cold. The winter of 1856-57 was going to be colder even than the previous winter, which was colder than the winter before it. So on the morning of November 15th, 1856, when the remaining prisoners were told they were being transported to another "facility," Patrick was able to convince Roger that any chance at escape would be seized. They agonized and planned it all day long, worried about getting shot in the back as they ran away, about being captured and tried for two crimes. How odd it was, then, when the lieutenant who had originally ushered Patrick to the infirmary and chased off the men of Lecompton as they laughed at the hornet-stung Irishman, appeared at the gate and opened it.

"Go over there," he said, pointing to the small cabin that served as the guards' barrack. "Gather there and we shall begin the transfer."

"There?" said one man quizzically. "You mean, just go stand there?"

"Yes, and wait for me." The lieutenant winked. "Sheriff Jones's and his men are due in the next quarter hour with some stages to transport you to a jailhouse in town, or maybe up to Leavenworth. I don't know. I just thought it may expedite the process if you weren't inside the fence when they arrive. Over there you shall be ready to board the coaches. I will be inside."

"You mean just stand over there and wait?"

"Yes."

They did as they were told, and as the lieutenant went inside and drew the curtains, many stood around looking at one another.

"I think he is letting us escape."

"Why would he do that?"

"Because it's a farce," said Roger. "And he knows it."

"We need to show the nation this farce and stand trial," said one man.

"You need to. I'm going home," said another. "And I advise you all to do the same. If you still have faith in the justice of this nation, you are a complete fool."

"They'll hunt us down."

"No they won't."

"Goodbye all!" said a young man as he trotted off. "I'm sure I will see you again!"

Patrick and Roger looked at each other, brows raised, nodded, and began walking home.

V

Crouched in the frost-covered scrub oak on the east-40 of his claim, Joseph James Hawkins realized it had been a whole year since the Wakarusa War. 1856 had changed everything for him. In November 1855 his father was still mostly a memory, his mother was miserable, his wife was happy and pregnant, his neighbors were friends (all but Roger, anyway), and Oliver John . . . was alive. He was still recovering from his smashed pelvis, but he was alive. At least Oliver John was alive. He'd take that any day over a doting mother, involved father, and quiet wife. Yes sir, them was the good ol' days.

He thought about what drove him to Lawrence twelve months ago. Yes, the Yankees were a threat, he thought, and still are. Their factories and indenturing of the poor whites who built this country would flood west like a barbarian hoard. He didn't know much about his family—on either side—but enough to know the Hawkinses had helped define the American dream. He knew they were poor somewhere in the Scottish borderlands hundreds of years ago, thousands of years ago, and remained poor somewhere in the Appalachia in the 18th century, and had eventually somehow made a name for themselves. George Sherman was born to well to-do parents, that's all he knew. And that's all he needed to know. It didn't matter that the idiot had thrown it all away so he could have his Indian mistress—and all the white ones along with her—all that mattered was that the Hawkinses had made it in America before, and they could do it again.

But only in the South. If the Yankees took Kansas all there would be would be giant dirty cities full of destitute whites, babbling immigrants from Europe, and free niggers. How a Hawkins would get along in a place like that was beyond Joseph James. Western Missouri was far preferable, but he'd left that behind, staked his life in Kansas. He belonged here in the crispy fall brush hunting, crouched with his coffee and hard-tack and slice of ham, ready to make of this wilderness a wonderland of agrarian bliss. So why he would leave this claim and scamper about Douglas County with a bunch of drunks to try and burn down a city made sense on one hand, but not on the other. He should have stayed put. Then maybe Oliver John would still be alive. One thing was sure—no matter what all them militias did, the Yankee hoard just kept a-comin'. Instead of trying to protect Kansas, he should have just protected his home, his land, his family, his own life.

Oliver John would love it right about now. So still and delicate were the woods, so colorful the prairie, so very perfect this land. From his spot he could see the game trail that led to the little stream, and had a perfect shot into the clearing just before it. Any deer that wanted to drink this morning would have to stop there, look around, and eventually, silently and alertly, step out into the clearing. And it would feed them. Hunting for Joseph and Oliver John was the furthest thing from killing imaginable; it was the essence of life, a communion with the land and its beasts, with whatever God had ordained the law of claw and tooth in the first place. In venison they became the earth, the earth grew within them, and the marriage was blessed forever and ever.

Oliver John had made that final consummation. Joseph could also see, in the distance, the tops of the cottonwoods that skirted his gravesite, the place where he, too, would one day be buried. Where Del would be buried. Where, perhaps, Missy and her future siblings would be buried. Hell, maybe even George and Sarah Sally would want to lay with their child there, too. And he wouldn't oppose it. No, no sense in that. For when they partook of the deer they became it too, just like Oliver John. If only George would get his lazy self up and help the hunt, that would be nice. Oliver John's eyes and ears were sorely missed right about now. He always saw the prey first. Always.

Joseph James could feel him right now; a-settin' there in the bush with him, the steam and heat rising from his neck and shoulders, his smell—that seemed to have never changed since he was a young boy—filling the little hunting nest he'd made. He could feel the tap on his shoulder, the eye-contact, and the pointing as Oliver John saw the deer make its way toward the clearing. He was there, risen up out of the earth like corn after the planting rain, come to help his brother hunt. Oliver John was a part of this place now, and would always help point out the prey, Joseph James realized. And there it was.

Just in front of the clearing, exactly where his brother indicated, he could see the angles of moving legs through the underbrush. There were still enough leaves on the smaller growth to make the sight difficult, but it was clear that the opening and closing triangles of shadow were legs. And he could hear, now that a slight breeze died away, the distinct sound of footsteps in the forest. His heart skipped a beat as it always did at this sound. Especially when it was human.

Because these were definitely human legs, and there were at least four of them, and they were walking very cautiously along the game trail, obviously to avoid being seen or heard. They weren't clumsy, either. Had Joseph not been sitting there still and silent for so long, so intently watching that one spot—and had Oliver John not pointed—he would not have seen them. He would have walked right by these men (or group of men) and they would have seen him first. He didn't like that. Not at all. His heart beat in anticipation and also now in a little fear. These men were on his property and could not be up to good.

Just as the thought came to him that this was all he needed right now, the self-pity of a man in trouble, he knew he could not allow himself to think that way. Like it or not he was in yet another potentially life-threatening situation. Maybe someday he'd get used to it. More likely not. And at least he knew what to do. He couldn't just shoot them, wouldn't just shoot them. And if he fired a warning shot they may see the origin of the smoke from the barrel of the gun and fire back. He had no choice but to call out and stay crouched in the bush.

"Who goes there!?" Immediately the snapping of branches stopped. He could make out the form of one man and part of another. "I asked who you are." He chose his tone carefully now. "You're on my land and I want to know if you are friend or foe. I am armed and have a bead on you."

After a silence that was just long enough for a decision to be made, the forms in the trees made a run for it. "Damnit," Joseph James cursed as he took chase, knowing he would be able to find his coffee in the bush again but wishing he didn't have to leave it.

He ran deliberately to his right of the men, watching the lay of the land. He had a feeling they would head for the area of Oliver John's grave, there being the dry bed of an old creek a hundred yards or so away that would lead them toward it, and then they would cut back toward the direction they were currently heading. So Joseph James ran for Oliver John. He kept his eye on the men, but did not follow them, instead running straight for the grove of cottonwoods. He could get there before the men and surprise them. He began to feel light of foot, the cold air cooling his skin as it began to bead with sweat, each step springing off the earth as if it were made of rubber, the air buoying his weight.

"Hold it right there!" he screamed at them as they arrived in the clearing.

"Oh my god," said Patrick Dugan. Roger stood beside him in shock and the blood drained form his face. "Are you a ghost?"

"Well if it ain't the Dugan brothers, brave veterans of the Battle of Hickory Point. Last time I saw you Paddy you had a gun pointed at my chest. And you pulled the goddamned trigger."

"But, I thought…"

"You left me for dead, eh? Gotta do more 'n 'at to kill a Hawkins. You shoulda shot me twice."

"I wish I hadn't at all."

Joseph James spat as the two stared at one another. It occurred to all three now that this was the exact spot where Joseph James had forced the Dugans to kneel in 1854, put a gun to their heads, and threatened to kill them if they didn't move their cabin.

Roger spoke, smiling. "Would you like us to kneel again, Jimmy?"

***

"You've got a lot of nerve come 'cross my claim, Dugan." Joseph James gripped his rifle as hard as he could. His hands remembered Patrick tearing the weapon from them in the Battle of Hickory Point, the surprising gorilla strength coming from the otherwise placid Irishman. Oliver John's grave was just behind him now, just as it had been when he'd faced Patrick at Hickory Point. The tree that had been lifted off Oliver John was there, too, and the earth had yet to heal from the digging of the grave. He could never forgive this man.

Patrick's face was even whiter than usual. "I thought…"

"You thought I was dead? Well, I ain't, is I? And if I was you'd be trekkin' cross the land of a man you just killed. Ain't that disrespectful in Ireland?"

"I can't say I…" Patrick stammered.

"Nevermind." He spat. "I outa shoot you back. An eye for an eye, as the Gospel says."

"The Old Testament," Roger corrected him, smiling again.

"What?"

"That passage is in the Old Testament, not the Gospel. Oh, nevermind."

"Yer damn right nevermind!" He turned the gun on Roger. "I outa shoot *you* for a whole hell of a lot of reasons you smart sonofabitch."

"I think I would feel the same if I were you, Joseph," Roger said calmly. "I know I would."

"Yer damn right you would. What're you all doing here, anyway? You is comin' 'cross, ain't ya? I mean, your line don't head to the house. I'd be damned if you came an knocked on the door of a man you killed."

"I didn't kill you."

"You thought you did."

"We're heading home, Joseph. We're cold and tired. We've been imprisoned since the . . . since Hickory Point."

"Is that so?" Joseph James smiled for a moment but it faded. "You all were taken by the Army and held at Lecompton under Jones? That bunch a men?"

"Yes."

"I heard it wasn't pretty in that camp." The barrel of the gun dropped a little.

"You heard correctly."

"And you," he motioned to Roger's lower body with his rifle, "How's yer leg?"

"Good enough to genuflect." Joseph looked at him quizzically. Roger smiled again. "To kneel and stand back up again."

"You are the smartest ass kid I ever did know." There was the hint of a smile in his scolding.

"And Oliver John…?" Patrick almost whispered.

"He's buried right there."

"I'm sorry Joseph."

"Me too Paddy. More 'n you'll ever know. Unless I shoot Roger right 'bout now."

"Please don't. It won't help you feel any better. Trust me."

"Tell me why I shouldn't. You give me one goddamn reason why I shouldn't do whatever the devil tells me to do with you two."

The Dugan brothers looked at each other in hesitation. Roger could only think of reasons why he should shoot them, but certainly did not want to offer them. Patrick could only think of one thing: what would Maria say?

"One last chance, you dumb Irish bastards. Tell me why I shouldn't shoot you right now."

"Be—because we're neighbors, Joseph. Whatever's happened hasn't changed that. We're neighbors in a godforsaken wilderness. We need each other."

Joseph James stared at Patrick Dugan, then spat. "I don't quite see how no more."

Patrick hesitated again. "Why did you tell me you killed Maria?"

"I thought I did. I—" he hesitated and glanced toward the Dugan farm. "I thought I may have." He looked down, then at the barrel of the gun. He could taste it again. "It woulda been an accident."

Patrick's jaw clenched and his gaze hardened, something they rarely did. He was angry. "That makes us even."

"The hell it does! Look at that grave you bastard! Look at it! You ain't a-buryin' anyone!"

"We didn't kill him, Joseph," said Roger.

"Your people did! Them Yankees a-killed 'im! Lane's men! The man Maria helped into Kansas, the man you fought for and with!"

"We are not Yankees, Joseph; we are farmers," Patrick spoke again. "You know that. And you, you hurt my wife. A woman! Does Del know?"

"No! I mean, I didn't intend to Patrick, never intended it. Just wanted to teach you and her a lesson and she had to go and…"

"What?"

"Attack me."

"With the shovel?" Roger chuckled.

"No, with the frying pan." And, despite all his fighting myself not to, Joseph James Hawkins chuckled too. "She did this with the shovel." He held up his broken arm.

"When did she do that?"

"The other day. I went there to see what'd become of ya'll, and her. She was a-waitin' behind the door, I guess."

The three stood frozen in the November frost, knuckles and ears and the tips of noses aching just a little. They all could picture Maria tucked behind the door with the shovel held up expertly like a woodsman wields an axe or a knight a sword. And they all knew they would have suffered the same fate should they have found themselves in Joseph James's shoes that autumn morning.

And they began to laugh. The tension that surrounded them just a moment ago lifted like a fog, and the humor came to them like sun shining through it for the first time in a morning. They laughed again, thinking about how they had gone from wanting to kill one another to laughing together so quickly. And they laughed yet again, reflecting briefly on the year they had had, from battlefields to holiday suppers, they lived the lives of a farce. A neighbor in Kansas was worth a thousand friends and a thousand enemies anywhere else on earth.

But all fits of laughter, especially delirious ones spurned partly by fear, must end, and this one did too. As it did a giant, brilliantly-colored bird, the jayhawk, rose almost silently from the cottonwood grove surrounding Oliver John's grave and lifted into the sky, casting no shadow, showing no sign of hurry, making no call whatsoever. They all watched it fly overhead.

"Get outa here," said Joseph James Hawkins. "Get offa my land."

VI

By February of 1857 Maria decided she should see a doctor. She realized, as she watched her husband disrobe in the doorway, having been out in the snow feeding the pigs and chickens, that she had never even told him she thought she may have lost the baby last fall. In fact, they hadn't even mentioned the baby at all since the day he left for battle last August. Maybe he was smart enough to have assumed she lost it during whatever altercation she had had with Joseph James and his cronies.

"Whew, it's cold out there," he said, smacking snow from his overcoat and interrupting her train of thought. Of course it's cold, you idiot, she thought. It's still winter.

Then again, maybe he was stupid enough to have forgotten all about the baby. When she told him he was distracted, of course, having just been threatened and finally deciding to take up arms for the Free State cause. Not to mention having just learned his father, J.P., was not only alive, he was coming from Australia because, as he put it, Kansas was the center of the struggle for world freedom. And since that day her lovely husband had been in two real battles, seen his brother injured in one of them, spent weeks as a prisoner of war, and then made a mad scramble to prepare for winter and get healthy again. Every structure on the farm needed repairs, the frosty grass was still useful to mow and put up in the little barn, and on and on with farm things that seemed to preoccupy Patrick Dugan more than most men. Yes, she decided, he is stupid enough to have forgotten, and it was almost forgivable. Almost.

"Don't you think I should see a doctor?"

"Sorry, love? My, it's cold out!"

"Of course it's cold. Don't you think I should see a doctor?"

"Why, yes, I suppose. Are you not well, so?"

Maria stared at him. Patrick drew back slightly in his chair, having taken a bite of the bread she had made him. He glanced at Maria's shovel, which stood behind the stove, and back at her. It must be three steps away, so if he had done something really terrible and she went for it, he should have time to run out the door. It was so cold out, though. He would have to remember to grab his coat and boots. That could give her time to catch him. The thought of the shovel coming down on the back of his leg made him draw back again.

"The baby, Paddy. Remember?"

"Remember what?"

"The baby!"

"What!? Are you asking me if I remember that you are with child?"

"Yes!"

"Do you think I'm stupid?"

She blushed. "Yes!"

"Well, I'm not that stupid. Of course I remember. That boy is our future."

"Boy?"

"Well, child, so. And yes, I suppose you should see a doctor, now that you mention it. I'm sorry I haven't suggested it myself, love." Patrick's muscles relaxed. The shovel didn't loom so large anymore.

"I'm not sure it's well, Paddy."

"The baby?"

Maria sighed and shook her head. Both of their tones changed now, and the cold outside seemed to be pushing in on the walls of the little cabin. "Yes. It's . . . I think it should be kicking by now, Paddy. I know it should."

"And it's not?"

"You are stupid," she said flatly.

Patrick smiled. "We'll go to town tomorrow." He stood, came around the table, and put his hand on Maria's belly. "Maybe he's lazy."

"Yes, well, he is a Dugan." Maria put her hand on Patrick's and looked at him deeply. "Paddy, I don't want to lose this one."

"Me neither, love."

"I thought I did already." Patrick looked at her inquiringly and sat down next to her. They were still holding hands. "When Joseph and those Missourians were here and tied me to the chair.

I bled some. Enough that I was worried I'd lost it. But I didn't. But she's not kicking."

"Not at all?"

"Nothing." She looked away. "But it is growing. Oh, Patrick, I can't stand the idea of it growing—dead—inside of me."

"Now who's stupid!? Dead things don't grow, Maria."

"Well, maybe I don't mean dead, exactly. Maybe—"

Patrick held up his hand to silence her. "I think it's better not to use the word 'maybe' when it comes to babies, girl."

"Yes." She looked down and sighed, letting her hand slip from his.

"Maria, what happened that day? I know you—" he chuckled a little.

"What?" she smiled too, despite herself.

"You hit him. With a frying pan?"

Maria laughed. "Yes. He told you that when he caught you on his claim?"

"Yes." Patrick's smile was the most sincere she'd ever seen on a man, thought Maria. "You should have heard the sound of it. Like a bell. And his grunt was like a cow going to slaughter."

"Ha! How did you get at him in the first place?"

"I ran. He tackled me, and I hit him with the pan."

"I should have loved to see it."

"Yes, well, all things considered I suppose I'd rather it not have happened." The two breathed deeply and stopped laughing, both knowing that what had followed was not funny. Being tied to a chair and left in a lonely cabin in Kansas just wasn't funny.

"And a perfect stranger just showed up later that day and freed you? Did you get his name?"

"He was Frenchman by birth and married a Kickapoo woman. Pa—"

"Paschal."

"Yes. You know him, then?"

"I have met him before." His eyes shifted and he stood. "He . . . seems to appear out of nowhere at the most interesting moments."

"Well, we owe him, should you see him again."

"Yes."

"Oh Paddy," Maria stood, somewhat excited now. "I want to laugh more. I want this horrible winter to lift. I want all this strife and bloodshed and disease and death to leave us. I want to enjoy Kansas. I want the world to leave us alone." She began to cry a little. "You were right all along. We should never have gotten involved in this bloody affair. We should have let the Americans settle their differences and kept to our farm. I was so wrong, Paddy, so very, very wrong—"

"No," Patrick said forcefully. "You were not. We are Americans, girl. God help us, we are Americans now and their fight is our fight whether we like it or not. Roger was right all along."

"I want—" tears tumbled down her cheeks. "I want this baby to come." She began to stutter. "I want it to be healthy and happy." Patrick stood and embraced his wife, who buried her face in his chest. She pulled a clenched fist to her teeth. "That's all I want, Paddy. That's all I want."

"That's all I want, too, love." He embraced her tightly. "That all any of us want."

***

Roger couldn't help himself. Living in Kansas but not being involved in her politics and sectarian violence was a hungry dog buying the carcass of a deer without eating any. Since the violence of the previous autumn he had helped his brother restore the Dugan farm to its former promise, but had also spent every moment he could with Free State party leaders and activities. They were cold, hard rides from Atchison to Topeka and Lawrence, but they were well worth it. Hell, Roger had even met the governor.

"You know my sister," he had said to the young executive at a gathering inside the lobby of the Free State Hotel. It had been razed by Missourians in the summer and was slowly being rebuilt. Smoke stains were evident on the stone behind the wooden ceiling joists. "Maria Dugan. You were generous enough to escort her to see us in the prisoners' infirmary after Hickory Point."

"Ha! Yes, generous enough indeed." The governor rocked in his boots. "Your sister has a way . . . she is very persuasive."

"Did she hit you with a shovel?"

The governor's mouth took a shape of confusion behind his beard. "Why no, of course not. Come to think of it, Mr. Dugan, I don't recall your having stood trial following that imprisonment. I don't suppose you are one of our escapees?" Roger stumbled on an answer. "Don't trouble yourself, young man. I have pardoned you all. It became rather clear to me that you were arrested under, shall we say, partisan pretenses."

"We certainly were, Governor."

"And that Sheriff Jones. What a man. Not the kindest of wardens, is he?"

"Why no. Worst month of my life." He paused. "And I crossed the Atlantic in the winter on a wooden boat."

The governor paused, bounced on his feet a little, looking out of the crowd, and firmly hooked his thumbs in his belt loop. "Worst month of my life too, Roger Dugan."

Their conversation was interrupted by Charles Robinson. Governor Geary had released him from prison in Leavenworth and the Free State leader had relinquished his title of "governor" following the pardon of the Hickory Point prisoners and several discussions with Geary. "We must give the governor a chance," he preached to his Free State officers. He slowly idled up beside Geary, pardoned himself to Roger, and began in his polite way.

"Good evening, Governor. It's a pleasure to have you here. We are honored."

"You know I'm obligated to be here, Governor. Besides, you have the best parties in Kansas."

"I am glad you enjoy spending time with us, but I'm not the governor, Governor. You are."

"Yes, well, should I have the opportunity I will let you take the title, Charles. 'Tis a dangerous one to hold, as you are all too aware."

"Indeed!"

Samuel Pomeroy, another man and a woman now joined the group. Roger had met Pomeroy very briefly during the Wakarusa War but had been in the same room with him many times, but the other man, with a long red beard, and the woman, who appeared to be Indian but was dressed as a white woman, and a pretty one at that, were unknown to him.

"Gentlemen!" Pomeroy bellowed as he joined them, patting Geary on the back a little harder than most would. "Just the small gathering I desire. Have you given my offer some additional thought, Governor?"

"Yes, but it has not changed my mind, Samuel. I do not think it appropriate for me to speculate on the land of a territory I govern." Roger felt suddenly tired. This lobby had been the scene of so much excitement over the last year, it seemed odd to be bored here, speaking of land transactions instead of the currency of right and wrong.

"Governor! You are a citizen, are you not? You are at least twenty-one years of age. You have to live somewhere in Kansas, and I presume you would improve any land upon which you did settle."

"We have secured this land at the very best possible price," said the other man. "My wife has, in fact," he turned to the woman next to him. "I intend to name the town after her."

"I don't believe I've had the pleasure—" bowed Geary.

"Guthrie," said the man, "and this is my wife Nancy. She is a Wyandotte Indian—a very civilized and Christian tribe, I assure you—and secured their land at the best possible price." The woman smiled and offered her hand in a way that was lady-like, but also confident.

"Come, Governor, there are many business opportunities in Kansas," Robinson joined Pomery's chorus, "but this is the best of them all."

"There are perhaps too many business opportunities, Charles."

"Yes, the strife is not good for business."

Roger suddenly couldn't swallow his drink. A warmth rose from his heart into his neck and he thought about his brother's farm.

"The strife is my business, Mr. Robinson," replied the governor. "And I shall let the business be your strife!"

They laughed, Roger wondering why, but through all their joviality there was an abiding seriousness. "But Governor, they cannot be separated, clearly," Pomeroy returned to that theme of there being something at stake.

"Quindaro is a prime example of this dilemma, Governor," Robinson chimed in.

"Yes, so you have said."

"We are actively selling stock now, Governor. You know the average northeasterner is not interested in de-boarding at Leavenworth. Qunidaro is a safe place, a welcome place. Many opportunities for Free State investors are provided there."

"I understand, Charles. And it shall remain a safe place as long as I am governor. All Kansas will be protected by federal law by federal forces."

Robinson let the statement have its moment, but Guthrie, the red-beard with the Indian wife, glanced around and decided he could continue. "And Quindaro will be profitable! We can offer lots as low as $500. And the ferry business is just the beginning, Governor. The railroads will soon come to Kansas. We intend to make Quindaro a hub by way of the St. Joseph and Hannibal line. Quindaro shall flourish."

A moment of silence fell over the group. Robinson, Pomeroy, and Guthrie and Nancy knew they could not push any longer, but also that it was the governor's turn to speak and decide the topic of the conversation. Roger felt lost in it, and began to feel suspicious of these men. "'Quindaro,'" Geary said after sipping his drink and brushing his beard with a cupped hand. "An interesting name."

"Yes, it is my wife's Indian name," Guthrie replied. "She is Wyandotte, a very civilized tribe. As such she was very helpful in negotiating the land purchase from the tribe," he repeated, and Nancy Brown Guthrie, or Seh Quindaro, stood simply, her expression totally inscrutable. "It is another reason why we can offer plots as low as $500."

"Yes, so you have said." The governor took another sip and stroked his beard again. "Tell me Mrs. Guthrie," he turned to Nancy. "What does 'Quindaro' mean?"

But Charles Robinson interrupted her, smiling, and the quality of illumination about his face, especially his eyes but also his skin and hair, pronounced itself. The leader of the Free State Party of Kansas was glowing from the inside out.

"Strength in unity," he said.

VII

Delilah J. Hawkins woke with a start in a pool of sweat. She knew instantly she would not sleep again this night. The thought that took shape from the strange place in her mind that she had learned told her things was, Something is wrong. It took shape like smoke rising from smoldering kindling, and once it started it usually didn't stop until it was alight. Grandma had taught her how to caress and sustain it. "Blow as hard as she'll take it," she would say. "Go on, the more smoke there is the harder you can blow." And sometimes she didn't have to encourage it at all; in fact, on nights like this she couldn't stomp it out if she tried.

She got out of bed, Joseph James snoring and little Missy breathing deeply beside her. She dressed and crept into the corner of the cabin that served as the kitchen. She lit a candle and placed her bible upright beside it, between the flame and where George and Sarah were sleeping, so the light wouldn't spill onto their faces. A rectangle of shade framed them instead, and the entire room, an orange and yellow flickering dancing about the walls and ceiling. They slumbered in the shadows of the good book this way, and did not notice as Del busied herself with her morning routine. She knew all she could do is wait until the smoldering of knowing grew and told her more.

She realized she'd left nothing between her husband and baby and returned to the bed. She placed a rolled up blanket between them so the man would not crush his daughter, and in glancing at her baby's face while doing so the next thought came to her: Maria. Maria. Maria. It was Maria. Something was wrong. Maria. Del could see first her name, hear it too, and then her face. It was still and serene, but a hint of anguish about the corners of her nose and mouth and eyes. Maria. Something was wrong with Maria. And then the knowing grew within her and she had her next thought: the baby. Maria's baby. That was it. Something was wrong with Maria's baby.

In front of her was an issue of the *Sovereign* from last November. Why it was still in the cabin was curious, and why it was placed out on the table even more so, and how in the world it could have been placed there without her cleaning it up immediately was nothing short of miraculous. Her eyes were drawn to an article that was tantamount to an advertisement for Atchison—how it was farther west than any town on the river and perfectly suited for outfitting; how well-established it was with boarding houses, butchers, and bakers; how the *Sovereign* had the largest circulation in all of Kansas and was read in the east—and then her eyes stopped near the end of the page. It read "A fine supply of professional gentlemen of all branches constantly on hand to equal demand." Her eyes crossed between the little squiggles of letters in the storm of white, and the phrase turned over in her mind like a snowflake.

And then, clear as anything this part of her gift had ever given her, she knew what to do. It spoke itself to her in an unmistakable voice, and she looked into the shadow of the bible, thinking perhaps her father in-law had said it. She not only heard it, she saw and felt it.

"Go to her," it said.

And so she did. Del scrawled out a little note and left it on the table. "Gawn fer a ride. Will retern after breakfast. Eggs in the coup, potatoes in the bucket in the shed." She thought about leaving a more detailed note, knowing that at one time she would have had to. But now, with her mother in-law Sarah Sally having changed so much since Oliver John's death, she knew the old woman would see to it all were fed. The baby may cry for a while, but Sarah Sally would figure it out. It wouldn't kill nobody to let a child cry some. Hell, might be good for them to do without her for a few hours.

Still, she returned to the note and wrote at the bottom: "No, the other shed."

She fed and saddled the horse, and while trying to stay warm and wait for her to eat, Del realized she had left the bible next to the burning candle. Would be a shame if it tipped over in a draft and caught fire, or worse yet, if it caught the damn table on fire and burned down the cabin, killing everything she loved. So she went inside, blew out the candle, and put the bible down on the table. But the voice came to her again.

"Take it with you."

The full moon hung very low the morning of February 9th, 1857 when Delilah Hawkins made her way to the cabin of Maria Dugan. Bible in hand, she knew she'd come to tell her friend that something was wrong with her baby, but didn't yet know what it was. It was cold and frost colored the land with a crystalline white, a giant snake molting its skin. Tiny castles of ice fell from some of the trees, and she was thankful her shawl was broad enough to cover her head and still reach well enough below her shoulders to keep it from bouncing above her neckline as the horse pranced northward.

It didn't matter that she had yet to find her words for Maria. She knew, as the kindle continued to burn in her "second-mind," as her grandma called it, that they would eventually. They always did. She slowed the horse, fearing it may slip in a particularly open, wind-exposed expanse of prairie, where the still snowy grass rippled southeast as if it were a little lake smoothed over with ice. She was so warm inside. All the grey and white and silver of winter fanned the flames even more, and slowly her message to Maria came to light. The sun had turned the black of night to a dull grey, but the full moon yet stood wide open.

But the words her mind told her to say were interrupted by a noise overhead, a slap that she couldn't immediately locate due to her hood. She threw it from her head and looked up into the barren sky. Even the horse stopped breathing, standing still in the icy clearing, waiting to see what had happened. Then a silhouette of giant wings moved overhead. The horse stomped, cracking the crispy grass. She kicked it forward, sending snow and ice scattered about. And the wings circled the clearing, and the beast landed in front of her.

"Back," Del said calmly. The beast stomped its feet too. "Leave Maria alone," she said. Del clutched her bible and closed her eyes. When she opened them it had disappeared. She looked around at the quiet Kansas morning and breathed deep. She was sure she had seen it. The damn horse had seen it.

She rode quickly to the spot where it had landed and found its tracks in the snow. They looked like those of a giant cat. Paws rather than talons. Claws, but they weren't a bird's. She'd never seen anything that large, either. Wheeling the horse around, she could see her own tracks back through the clearing, but still nothing else there, nothing at all. Turning back northeast, she spurred the horse.

"Git!"

***

Joseph James was quite upset to find his wife gone. His mother tried to calm him.

"Where's she gonna go?" he said, gesturing in the exact direction she had gone without knowing it.

"Somewhere where's she's needed, you can bet on that," Sarah Sally said. "Besides, ain't nona your business anyway."

"Nona my business?" His eyebrows arching an angry cat, its follicles raised and twitching. "Nona my business? I'm her goddamn husband!" Something in the final word felt like whiskey in his chest.

"Hush. You'll wake the baby."

"Del is out there in the cold on a horse that even I don't totally trust yet and you're a-worried about wakin' the baby? What's the matter with you!? Do you know what happens if yer thrown from a horse and break a bone and it's this cold out? You don't wanna be alone, that's fer certain."

"I said shutup Joseph!" She glanced toward the sleeping infant and quieted her voice. "Your Del knows exactly what she's a-doin', Joseph, and you know it. Now jes' act like a man 'n do what yer wife a-says to do!"

Joseph James stomped off into the chill morning without his hat on for the first time in nearly twenty years. He was that mad. Just exactly that mad, and he wanted everyone to know it, even the trees and the ice and the livestock. The chickens sure knew it, as he slammed things about while feeding them, sending them into their characteristic hysterics. He was just that mad that he would frighten the chickens, which he never did. Just that mad. The cow didn't know it, but the stupid cow didn't know Joseph. He almost kicked her, just to show he didn't care about her yet because she was so indifferent and his wife's charge.

When Joseph James returned to the house, thinking he had calmed, his father was awake inside, and he asked what was wrong.

"Yer son is a pigheaded ass, if you ain't noticed," replied his mother. "But you'd have to be 'round him more to notice, I s'pose."

George glanced over at his son who pretended to be busy at the table. "That's every day, Sarah. What's it this fine morning?"

"It ain't any 'it' anymore 'n it's a fine mornin', George. 'It' is just that it's them."

George closed his eyes and sighed. Joseph James thought that in some ways, she really did deserve all that this man had done to her over the years. "I mean to say, Sarah, why did Joseph run out so violently?"

She looked at him, paused, and said, "Why did you?"

Joseph James left the cabin, suddenly not mad anymore. It was a beautifully still morning and he caught his reflection in a small puddle. He couldn't remember the last time he'd studied his own image. He wasn't so bad looking, but sure didn't take very good care of himself. He looked like a man who had started shaving but was interrupted; a man who forgot he was bathing and emerged half-clean and half-dirty. Removing his hat, he saw just how thin his hair was getting, how there was grey in his temples and on his neck.

Somewhere inside his image he saw himself as a child. On his chin there was still a scar that hot grease had made when he tried to fix supper for himself one day when he was maybe eight years old. George had left and Sarah Sally had been in bed for days. He'd tried to fry some squirrel meat in oil and had added water as it began to dry out, as the oil was gone. It jumped out of the pan and onto his chin and neck. He and Oliver John ate it, and later that night Oliver John snuck out into the night and returned with a cool cloth for his brother to put on his burn. For the first time in his life, Joseph James Hawkins felt pity for himself.

He walked to Oliver John's grave and sat, spending the rest of the morning listening to the birds.

***

Patrick was out feeding his chickens when Del arrived. He didn't look quite as surprised to see her as she thought he'd be.

"Del? Is all well?"

"Patrick." She stopped her mare, dismounted, and walked up to him. "Is all well?"

"Yes. Why yes, it is, Del. What's the matter?"

"I—" she stopped and looked at him. She looked desperate to him but he looked unaware to her. "I—why, nothing. I suppose. Is Maria in?"

"Of course. Here, I'll take your mare."

Del handed her neighbor the reigns to a horse that had once opposed him on the battlefield. They both held the fraying leather for a moment, and it seemed charged. Del smiled. "Thank you," she said.

Inside, Del found Maria fixing tea. "Oh, Maria," she said, removing her overcoat and slumping her shoulders in relief. "I'm so happy yer well!"

"Why would you have thought otherwise, Del? I'm perfectly well."

"I have a gift, Maria. I know things." She had blurted it out without even pausing or looking directly at Maria. She was surprised at how nonchalant and blunt she'd been about it, given that she'd rarely told anyone about this belief in herself at all.

But Maria was totally undaunted. She sat and held her hands out to Del. "Tell me what you know."

For the first time since arriving, Del realized she hadn't yet had her revelation. By now she was supposed to know exactly what to say. But she didn't. There was nothing there, not even the smell of a fire. It was a cold, acrid, black glob.

"I don't know."

"But you knew?"

"Yes. Well—no. I knew to a-come for ya. And bring the bible." She removed it from under her coat and put it on the table. "Go to you. Bring this with me."

"But why?"

Del knew she was supposed to know. Knowing was the whole point. But she didn't. "I don't know."

Maria sighed. She looked perturbed. Her hands wrung in her apron and looked out the window. "Del, I thought I had lost the child originally. I even—I accused Joseph of killing her. But it grew. But—" she stood, tears coming to her eyes. "She isn't moving."

And then Del knew why she had come. The voice said it with her. Said it for her. And it couldn't come quick enough. "Your baby is fine. I know yer worried about it, but you shouldn't."

"What?"

"That's why I came. That's what it told me. Your baby is well. He is loved by his God. And you need to hear this from me. No one else."

Maria slipped her hands from Del's and sat back in her chair. "He?"

"Yes, you have a son in your womb, Maria. His name shall be Lawrence."

"How did you know?" The women looked at each other and clasped hands again. "Why the bible, Del? Why did you bring the bible?"

"To protect you." She hesitated, hoping Maria would not ask what from.

"Del, Paddy and I were going to go to Atchison and see the doctor today. To see about the baby."

And with the same force, the voice came to her and said, "Don't go."

***

Even after his son left the cabin, George had absolutely no idea what to say to Sarah. He knew, in fact, that she knew he did not know what to say and that she didn't actually expect him to answer this. Certainly, he had left because he was a scoundrel. That was the long and short of it, really. He was a philanderer. A philanderer with two families.

Ah, Rebecca. She was a sweet one. Her wavy black hair, off-centered dimple in her nose, and slender yet voluptuous-in-all-the-right places body. Everything about her was like a woman's form inside a gown. She was a shape inside a dream, something not forbidden but so mysterious it was unbearable. Rebecca was an absolute angel. And she, too, was alone with children to rear. And he was gone.

"Don't answer it, you scoundrel. Don't tell me why you left. I don't want to know."

"I don't intend to."

"That is why you are a scoundrel."

"I don't intend to because I don't have an answer. I don't know why I did it to you. Or her."

"Your Black-Red Whore?

George clenched his jaw. "No. Rebecca."

Sarah Sally clenched her jaw. And her fists.

Soon, the baby was awake.

***

But Maria went anyway. She needed to see a doctor. It wasn't a choice. She knew Del had the gift of knowing, had known it all along, but this gift had been a curse too often in Maria Dugan's life for her to abide by it. She knew the sensible thing to do was see a doctor, and she just couldn't risk the irresponsibility of neglecting medical attention, regardless of what Del's dreams told her. If the boy—if it was a boy—was well, the doctor would know. If the boy wasn't well, the doctor may know that too, which would be a good thing, to discover it. If the boy—if it was a boy—was well, that would be wonderful. Truly wonderful. It only made sense. It was reasonable. She had to go. Another Dugan bo—

Interrupting herself as best as she could, Maria found Atchison to be different than she had left it. How long had it been? A few weeks? Months? Atchison had grown. There must have been three times as many buildings, and most of them looked quite well built. The sawmill was large and obnoxious, and there must have been a baker's dozen each of hardware stores, blacksmiths, even lawyers. Additions to the east and south were platted, ready for investment. Commercial Street was coming to life, and it rose from the river like a tributary that drew from the river instead giving to it. The Missouri slunk to the south un-depleted by it, as if it were an infinite source of life.

There were almost as many doctors as lawyers now, but Maria couldn't find any of them except Stringfellow, the same horrible man who had all but pronounced her dead a year ago. The same man who was editor of the *Squatter Sovereign*, a vehement Pro Slavery monster of a man who advocated violence against "abolitionists" and considered anyone from anywhere but the South an abolitionist. To trust your body to such a man was worse than the worry she already felt. Something compelled her into his office anyway. Patrick held the door for her.

"Well, well!" Stringfellow boomed. "You survived the last one and now you're with child again, eh?"

"Yes."

"They make 'em tough in Ireland, I suppose!" he winked at Patrick, who stood silent, stiff, and still.

"I just want to make sure the baby is healthy, doctor. I am not in a mind for conversation."

"My, my. Why, I imagine he's as tough as they come, Ms…what was it again?"

"Dugan. Call me Maria if you don't mind."

"I don't mind if you don't. As I said in that cabin last winter, I'm not only surprised you survived that ordeal, but that you can have a child at all. Much less so shortly after. That baby has got to be a tough one. You sure he don't have any southern blood in 'im?" Maria's look frightened him. "Apologies. Where are my manners this afternoon? Now then, let's have a look at ya. Mr. Dugan, you'll have to—"

"No, he stays," Maria said.

"Whatever you say, Maria."

Maria lay down on a cold table and Dr. Stringfellow prodded about her abdomen. "Everything feels alright in there, Maria. Yessir, here's his head, body . . . maybe a knee. I think he's a-movin' in there, too. He may be breach but it's too soon to tell." He turned to a table by the bed and produced a somewhat crude stethoscope. "Look at this amazing new device. Perhaps we can hear your baby's heart." He smiled as he found it. "My, my, that is amazing. Here." Patrick and Maria took turns listening as the doctor explained how to distinguish it from the mother's. Both had tears in their eyes. "That's about all I can tell you. Parts are in the right places, heartbeat's as strong as an ox. So far so good."

Maria was shocked. The baby had indeed started moving. Just as she arrived in Atchison. "But the last one…"

"Yes ma'am. Could happen again. There is no way of tellin' though, I'm afraid. Some of 'em just don't take, as we say in Missourah. My wife, for instance…"

"There's something else." She looked over at her husband. He had retreated into the corner of the room as if he were hiding. She hated him for it. She hated her sweet, supporting, loving husband and hated herself for it.

"What's that?"

"I—I was assaulted." Stringfellow's mouth fell open and the dent in his lip where his cigar often nestled itself became apparent by a slobbery reflection. It wasn't until his brow furled that Maria clarified. She was shocked at herself, at her own careless use of language. "The child is my husband's! I was attacked during the recent . . . unpleasantness. This summer. I fell and may have crushed the baby." Patrick looked mortified and stepped strongly forward, grasping her hand. She loved him again, for the very reason she hated him a moment ago—he held his tongue.

The doctor's face relaxed again and he laughed. "Ha! That baby is fine, Maria. Your son," he smirked at Patrick, "is fine."

"But—"

"Trust me," he said. "I'm a doctor."

Dr. J. H. Stringfellow turned with purpose and replaced the stethoscope. "Now, for the real business at hand," he said as he faced them again, wringing his hands.

VIII

Roger felt triumphant as he rode back to Atchison. His horse felt wider and taller than it ever had before, and so did he; utterly impervious to the winter wind and frost. The cadence he and his animal had together was unprecedented too, and he felt all the swagger of a rooster. In his chest there was air, in his head a hum, in his legs a spring. That little town meant nothing to him anymore. Atchison. Ha. He knew the governor himself. The governor of all of Kansas.

The old military road near Leavenworth was worn with a hundred generations. Men and horses and wagons had followed this path for millennia, long before the settlers of Kansas used her as a means of commerce. From here the vast grasses were once found by men in hats that would forever mark their age; armies and trains of wagons embarked from here to seek gold and expansion; why, even Joseph James knew this road long before he laid the foundation of his cabin, for he had begun his long march to Mexico from this road. But long before that, the Kanza traveled parts of this path on their seasonal hunts.

And so they looked quite at home beside it, Roger thought as he came upon a small group, perhaps two families. So at home, in fact, he almost passed them as if they were merchants along a wharf. They seemed simply a part of the road and hills through which it meandered, clad in deerskin and a motley assortment of furs, adorned by things far older than this road. His thoughts were of the road as he took a wide berth around them (two columns of infantry could pass abreast here), not of them. But a shot rang out, ringing his left ear, startling his horse. He calmed and sat her, then turned to the Indians.

A small pony lay in the final twitches of life at their feet, its tongue turning brown with the dirt of the road, its blood blackening as it crept out from under its head. Some men dragged it off to the side once it breathed its last, an older woman with two very skinny children standing with many things at her feet watching carefully, their backs to the wind, a stolid resistance on their faces. Only now, only now, did Roger see the man beside the road, laying limp, still warm, and still two other men scratching his grave in the earth. Roger watched their hands move the earth, numb and purple, timeless. He dismounted and walked up to them, and they all stopped what they were doing and stood, facing him.

"Hello," he said, unsure if they understood him. "My name is Roger. Roger Dugan. I am wondering if you need help?"

They all looked at him, neither quizzically nor distrustfully, but something between the two, and they turned to one of the children, a girl about Kathy's age, and returned to their work.

"Uncle has died," she said, nodding to the corpse.

"I'm sorry to hear that. Was he ill?"

She seemed utterly confused by this question, but answered easily. "Yes."

Roger pointed to the pony. "And the pony? Was he ill?"

She blinked. "Uncle's."

Roger smiled, then stopped himself. "You can't get it from the pony," he said, but she offered no response. "Your uncle's illness—you can't contract it from the pony."

She looked at her uncle and his animal, then back to Roger. "Uncle's. He will need."

The girl's uncle was being buried now, large stones being placed atop his body, and the pony beside it. The old woman left the children and placed one of the satchels beside the corpses.

"He will need that too?" Roger asked.

The girl smiled, and in this smile Roger saw a beauty he had never seen before. "Yes," she replied as if to congratulate him. "Uncle's food. Must eat," said she, making a motion with her hand to indicate eating.

Roger tried not to furl his brow, as it felt rude, but he had to ask: "But you could eat it," he motioned to her body, nearly emaciated.

"No," she shook her head, "Uncle need."

The men finished placing stones upon Uncle, and with a simple touch here and there, the family picked up their things and began the long walk to their reservation in the west. He watched them a long while, until they nearly disappeared in the distance. Low, iron, flat clouds moved atop the horizon, great barges along a river. He wondered how many Kanza had passed down this road before, how many would ever pass down it again; how many he had passed, or could have passed, during his time in Kansas, without giving them a moment's notice.

Then he mounted and rode after them.

Startled, but exhausted, they spun languidly around as he came upon them.

"Here," he said, handing the reigns to the girl as he hopped from the saddle. "You need her more than I do. She's a good horse, very loyal."

The girl took the reigns, glancing at one of the men, who looked hard and suspiciously at Roger. Roger nodded at him, and the man walked to the horse, deftly unbuckled the cinches, and removed the saddle.

"You take," said the girl. "Indian ride bareback." The man now lifted the girl, then two other children upon the back of the horse, then returned to Roger, placing a hand upon his shoulder. No words passed between them, but in the man's deep, brown eyes Roger saw something he had not seen in a long while. It was both the dullness of an unjust, interminable suffering, and the sharpness and clarity born in faith. Faith that beyond and within this world, this pain, there was grace, wisdom, some indescribable beauty that a benevolent, masterful hand granted only to those who accept. Who let go. Roger had seen it in the faces of the starving Catholics of Ireland. And now, in the people of the South Wind.

Roger shouldered the saddle and began the long walk to Atchison, feeling he had all the height and power of a mounted rider within his legs alone. He stopped at the grave of Uncle. What had first appeared to be a hurried, messy grave was in fact a very carefully constructed tomb. No coyote or fox or bird would disturb this man in his journey, and Roger left him and his pony beside the old road, continuing his own, knowing that one day their paths must meet again.

A cold, misty rain, soon to turn to snow, began to fall, and in the east the river carried all to the beginning.

***

Roger's heart did skip just a little, he had to admit, as he saw Pat Laughlin on the street as he entered town. Laughlin had boarded Roger two years earlier, taken him under his wing in the Free State's militia, the Kansas Legion. But Pat Laughlin turned out to be a traitor, spying for the Pro Slavery forces, and had exploited Roger's relationships with Free State leadership to do the same. And, when at last caught and confronted on this very road at night by a good man, a man with a wife and children and abiding desire to see a better world for them, Laughlin had simply shot him in the face. That was the last time Roger had seen him.

Pat didn't look drunk but he didn't look sober either. His left boot fell a bit heavily on the wooden planks of the walk-way along Commercial Street, which had bowed and discolored some since it was built. Still there was more mud than plank, and the businesses were growing weary of mopping their floors. Pat stomped along happily, unaware that a man who had witnessed him murder an innocent was just behind him.

"I don't know if I should hail you or hail the sheriff, Mr. Laughlin." Pat spun around at the sound of Roger's voice. "Or maybe I should just shoot. Maybe I should just shoot you right in the face and split your head in half like a log. Just the way you did to Sam Collins."

Pat Laughlin studied the boy carefully. And smiled. "I don't believe you'll do that, *Mr.* Dugan." He took an unsteady step forward. "In fact, I know you will not, son. And further yet, I don't know what in the name of the Lord Jesus you are referring to."

Turning, he walked up the planks toward the hardware store. "Turn around." Roger didn't follow him, only projected his voice and stood tall. "What are you doing here? In town. In Atchison. You should be in prison."

"I don't believe we have met," he said, returning the few strides and offering his hand. "My name is Patrick Laughlin."

"Don't you dare pretend you don't know me." Roger slapped his hand away. "I know where you live. I know your wife. I've eaten from her table and slept on your floor two dozen times. I know you are a traitor and a disgrace to all righteous causes in Kansas. In the Good Book Itself, for that matter. I know you are a murderer, Pat Laughlin."

Laughlin smiled as he had before. "Whatever are you talking about?" But, to Roger's surprise, he took a step closer and gently touched Roger's elbow, seemed suddenly very sober, and in a near whisper, said. "Roger, my boy, did you not see that Collins was armed, so?"

Roger remembered, in fact, that Collins had indeed been holding something that glinted in the moonlight that October night. That he had stepped out from the trees. That he had accosted them dangerously.

"Roger," Laughlin looked around, "That man threatened me. I may have been a traitor, but—"

"—there is no excuse for that, Pat."

Pat's face curled in bemusement. "My boy, we were all traitors to the Crown, were we not?" There was a pause. Roger felt young again. "Do you know why I betrayed that damned Legion, Roger? They were and are hypocrites. They care nothing of slaves, and think even less of us Catholics. What they really want is to send the Africans to Africa and enslave the rest of us." He grit his teeth. "Perfidious Albinon."

Roger pounced on him. To compare his beloved Free State movement to the English was heresy. Within seconds the two rolled off the walkway into the mud. Another man approached and pulled the two apart. He was a South Carolinian from the way he was dressed, and he soon knew he had two Irishmen before him. "Why're you a-fightin?" he asked.

"This young man is a Free Stater," said Laughlin. "I meant to teach him a lesson he'd not soon ferget about Atchison."

The Southerner took one look at Roger and punched him in the eye. Roger fell into the mud, a crackling sound in his head. He felt the ooze of the mud in his fingers and armpits as the man held him down and beat him, as well as his own blood, first running down his check and then smeared on the man's hand as it pummeled his forehead. And he felt the cold rise away from him as someone else attacked the man in his defense. Someone was balancing the fight, and he lifted himself from the ground, as if instinctively. It was an older man that defended him, an Irishman if he ever saw one. And he could fight. How could he fight! The drunken South Carolinian fell to the mud alongside Roger, got up, and walked away with mud on his face.

The older man took Roger by the shoulders, picked him up, and pressed a handkerchief to his bleeding face.

"That's a nasty cut on your eye," he said. He held Roger still when he stumbled, hugging him and digging into the slop around his feet. "What's your name, son?"

"Roger. Roger Dugan."

The man froze. He pushed Roger a bit away from him and looked him deep in the eye. And Roger saw, through the swell and the smear of blood, who it was. "And who are you?" he said anyway.

"Pappa," he said. "It's Pappa, my boy."

J. P. Dugan held his boy to his chest, and Roger could smell the clean rain.

***

Joseph James Hawkins stood, took a deep breath, and looked out at his land. His land. It sure had a ring to it. It was a beautiful stretch of land, but looking at it this way didn't make it seem so. Didn't do it justice. The little clearing he'd been able to accomplish, the angle of the house, to the river and the line of trees to the northeast, to Ollie's Grove, made it obvious he'd built and planted in a hurry. Almost shoddy and disheveled and ill-advised. It wore its woods awkwardly, this land. The water ran across her like something spilt, not drained or drank. He wasn't ashamed of it, but he could do better. He would have to if he stayed. If he survived.

Over the trees to the east, as his breath rose into the February sky, he saw a form. At first he thought it was that damned bird. The damned bird that showed its ugly face every time things went awry and a man had no means to kill it. The bird that knowed. But after a few twists and turns over the treetops it looked more like a dragon. With a long pointed tail and legs a-hangin' over the land. And it swished and swashed its way across the sky like a snake, a fish, an otter.

Joseph James Hawkins ran to his cabin for his gun. At the back of his skull somewhere was the beast's cry, a groan or growl or grunt that carried across the prairie, and he stumbled, clawing the frost-bitten grass like a four-legged creature and scrambling his way to the door. He wasn't sure if he actually heard the beast or if somehow his mind knew about its sound. Somehow in the back there somewhere was this thought, this memory, this idea or this dream, that knew what that slithery thing in the sky was. He thought of Del. That's why she'd gone. To Maria's because something in that part of your head told her to.

And this thing was out to stop her.

***

Del saw it too. She knew as she left the Dugan claim that it would be there. And now she knew that Joseph James knew. She knew from that part of her mind that loved her husband so immensely it was painful and dangerous. In the horse she could feel it, the bulge of its muscles and hesitation in its step. The beast and the knowledge that her husband would be coming with a mind to save her from it, as if he needed to, while at the same time knowing he didn't need to anymore. Del braced herself for this giant bird to crash to the earth. She reached for her bible, her own panic making her panic all the more. For it is a part of knowing, isn't it, to have a moment's doubt?

Then, in the clearing, there he was. Her Jimmy. He rode steadily to her and as he grabbed her by the elbow and let the horses steady themselves, he asked if she was alright.

"Yes."

"I told you not to go."

She smiled. "No you didn't."

"Well, I would have."

"But you didn't."

"But I would have." He smiled. "You are a naughty girl."

"I told her not to go to Atchison, Jimmy. She shouldn't go there. Not right now."

"What's so bad 'bout goin ta town that you'd go and risk her life for it, woman?"

She looked into the sky where the beast had been. "Because the real monster is in town."

"Of course. Real monsters always live in cities."

"She doesn't need a doctor anymore 'n she needs a priest. She needs peace and quiet."

"You did what you could."

"What I must. Only that."

"That's all we can ever do, Del. You know that."

Del looked at the sky again, twisting in her saddle to see the land around her. It was so beautiful, Kansas. The tangles of trees reached up from the river bottoms as if to leave no part of the earth too sunken or forgotten, and though the winter sun shone it was dulled by the crystalline moisture that hung like a grey curtain over them. "We can't stop it," she said.

"No, I'm afraid not. Slavery or no slavery, the beast is coming. All we can do is protect our claim, Del. Let the Dugans protect theirs."

"But . . . they are our friends."

Joseph James thought of this. Patrick had said it too, and it did make sense. But how can you be friends with someone who has tried to kill you? With a man who brought such a beast to the land, whether he knew it or not? Soon, railroads and factories and iron and choking smog would come. Soon, the rabbit and the fowl and the furry creatures dug into the mud would disappear. Soon, the land would never be the same. The river would choke and men in shoes that could not even carry him across a garden would come.

Even if you kept the niggers in chains, the Yankees would still chain the rest of us in the West, thought Joseph James. There was no stopping them.

***

George Sherman Hawkins liked to dress up whenever he got the chance. And he figured now was as good a day as any. So he dawned his best—his starched white shirt and his vest, even his waistcoat watch (that hadn't ticked in years but still looked as sharp as ever)—and came out into the garden. He stopped and put his tallest hat on, brushing his beard to his neck, and walked into the mud.

"Sarah," he said.

Sarah didn't answer. She knew he was there, and could even tell he was dressed differently by his mid-morning shadow, but made a valiant effort in pretending she did not. She continued preparing the garden for the spring rain, expanding it to the north beyond the cabin so it would yield more than a pittance. Pathetic little plot Del had chosen. All wrong from the looks of it. But she remembered Oliver John, remembered that she wouldn't be that way anymore. There wasn't any room for pettiness in Kansas anymore.

"Sarah," George Sherman said again. "Sarah, I wonder if I might help you."

Sarah stood, arching her back and placing the back of her hand against its small, worn and knotted curvature, and turned. Seeing him she laughed. And she laughed again, saying in her incredibly odd accent, "Them ain't your best clothes to be a-helpin' me, is they now George?"

"Depends on what you need help with, I suppose."

"Don't play coy with me, George. That time is past. I need help with the garden, not with dancing."

"I am not too sure there is much of a difference, Sarah. Making an Eden out of a hell is the same any way you cut it."

"Or sow it."

"Precisely."

"Here." She deftly tossed a garden hoe to him, extending it halfway with a strong wrist and tipping it forward. "Then get to work and do the work of God."

George Sherman Hawkins did exactly as he was asked by his ex-wife. He walked carefully around the plot from south to the north by way of the west and began chopping the semi-frozen topsoil to reveal the clayish mud below, tossing chunks of sod into the pile Sarah had started. He worked for an hour straight in this way, allowing every droplet of snow and mud to splatter his best shoes and the hems of his pants, leaving his top-hat and overcoat on all the while, despite the odd sensation of freezing sweat beneath both.

Until Sarah said with a chuckle, "You are an idiot, you know that, George Hawkins? A complete nincompoop."

"Why yes. Of course I do." He dropped his hoe and walked over to Sarah. "And now, a dance?"

"Yer even stupider than I supposed." But she was smiling.

"Who is stupider," he said, taking her hand and placing her other hand around his waist, "the idiot or the woman who dances with him in the mud?"

***

"We're all Kansans, when you think about it," said Dr. J.H. Stringfellow as Maria sat up and gathered her dress about her. "And Americans. At least, in the eyes of the law." Patrick took a step back and brought his wife with him. "There is no need for distrust, let me assure you, Patrick." The shadows in the room were odd, the light colored a muddy orange-brown, like the river that tugged the earth, its light and its shadows, to her lowest points.

"My friends—my real friends—call me 'Paddy.'" Even Patrick wasn't convinced by the attempt at sternness in his tone.

"I don't suppose I am that close to you yet, Mr. Patrick Dugan. But I aim to be."

"You have threatened me." More convincing now.

"Why, not personally, you must know." The older man pushed his plump thumbs into his waistcoat pockets. "Only in principal." He had an odd smile on this face and the color of the light made him look quite ill.

"Principals are personal, Doctor."

Stringfellow laughed. "Not in America, Patrick. Not in 1857, anyways. At least, not when business is involved."

"What do you mean?"

"I intend to propose a business proposition. A small one, but one nonetheless. You see, for all the intent of my paper, the *Sovereign*, and my political and cultural beliefs, the truth is that this town of Atchison (and Kansas, in her totality) is for me a business venture. You see, I perceive slavery as a good thing for Kansas, and for America, for all of us. But slavery at the expense of business, why, that would make very little sense indeed."

"I am not interested in dealing in slaves."

Stringfellow bellowed. "Why, you could not afford a slave, Mr. Dugan! And even if you could, an Irishman owning a—I dare ask, what would you have him do!?" He shook his head, incredulous. "I would never insult you by offering you one. If truth be told, I have none either. I propose a simple arrangement that is for our mutual benefit, one that involves no slaves whatsoever. A bank account, Mr. Dugan. A simple banking arrangement. You shall need to have money if you are to purchase your claim from the government, shall you not?"

"Yes. Of course." Maria had now gathered herself completely and stood as tall and soundly as ever. Patrick looked over at her. She was obdurate.

"Well, you would be quite the simpleton if you were to be saving dollars under your mattress or in a jar up in that hideaway you have. I can offer you interest, Mr. Dugan. Return on your investment."

"How so?"

"An account of course! An account in the Kansas Valley Bank!" Overhead, a rumble of thunder could be heard. It sounded like the river bounding over her banks and spilling up the streets of Atchison like the town were a thirsty tree. Stringfellow had to pause before continuing. "It is just chartered with the Territorial government and I am soliciting shares. We anticipate as much as five to ten percent per annum. A solid investment."

Patrick looked at him blankly. He had never had a bank account, of course, and was not sure that giving money to make money made any sense at all, but knew it could be and was done. The English did it. The English did it at the expense of the Irish. His father had told him so. And in America, apparently, even the Irish could do it. Hell, if the Irish could make money from money anybody could.

"Who is 'we'? I have no reason to trust a man who had preached violence against his fellow 'Kansans' and 'Americans,' as you so nobly call us." His tone betrayed him again.

Just then there was a knock at the door, and Samuel C. Pomeroy let himself in. "Why, speak of the devil!" said Dr. Stringfellow. "Allow me to introduce my partner in the Kansas Valley Bank, Mr. Dugan. This is Sa—"

"I know this man," said Patrick in an unmistakably sincere tone. "He is a Free Stater if there ever was one. Your opposite, Mr. Stringfellow."

Both men smiled. "Kansas has a way of making strange bedfellows," said one of them, the other laughing.

Another rumble seeped into the room and it began to rain suddenly. They could hear the water hitting the plank walkway outside. It sounded like a stampede.

IX

Joseph James and Delilah J. rode quickly to their farm, only to halt the horses suddenly (their new and rather dull-witted gelding needing to be told twice) when they arrived. In the garden was the most bizarre and surreal sight they had ever seen. George Sherman was dressed to the nines and was dancing in the mud with Sarah Sally.

"Looks like she's a-dancin' with the devil."

Del thought a moment. "No, he's not the devil."

"You sure 'bout that, Del?" Joseph wheeled his horse toward the barn in effort to make noise that would interrupt his dancing parents. "A man with two families in two states, maybe more, and an Indian whore he keeps around like a dog? Seems like he's one selfish greedy sonofabitch to me."

Del thought another moment. "He's changed. I can feel it when I'm around him." She wheeled her horse, laughing at the gelding who'd turned the wrong direction, before they trotted toward the barn. "Forgive yer pappa, Jimmy," she paused, smiling. "Just let it go."

As they unbridled the horses and fed them, Joseph and Del wondered what George and Sarah could possibly be talking about. He was telling her about Rebecca, perhaps, and his other family. Or maybe all the places he'd been in the last years. They could see through the gaps between the planks on the barn walls that they were not dancing anymore, but were still struck in that pose and conversing.

"That's about enough of this," said Joseph, heading for the door.

"It's nice, you know, Jimmy. We ain't danced in years."

"Aw hell, Del. That man is the devil!" he said, but walked back to his wife and took her in his arms.

***

Roger was perturbed that Patrick and Maria were not at home when he burst into the Dugan cabin with J.P. Something seemed very amiss about it. That the two of them would be gone was an anomaly, for sure. A trip to town was usually the job of one person, normally Patrick. Still, it didn't seem wrong, exactly. Not exactly. But he felt an odd sense of embarrassment.

Roger looked at his father to see his reaction. The old man, the Irish rebel who had fought the English and been expatriated to Australia, only to make his way to America to join his grown sons as they had expatriated themselves from a land of oppression and starvation—smiled. He smiled in the most satisfied manner possible.

"Why, this is one impressive piece of work, son. One impressive piece of work, I must say. The Lord himself would be proud. Why, this is an excellent farm. An excellent homestead. The best homestead in all of Kansas I am sure!" The old man's smile grew gradually larger as he said this.

"Patrick deserves all the credit, Pappa. He has built it while I have been—"

"Fighting!" The old man patted him on the back enthusiastically. "Of course!"

"Well, he has—"

"I know my sons, Roger. I know that you have helped him homestead and he has helped you fight, so? I know we left one another all too young, but I know your characters."

Roger turned around and sat at the table. "The place does need some work, Pappa." He smiled and waved his hand. Not just Kansas. This farm. He looked around. "I don't know why they are out. One of them should be here."

"Oh they are busy in town, boy. Farming is not just working the land. It is a business. Ever more so as the years go on. You should know that. I am quite sure your brother does."

"Yes, he does, but yet—"

"Hush. He is fine. Now, I am quite sure there is tea here. Make me some, why don't you. I've come across the globe to see this little cabin in Kansas and I intend to take your brother's absence as an opportunity to poke around."

Roger did his best to make tea without leaving traces that he had used Maria's beloved stove. He had been expressly forbidden from doing so many months ago after leaving a mess of eggs on the stovetop and, apparently, the coals improperly ventilated. His hands shook as he boiled the water and stoked the fire, but he didn't want his father to know it.

Meanwhile J.P. carefully examined every corner of the cabin, as un-intrusively as he could, if that is possible. He sauntered and meandered about like a tourist in an old quiet church, inspecting everything from the floorboards, which he admired greatly, to the eaves and the juncture between wall and ceiling, which he thought was a touch sloppy.

"Your brother has read Thoreau, has he not?"

Roger smiled as he tried to make the burning logs reduce into shapes similar to those that had been left before. It was nice to hear his father speak, and Roger became somewhat self-conscious of his own evolving accent. "He has indeed. Did you see it in his room?"

"No, I can tell from the shoddy roof joist placements. Too much reclaimed wood up there. Paddy should know his cabin is not the experiment of an artist but the permanent home for his family."

Roger smiled. "He knows that, Pappa."

"Why yes, I am sure you are right, so."

J.P. sat down and suddenly grew distant. His exhaustion only now became apparent, this being the first moment he had allowed his thoughts to wander since saving his son in town. Roger took the tea to the table, and after being chided for not having them, returned with saucers and spoons. "Mother would not be pleased about tea without saucers," J.P. had said, and grew quiet.

"Pappa, you haven't said yet what you did in Australia all these years."

The old man looked out the window and sipped his tea. His distance grew at once but then quickly closed. He looked at his son, then down at his hands resting on the table. "I was a convict, son, a criminal. I spent some time in chains, but much of it at work in labor camps. It was hell, to be sure, for several years. But, at some length I was released and I tried to make a go of it. I built a cabin, had some land, and tried to settle in. But—" he grew distant again, looking out the window. "I became somewhat obsessed with finding you. You and Mamma. My little farm went fallow as I wrote letter after letter to everyone I could remember. I finally found Maria's name, then her family in Boston, who knew where you were."

He took a deep breath and laughed. "And then I read everything about this Kansas place that I could get my hands on, which was not much, let me tell you. But the troubles here this summer were widely publicized, and I read all reports voraciously as I prepared for my journey. You took part in an international revolution, boy." His face took on the passion that Roger had so well remembered, as J.P. threw his hands about at night while mother cooked. "*International,*" said he.

Roger felt his moment. This was his moment to show his father he understood the struggle in the broad sense of humanity, not the petty politics of the territory, the westward expansion, or even the nation or even slavery. It was a global struggle, and J.P. had returned just so he could have his chance at proving he understood it. All his life led to this very moment.

But just as he opened his mouth to speak, Patrick and Maria walked in the door. They hadn't even heard the horses in the yard. Both stood just inside the doorway, mouths agape in astonishment.

"Father?" said Patrick.

"Who's been using my stove?" chided Maria.

***

Something about dancing in the mud allowed Sarah Sally and George Sherman to talk for the first time in years. The feeling of the slick, warming soil beneath their boots, and the sucking sound it made when they lifted each foot, so slightly and gently, and the rhythm of their bodies keeping time with the smattering of gold finches and red-winged blackbirds made it feel like 1835 again, before George went back for Rebecca, before life changed and made a cruel prank of love.

"You are one selfish sonofabitch," Sarah Sally said to him. "What you did to me you are doing right now, as we speak, to her. Yer a filthy scoundrel, George Sherman. And I'm a whore for dancing with you."

"You're a lonely woman, Sarah. And a beautiful one."

Looking into his eyes, she said, "How old is she now?" and he looked unsure. She was disgusted. The lines around his mouth were the same she saw all those years ago when he first explained it to her, like a child, a cowardly boy. "My God, George. Do you even know how old you are? How old I am?"

"Yes."

"Too old to be married to young women and have babies, that's fer sure. You disgust me."

"Indians grow old, too, you know, Sarah." They danced a moment longer and Sarah let her head settle into his shoulder. "I know I disgust you," he said, and she could feel his voice reverberate throughout his chest, and her head. "And I understand why. But you know why I went back for her, Sarah. And why—" he swallowed and she lifted her head but the chin. "—why he had to stay with you."

This hung in the air with all the smells of the river, and he held her out from his body a few more inches and stopped rocking in the mud. "The thing is, Sarah, I think you understand exactly why I'm a scoundrel, and why it doesn't make me the devil. I can see it in your eyes."

Sarah Sally caught a glimpse now of her son and daughter in-law in the barn. She could see they were dancing. "Goddamn you, George. You are the most romantic man I ever did meet." Her head sunk back to his body as if of its own accord, heavy with the years and the lies.

Suddenly it felt both bizarre and familiar to George Sherman; dancing in the mud to the music of strange insects. He smiled, touching her hair for the first time in almost twenty years. He looked away, then back, hesitating, and took a deep breath. "Does this mean you'll let me stay?"

"Let you stay!?" she pushed herself away from him. "It ain't my decision, George. I'm a weak woman and can't imagine ever a-turnin' you away. Yer son, on the other hand," she motioned to the barn, where Joseph James was just emerging, and lowered her voice, "why, you leavin' just about a-ruined his damned life,

George. You gotta understand that. And Oliver John—" her lip quivered, "he was a sad boy, you sonofabitch!" She slapped him on the chest. "And a-think of Rebecca and her children! You don't even a-know what you mean by 'stay.' I don't think you do neither." She looked away, then back. "I feel sorry even for her. You're a scoundrel."

George looked at his son and his wife coming out of the barn. They were holding hands and their feet melted the snow as they walked, turning white to black, giving the spring grasses below room to rise. He thought about their lives here, the promise of the future that was coming out of the earth after the horrible winter in which they grieved their brother, more like their son. Inside was their daughter, napping; behind them their barn and healthy horses; and all around them, almost as far as the eye could see, was their land. *Their* land. It had a ring to it, The Hawkins Farm. In the soles of his boots he felt as if poison escaped. He didn't belong here.

"You ornery old man!" Joseph James said to his father. "I done caught you two a-dancin'."

His son's smile was childlike, hopeful, so he looked to the west and said, "How's about you and I go huntin'," looking back briefly at Joseph James, light trying to push through the dullness his brother's death had brought to his once bright blue eyes.

"Go a-huntin' with my Pappa!? Jes' try 'n stop me." He bounded off into the house.

Delilah stepped between her parents in-law, taking them by the arms. "I'm so very glad we're all here," she said. "We are so very fortunate. We must honor Oliver John. A piece of that boy is in all of us. His simple joys. His forgiveness. His wonder."

It grew very quiet on the Hawkins farm, and the sounds of spring could be heard about them. The trees rustled with the squirrels coming out of hiding, new songs from dormant birds slowly filled the sky, and the dripping of melting snow and ice could be heard like thunder. The damp, thawing earth filled their nostrils, and the creeping of the growing grasses and crops could be heard like a river in winter. Even a frog awoke in the distance.

"Oliver John loved frogs," Sarah Sally said in a faltering voice.

Inside they could hear Missy waking from her nap, her gentle gurgles and groans rising from the cabin and into the brightness of the sky. Del went in for her, and Sarah Sally turned to George Sherman.

"You have to tell him," she said, and her voice fell away, a tree frog growing suspicious at the sounds carried by the moonlight.

***

George Sherman didn't quite realize his brilliance in asking his son to hunt in order to tell him something difficult to hear. Men often forget themselves in the bustling and the ways of the world, the need to persevere and preserve. Gentlemen all, in town and city and country alike, the game must be played. But in the woods, the wild, and on the hunt, the softness of their souls is unleashed.

It is also often the case that men on the hunt do not hunt. Unleased souls rest against trees and on hillsides, against boulders and the banks of rivers. They cross their boots and smoke, snort whiskey, toss rocks and tap pinecones with sticks. And in the arc of a tossed clod of moss between one man and another, the best words pass between them.

They found Joseph James's hunting blind near the northwest corner of the property, hidden at the edge of a wood with a few of a clearing. Crouched against stumps, picking ticks from their ankles and waists, they spoke of the biggest bucks they'd ever slayed and fish they'd caught, and son related to father both the drudgery and excitement of wars, in Mexico and Kansas alike. And they arrived at last at Oliver John.

"We were camped along a crick something just like this. For the second time in my life my captain let the men get drunk—" he swallowed, spat, cleared his throat. "—and someone I loved a-payed fer it."

A jay called in the tree nearby, both men glanced at it as if to acknowledge what it had to add, but continued. "What—" George Sherman began, faltered, "What happened?"

"I think he got up to pee," Joseph James stood, slowly, with his rifle, and sighed. "And someone shot 'im. Jes' like that." His father's face, not glancing again at the jay and not looking away, asked him to continue gently. Turning, the son looked out over the pasture and saw a large buck emerge from the trees opposite, but he continued. "His bedroll was cold, so I went a-lookin' for 'im. You know when he was a kid—" he turned back now, but George Sherman shook his head ever so slightly in shame, so he turned back and watched the buck take careful steps into the grass as he spoke. "When Ollie was a kid he'd get up in the middle of the night and you'd a-go find 'im somewhere sleepin', by the fire or out in the yard or somethin'. I figured he'd a-done that, so I went a-lookin'."

"And you found him."

"Yeah," he turned back now. "Yeah, I found him. What was left of him."

George Sherman stood next to his son, and they watched the buck as he came into full view in the middle of the clearing. "That's one hell of an animal," he said, touching his son on the shoulder carefully. "Don't get much prouder than that."

Stepping back a bit and facing his father, Joseph James said it. "It killed that poor boy, you know," he said, realizing he was able to swallow, didn't have to spit. "You a-leavin' us like that."

The father didn't, as the son expected, bow his head even lower in even more shame. Instead he raised it, stuck out his chin, and looked again at the buck, who by now had nearly passed through the clearing. And he said, "I had to save someone."

"Save who?" the son asked. "Rebecca or that Indian whore Mamma's always on about?" He saw the pain in his father's proud eyes now, and regretted using his mother's nasty word.

George Sherman sighed and turned, kicking the dirt with his boot, and the buck bounded off into the woods. "Both," he said, and turned back to his son. Looking him in the eye, and seeing his pain, he said softly, "they are one in the same, son."

"Wh—what?" Joseph James shook his head, let his arms fall to his sides, the buckskin of his coat slapping together.

"Rebecca is the Indian, Jimmy. And what you call a 'nigger,' in fact. Rebecca is my wife." He shook his head at his son's unmoving expression. "Jimmy, the Indian is my wife."

Joseph James didn't look as stupefied as he might have. His stolidness held and he chose one question from as many as there were leaves on the tree above them. "Why would you lie about that?"

George Sherman took a deep breath, sadness and smile flashed across his face all at once, and his son braced himself.

"Jimmy, she's your mother. Rebecca is your mother."

X

"Them pigs need a-tendin' to," said Roger, hurriedly grabbing his coat and heading out the door.

"Roger!" Maria said, stopping him immediately.

He pointed at his father. "He made me do it, Maria! He made me make him tea, I swear! I didn't want to use your stove! Pappa made me do it!"

J.P. interrupted. "Maria, I like you already, love. I apologize that I had my son use your stove. It's been a long time since I had a cup of tea with family."

Maria smiled. "Let me make you some." She threw Roger a look that made him flinch and scramble out into the bright afternoon. "Properly."

Patrick stood as if he were a frozen statue while Maria and J.P. introduced themselves, hugged and kissed, and the old man sat at the table describing his trip to his daughter in-law while she made tea and toast and washed the last batch of carrots from the previous fall. She listened to her father in-law while she did this, but the shape and color of the carrots took her back to pulling them out of the ground last September, wondering if her husband was alive.

And Patrick still stood there, dripping onto the floor, until his wife told him to wake up and "make himself useful if he still knew how." He did, removed his coat and hat and gloves, mopped the entryway without being asked, and sat down across from his father, all without taking his eyes of the old man or even blinking. He barely breathed.

At length, the old man reached across the table and held his eldest son by the hand. "You look as if you've seen a ghost, boy."

"I fear I have, Pappa. Is that really you?"

"I'm afraid so."

"Even after I received your letter last autumn I still thought you were dead. Or that you would die on your way to America. I simply cannot believe my eyes."

"Sometimes eyes are not to be believed, son. You know that, I'm sure. But in this they inform you correctly. I am here. I am old, but alive, and thank Mother Mary, I am a free man once again." He looked to the heavens.

"I don't know where to begin."

"You are a man now, Paddy." The old Irishman smiled. "And I am an old man now. When we last saw each other, I was a man and you were still a child. Perhaps we should start there." He saw his son hesitate. "Tell me about mother."

An image of her came to Patrick's mind. She was tired, maybe frightened. "I don't know if I can, like."

"Perhaps not now, but you must, son. I must know."

"Yes. Well—" Maria sat at the table and served the tea and food. "She died of cholera on the boat, Pappa. It was quick, but it was terrible. Mostly for Roger, I believe. She said goodbye to us."

"I have heard those ships were deathtraps."

Patrick looked at his hands. They were shaking. His heart fluttered, something that worried him from time to time. But it didn't matter just now. "Yes, I'm afraid so, Pappa. I'm afraid so. Mother was not alone. But," he sighed, one hand grasping the other, his father grasping both, "the ships were better by the time we left. It was," his voice cracked, "it was at home when things were the worst. I often wonder if we stayed too long. Perhaps if we left sooner Mother would—"

"You raised your brother, Patrick. God will smile kindly on you. You are courageous and loving. I am proud of you."

Patrick looked at Maria. "We raised him. As our own. As best we could." He smiled. "Roger is at times a horse that cannot be broken." He looked at Maria again, and then at his father. The afternoon light streamed in the windows and gave the scene a supernatural quality, a heavenly glow. Dust danced in the light. "Is this really happening?"

His father laughed. "Farm metaphors with you, so?" He laughed again. "Ah, you are my son indeed. You love this land, don't you? And you see it sometimes. Tell me, Patrick Dugan of Kansas, what little ones are in these woods?" J.P. was beaming now.

Maria began to speak. She wanted to stop this conversation, but Patrick interrupted her. "It isn't small. It's a bird. A great bird."

The old man's eyebrows raised. "Yes," he said. It was part exclamation, part question.

Maria sighed heavily and looked at her hands. "Eat, boys, eat. You have plenty of time for this nonsense."

"And the spirits of men." Patrick was only slightly aware of what he was saying. "A Frenchman, for one. And a ferryman. And the ghost of a hanged slave, Molly."

"Yes!" The elder Irishman's eyes were wide with a familiar wonder.

"Nonsense! Stop it, the two of you. This isn't Ireland!" Maria's face looked older than it usually did.

"Paschal saved you!" he snapped at his wife, wondering how such a brilliant woman could close her own wisdom at times, a hen sitting a rotten egg.

"I don't have time for this." She stood and busied herself near the stove.

"And the bird, Maria. You saw it," Patrick said, restraining himself as best he could. He wanted to shake her, turn her upside down like a newborn and make her breath and cry to be sure she was alive.

"Yes, I saw it you bumbling idiot! But we are not to speak of these things!"

J.P. interrupted his son as he began to reply to his wife. "Maria is correct, son. Now, we must appease the sprites and go tend to your land." The two men stood and Maria watched them go, holding carrots and tea in her hands, protesting silently.

***

For the first time in his life, Joseph James Hawkins wished he had a mirror. Once or twice someone had said something to him about being Indian, but he'd only seen his own face a dozen times or so. The way the dust of New Mexico settled on his skin, for instance, reminded at least one fellow Missourian of a Puebloan.

"You sure you ain't Indian, Hawkins?" the man had said. "Yer pretty dark, and that nose looks downright Cherokee to me. Hell, I'd a-bet you could stay right here with a change of clothes and these folk'd never know the difference. If you could keep yer mouth shut, that is. Which you cain't."

But it wasn't those comments that made him know this to be so—that Rebecca was his true mother—it was the way she felt in his arms the day they buried Oliver John. The whole thing had happened as if in a dream, and as it is with many dreams, he'd not given the moment a second thought since. But how odd that this woman would embrace him like she did; where she did, when she did, as if they were two trees finding they could share the world, gently. Only a mother could do that. Appear like a cloud out of nowhere, blessing with shade and rain just when the scorch of grief becomes unbearable.

Sarah Sally sat quietly, as small as possible, in the dark corner of the cabin. He must have been the runt of the litter to her, the oddly-colored hide, awkward, misshapen, strange and alien; the one that bit the nipple, fumbling with crooked hands as it tried to suckle. And yet she made him feel loved every now and then, kept him warm and fed and never once told him the truth. Her lie, her sin, was for him.

He looked at his hands and said, "So you went back for her." In the fading light his hands looked clean, though he knew them to be dirty.

George Sherman sat next to Sarah Sally. She rocked and pursed her lips. She was downright nervous. "I did," said the man. "She would have died, Jimmy."

Joseph James turned and looked out the window, aware of the cup of coffee in his hand, the way his profile may have looked to those askance him, and straightened his back. Suddenly he saw himself in reflection, utterly, as if he'd only ever seen himself in a mirror and nothing else. "They'd a-marched her to Indian Territory." He turned. In the reflection, where his wife would see it, he felt wise and strong as a buffalo. But to him, to him, this man was a monster.

"Yes." His father, his beard seeming to carry the dust of decades in it, looked over at his not-mother again, and touched her leg. She moved it away. "It was over by then. They were going to force them all. Remove them all. I went back to help."

Sarah Sally looked away, as far away as anyone can look; into the pain of her youth. George Sherman sighed and sat back, removed his hat and rubbed his hair, and the woman next to him said, as if the wall or a person long since removed from it, "I never had any help."

Joseph James sat, seeing himself trying not to rub his hair the way his father did. "I'm a mite surprised Rebecca had you back, Pappa. Why didn't you just a-marry her in the first place? Why—" his elbow came to his knees, his dusty now-nigger-Indian hands grasping each other in his lap. "How . . . what . . . ?" he stammered like an idiot.

"She didn't want to marry me, Jimmy," came a flat reply. "We had you. Her family—her father—didn't especially—"

"Want his half-breed grandson?"

A nail appeared, as if out of nowhere, in George Sherman's fingers. He twisted it over a couple times, as if examining it to be sure it was straight. "It wasn't that, son," he sighed. "He was a good man. His daughter was a 'half-breed,' as you say—her mother's family had an African in it. So it wasn't that. Not really, anyway." He stood and let the nail drop on the table, turning to look out the window. "He didn't like me, son. White, from a well to-do family in North Carolina." He turned back around and sat again, playing with the nail on the table top, smiling and shaking his head. "And it wasn't even that, I don't think, that mattered most. At that time, she wouldn't leave him. Wouldn't leave the tribe. She wanted to stay, on her farm, her homeland, the trees and rivers and rolling hills. She didn't love me enough."

"And so you—?"

"Met your mo—" he looked over again, pausing. The woman beside him was still well beyond the wall, way long ago. "I met Sarah Sally here. And I fell in love," he said in such a way that he sounded convinced but uninterested in sounding convincing. "We—all of us—thought it better you be raised by a white woman. That you be raised white."

His hands, thought Joseph James, were big. Their creases were deeply inlaid. They appeared to be chiseled by a master craftsman. They had known love. There was no denying it. But they had also done unspeakable things. "But still you went back for her."

At this, Sarah Sally's head swiveled right back to the room, and fixed its gaze up on the man who, yes, had gone back for her, and yes, had also left. The man who could do both, and neither. She waited for his answer.

"Yes," he said, rising, and walking over to his son, gentler upon the floorboards than usual, as if his boots were lighter and softer. He placed a hand upon the half-breed's shoulder, so wide and proud and strong. "It's a curious thing, love," he said. "We have too much of it. More of it than we can give to one person, more than one person can accept."

Sarah Sally didn't move. She agreed, goddamn her. But her now-not-son wasn't sure.

"Some folk give love just so they can get it," the son not-son said, looking at them both in equal measure. "So they aren't a-givin' at all, if you ask me. They take and they take, and even when you think they're a-givin', you get downright tired around them." He took a step toward the bedroom and stopped. Looking straight at his now not-mother, he said, leaning forward, "You hear me? I said I'm tired. Tired of it all."

And he went in his room.

***

Sometimes we have to divide our lives like our land, thought Patrick Dugan as he picked up his hoe and waded into his corn. His wife and brother were in one section, his father another, his mother in-law yet another; the Hawkinses had their place, and so did the others, like Paschal and Molly and the jayhawk. Ghosts belong not upon the surface, he thought, like the rest, where the surveyor's chains, hedges of mulberry and limestone walls divide us. Ghosts are just above, dragonflies flitting about the place in terrible acrobatics; just below, moles, undying, blind determination. Like crops must grow in rows, men in squares, the fairies have a shape, too. Orbs and an oblong fuzziness.

Somehow J.P. Dugan still belonged in his own shape, divided from the rest. Every single time Patrick saw his father these categorizations that made husbandry easier were bereft of any sense. Where was he? What was he? He seemed to belong to something else, a new division Patrick had yet to encounter; or, at the least, hadn't encountered for a long time. Truth be told (and when it was Patrick had to set down his hoe and wipe his brow, despite it being cold), he was afraid of his father. Afraid of what he might have been, what he might still be.

But hush, there were weeds in the corn.

***

His things were piled expertly by the door, which was ajar, and through which the dull light cast an odd shape on the floor, and Joseph James knew that outside his father sat, coffee in his hand, waiting for his son and his family to rise, so he could leave them. Once again.

He stood when he saw his son and shook the last dregs of coffee out of the cup.

"Back to Indiana, then?"

The old man smiled, and looked somewhat younger in doing so. One last lie to divulge. "Indian Territory."

Joseph James was not surprised. He'd seen the smile. "You never lived in Indiana?"

"I wouldn't say 'never.'" He smiled again, even laughed with his eyes. "Just not exactly."

Mysteries, thought Joseph James, come in all shapes and sizes. He had first learned this as a boy, calving a cow with Mr. Anderson—the farmer who employed him (and nothing more)—in Clay County for much of his life. How could such an animal be inside another animal? Why didn't the hooves, or the sheer weight of the thing, just tear open the heifer's belly? They never did, but sometimes, he found, the mother seemed to feel so; refusing to nuzzle and wash her calf. Ever since he'd seen mysteries in all the world. Frogs surviving winter. Insects drawing blood from things a million times their size. The dragon wrapped back and forth many times in the trees of Kansas, and the fact that one can live so long and not know one's mother is not one's mother. A mystery to himself. He felt ill now, like yesterday when he went to bed in daylight for the first time since he was last ill, some twenty years ago, maybe.

"You went back to Tennessee to save a woman from being forced to move to Indian Territory, just so you could take her to Indian Territory." It wasn't a question. Just a point of clarification.

"Yes," he said. "Yes," he said again, and a breeze rose from the northeast, making them shiver a little. He offered his hand to his son, who took it. "You should come down there one day, Jimmy. Your mo—" he paused, "—Rebecca would be overjoyed if you were to meet her people."

But Joseph James didn't smile, and his brow didn't unfurl. In fact, it wrinkled up like an apple left in the sun. "Don't run from it," said the father to the half-breed. "You can't. Believe me," he laughed now, heartily this time, not because it was amusing but because life has this odd way of curling back upon itself. "Believe me. The world is round."

Seeing his son would not reply, would perhaps never even have anything else to say to him ever again, George Sherman Hawkins took his things, mounted the horse hitched just outside, and rode slowly to the south. He'd always ridden north. But this time he rode south.

Mysteries, thought Joseph James, and lies, often come in the shape of fathers. Fathers and mothers, grandfathers and grandmothers. For the past is nothing but mysteries and lies.

XI

By May of 1857, both the Hawkins and Dugan farms were prepared for the coming warmth of summer. Cash crops had been sown, gardens were sprouting, baby chicks were being hatched, and the Hawkinses had even managed to see a sow through pregnancy and now had several squealing piglets. Missy had begun to walk, Del was pregnant again, and Maria was due to deliver her child any day now. Joseph James hadn't spoken to his now-not-mother in months, but that wasn't anything completely unique and didn't ever have to change, really. The Kansas spring was full of promise.

And when the spring is full of promise, women want better things. Del sat down one evening as the sun turned toward the western horizon and decided to write Maria and invite them over for supper again. Joseph James wasn't too happy about it, but she figured he'd grown up a lot in the last few months and he'd get over it. She smiled and began to write.

Dere Mariah,

I hope I spelled yer name rite this time! Not too bad fer a gurl who tought herself to read and rite. Truth is, I been studying a lot and am determind to have Missy go to skool. I here they been starting to bild a skool in town and I figer it aint too long before they bild one out here for the farm folk. Have you seen how many claims been comin up round? Why, wont be too long before we have more naybors n we kin shake a stick at.

Mariah, I know our familys have had some trying times of late, but the Good Lord always has a plan for us. And rite now He's tellin me we is naybors and will always be, and that it's time we put last summer behind us. Jimmy done healed up nicely, and I hope you have too. I know my husband, and I know he probly deservd whatever you done to him. I'm sher he did. He can be pigheaded at times. I hope you and yer boys are getting along nisely and are enjoying the springtime.

*I propose we have a supper, Mariah. Let's get these darn
men together and who knows, mebbe after a drink or too they will
forgive eachother. Stranger things have happened round these
parts, and the Lord preaches that we forgive and treat our neybors
as we want to be treeted ourselvs.*

Let me know what you think.

My love to you and yours.

Delilah J.

"You realize yer a-askin' me to invite the man who shot me
over fer supper, don't you? And the woman who broke my
hand?" said Joseph James as his wife handed him the letter. "Are
ya as crazy as that?"

"You are inviting your neighbors over for supper, Joseph.
And your oldest friends in the world, too, if you didn't a-think
of that."

"He tried to kill me, Del. I fought him in battle! The Battle
of Hickory Point!"

"Oh hogwash. As far as I can tell this whole Bleeding
Kansas thing is just a schoolyard fist fight between a bunch of
boys. You've a-been in bar brawls bigger 'n that 'Battle of
Hickory Point.' This ain't Mexico, Joseph."

"Padd—that goddamn Irishman tried to kill me!"

"You were a-tryin' ta kill him too, weren't you?"

"Del—"

"And whatever you did to Maria, well, I think yer lucky if
they accept, Joseph James Hawkins."

"Del, I fought in Doniphan's army in Mexico, at El Brazito
and Buena Vista and Sacramento, and I'm a-tellin' you—"

"Oh hush," she shoved the letter farther into his hand. "I
don't care what the papers are a-sayin'. It don't match the reality,
Joseph. If you'd a-believe the papers you'd think everyone in
Kansas was dead by now. Look around you," she made a
sweeping motion around her. "This is one helluva farm, Joseph

James. If you were caught in the middle of a war you think you coulda done this?"

Joseph James was mad now, and he spat and clenched his teeth. "Oliver John. They killed Oliver John."

Del was quiet for a moment and lowered her voice, softening her tone. "I know, Jimmy. And I miss him more than anyone. That's another reason to invite them over. We can't war with our neighbors forever, Joseph, and the Dugans ain't a-goin' nowheres. Oliver John would understand that and you know it. A more forgiving child was never a-born to this broken world."

Joseph James spat again and stomped off toward his barn.

***

Paschal had been waiting for Patrick since last fall. It was the night of June 7, 1857, and a wet day had given over to a clear, muggy night. Paschal smoked his pipe and waited, knowing that this night the Irishman would arrive. He wouldn't be able to sleep, knowing that the next day he was to share a meal with a man who tried to kill him, and he would wander toward the spring, the Eternal Spring that Patrick knew was a place of knowing. A place of reflection and silence.

Patrick seemed to be a ghost as he strolled into the clearing where the mound and the spring that rose out of it lay. He was so tall and gaunt, and looked older than he did just last year. His skin had a transparent, sickly quality to it in the light of the full moon, and his gait was so lazy he seemed to hover above the now knee-high grasses.

"Irishman! At last, you arrive!"

"Hello Paschal. Fancy seeing you here."

"Yes indeed! My, it has been some months, has it not?"

"I suppose so."

"I have been waiting for you."

"I know."

"Yes indeed! You are beginning to listen, I believe."

"I don't like what I'm hearing."

"Why not, Paddy? Here, sit, my friend."

Patrick sat next to the Frenchman on the limestone platform beside the spring. He could see that many of the Kanza Indian relics scattered around the mound had been disturbed. "Someone has been here. Someone else."

"Yes indeed. You are beginning to listen, and you do not like what you hear."

"Why not, Paschal? This time last year I was raising a gun at fellow human beings, and they were raising theirs at me. 1857 has been quieter than 1856, more peaceful. Why, I haven't even seen the great bird."

Paschal laughed. "Why yes indeed! But perhaps you are not listening carefully enough. It is there." The Frenchman began to glow, as he did when he was most frightening. "1857 quieter than 1856? There is something more sinister than guns, my young Irish friend."

"Where? What?"

"Why, there!" Paschal pointed to the trees where a year ago Patrick had seen the bird for the first time. It was there again. Or, something like it but not the same. Its silhouette was long and sleek, seemed to go on forever in the trees, like a giant snake.

"What is that? That is not the same bird. The jayhawk."

"You have named it!? Oh, I wouldn't name it, Mr. Mudfaced Irishman. I wouldn't name it any more than I would follow it." He licked his lips and stoked his pipe. "Bad luck. An Irishman should know that."

"Many of the men here, the Free Staters, call themselves jayhawkers."

"My, my. Perhaps I underestimated you, Irishman. You are listening, and quite well. Yes indeed!"

"But that is not the jayhawk. And why does it stay so still?" Just then the beast rose into the sky, and Patrick could see it well in the moonlight. It was the bird. But it was different. It seemed part fish, part lizard, part bird, part mammal, part man, even. Nasty. Mean. Frightening. But its face smiled kindly. "Dear God in Heaven."

"No indeed!" Paschal laughed. "That ain't no god, Irishman." He laughed again. "No god you'd wanna worship, anyway." He grew serious and took a step toward Patrick, grabbed his lapel and pulled the taller man toward his face. Paschal smelled less like tobacco than Patrick expected. He had another smell. An earthy one. "And what makes you so sure that ain't the same beast, Mudface. Hm? You may be listening better, but your eyes deceive you, son."

***

Maria and Del had convinced Patrick and Joseph to shuttle letters back and forth between the farms for two weeks, and in so doing this conversation had resulted in the supper being held at the Dugans'. Maria insisted that it was their turn to host. Though she had sheltered and fed Oliver John for several months in the fall and winter of 1855, and Joseph for part of that; though she had indeed had them over before, she was adamant that Sarah Sally had not attended, that the meal had been ruined by politics, and that J.P. would decry his daughter in-law's lack of hospitality if she were to allow Del to host.

Del protested that the last time they had spent time together at the Hawkins house, the night had been ruined by the stillbirth of Maria's first child. But this point was used against her by Maria, who said that it was all the more reason for her to host. "I feel I have been pregnant for far too long, Delilah, and that I may explode into labor any day. Please do the honor of being home, should that occur." That was that. The supper was scheduled for June 8th at Maria's house.

The night before, as Patrick returned from his moonlight meeting with Pascal, Roger stood in the yard, waiting for his brother. He leaned against the sole remnant of the old shack they used back in the winter of 1854-1855—a solitary cottonwood plank nailed against a hickory tree with a flap of tattered canvas hanging from it—smoking a pipe.

"Brother! You return from your walk."

"Roger?" Patrick said disappointingly. "You're smoking?"

"Father gave it to me."

"Give me that." He took the pipe and smoked it. It tasted like Ireland. Like home. He thought of his mother. "My, my, that is good, isn't it?"

"Reminds me of something."

"Home, Roger. Pappa smoked this back in Cork."

"That explains why he was so excited to give it me, so."

"Yes indeed. Here." He handed it back to his brother. "I suppose you are old enough." Roger raised his brows in question. "And..." Patrick sighed and looked up at the moon, shoving his hands in his pockets, "that you don't need me to father you anymore."

"Haven't for some time, brother!"

Patrick smiled. "Yes, I suppose not. It seems a long time ago now, doesn't it?"

"What? Ireland? I don't even remember it."

"No. Osawatomie. Hickory Point. Last summer. Our . . . troubles."

"Our victory! Seems like yesterday to me. I relive it every moment I have." He scratched his leg where the scar of his combat wound was, though it was almost indiscernible now. A moment of silence passed. Roger packed the pipe again and handed it to Patrick. "Tell me, Paddy. What do you do out there in them woods? Why do you walk into them at night?"

"Paschal."

"Paschal?"

"You were delirious with fever when I told you about him. Do you remember the bird?"

Roger looked off into the distance and frowned. "I thought that was a nightmare."

"Oh it was! It was indeed."

"But . . . it is real?"

"I don't know how to answer that question, boy. Paschal is a . . . a man, I s'pose. A French trapper that lived here before, with the Indians. He . . . he is sometimes out there." He pointed to the rugged country to the north and east of the cabin. "He showed me the bird. He taught me not to follow it."

"A man? Out there? Does he have a claim?"

"No. I'm not sure anyone does, not really."

"You're starting to sound very Irish, Paddy."

"It's been many months, but I met him tonight. The bird, Roger . . . has . . . changed."

"What do you mean, changed?"

They heard the front door of the cabin open behind them. It was J.P. He joined his sons on the site of the old shack and lit his own pipe. "Like father, like sons," he said. "Full moons make it hard to sleep. A good smoke passes the time, so. You two look serious. Have you seen a ghost?"

"Patrick has."

"Has he now? Tell me about it son."

"Maria said not to."

"Ah, yes. The ferryman?"

"No, the trapper. Paschal Pensenou. And . . . the bird."

"Spirits, you think?"

"I have no idea."

"Mm, better that way." The old man took a few steps away and yawned, stretching toward the stars, then returned to his sons. "Here, take this." He handed Patrick an old, dirty pipe.

"I have one, Pappa."

"I want you to have it. It was your mother's." He saw surprise in his sons' faces. "Don't look alarmed boys. Your mother was an ornery one at times, so." He smiled. "A true woman."

"She smoked?"

"Occasionally. She hid it from you boys, among other things. She hid it from me for a while, even. It angered me. I shouted at her." He shook his head and puffed his pipe. "My, how insignificant. How petty. How deceived we become in this life, gentlemen." He paused again, rocking forward to the balls of his feet and back again, and looked around. "This is one beautiful country, Patrick. You will do very well here." He turned and looked at his eldest. "Listen to your wife, Patrick. Listen to her. Follow her, even. Do as she tells you." He exhaled from his nose. The curling smoke reminded Patrick of Paschal. "These people . . . this family coming here tomorrow. Remember they are your neighbors. They are not your enemy." He looked at Roger. "It is easy to see your enemy in people who tend to agree with them. But they are not."

"The English—"

"An entire ocean, two wars, and nearly a century lay between us and the Parliament, boy."

"But—"

"Protestants are not our enemy, Roger. Hell, as I've aged I've come to realize the English aren't either. It is the rich, sons. The wealthy. The powerful. Greed is our enemy. Avarice is our enemy. The Hawkinses, it seems to me, are not these things."

Roger looked away, toward the old shack. Consternation darkened his face even in the night, and he looked younger than usual. "Then what are we to do about the wealthy, Pappa?"

J.P. Dugan's yellow teeth smiled through the curling smoke. "Beat them at their own game, Roger, my boy."

Roger looked back again, a glint of understanding in his eye. "But how?"

"Land, Roger, land. Kansas is the greatest investment opportunity there ever was."

Roger chewed his pipe. "I know a place," he said as if divulging a secret.

"Do you now?"

"Quindaro. A town downriver created as a Free State ferry-landing and, one day, a railroad hub. Bought at good prices from the Wyandotte, they are even part owners. The Wyandotte are civilized." He looked uncomfortable, as if the words were misshapen in his mouth, but continued. "If investment is what you want, Pappa, you may as well invest in land with a righteous cause, don't you think?"

Patrick sighed impatiently. "We've an entire generation of farm-work here, boys."

"You won't get rich farming, Paddy," said his father.

"I don't want to be rich. I just want to keep this claim."

"If you aren't rich they'll take it from you, Paddy."

"Not here," said he. "Not in America."

A patronizing smile glinted on the old man's face. "This land is as capitalist as it is democratic," said he. "Tell me more about Quindaro, Roger,"

But just then Maria emerged from the cabin, a pipe in her hand. "Mind if I join you gentlemen?" said she.

XII

Joseph James Hawkins could not sleep the night of the full moon, June 7th, 1857. While the Dugans stood around the yard outside their cabin, just a quarter-mile away, Joseph lay in bed staring at the ceiling he had built with Oliver John. He would think of his brother, his neighbors, the work that needed done on the farm. He thought of his now-not-mother and father, the mysterious black-Indian woman in his soul, his childhood in Missouri, and cycle back to Oliver John. His back hurt. His right leg ached. He decided tomorrow he'd mow the front-quarter pasture and re-stuff the mattress with new grass. Maybe he'd sleep better if he did that.

And then he began to think of the war in Mexico. Once that started, he knew he was doomed to at least another hour of insomnia, so he dressed and stepped outside with his pipe and a cup of whiskey. He sat next to the well, in sight of Oliver John's grave. Pegasus was just emerging from the east, just as it had on some of the long nights on the march to Santa Fe. The longest march since Alexander the Great, they said. Nearly 6,000 miles, from Leavenworth to Santa Fe to the Sacramento River to the Gulf of Mexico. He was cavalry, so much of his was astride Ninny, his old horse, who died on New Year's Eve, 1856. My, how he missed her. But he walked a lot too, giving Ninny needed rest. That's probably why his back hurt now. All those miles in the saddle and on the trail.

He thought about what he had told the men in his picket party last winter during the Wakarusa War. "Discipline," he told them. That was the difference between Senator Atchison's and Sheriff Jones's drunken siege of Lawrence in 1855 and the New Mexican campaign of Colonel Alexander W. Doniphan in 1846 and 1847. Discipline. And it was true. At El Brazito and Sacramento the Missouri volunteers did exactly as they were told. They were sharp and quick and calm, patient and unflinching under fire, holding their ranks, advancing and flanking only when ordered. But really, the Mexican War for Joseph James and his 1,000 comrades in Doniphan's regiment was interminable marching. Thousands of miles across prairie and desert. And it wasn't disciplined. It wasn't very orderly at all. Doniphan let the men move as they wished. They came home heroes, and ever since Joseph had idolized Doniphan, but now, in the full moon with his whiskey, he wondered why the Colonel had allowed that sort of disorderliness. If he never knew his own mother, and her people, maybe he didn't know his heroes either. Maybe the past was never what he thought it was.

Really, as he thought of his childhood friend, Dan Baumgartner, who was critically wounded at El Brazito, losing an eye and scarring his face beyond recognition, it was Doniphan's fault. Dan had been drinking that morning. All the men were drinking, playing cards, including Doniphan. Sure, it was Christmas, but there are no holidays in the army. At least, there shouldn't be. Had Doniphan ran that campaign with a firmer, stricter hand, perhaps Dan would still have his eye. He wondered how his old friend had gotten along these last ten years, knowing probably not too well. Maybe nobody from Clay County ever amounted to much. Maybe there was some curse across the land. Maybe they were on the wrong side of Bleeding Kansas, the wrong side of history, the wrong side of the river, the wrong side of—everything. Maybe he—Joseph James Hawkins—would always be this way. Poor, tired, and in pain.

He gulped his whiskey, puffed his pipe, spat, and began to think again of sleep, when suddenly he heard footsteps behind him. He spun around, ready for a fight, and saw it was Del.

"Don't worry," she said. "It will leave."

And only then did Joseph James realize the beast was lying between him and Oliver John. It slowly rose from the grass like a whale surfacing from the sea, and gently took to the sky.

"I didn't even see it," he said. "I'm a blind man, Del." He turned around to his wife. "My whole life." His head sunk. "Blind."

She smiled. "Nonsense," she said. "You are the most wide awake man I ever did know," she said, clasping his face in her hands and turning it like a precious vase or sculpture, aloft in the starlight. "You hear me?" He nodded and she smiled. "Good," said she, "now," taking the whiskey and pipe from him for herself and sitting on his lap. "Mind if I join you?"

***

Both Patrick and Joseph had never felt stupider than when Joseph arrived at Patrick's house with a plate full of biscuits in his hands. The women hugged and exchanged greetings, smiling, and introductions to J.P. Dugan were made. Even Roger seemed at ease, smiling at the absurdity of the evening and shaking hands, stealing bites of this and that, gnawing with a cocky chomp in his jaw. But Joseph and Patrick looked around, fidgeting their hands, chewing their lips, exchanging very brief, awkward glances with each other. Joseph James had an irrepressible urge to spit, and Patrick just wanted to drink. Either that or curl up with his book in bed, take a long walk, or say his rosary. Anything but dine with a man he shot and left for dead. Truly, this was an incredibly bizarre dinner party, one fit only for Kansas. Only in America.

Finally it became clear the rest of the party were waiting for Patrick and Joseph to greet each other, so they did, as two repellent magnets might. But when Patrick saw Missy he found his opening.

"Your daughter, Joseph, is adorable."

"Yessir, she sure is. Seems to like you, too. Missy, this is Paddy—er, Patrick Dugan. Mr. Dugan to you." He smiled. "Look at that. She wants you to hold her."

Patrick took little Melissa Carrie Hawkins in his arms and melted. "Joseph, I'm—I'm sorry. I'm just sorry."

"Me too, Paddy. That ain't no way fer—fer two grown men to act. I guess."

Roger laughed, bits of carrot falling from his mouth. "You're mortal enemies!"

"Roger!" Maria chided, smacking him in the arm with just enough force for it to be understood, by everyone in the room, as quite serious.

"Roger," J.P. interrupted, "why don't you see if Maria needs some help."

"Yes sir," he laughed and shook his head.

"I was blind with rage, Paddy," Joseph James shoved his thumbs in his waistline. "Blind."

"I would have been too. I can only imagine if Roger . . . I have at times, in fact."

"I know."

"Young men have passions," J.P. said, patting Missy's head. "It's well and good that they do. But they must direct them appropriately. In time I believe you will find you have common enemies."

"That's enough," Maria interjected. "What's done is done, gentlemen. If my brothers didn't try and kill each other at least once a year, why, it wouldn't be Christmas in the Kenny house. Now, who would like some whiskey?"

It wasn't long before the families felt as they did many months ago. They talked about Maria's pregnancy, Missy's recently found ability to walk, how the promise of the early spring had faded and dried away, and that perhaps they had gotten the corn in too early this time. They talked about the birth of the Dugan's new calf and the Hawkins's litter of piglets, repairs to fences and stables and barns, and the time passed quickly. Even Roger seemed to be enjoying the evening, not its absurdity, and J.P. and Sarah Sally found a quiet corner to discuss their long, storied pasts. Eventually, however, being in Kansas meant they needed to discuss what was still one of the nation's most controversial topics: Kansas.

"We should both need to purchase our claims soon, Joseph." Paddy realized the whiskey was getting to him, felt a wash of appreciation that Maria trusted him to partake. "You know that, of course."

"I do indeed, Paddy. I do indeed. Not sure how I'm a-gonna do that."

Del and Maria grew quiet. Del glanced up frequently and quickly at her husband. "You have no cash?" Patrick asked.

"No. We didn't produce anything last year, Paddy. You know that. And my fa—well, you met George. He helped some, and I hate to say it, but he was another mouth to feed. We been a-buyin' supplies in town for over a year now. Got almost nothin' left."

"Perhaps you'll have time."

"Before the land goes to public auction? I dunno. I saw that goddamn government surveyor—Kuhn I think his name is—come through here a while back and almost shot 'im in the back. Figured I'd a-just stay hidden in the woods instead. Only a matter of weeks, I figure, before they have all the lines drawn and pre-emption is done. They'll sell the land at auction."

"I can vouch for you, Joseph. That you've been on the land and improved it long enough. I don't think it would be included in the auction if you had witnesses."

"Hell, I dunno. If anyone of these aid companies—and I mean on either side—stands to make a profit, they'll a-take it, Paddy. You know that. The government and the rich go hand in hand, North and South. I'm a-willin' ta bet it was that way in Ireland, too."

"Yes, it most certainly was. But we have a chance here. Do you have an alternative plan?"

"Yessir. I'll go into Atchison and work once the crops are good 'n set." He looked at the ceiling, raised his hands, and shook them. "God please let it rain!" Took a deep breath. "I have a lot of pork but the prices are down right now. That's a helluva lot of bacon to sell! If I can't wait until fall and get the potato and corn outa the ground, that's all I got. Some pigs and the hours in the day to slave for someone in town."

There was a moment of silence in the cabin. J.P. and Sarah Sally were listening. Roger was listening. Del and Maria were listening. Maria knew she should consult her husband first, but decided it wasn't necessary. If he didn't agree she'd have had to force him to anyway, and didn't want it to be necessary.

"And us," she said. "You have us."

Joseph and Del looked at her. The passing moment had been long enough that they weren't sure what she meant, but Joseph figured it. "I appreciate that, Maria. After all—after all the things that come between us—that you'd vouch for us. But I don't think we could live on your claim again. Just wouldn't be right."

"No," she wiped her hands on her apron after setting down her knife, and came a step closer to the seated men and stopped, deciding it was best not to be too close to her husband when she said, "that's not what I mean. I mean, we can help you. We have enough and then some. You can have our beef cow." Patrick spun around and glared at his wife. Roger looked angry immediately. Even J.P. looked shocked. "Beef is at a good price. If it doesn't work out for you, it should be plenty." She looked around the room. Even the Hawkinses seemed not only dumbfounded, but insulted.

Eventually Joseph spoke. "That's right Christian of you, Maria. And with all due respect—God knows my head and hand know your power—I'm not so sure that cow is yours to offer."

"I know Joseph. I know, love," she said to Patrick, her palms turned to the ceiling at the end of outstretched arms, an entreaty to the room. "I know everyone! And I apologize for not consulting my family first. I should have done. But think on it. It's the right thing to do. We all know that. And it can be a loan. We ask only that you help us one day. God knows in a wilderness like Kansas one needs favors. It can't hurt to be owed them, either."

"I don't like owin' folks, Maria."

Maria returned to her busy work with fervor but kept talking. Her mouth moved as fast as her hands. "If you don't own land you will owe someone something for the rest of your life. If you don't own this land you shall be forced to move west. Into Indian country. And it will start all over again."

Another moment of silence passed. Del interrupted it. "Maria, you are a good woman and well-named. But that is too kind. We cannot accept." She moved to her husband. "It will work for us. I know it." She smiled and placed her hand on his shoulder.

But inside her, from the place that knew things, she wasn't so sure, and in the tension between her hand and his shoulder, both husband and wife knew the other knew.

And through the cacophony of crickets and frogs outside, the two families began to hear a faint scratching noise on the roof. Kansas may have ceased bleeding, but her monsters were growing.

***

It was the same the night of the following new moon. Del touched her sleeping husband's shoulder with the same unnatural posture in her hand, a buzzing coming through her fingers. He woke, but did not stir, not until she squeezed harder.

"Jimmy, wake up, Jimmy. I hear something outside."

And it was the same inside her mind, the place of knowing; she wasn't sure. Usually this place of her did not fail, but it did tonight. Only her ears heard the sound, and she was perturbed that such a crude organ should do her sensing for her.

"I'll go and see what it is."

He sat up, pulled on his trousers, grabbed his rifle and slipped into his boots without breaking stride toward the door. He could hear Missy's breathing just before he heard horses outside, riding off toward the east. He ran. But he was too late. They were gone, leaving only an invisible trail of dust in the utter darkness.

And then, from his own place of knowing, Joseph James knew what had happened. He'd been robbed. By jayhawkers, probably, Free State guerillas roaming places like Atchison, stealing horses and livestock, rummaging through cabinets and sloppily drinking whiskey. He ran through the humidity and the screaming frogs and crickets toward the barn.

The horse was there. Thank God. He'd come to like this one, was thinking even of naming him. He hadn't named a horse since his Ninny died. Good ol' Ninny, who rode all the way to the Gulf and back.

He ran to the chicken coop. It looked unmolested and he could hear the chickens inside. And then it came to him. The pigs. The ham. The cash that would come from them so he could buy the land. God no, not the pigs. But surely the jayhawkers had taken something.

And they had. The gate to the sty was broken and he could smell the dust settling. Not a single pig was left. All of them were gone. All of them. Goddamnit, they'd a-taken his ham! He bit his fist and screamed into it silently, spinning around, looking for anyone, anything, he could shoot and kill.

On the roof of the barn he saw the beast, curled along its apex like a seductress, flipping its tail like a contented cat in the sun. He fired at it, and it slinked away to the other side, the darkness in the woods. Suddenly there was no sound at all. It was over. All over.

***

Maria was woken by the part of her she had always been told to silence. It caused worry, old Maggie Kenny used to say. Worry and dread and heartache, and nothing more. "Close it off inside of you," she would say. "Lock it tight and never open it. It may seduce you from time to time, but believe you me, what it offers in beauty it costs dearly in terror." But in sleep it was hard to ignore, and now it woke her.

"Paddy, I think I hear something. Something outside. Something's not right." Her husband grunted. He smelled. "Damnit Patrick Dugan, wake up! There's something outside!"

He had his boots on before his eyes opened and stumbled toward the door. He could see commotion in the dark near the barn and went back inside for his rifle. A fox, probably. Maybe a coyote, even a skunk or raccoon. The chickens were always the first to go. He'd lost so many during the first eighteen months in Kansas he could hardly keep count. But he'd learned how to reinforce their coop and hadn't lost any for over a year.

As he turned back toward the door, though, something occurred to him. It wasn't the coop that was the center of the commotion. And he didn't hear the telltale sound of panicked birds. The noise came from behind the barn, maybe inside it. Horse thieves. Missourians. Bushwackers. Hickory Point all over again. Better to lose a horse than a few pints of blood, or worse. He backed off and listened, crouching beside a tangle of scrub-oak next to the cabin.

As his eyes adjusted to the light surrounding the barn the shapes began to emerge. Slowly but surely he could tell, from the silhouette of their hats, that they weren't likely Missourians at all. They had overcoats and wool gaiters around their boots that were more common in Ohio or Illinois. These weren't Bushwackers from the other side of the river or from Atchison. They were jayhawkers. Free State guerillas. His comrades in arms just a few months ago.

And they were stealing his cow.

XIII

"Who is there?" Patrick shouted. The sounds of men hushed in the dark and their silhouettes slipped into the shadows. He could still hear the sounds of animals moving away from the men, and soon saw the heifer make her way to the farthest part of the holding pen, which told Patrick where the men were—exactly opposite her. All grew quiet now, and Patrick trained his rifle into the shadows where the men must be hiding. He held the ground.

"I say who is there? I have my sights on you. You may as well give yourselves up."

Three men emerged from the darkness, their hands held high in the air. He could see their long beards and teeth before anything else, and as their faces were illuminated by the moonlight he knew he did not recognize them. Yes, they were certainly jayhawkers, but he didn't know their names.

"That's close enough. Who are you? Give me your names."

"Charles," said one. "Charles Metz. And I believe we have the wrong farm."

"Why is that?"

"We are countrymen," said a second man in an Irish accent. It was distinctly Kilkenny. "In more ways than one."

"I would speak plainly if I had a Sharps pointed at me."

The third man spoke. "We are Free Staters," he said. "And it appears you may be one as well. We thought otherwise and are here by mistake."

"You are thieves. Your politics matter not. You are stealing my cow. Why my cow? And not my horses."

"We have the wrong house."

"No. You know what you are doing. Maybe I should tie you up until the Sheriff arrives. Atchison County may be blind to thieves of one kind, but not yours. I'm sure they will be happy to arrest you."

Finally the Irishman's body relaxed as if he were capitulating to himself. "You are a traitor, Mr. Dugan. A disgrace to the Irish and to freedom-loving Kansans. To think you fought at

Osawatomie and Hickory Point and were a prisoner of war! You
are a disgrace!"

"Why? How do you know my name?"

"You've aided and abetted the enemy! A Missourian has
lived with you! You have fed him, and now you intend to help
him secure his property rights in Kansas so he may vote against
us, against freedom, against decency! You may as well be
English, Perfidious Albinon!"

"How do you know that? Is that why you are stealing my
cow? How could you possibly know that?"

Just then Roger and J.P. emerged from the cabin. Roger was
smiling. "Got yourself some Bushwackers brother?"

Patrick turned a looked at his younger brother and his
father, lowered his weapon, and heard the men scurry off into
the woods toward Atchison.

"Horsethieves," he said. "Mere criminals."

"That's a shame," Roger smiled. "Did they get anything?"

Patrick didn't like the way his brother smiled.

***

As Patrick and Joseph rode north toward Doniphan, Patrick
thought of the bird. It had been there the night the three men
(Metz was the only name he got) failed to steal the heifer, and
had been there two nights later, when somebody did get the cow.
It had to be Metz and the Kilkenny man. They didn't take a
horse, any pigs or chickens, and Patrick found only the giant bird
in the barn when he finally awoke. So odd that it pretended to
seek shelter in the barn, almost making a display of it like an
actor might. Yes, I see you are seeking shelter. What is that
supposed to mean? What are you trying to tell me?

Now, learning that Joseph's pigs were stolen the night
Patrick found the men on his farm, it became almost
unavoidable to think Roger may be behind it. Roger knew the
Hawkinses were depending on the pigs and the Dugan cow to
pay their preemption. Yes, Maria and J.P. knew, but neither of
them seemed likely to hate the Hawkinses the way only Roger
could. But Roger would never do such a thing. Never.

"Funny yer cow and my pigs should get stole on the same night," said Joseph James, spitting.

"Not the same night. But they were there that night. I caught them."

"Still. Kinda funny, don't ya think?"

"It could be a coincidence."

"Hell, Paddy." Joseph James sighed and looked away, then turned back sharply. "Like hell! It's hard enough to put the past behind us, Paddy."

"I realize that."

"We don't need secrets."

"I don't have any secrets, Joseph."

"But don't play dumb with me neither. You know what I'm a-drivin' at."

"Yes!" Patrick sighed, closed his eyes, and stopped his horse. They were just entering town and needed to find the Land Office. "I don't know what to say. I understand your suspicion."

Joseph spurred the horses back into an easy pace. "Like somebody's got it out fer us, Paddy. Or me, that is, me and my family. Like they don't want us around. Almost like they done knowed exactly what my plan is to pay for the land. Almost like they was in the room the night..."

"There is the Land Office," Patrick interrupted. Joseph stopped his horse and stared at Patrick. He spat. "Alright, Joseph. Alright. I'll speak to him."

***

Maria knew she would go into labor the day Patrick went to Doniphan. She knew it from that place her mother had told her to ignore. Still, mamma had been right. It was a part of her soul that was sometimes right but often wrong, and in the wrong there was more worry and heartache than there was wisdom in the right. Only God could know, truly know, and the pious left it to Him. At least, it made man happier to think so.

But she couldn't deny, as her water broke all over the kitchen and Roger sauntered off toward the well, swinging the pail in his hand like a young boy would, that she knew today was the day. She had known, despite ignoring it. Somehow the knowledge that her son would arrive today—that he was a son in the first place—made its way into her consciousness despite her having shut it off like a spigot. But it leaked its way in anyway, and as she watched the fluid that had suspended her son these last months seep its way into the floorboards, she knew she could not shut it off any longer. It was useless. Kansas was a place of magic. There was no use in fighting it any longer.

"Roger!" she called out the door, smiling. "Roger, it's happening! Fetch some extra water, would you!?"

Roger ran this way and that in a sudden panic, and Maria watched him from the doorway laughing. First he ran back toward the house, then toward the well, back again, back again, lost his hat, picked it up, ran in a ridiculous direction, then found his way to the well and began filling as many pails as he had on hand, splashing all over God's creation. She'd have to have him fetch J.P. after he brought the water, unless he found his wits on the way back. Men are so useless, she thought. So endearingly and lovingly useless.

***

Henry Kuhn sat alone in the one-room Doniphan Land Office chewing on a pencil. Hung on nails about him were his surveying equipment—chains and nails and hammers and compasses—and the smell of tobacco and camp-fires emanated from his coat. He was in the Land Office to check in and make some minor adjustments to the county map, a beautiful grid, but the commissioner was nowhere to be found. Kuhn already missed being out in the country with his men and equipment, smoking and laughing and working under the open sky. But all that was over now. It was time to chew pencils and jerked meat, wash the coat, and settle down.

He would still be very busy. He had schools to build, voter registries to complete, and a bank to organize. He often wondered why he had chosen Atchison. The new town downriver may have been a better choice, had he waited another year or two to move to Kansas. Sumner, it was called, and it enjoyed all the benefits of being at the river's western-most point, like Atchison, but didn't suffer from the yoke of Southern life. Atchison was slowly killing herself by treating any potential investor from the west or the north like an enemy. His map lay rolled out on the desk and he saw the two towns—the "upper landing" and the "lower landing"—and wondered if they were the modern Sodom and Gamorrah. Instead of fire, God would destroy them with water. The river would take it back. Even if a great city were erected on these prairies, he thought, Kansas shall always be wild. Always.

Finally, just as he was ready to close the office and return tomorrow looking for the new commissioner, two men walked in. They were an odd couple to be sure. One clearly a Missourian, the other an Irishman. A dispute! It had to be a boundary dispute. There could be no other reason in Kansas for two men such as these to accompany each other to a Land Office. At least they hadn't shot each other first.

"Can I help you gentlemen?"

"Yes, sir," replied Patrick. "We are here to file our claims of pre-emption. We are also curious as to when the lands may be offered for auction?"

The surveyor seemed to hesitate. "Please, sit down and make yourselves comfortable. Would you like some coffee?" Patrick shook his head "no" but Joseph said "yes" and after shaking hands and introducing themselves, Kuhn was soon up making the coffee on a little wood stove in the corner. "I hate using the stove in the summer," he said. "But I do enjoy an afternoon cup of coffee."

Patrick glanced at Joseph James, who looked about for a spittoon. "Mr. Kuhn, are the lands slated for auction?"

He sat down and rubbed his hands on his knees. Something on his person clinked like metal. "It is surveyed and ready. Only paperwork and an order from the President remain. A matter of weeks, I should think." Both the Irishman and the Missourian seated before him drooped their heads. "Now, you have a boundary dispute, I presume?"

"No sir, we don't," replied Joseph. "We sorted that out the autumn a-fore last," he grinned at his partner. "We just wanna stake our claim."

"I see. And how long have you been in Kansas, gentlemen?"

"We both came in the summer of '54, Mr. Kuhn. We have had almost no absences since. We are neighbors."

"Neighbors? In all these millions of acres you decided to live side-by-side? In 1854?"

The two men looked at each other. Patrick spoke. "It may be somewhat more complicated than that, I'm afraid. But like Joseph has said, we sorted that out many months ago."

Kuhn retrieved the coffee and sat again. "Indeed." He then tapped the large map on his desk. "Now, show me where your claims lay, gentlemen."

They all strained backs and eyes over the map. Patrick found his first. "Here, I do believe. I am just up on the ridge overlooking this tributary to the Independence. Fewer bugs there but it's windy."

"My," said Mr. Kuhn. "You could not have known, but you chose the extreme corner of that quarter section."

Joseph James then found his. "And I'm just down off the crick some toward town, over this here ridge. Right about here, I'd say."

There was a moment of silence, then Patrick spoke. "I think you are farther over to the east some, don't you Joseph?" He pointed with a pencil.

"Nah, ain't that far."

"I believe it is."

"Well it ain't."

"But you see the surveyor's lines, Joseph. I believe you are on the plot over from mine? We can't pre-empt the same claim."

Mr. Kuhn interrupted. "You are where you are, Mr. Hawkins. But there is time for adjustments." Kuhn glanced at his eight-foot chain that was used to mark off Kansas, mile by mile. It looked lonely and he'd be happy to measure an adjustment.

"Adjustments? To what?"

"Well, it would have been fortunate had you found me during the surveying, but the lines can be adjusted some. That, or you can move your house."

"Again!?"

"Again? You realize, Mr. Hawkins, you cannot remove from your home during pre-emption."

"I mean we spaced it out some after we built the foundation. We made damn sure we were more than a quarter-mile apart."

"Yes. But you've done so on the diagonal, Mr. Hawkins, and what's more, a quarter-mile isn't far enough. Your 160 acres are one-quarter of a square mile in area, yes, but that means your property lines (assuming it is a perfect square, which is a difficult thing to do on a globe in the grass and mud) are one half-mile in length." The two men looked at him blankly. He produced a piece of paper and ruler, drew a square with a diagonal line through it, and began a geometry lesson before he was interrupted. Why wouldn't they be interested in this? he thought. Any settler should know basic geometry, perhaps even a little astronomy to help. For a moment he considered a geometry test being a part of the pre-emption application.

"I get it, Mr. Kuhn," replied Joseph James. "We need to be a half-mile apart."

"You need to be a half-mile apart due north, south, east, or west, gentlemen. If you are on a diagonal from a cabin located on a section such as Mr. Dugan is. . . " he looked to the ceiling and rubbed his fingers together, which he often did while calculating in his head, "you should be at least seven-tenths," he glanced at them again, "oh, never mind." Kuhn opened the drawer of an oak cabinet and removed a bundle of papers. After quickly perusing them he said, "Now, I am not the man you need to see, but he is out now and I know his business." As he studied the paper his brow furled. "My, my, what a dilemma."

"What now?" Patrick and Joseph said simultaneously.

"I'm afraid someone else has already declared their intent to pre-empt on the plot to your south-east. Another Dugan, in fact." Kuhn noticed the two men eyed each other now, almost suspiciously. He looked back down at the neat grids and lists of names.

A deep memory from Patrick's childhood came to him, of his father and a map and the farmers about him; the English had divided and subdivided all of Ireland, and now families that once owned hundreds of acres were reduced to leasing a half an acre.

"In fact, you are surrounded by claims," continued Kuhn. He looked out the window. "My, you are surrounded by Irish and Germans," he said, almost as an aside, "but aren't we all?" He again returned to his drawings. "That means I cannot adjust the line."

"And I can't move the house."

A moment of silence passed, during which both men thought of Oliver John. His grave, his injury two falls ago, the grove where he now lay was not on the Hawkins land. "Well," replied the surveyor, "if you didn't have a boundary dispute when you arrived, I'm afraid you do now." He didn't have the heart to tell them that ultimately, in the end, neither of them could have this land. That would wait. "You must be the two most geographically unlucky gentlemen I have ever met."

The sharp cry of the jayhawk slipped in through the windows and Patrick spilled his coffee on the neat grids of the surveyor's map.

***

Del knew. She knew she should check in on Maria while the boys were up in Doniphan asking about the land and surveying. She knew this not from the part of herself that knew things. She knew if from the part of herself that what was sensible. And, from her mother in-law.

"Alright then, Delilah. I'm a-gonna get up to that Irish farm and check in on Maria. Bad enough Jimmy leaves you here with Missy and another on the way—" she read her daughter in-law's face. "—don't pretend I don't know."

"Jimmy doesn't, so don't you go and say anything."

"I won't, I won't. You know that. At least that helps explain why he abandoned you."

"He didn't abandon me. There's business to attend to, Mamma. You know that."

"Business. Ha. Is that all men ever do nowadays besides bully each other around with their fancy new-fangled rifles? Business. All that word means is they's messin' around with other men without guns."

"This is new to us, Mamma. Owning land is different than leasing and being a farm-hand. We haveta follow the rules and be responsible."

"Follow the rules and be responsible? Then you don't want to be in business, Delilah."

"Well, ain't no helpin' it, Sarah. Jimmy had to go."

"Yes, and I'm sure Maria would say the same for her husband. Yer nice ladies, you and yer friend. I'll give ya that. So, I must go and check on the nice Irish woman next door. My!" she sat back down and fanned her face with her hand. "It's so hot!"

"Alright, mother. I'll go."

"Oh, will you? Bless your heart."

***

"Where is Paddy?" Roger blurted out as he came in the door, splashing water inside the door.

"Mind the mess, Roger." Maria was as prostrate as she could be in a chair beside an open window. "You know where he is."

"Where's Pappa?"

"In town."

"I can't do this alone."

"You have me here, my lad!"

"I'll fetch the doctor."

"Not Stringfellow."

"Maria—"

"No! That man has taken so much from us already. It's not wise to trust both your money and your health to the same man."

"Money?"

"We're going to bank with him."

"Bank with him?"

"Can we talk about it later?" she moaned as he her back arched, almost violently.

"You should be in bed."

"Not yet."

"You don't look comfortable."

"I'm not."

"What can I do?"

"Cover the water and keep it clean. Stoke the fire in the stove and be ready to boil it." Roger had moved closer but now turned toward the stove. "And Roger?"

"Yes?"

"Thank you. And don't worry. Paddy will be home by dark. We can always fetch Del—" Just then Del walked in the ajar door.

"I knew it," she said, removing her boots and washing her hands in the washtub on the table.

"I knew you knew it. Do you ever not know?"

"Of course. Where's J.P.?" Del asked.

"In town." Del looked perturbed. "What is it?"

"Nevermind. The men should be home soon. You have water, good. Roger, stoke the stove."

"Yes ma'am!" Roger was beaming in relief.

"I'll get some clean linens."

"In the bedroom."

"And ready your bed."

"Thank you Delilah. I owe you one."

"Well, it won't be too long a-fore you're able to pay this debt."

"You're pregnant?"

"I am. Don't tell my husband." Del stopped and stood pensively for a moment. The part of her that knew things was smoldering and she had to fan the flames gently, just for a moment. "Maria?" She turned to her friend.

"Yes?"

"It will be alright this time. Your baby is strong. And so are you."

"Thank you Delilah. But you must tell me what the trouble is, then."

"With what?"

"With town. With Atchison. Why you don't want people going there."

"I'll tell ya tomorrow, but only if you tell me what you're going to name your child." She placed her hand on Maria's stomach and closed her eyes.

Maria smiled. "So, a boy. Right, so." She smiled, thinking of her father.

"What will you name him then, Maria?"

Maria looked at Del. All her years in Kansas she had felt this day would come, that all the times she had said that Kansas is no place to raise a child were slipping away, and if "Kansas" were an acceptable name for a son, she would have named him that. So she chose the next best thing. "You know his name," she said. "Lawrence. I will call him Lawrence."

XIV

By the time the men returned from Doniphan and Atchison they were all, at long last, fathers. Maria was in labor only five hours, and Roger and Delilah had little more to do than watch, wait, and wash. How her first labor could have gone so horribly and the second so very well was striking.

"The Lord grants only as much suffering as we can bear," said Maria.

"And not a drop less," said Del.

Roger had seen a man's head blown apart by a revolver; he had once torn a man's shoulder nearly off with a rifle; he had seen his own leg splintered by a bullet; and he'd watched children starve to death in their own filth in Ireland and on the boat to America, but nothing prepared him for the gruesomeness of childbirth. When his brother and father arrived at the farm, several hours apart, he was found both times sitting outside the cabin, near the old fire-pit, his face drained of its blood. It was the afterbirth that especially bothered him. He'd tried to clean it from the linens as Del told him to, but found it didn't want to be cleaned. So he buried both.

In the excitement nobody thought to ask J.P. why he had been gone so long. What he could be doing in town all those hours, and return empty-handed, would have been suspicious if anyone thought to think about it. But the birth of Joseph Patrick Dugan's first grandson provided cover for his activities. Nobody asked. They just cleaned and cooked and ate and slept, and near midnight he found himself outside with his pipe, content.

And as his tobacco smoldered in its bowl and wafted into the summer night outside, so too did Del's dreams. She wafted along them into consciousness, and then out the door and toward the man with whom she had had only very brief and superficial conversations. But as she reached a distance of conversation from him, she knew what she had to ask.

"Nice evenings we have here."

"Yes indeed, love. You've done well for yourselves."

"J.P., can I ask you something?"

"Of course."

"What were you doing in town today?"

The older man shifted his weight uncomfortably on his stump and curled his lips so his moustache protruded from his face in an arch, like the tuft of a proud and strutting pheasant. He pushed the smoke through his nose and the facial hair, dispersing it in the moonlight.

"Exploring options," he answered.

"What sorta options, if I may ask?"

"Well, I don't see how it's quite any of your business, lass, but I'll tell you. Investment opportunities. I have some money from my time abroad, and am looking to increase it. I would like to help provide a life for my sons and grandson, whatever they name him, in Kansas." Del sat delicately next to him and he offered his pipe. "Care to join me?"

"I have my own, thanks." She produced her own pipe and lit it. "J.P., I think you should be careful. Atchison is . . . changing."

J.P. smiled. "I can see why you and Maria get on so well."

Del smiled back. "Yes. And do fergive me. But I must ask, and I must tell you." She stood and took a few steps away, looking into the stars toward her own cabin, where her husband, daughter, and mother in-law were resting. "J.P., I can't tell you how, but sometimes I know things. I know them like I know how to breathe or blink. I know them without knowing I know them. At least, when I was a girl—" J.P. stood now and placed his hand on her shoulder.

"I understand. My grandmother knew as well. Back in the old country many of the old ones told us things. You don't have to explain it to me, love."

"Well, it's telling me that you are putting yerself in danger, Mr. Dugan. Whatever opportunities yer a-lookin' fer, well, the wrong ones are a-gonna find you first." She pointed at him with her pipe.

J.P. considered this and began to pace a little. He resembled both of his sons in one way or another. He had the bulbous knees and elbows of lanky Patrick, but the round cheeks and pointed brow and nose of Roger. He was not as good looking as either, having not aged as he might have in life shorter of suffering, but had more confidence in his posture than the two of them put together. He took a long pull from his pipe, tapped it out on the stump, and sat again.

"Kansas is fertile," he began. "Not just her soil, but a great many things, Mrs. Hawkins. I hardly know where to invest first, if I am to be quite honest with you. Outfitting the wagon trains, for instance. I'd wager you could have a hardware or blacksmith's shop for every man woman and child in Atchison and still have plenty of work to go around. There's land, of course. I could buy plots all along the river if I like, once they go to auction. But Delilah," he stood again and packed his pipe. "I'm intrigued by two things: newspapers and railroads. I met with a man—"

"Who?" Del asked forcefully.

"Stringfellow's his name. Do you know him?"

Having seen Delilah J.'s expression, J.P. stopped talking. He knew this was the matter that had woken her this night; this was the person, the opportunity, that kept that part of her that knew things smoldering in the night, glowing like the embers of a distant brush fire.

He didn't say so, but it was too late. Stringfellow had already secured commitments from the Dugans for nearly the entirety of their savings, and the Kansas Valley Bank was sufficiently capitalized. And he didn't need to say so, because overhead, in the crisp light of the moon, a beast slithered across the sky as if it were swimming up the river of stars.

They both knew it was too late.

***

Last summer had been so eventful Roger had already forgotten how miserable summer in Kansas was. Two years ago, in 1855, while they were doing the monotonous work of building the cabin and going back and forth to town for work and supplies, the weather was not something he could ever ignore. But last year, in 1856, with so much violence and terror, he only thought of it at night while the mosquitoes, ticks, and chiggers crawled all over him. But this, his third summer in Kansas Territory, 1857, was boring again, and all Roger could think about was how damned hot he was all the time. He needed something to do. Something needed to happen.

The birth of his nephew, Lawrence, had provided some excitement a month or so ago, and for a moment or two it seemed the thefts of their cow and the Hawkins swine would prove interesting, but all in all it had been the drab summer of a simple farmer. Every Saturday he would read the *Sovereign*, waiting for some news of a militia roaming here or there, a murder or a convention that could incite a riot or an election that could prove fraudulent. But for some reason he hadn't seen the paper in some months.

One morning he was clearing stone from along the creek on the north-east corner of the property. He preferred work such as this. Plowing up the native grasses made a snapping and popping sound that seemed overly violent, so obvious it was that the work undid, in a manner of seconds, tens of thousands of years of the earth's work in growing these roots. It was just as exhausting, true, and the creaking of the leather and metal rings, the breathing of the animals was so fine; but the pain stump and stone clearing caused in his back also enabled him to look up now and then instead of always at the back end of Paddy's horses, endlessly cajoling them to carry on. And then, looking up, something happened.

Silhouetted against the southern sky, the man riding up the ridge between him and the cabin was unmistakably his father, J.P., Joseph Patrick, and he was heading west along the ridge, as if returning from somewhere to the east. He watched the posture that he'd known for so long carry itself beautifully in the saddle as it slowly made its way to the crest of the ridge, stop, and wheel around as if surveying the landscape. J.P. was looking for him. They were supposed to meet Patrick before lunchtime by the creek to discuss the rest of the afternoon's work.

So Roger Dugan stepped out into the clearing at the bottom of the hill and began to hail his father. The silhouette began to look like that of a single animal, some mythical man-horse beast, and as it turned there seemed to be an obvious recognition—

the beast stopped as it faced Roger—but it continued to rotate until it faced north again and crept over the crest and disappeared. Roger had a feeling that his father had seen him and pretended that he didn't. And the feeling reminded him of something.

As a boy he had nightmares; like all children perhaps, but the dreams he had when he had a fever, which was fairly frequent, were truly terrifying and unforgettable. He would wake sometimes but they would follow him into reality, morphing the walls of their tiny cabin into a fluttering silk-screen, the firelight and shadows dancing on it like puppets. Sometimes the walls would cave in and he'd scream at them, protecting his mother. Sometimes a puppet would slip down onto the floor and scurry off under something, hiding there in the dark with glowing eyes. The eyes would be that of a witch, or a boy who wanted to beat him up, or some other kind of beast that was neither mammal nor fowl nor fish, but somehow furry and scaly and feathery all the same. One of these ran under his father's chair one night.

Roger had been sleeping in the middle of the room by the fire, his mother dabbing him with a cool washcloth, but she'd stepped out into the cold, headed for the outhouse. He remembered that much, soberly and clearly—the snow swirling in as she left—as she had told him in his half-sleep feverish delirium, and he'd remembered it. She had said something to his father and J.P. had nodded while he read his paper, smoking his pipe. He was warm and happy for a moment and slipped away.

He opened his eyes in panic. Only a few seconds had passed, as his mother was still out and his father in the same position, but the puppets were playing on the walls, his heart was racing, and he was swimming in a pool of sweat. He watched his father rocking slowly, reading and smoking, as several of the puppets gathered together into a grotesque form and slipped under his father's chair. They stared back at him now, their eyes smiling, and he decided he had to keep his eyes on this father. J.P. would save him.

After what seemed an eternity his father looked at him. Roger knew J.P. could see the terror in his face and probably hear his quick, shallow breathing. He knew this was all he had to communicate. As long as he gave his father the look of panic and fear, and did not under any circumstances look at the puppets under the chair as they cackled and squirmed, J.P. would save him. They held eyes for a moment, and Roger was sure the old man would get out of his chair, squash the monsters, and lay on the floor with him. But he didn't. He looked deep into the hole in his son's blankets, saw his face, and turned away.

He looked at the door, then his watch. Roger would have to wait for his mother.

Yes, J.P. was up to something.

***

As lunchtime approached Roger finally saw J.P. and Patrick walking up over the ridge, around the plowed field, and come up just along the creek. The son walked in front of the father. Just a step or two, just enough that made Roger smile for his brother. This was what he wanted. His family was here together, today, tending the fields and his son, their future. The sun stood centered, framed to the north and the south by the very trees that framed his property, drank from its water and ate from its soil, and unfurled its light like a quilt on the backs of the men and the crops. As they came closer Roger could see that Patrick was happy. Truly happy.

J.P. walked with his hands in his pockets, and he also appeared content. He seemed to steal glances at his eldest son now and then, and also at the east. The closer they came to Roger the older his father seemed, and the more he seemed to be interested in something afar. His contentment waned until it nearly disappeared altogether, forming itself into the knitted brow of worry. A bird called from the east and the old man stopped for a moment, just a moment, halting in his stride like a foal hesitating before a fence. Aged weariness and youthful fright made an odd outfit to wear.

"Well done, lad!" Patrick called, surveying the work his brother had done. "You've nearly finished!"

Roger beamed. "'Tis good work, Paddy!"

Patrick chuckled, closed the remaining gap between them and said, grasping Roger's shoulder with a firmness somewhat out of character, "You don't mean that, but I appreciate your saying so." J.P. joined them, and as he looked at Roger his contentment snapped back into his face, easing the brow and tightening the lips. "I'd figured this a day or two, and he's done it by lunchtime."

"A strong back on that one, Paddy. He's a Dugan, after all."

"I hope Lawrence can see me through my old age as you have my youth, Roger."

"Don't curse the child already, Paddy. He may not be a farmer."

"Precisely."

They sat down beside the water in the shade of the cottonwood. If it weren't for the mosquitoes it would have been pleasant to anyone. Nonetheless, it was to the Dugans, to Patrick in particular. The cold crisp water complimented the cucumber and hard-boiled eggs. He was a good farmer, it turned out, and all three knew it. They knew Patrick's good fortune with the land relative to most Kansans was in large part attributable to his hard work and wise decisions, from where he chose to squat, where he chose to plow, what he chose to sow. For him, the earth breaking under his plow was the sound of hope. From their vantage point the contour of his land and what he'd done with is was wonderfully apparent. Hope was everywhere.

The cabin was far enough away and elevated from the water to avoid floods and bugs, yet close enough to keep it accessible daily; the little stock-yard downwind of the cabin yet even and level with it; the barn next to it on one side but also abutted the fields, every one of its doors wide enough and close enough for their intended use; and the garden, a new well, and now nearly ten acres of workable fields that Roger was beginning to extend to the north were fitted to the gentle rolls of the earth like they were her very skin, or ornaments to it that increased its beauty. Patrick farmed as if he were listening to the earth, letting it tell him what to do, and where.

"It's a shame the wheat isn't ready yet," he said with a full mouth, choking a bit so he had to gulp some water, "'twould be a good day to start cutting it. I really do appreciate what you've done this morning, Roger. You've certainly put your back into it." He looked out over his land, remembered how last year he'd felt the world was coming to an end. Last year at this time he sat eating with lunatics in the woods, wondering if he'd be shot, horrified at how the world had followed him across the Atlantic and half the continent, worried he'd never escape it. And now here he was, with his father and brother, his wife and son safe inside, fed and happy and healthy. "One day Lawrence may be as appreciative as me."

Roger chuckled. "Really, Paddy, he is too young for such talk."

"I don't see why!? Think of it, you two. Think of how far we've come, and how different his life might be!" He made a sweeping motion across his land, the sun moving just to the right of center now.

J.P. swallowed a bite of egg. "Your brother may be right, Paddy. His world will be different than ours."

"Indeed! He will inherit something!" There was a moment of tense silence. They all knew Patrick did not, could not, intend for it to seem indicative of what J.P. had not been able to do for his sons what Patrick might for his, but it caused a silence nonetheless. "I didn't mean it that way, Pappa."

"The opposite is true," said Roger, turning to his father. "Your courage led us here. This would not have been possible in Ireland."

"True," said the other son. "I've often cursed you in your absence, Pappa, I must admit that. But your loss gave us this, all this."

J.P. did have something to say, the boys knew. But he did not say it at first. The contentment waned again and he shuddered, almost imperceptibly, from hesitation. He sighed and stood, brushed off his pants, and took his pipe out of his pocket. "What I did in Ireland did very little to help you boys." He held a hand up to indicate he was not to be interrupted. Both boys remembered this gesture from years before. It was a comforting sort of directive.

"It had to be done. I'm sure of that. In a sense you are right, Roger, and I love you for seeing it. To cling to nothing in Ireland was not an option. Not for us. Your grandfather—" He hesitated and lit his pipe. The inhale choked back his tears. "The last thing your grandfather said to me was, 'Don't let them do to you what they've done to me.'" He exhaled pointedly, the smoke escaping into the sunlight that streamed between the leaves above them. "I had to fight. I had no choice."

Patrick and Roger stood now, as their father turned away. They waited.

"But what I did in Ireland made me an international criminal and you boys orphans. And your mother—" again he puffed his pipe, "Your mother a widow, then you orphans."

"I was grow—"

"I know you were grown, Paddy, but yet—the truth must be told—I didn't do it for you." He dropped his pipe now and bent over, the tears more powerful than the smoke.

"I didn't do it for you boys. Forgive me," he cried, "I didn't do it for you and I am here to make amends."

XV

The night of August 24th, 1857 was very dark. Why Joseph James Hawkins chose this night, of all nights, to cross the river looking for Dan Baumgartner made no sense at all. Not a lick. Not only was it dark, he had work to do. He had finished bringing in a fair wheat crop and had readied the field for another planting, but the corn was almost ready and he still had to sell the wheat. He had spent his last dollar on the ferry, dragging George Million out of his saloon and paying him double the usual price to cross in the dark this late in the season. No, it made no sense.

But if anyone could help the Hawkinses now, it was Dan, and Joseph James was desperate. Dan's father had somehow managed to purchase a tobacco farm in Clay County in the early '40s and save a small inheritance for his son. With the wheat at a good price and if the corn came in the way it looked it might, Joseph figured he needed to borrow twenty to fifty dollars to have enough money to secure his land, whatever happened. If he had to pick up that whole cabin and a-carry it to another square on Kuhn's map, or pay some German for theirs, he'd do it.

Asking anyone was humiliating, but it was less with Dan. And he must, at all costs, secure his land. The thought of moving back to Missouri as a tenant farmer or farmhand made him spit. No, better to cross dark rivers with drunken ferrymen and beg than to spend the rest of his life the way it used to be. Dan was his last hope.

Now that he was out of Weston, it was darker than he thought it would be. Weston had changed since he last saw it. It had grown and recovered, but a fire had destroyed the wooden facades downtown that he had known as a boy. There was a sense of resentment in the faces of its citizenry, a tension that reminded him of Atchison. Bustling from immigrant traffic, its prosperity was somehow overshadowed by something gloomy. Like Atchison, Weston seemed swept up in history like the river had flooded and deposited centuries of sediment at its feet, in offering to something ungodly.

The road east was familiar to him, and he kept to it as the lights of the town slipped away behind him. The Baumgartner place was hidden in a copse of walnut trees a few foot above and to the right of the road, if he remembered right. As a boy he had come with Dan to this house once or twice, after his father had purchased it and begun to move his family. Dan and Joseph were young and often in trouble with the old man, but they were always welcomed by his mother, a short woman of German stock and a hearty cupboard. She loved Joseph.

Just as it couldn't get any darker, Joseph James saw a horseman approaching. The hair stood up on the back of his neck. Perhaps it was Dan, or someone from his house. As the riders drew near each other Joseph recognized the copse of walnuts and an opening in them that would lead to the Baumgartner's, but the other rider passed it. He was headed to Weston, and any man heading to Weston, Missouri at midnight in 1857 was a potentially dangerous man. Joseph unbuttoned his holster.

"No need for that, sir," the other rider said in a voice that was not a whisper but was careful and hushed nonetheless, as if he were calling across an empty church. Joseph was amazed the man could see his hand from that far away. "I pose no danger."

"Who are you?"

"I may ask the same of you my friend," said the stranger just as they drew near enough to see shadowy faces. "As a matter of fact, I do believe I recognize you." The shadows on his face shifted as he furled his brow and peered into the starlight. "Have we met?"

Joseph James could hardly believe his eyes; but then, he didn't even need to see to know who it was. This was why he came on this darkest of nights—to see not only Little Dan, but this man. "Lieutenant Joseph James Hawkins, Colonel," he saluted. His voice faltered.

"My, my," he replied in the tone used for nieces and nephews that have grown so much since the last holiday. "At ease, soldier. Those days are over. Or, not yet resumed, I might say." He offered his hand and Joseph shook it.

"It's mighty good to see you, Colonel Doniphan." An image and the smell of Dan's blood, clotted brown in the dust of New Mexico, came to him, and he wondered if he had the guts to say something about El Brazito, about how he had long idolized Doniphan, only to realize in the bright light of the past that he was no idol. Why, he'd even disobeyed the governor just so he could save that Mormon Jesus in '38, as Clegg told him. Maybe he should mention that too.

"Please, Alexander will do just fine, Mr. Hawkins."

"Joseph, then, sir."

"Very well then, we are both on familiar terms. Tell me, where are you heading?"

Yes, yes, he would have to mention the eye. "A friend of mine, and a fellow dragoon at that, lives up the road a-piece. Baumgartner. Dan Baumgartner. In fact—" Joseph James began to say, thinking he would ease into it somehow, mention the injury without mentioning the blunder, the disorderliness of Christmas Day 1846.

But look of sorrow drew the shadows in Doniphan's face inward until they spiraled out from the nose like a pinwheel. "Baumgartner. A casualty if I remember correctly. One of only a handful at El Brazito."

Joseph didn't know whether to smile or cry. "Yes, sir. I—am—glad you remember."

And he felt like saying Damn you, you let a boy get drunk in a war and now he can't see, but Doniphan looked into the distance for a moment. His gaze travelled across the prairies to the deserts, across the seasons. "I am fortunate to have had few enough that I try to remember them all. Please send my regrets. How has he been all these years?"

The pinwheel of shadows opened and eased some, a little flicker of light emerging from somewhere deep in the middle of the colonel's face.

"Can't say I know for sure, Colo—Alexander. Been a long time since I saw him."

"It was his leg, correct?" he said, unsure.

"No, sir. His eye, I'm afraid. Just got tore up by one of them few shells that his us in that first charge." He paused, and decided to try this hint: "The charge that caught us by surprise."

The pinwheel of shadows pulled tighter together again, as if a galaxy of darkness were centering its mass upon Alexander W. Doniphan's face. "El Brazito was a blunder. That should have been my eye left behind in the desert."

Joseph paused and spat. Suddenly he pitied his hero, and chafed at the suggestion that anything the 1st Missouri did could possibly be described a 'blunder.' "With all due respect, Colonel, we whupped them damned Mexicans anyway."

A wry smile finally broke the swirling shadows. "I should have known better than to let my army have a holiday. No army seems to respect the birth of the Son of Man. Not even a Catholic one." He sighed and looked into the night. His horse shifted its weight. "Christ forgive me, for I shall not."

And suddenly Joseph James Hawkins saw a sun in the face of Colonel Alexander W. Doniphan. Funny, he thought, that after seeing this man's face under the hottest of suns for so many months, that he should only now see it in the light of day, on the darkest of nights.

"You were young, Alexander," he said gently. "We all were." He could see this eased the pain, but that it would remain as long as Doniphan lived. And a wave of pity came over Joseph. To pity your hero, he thought. To pity your hero. "And we whupped 'em, sir." He clenched his teeth. "All the way to the goddamned sea!"

An actual smile eased across Doniphan's cheeks and more prominent forehead. "Yes, I suppose we did." He sighed and looked up again. A different shadow seemed to fall upon him. "And half of us are still fighting." His horse seemed impatient. "You spend so much time a-tryin' ta make sure they come home from one war, and they go off and a-start another." The colonel seemed old now.

"I s'pose so, sir."

"But it's all the same is it not?"

"In what way, sir?"

He seemed wise again. "Land, Joseph, land. The Mormons in '38, the Mexicans in '48, the Yanks in '56. We fight over land, the right to own it, to reap it, to rape it, even. We've lived our lives on the frontier, you and I. It's all about the land. Always has been, always will be." Sighing, he stroked the neck of his beautiful stallion, trying to ease him some. "And the land don't care too much for a-bein' owned, does it?"

The same spiral of darkness came over Hawkins's face now, and he could feel it pushing on his skull. "No, it sure don't, Colonel."

"You have gotten involved, then?"

"Yes, sir. Willingly at first. But now I just want to secure my claim in Kansas and raise my family. I—I lost my little brother in this mess. At first I wanted revenge. Now I . . ." he looked into the sky. Behind the trees the stars seemed to swirl, draining away and beyond into the black. "Now I just want to be left alone, but I am not too sure I can stay. I don't have the money and jayhawkers have stolen my stock and last year's crop was ruined by the war."

Doniphan sank a little in his saddle. "I'm very sorry to hear about your brother, Joseph. Very sorry indeed. And about your farm. War has a way of suddenly destroying what takes years of dedicated husbandry to build. When is your land up for auction?"

"Don't know yet. Soon, I fear. In fact, Col—Alexander—I'm a-comin' to Dan for a loan." He didn't know why he said it, but was not embarrassed.

"I may be able to help you, Joseph," Doniphan said without a pause, as is he was in the business of giving money to old friends on dark roads.

"No, sir, I—"

"Nonsense. It's the least I can do for a veteran of the Volunteers, and if I can do it, I shall. Consider me your personal emigrant aid company. God knows both the north and south have sent their zealots, myself included, but should like to also send peace-loving moderates."

"I can't rightly take your money for any reason, Alexander." He spat, having wanted to say the following more now than ever, and had wanted to say it for ten years. "Serving under your command, Colonel, was the privilege of a lifetime."

"So do me the honor of allowing me the privilege of helping you, Joseph. If Mr. Baumgartner cannot, for whatever reason, call on me at the Weston Hotel at suppertime tomorrow and we shall discuss the terms."

"No, sir—"

"That is an order, Lieutenant. If Mr. Baumgartner can help, well, I shall see you again sometime, I hope."

"Yes, sir, Colonel, sir."

"Very good then." Doniphan saluted. "Until next time, Joseph."

He saluted in reply. "Until next time, Alexander."

Lieutenant Joseph James Hawkins rode away tall in the saddle, the dark night over Clay County suddenly full of stars.

***

And why little Lawrence Dugan would choose the night of August 24th, of all nights, to scream all the dark hours made no sense either. If the moon was full at least Patrick could go outside and get some work done. Otherwise, what he really needed was sleep. Much of his wheat was in but there was corn to harvest soon and a new field ready for planting winter wheat right after that. He wanted to get that in early, as this crop wasn't turning out as much as he'd hoped, probably a result of not planting much of it until leaving prison. The little Maria planted earlier in the fall was doing better, so he had better hurry and get it in the ground. Indeed, if he wasn't sleeping he should be working, not sitting awake in bed listening to the cries of a baby. But Lawrence had other ideas.

The child was so adamant in these ideas that Patrick soon found himself outside with his brother and father, smoking in the impossible darkness. Helping Maria with the baby sometimes proved fruitful, but not this night. She was happier with the men outside, it seemed, as she could give her undivided attention to little Lawrence. It also meant Patrick could give his undivided attention to his worries. He paced and stamped the earth with a walking stick, kicking stones now and then.

"Relax, Paddy," said J.P. "He'll go to sleep soon enough."

"It's already too late. If we don't get the rest of that wheat cut before it rains again—and the corn—and we need to turn the soil for planting the winter wheat—I don't know..." he puffed his pipe agitatedly.

"We will."

"Maybe if I put Roger on the corn tomorrow and you and I finish the wheat—"

"'Twill be alright, boy. I promise you."

Roger stood stiffly and rubbed his hands on his thighs. "Paddy, I'm going to Grasshopper Falls tomorrow."

Patrick's face drained of its blood. He felt unsure on his feet. "What!? Now!?"

"Yes."

"Why!?"

"I'm not a farmer, Paddy."

"I know that! Farmers don't have time to think about politics during the harvest! Hell, they never do for that matter! Or they find themselves in my predicament."

Roger sat again, on the same stump he'd sat on when he told Patrick he was going to Big Springs over two years ago, the same stump he'd sat on when he declared that the world was coming to Kansas, that it was the threshold of the future. There was something prophetic about this boy, at times, thought his older brother. But he's still a dangerous idiot, he also thought.

"There are going to be more elections, Paddy. And the bogus legislature is writing a constitution for Kansas. And so are we."

"We?" His voice cracked. He sat, wobbly, and tried to breath.

"Yes, we. I'm not a farmer, Paddy. I want to help the Free State government through the elections, in any small way I can. I want to help with the constitution. I want—I want it for Lawrence. Your Lawrence."

"For him!? Roger, he needs corn, not a constitution! He needs cash. He needs us to own this land outright, once and for all!"

"He needs a free Kansas, Paddy."

"No, *your* Lawrence needs a free Kansas, Roger!"

"Boys, boys, boys," interrupted the father, standing laboriously. "I can help."

"We all do!" Roger continued, ignoring J.P, standing from his stump and taking a step closer to his brother. "Your nose is always in the dirt, brother, and you forget the dirt is a part of a country." He sighed. "Do you even know what the Supreme Court decided in March, Paddy? Do you?"

"Yes, yes, Dred Scott, we all know—"

"But do you know, do you even comprehend, what that means?" He reminded his brother of the jayhawk, the way his arms fluttered about as he spoke. "For us all? Hell, for your precious wheat and corn?"

"No, why don't you tell me what Dred Scott means to my corn, Roger."

"Boys!" J.P. had seen this before—the boys inching closer and closer to each other. He couldn't help but smile, though inside him was a rotting dread.

"It means a slaveholder can buy up all the land around you, move an army of slaves into Kansas, farm it to dust through the blood and sweat of others, and produce more corn in a single season than you can in your life, Paddy. Prices would plummet. You'd be bankrupt in two years."

"Nonsense." Though Patrick had to admit it did make sense.

Roger was exasperated. "It's true, Paddy! 'Tis what the Ascendency did to us in Ireland. And it won't be long before the Catholics are slaves here, too Patrick Dugan! How can you not see what it means for our own freedom!? For Lawrence's freedom!? Your Eden in Kansas is threatened again, Paddy. The future of the world depends on a Free Kansas!"

"Boys…" J.P. said half-heartedly, having all but given up on stopping them. It had to run its course now.

"I'm not fighting again, Roger. Look what became of us."

Roger breathed deeply and shrugged his shoulders. The night came back into their circle. Frogs sang in the nearby copse of trees where the old shack once stood. "I know," he said, closing his eyes and shoving his hands in his pockets. "But someone must, brother. Somebody has to fight."

Patrick thought about letting it go now, but the thought of losing Roger's help in the fields was too strong. He needed this crop more than anything in his whole life. If he didn't raise he cash soon, he'd lose everything. "Governor Geary will ensure proper elections are—"

"Geary is gone, Paddy!" Roger exploded. "You've been so busy farming you don't know what's going on!"

"The *Sovereign* stopped coming!" Patrick protested.

"Boys—" J.P. tried to interrupt again. "There's a reason for that you may like to hear." But it was to no avail. He would have to wait until they were done.

"Geary left before the buds came to the trees! Sheriff Jones and his posse ran him out of the territory! He ran away in the middle of the night with nothing but a wool blanket and two pistols! We have a new governor, Governor Walker, and he's a former Senator from Mississippi." At times, when he berated his older brother this way, he seemed to be the older one, tutoring his student in the ways of the world. "Mississippi, Paddy— Mississippi! He's already told us that hanging for treason should be expected of anyone who opposes the laws of the legislature, the Ruffian legislature in Lecompton! The one the Missourians elected by fraud! Do you remember—"

"Of course I remember."

"No, think of it, Paddy. Remember it! They made you kneel before them and threatened to shoot you! Remember!"

"So what are you going to fight for!? What hope do you have?"

"Walker has promised that the constitution they've started drafting in Lecompton will go up for a vote in the fall. I'm going to Grasshopper Falls for a Free State convention, where we will decide our course of action."

"Elections in Kansas are elections for Missourians, Roger. You know that."

"Lane's Army—we—will ensure they are fair, Paddy."

"You saw what happened," Paddy pointed to his brother's wounded leg, "last time Lane's Army tried to police Kansas, Roger."

Roger sat again, exasperated. "We were successful, Paddy. We drove out a prejudiced governor and exposed the lawlessness of the Bogus Legislature, of the Ruffians. It's only a matter of time. The country will see we are not only in the right, we are in the majority." He rubbed his eyes with the palms of his hands. "And with places like Sumner and Quindaro attracting more capital, we will win the economic battle, too." Patrick guffawed at these odd words coming from his brother's mouth. Roger looked him in the eye. "Kansas must be free. At all costs."

There was a moment of silence, and Patrick knew it was time. "Roger, did you tell those jayhawkers about the cow, and Hawkins's pigs?"

Roger stared at his brother flatly. "Somebody has to do this, brother. I understand why you won't. Please understand why I must. We've had this argument one times too many. You have to understand that I am not a farmer." He paused and turned back on his brother with constrained fire. "And I'm not a thief either. Don't you *ever*" his voice shuffled off the constraints and he said in an inferno, "—accuse me of it again!"

Another moment of silence followed, and J.P. knew now it was his turn to tell his sons just what he had done for them. "Boys," he said, "there is something I must tell you."

XVI

The Baumgartner house was recessed in the shadows of so many trees that the porch was even darker than the moonless night. Some of the trees were ancient, and something hung from their boughs, adding to the eeriness of the front of the property. In the dark it looked almost like Spanish moss, but Joseph James knew it didn't grow this far north, on trees such as these. Before mounting the steps he walked up close to a tree and saw that it was not moss but the webs of silkworms. They covered the walnut trees completely. Nobody had tended to this yard at all this year. He had never seen so many silkworms before. The trees were like giant spider nests.

It hadn't occurred to Joseph James that calling upon an old friend in a new house this late at night may not be the most polite thing to do. An old army comrade aside, perhaps this was a too familiar, too forward, an act. Asking for money in the dead of night could only be the recourse of the truly desperate. Only now did he realize just how desperate he was, standing on the rotting porch of a man he hadn't seen in nearly ten years, prepared to beg. If only Oliver John were here. It would somehow be a more wholesome act. Alone, it seemed dirty.

"He don't like visitors," a voice came from the shadows, startling Joseph. It was a black man sitting in a rocking chair.

Suddenly the door opened and Joseph found himself at the end of a very old Sheridan rifle. He could tell immediately it was Dan's rifle, but the shadow of the man holding it didn't seem to be Dan's. He was shorter, more folded over, weaker.

"State yer name or 'll blow ya apart."

"Danny, it's J.J. Hawkins. Jimmy."

Dan Baumgartner lowered the gun. "You sonofabitch. I nearly killed you." He did not smile.

"Yessir." Joseph smiled. "It's been a long time, my friend."

"It has." He tightened his grip on the rifle, seeming to ready it again. "And why in the hell would you a-come at this time a night?"

After a brief hesitation he said, "I'm desperate."

"Ain't we all?"

"I figure so. I need ta borrow money, Dan. For some reason I figured you could help."

A "hmph" escaped from Dan's mouth, a sound Joseph had never heard come out of him before. "You can come in, J.J. It's been a long time."

The old black man laughed eerily as Joseph James stepped past. Inside, Joseph James realized that if the silkworm webs outside seemed like spiders, the spiders inside were an appropriate accessory to the decorative theme. And if there was one thing Joseph James didn't like it was spiders. He stopped in the doorway, turned around and spat on the porch. Little Dan laughed.

"I remember you wasn't too fond a spiders. Don't bother me none."

"Aw, me neither, Dan."

"Like hell," he said, sitting in a chair inside the parlor, just off the fourier. It was the only chair not covered in spider webs, and one of the only ones not covered or surrounded by what would best be called "stuff." Once Joseph could attend to anything but the webs, he saw that the whole house was full of stuff. He stood awkwardly in a clear spot on the floor. "You always spit when yer nervous. Just like El Brazito."

"I s'pose yer right 'bout that."

"I'd tell ya to sit but I can't imagine why you would. You ain't gonna stay long anyways."

"You look well, Danny."

Little Dan laughed heartily, looked at his old friend and laughed again. "You never used ta lie like that. Even when we was kids."

Joseph looked around. "Some a these is poisonous, Dan."

"I know it. Black widows, brown recluses. Hell, with any luck there's some snakes, too."

"What happened?"

"To what?" Dan leaned forward in his chair and Joseph realized how dark it was inside, once Dan's face became illuminated by the little starlight that seeped in through the window. His one good eye showed a smirk, and his bad eye looked dirty and infected. A raspy chuckle escaped from his lips, followed by another. "What happened to what?"

Tension swelled in Joseph James's throat and rose to his mouth, and he tried not to look like he had to spit. "The house. What happened to your daddy's house?"

Little Dan removed a flask from his breast pocket and took a long swig, wiping his mouth with the back of his hand. "I fired the help a couple years back. Ain't no niggers allowed inside no more."

"What about the man on the porch?"

"Elias? I can't get that damned nigger to leave. He works the land some, forages outa the woods I s'pose. Hell, I don't care what that old nigger does."

"Can you get a white maid?"

"I s'pose I could. I think I'd rather watch the place fall apart though, J.J. Ya know? Watchin' all my daddy's work crumble around me. Kinda romantic. I ain't got no kids anyway. Ain't no reason to keep the place goin'."

"What about your uncle? The one with the same name as you?"

Mention of this person seemed to bring the hint of a real smile to Little Dan's face. "Dan, Dan from Germany? Dutch Dan?" But all the mirth was soon gone. "Hell, I ain't seen him since I seen you last. Heard he moved over to your side-a the river and had a kid, though. Imagine that. Havin' a kid at his age."

"The fields?"

"Aw hell, the fields is still full a tobacco and niggers. I never go out there."

"You still farm them, though?"

"I still have an income if that's what yer a-getting' at. Probably a pretty good one." He took another draw from his flask. "I can't drink it all if I try. And believe me, I have tried."

Joseph James sat in a chair a few feet from Little Dan. He was conscious of the spider webs all over the chair but tried to pretend they didn't bother him. He held his hands well enough above the chair, in his lap, so no skin would touch a web. He took a deep breath and could see Dan as a little boy. Before he was a soldier, a casualty, as Doniphan said.

"When I asked what happened, Danny, I meant you. What happened to *you?*"

Little Dan pointed at the mangled side of his face. "This." He pulled the flask out of his breast pocket. "And this. First this," his eye, "then this," his flask. "And this," he held up the flask, "will really do you in." He chugged the remaining whiskey and laughed. "I have it backwards, don't I? it was this," the flask, "then this," his eye. "Remember? That sonofabitch sent us into combat drunk."

"It wasn't Doniphan's fault. We were surprised."

"Yes. Imagine a bunch a Catholics attackin' on Christmas. Imagine that."

"Dan—"

"Just shutup, Jimmy. I'm a-done with this here conversation. Take yer money and get the hell outa here." From the breast opposite the one that held the flask he produced a billfold. "How much do you need? You can take it all for all I care. I will be dead soon anyways."

***

By sunrise on the 25th of August, 1857, everything had changed. And it all started with J.P. Dugan.

"It was me," he said in the early tendrils of light. His boys stared at him as best they could through the lingering darkness. "It was for your own good," he said. J.P. had never imagined himself in this position. He imagined his boys would respond in some way. Say something, do something, cry out, attack him, thank him or hug him or—anything. But they stared flatly through the black, and as the chorus of frogs rose to a small crescendo, the whites of his sons' eyes brightened in the night like the light of a steamship approaching from downriver. It was still his turn to speak, explain himself, and this meant (and J.P. realized fully for the first time) that his sons were now men.

"I did it," he repeated lamely.

Patrick shook his head in confusion and perhaps a little frustration. "Did what, Pappa?"

J.P. hung his head and wished he could have waited for morning. Inside his grandson Lawrence had finally stopped crying, and he could be asleep now. But instead Maria emerged from the cabin and he waited for her to join them. She may as well hear it from him too.

"I had the pigs and the cow stolen. I hired some men to do it." Everyone stared back at him in amazement. "They are Free Staters, though. You'll be glad to hear that, so." He looked around at the stunned faces of his family. All stunned but a small part of one corner of Maria's mouth, which seemed to know. He wondered where she usually kept that part hiding.

"What? Pappa . . . why!?" Roger asked, sharing the exasperation he had with his brother with his father now.

"It isn't the Hawkinses. It isn't that they are, as you said when I met them, Roger, your 'mortal enemies.' It isn't even that they are Missourians. I just want the land. For us. For our families."

Patrick stood, removed his hat, and rubbed his face and scalp with a flattened palm. "I don't believe this."

Roger stood, removed his hat, and slapped it on his leg. "It *should* be that it is the Hawkinses! It *should* be that they are Pro Slavery Missourians who are spreading an evil across the land! It *should* be that you are investing in Quindaro to help a just cause! It *should* be that—"

"It isn't, boy," J.P. interrupted calmly, with an outstretched hand. "It just isn't."

"And it should be done with honor and forthrightness! Not lying and cheating and stealing!" Roger slapped his hat on his leg again and sat down. He was close to tears. "Why not Quindaro?"

"I'm sorry I've disappointed you Roger. But I don't see this family as your mortal enemy. And I don't think I see the methods of the last year as honorable as you do. And Quindaro is not as wise an investment as Atchison. The railroad will be here."

"You paid a band of criminals to steal! From your own son!"

"Let me explain."

"Please do," Patrick said, raising his head from his hands.

Maria sat, wondering if she should suggest they resume the discussion after a couple hours' sleep. But it was too late.

"I made a great deal of money in Australia, boys. That alone is a long story, so sufficed to say that I intend on spending it in Kansas. You have chosen an Eden, Paddy, and we are going to own it."

"Own it?"

"Yes, lad. Own it. Own it all." His face contorted into something mean, something the boys had not seen since they were very young. "Own every last inch of everything you can see from here." His voice turned quickly now, into a forceful, almost vengeful tone. "We are going to buy all the land in this part of the county and move all the Dugans and Kennys and Farrells here that we can. Hell, I don't even care if your mother's family joins us, wherever they are! We're going to build our own little Irish kingdom right here, in the middle of America!"

J.P. Dugan stood as he delivered this last phrase. It was a phrase that impelled him onward during the last decade of his life and he could hardly sit while delivering it. After his conviction for sedition for his involvement in the 1848 rebellion in Ireland, he labored in the public works camps of Van Diemen's Land and imagined owning soil in Australia and sending for his family. But after he was released in 1853, found himself in Melbourne, and was able to contact a cousin in Cork and began to piece together the puzzle of what happened to his wife and sons, his dream shifted to America. And when he found his sons were in Kansas, and that Kansas was bleeding the way Ireland had his whole life, he knew his destiny. So when he found his first nugget of gold in the fields of Victoria, he was unsurprised. He quietly put it in his pocket and kept digging. There would be more. Much more.

He looked down at the faces of his family, all of which took on ghostly qualities in the dark. "I know it sounds maniacal, I know it does, so. But it's possible. I've already started."

Patrick turned around and faced the north, where the Big Dipper had long sunk below the horizon, leaving a lonely, weak North Star hanging in the most unlikely of places in the sky. He couldn't face his father and ask this question. "Did you jump the Hawkins claim?"

"Yes." There was silence. "I mean, I claimed it for myself. They are on your land, Patrick. I checked the survey at the Land Office in Doniphan."

Patrick turned around and raised his hands. "And what now?" He raised his voice. "What now, dad!?"

"We remove them."

"Remove them?"

"They are on your land, Paddy. They don't belong here."

"What good is this going to do, dad? What gift is this?"

J.P. sat down again and re-lit his pipe. "As I said, son. I have money. Lots of it, and more coming."

"More coming?"

"I have made some investments. I believe you know Stringfellow?"

"Oh Mother of Heaven," they all three said in unison.

"I wouldn't call him that, so. She wouldn't likely be a great business partner, methinks. But I am in business with Stringfellow now. He and another man you may know— Pomeroy."

Roger stood and said stiffly, "An unholy alliance if there ever was one."

Maria interjected. "We gave them our money, Paddy!"

"We gave our money to the Kansas Valley Bank, girl," he replied cautiously. "Not to him."

"As did I," J.P. continued. "And a wise investment you have made with your savings. The only way to survive in a world of haves and have-nots, boys and girls, is to have. Pomeroy and Stringfellow have also started a railroad company, and I've invested quite heavily in that. And land. Of course land." J.P. stood again and made a sweeping motion with his arms. The sun was rising in the east and the smoke from the Hawkins chimney shimmered in the morning light. "Land, land, land!" he cried. "It's ours," he said. "One day, it shall all be ours. And when we have, we shall give." He smiled and, in his distant stare, seemed to forget he was even in the company of anyone else. It was as if he were still chained by the ankles and laboring on some strange, distant island.

Roger stared at his father in stunned disgust, and Patrick looked at him with a sadness only his face was capable of expressing. Maria watched her husband and was filled with a love she hadn't felt since they left Boston three years ago. The corners of his eyes were the most expressive thing in the world, she thought. And when he looked back at her they both knew. They knew.

Kansas did things to people.

"And that is why you haven't seen the *Sovereign* of late, Paddy. Stringfellow sold it to Pomeroy, and it shall be a Free State publication now. Smart business, I say. No sense in being so zealous about something you can't attract capital."

J.P. turned around and the sun pushed its beak through the shell of the horizon, unfolding around his silhouette, and above him the beast fluttered in the sky.

"What a paradise!" he said.

XVII

Del knew something was cursed about that money the moment her husband walked in the door. He seemed to be holding his body as far away from his breast pocket as possible, as if there were a hot coal or iron inside it. Neither did he seem in a hurry to show it to her.

"Well?" she asked, looking up from her knitting.

"Life ain't fair," he said, sitting next to her. He looked over at his mother and daughter. Both were sleeping soundly. "And it don't make no sense."

Delilah J. put down her knitting and placed her hand gently on her husband's thigh. "Tell me about it," she said.

"Dan gave me this," he said, removing the bank note from his pocket and handing it to her. "But he ain't in good shape, Del."

"This is three times what we need." She was repressing a smile. "He's generous, I'll say that."

"He just don't care. I coulda asked him for his whole property and he'd a-given to me."

"Why?"

"Booze, maybe. The war. Something he's mad at, his pappy, maybe. Hell, I dunno."

"I can feel it."

"Feel what?"

She stared at the note, folded it, and handed it back to Joseph James. "The sadness. In that piece of paper. It may be worth a lot of money but it comes with a price."

Now Joseph stared at it. "When we was boys ridin' out in the desert with Doniphan we used to talk about ownin' our own piece a land somewhere. Them Mexicans, ya know," he looked at his wife, "they know a thing or two. Their little casitas, some chickens and pigs and such, all the little hijos a-runnin' around—they looked happy. Here a foreign army's a-marchin' through their village and they just smile."

Del smiled and rubbed her husband's chest. "We have that now, Jimmy. We do."

"Only if we accept this," he said, sighing and looking up at the ceiling. His beard was coming in again and Del was reminded of the day she met him, at a barn dance near Weston, the smell of tobacco forever ingrained into the wood. "Danny has it, Del. His pappa left him everything you could ever want. Land, money, a house, hell, even a few slaves. He has everything."

Del stood and took him by the hand. "Except a wife," she smiled. "He's alone, Jimmy."

"Yer right. Poor man." He had taken her hand but dropped it now, then dropped his head into his hands. She could see he was fighting off tears. A daddy that left him alone to raise his little brother (and his mother), his arm broke by a shovel, his shoulder by a bullet, all the whips and beatings of a two-war combat veteran and a poor country life he could bear, but not the sadness of a boyhood friend. One long deep breath, and he looked back up.

"There's somethin' else, Del."

She slipped her arm around his neck and sat on his lap. "What is it?" She rubbed her hand along his gruff cheek.

"I saw Doniphan."

"Doniphan? Your colonel? Alexander *W*. Doniphan?"

"Yes. And he also offered me the money."

"What?"

"I met him on the road to the Baumgartner place and explained what I was up to. He said if Dan couldn't help he would, gave me his room at the hotel."

Del looked deep into his eyes. Why he would accept money from a tortured soul with nothing to gain instead of a true Missouri hero didn't make sense at first. But then, suddenly, it made all the sense in the world. "And you didn't go, because Dan did help. You're a man of your word."

"No," he said, looking up at his wife and placing his hands around her waist, or, what was once her waist and now his second child. "I just wanted to come home. To you and Missy, and..." She smiled at him, placed her hand on his, and nodded. "My god," he chuckled. "I s'pose we are gonna need the money, aren't we?"

She stood and took him by the hand again. "You're a good man, Joseph James Hawkins, and the Lord has a-finally seen to it that you have some good luck fer once. We will a-take that money. It was clean and bright the second you a-took it. Come, let's get some rest before the sun rises. Sarah will take the baby to gather berries for breakfast. It's a-goin' to be hot today."

They undressed as the birds began to sing in the pre-dawn grey to the east, and as Sarah Sally and Missy went outside to pick raspberries, they made love slowly and tenderly, and then, for the first time in their lives, they slept until noon.

***

The next evening J.P. Dugan ran into Joseph James Hawkins on the corner of 6th and Commercial Streets, outside the offices of the *Squatter Sovereign*, and now offices of the Atchison – St. Joseph Railroad Company and Atchison branch of the Kansas Valley Bank. Dugan was exiting and Hawkins was entering.

"Evenin' neighbor," Joseph James nodded as he hitched his horse in the dust.

"Good evening, Joseph," J.P. replied in a wholly uncharacteristically deflated tone.

"Somethin' wrong?"

"You might say that. Why are you here?"

"I'm here ta deposit this here check!" He removed Baumgartner's bank note from his breast pocket, which no longer felt like a hot iron. "I'm a-bankin'!"

J.P. Dugan shuffled his feet on the squeaky planks of the boardwalk. Everything within him wanted to resist telling his neighbor what had just occurred inside. All the years of suffering, of trans-oceanic crossings in chains, of landless poverty and even starvation and disease, told him to resist. But each bitter experience he had ever had over the last decade fell away with each grain of gravel that fell between the planks into the earth below, and, for the moment, just a moment, he remembered his own father. A man who stood both rigidly and

gently beside the fire on rainy Irish nights, and he knew he had
to do the right thing.

"I wouldn't do that if I were you."

"Why not?"

"There is a financial panic of sorts, Joseph." As he said it,
he felt his heart sink, and he thought again of his father. A
feeling he hadn't had since he was a boy came to him. He felt
cursed, lesser-than, inadequate. "Land prices in Kansas are
plummeting. Even grain is next to worthless right now. Railroad
companies are going bankrupt overnight. Stringellow tells me
his bank, and his railroad, are secure, but . . ." he looked over his
shoulder at the relative commotion inside, where men were
demanding their money, a bustle Joseph James only now just
noticed, "I am not sure I believe him." J.P. took a deep breath.
He had pushed his family across the world as a younger,
stubborn man, only to come across that world again so he could
ruin them, again. "If I were you, I would keep that money. The
worst thing anyone in this world can do right now is exactly what
I have done—invest in the godforsaken wilderness that is
Kansas." He'd ruined his son's life.

Joseph James looked stunned, and stood as still as his horse.
Though it had been building for many months, it seemed in
Atchison that the crisis had happened overnight on August 24th,
1857. "What the hell happened?" he said, folding the bank note
and replacing it in his pocket.

"The English," said J.P. Dugan. "And gold. The two things
that have plagued me all my damned life. Gold and the
goddamned English." He stepped aside, and as he mounted his
horse and headed north, the dragon of Kansas peaked its head
out from a lawyer's office across the street, and disappeared.
"And Joseph," he said, turning in his saddle. "The land will be
up for auction next June."

Thus began the Panic of 1857.

***

The pulpit was made of oak, and Roger nearly shed a tear
he was so ecstatic to be there.

"Welcome, my friends," began Charles Robinson. "Delegates, soldiers, investors, simple farmers and squatters— land owners and lovers of freedom, all—welcome to the first meeting of the future governing party of Kansas!" The crowd cheered and stomped their feet on the wooden floor. "I have no doubt we will win the imminent legislative elections, and that we write the constitution that admits Kansas to the Union. As a free state!" The crowd cheered again. "There can be no question we are in the majority now, and our majority is necessary if immigration to and investment in Kansas is to continue. And I assure you the governor understands this as fact."

He couldn't have gotten away from the farm quickly enough that morning, though he allowed Chance, his new horse, to saunter through Kansas autumn, the earth singing one final crisp and vibrant phrase before the silence of winter. An overwhelming sense of freedom and power coursed through his body like electricity and emanated from his fingertips as he rode, on the same trail Lane used a year before, leading his army into Kansas. He had only thirty miles or so to go, down to Grasshopper Falls, where the Free State meeting was being held. Grasshopper Falls was very near where he was injured last summer, in the Battle of Hickory Point. Returning would be, for many men, the reminder of a horrific experience, but it felt to Roger like a kind of homecoming, a triumphant return.

"Afternoon, young Irishman," Captain Samuel Walker had greeted him as he hitched his horse outside the hall, a Sharps rifle resting comfortably in the crook of one arm. Something about this man embodied the movement. The strength of his countenance recompensed his lame leg: there may be some fundamental weaknesses that kept him from moving quickly, but he sure as hell would keep moving. Sam Walker could hardly walk but he would always be the last man standing. Sam Walker was Kansas.

"Good to see you, Captain," he'd replied. "Is everyone here?" By that Roger had meant the Free State Party's leadership—Robinson, Lane, Brown, Pomeroy, and others.

"Now that you are here, they are," winked Walker, leaning forward on his lame leg so he could clap Roger on the shoulder.

And now that he'd taken his seat and Robinson was speaking, he felt so old and wise. The energy of every hoof that set upon Lane's Trail was within him, as if he'd imbibed it through Chance's legs all day.

"*You* are the governor!" a man Roger did not recognize yelled from the floor, a few feet from Roger. He looked newly arrived from someplace like Indiana, the way he was dressed. And Roger realized he didn't recognize most of the Party's rank-and-file at this meeting. The party was strong, its leadership had overcome imprisonment and battle, but many of its immigrants had left. Fire, ice, and cholera had done the work for the hairy Missourians. But the North kept coming, like a storm in the Atlantic.

Robinson smiled from the stage, a smile so bright and wide it seemed to embrace his audience. "Not yet, I am not." The crowd laughed. "The tides are turning, my friends. No honest man—and I do believe Senator Walker is an honest man—can continue to uphold the fraudulent belief that the elections staged in this territory thus far have been legitimate. The ruse is up for our Southern friends."

"They are not our friends!" hissed another man behind Roger, one he did recognize. In fact, the last time Roger saw this man, his face was contorted with fear in the Battle of Osawatomie, hunkered down in the grassy bank of the river, digging into it with his knees and elbows and wriggling his body like a lizard.

"Nor are they are enemies," Robinson held his hands up to settle the crowd. "They are our countrymen." Roger looked back at his fellow soldier from last year. His face was set, as if it had decided it would never contort again. "Gentlemen, I propose our path to be one of the moral highground, as it has been, and as it has served us thus far. We shall let the Pro Slavery party use words such as 'enemy.' We shall let them lie, cheat, and steal, while we embody the principles of democracy. We shall show Congress that squatter sovereignty was the correct policy, insofar as the law-abiding citizens of this nation are concerned."

The order of the day was the party's strategy for the upcoming elections. In October a new legislature was to be elected, while the current Pro Slavery legislature was writing a state constitution in Lecompton. Governor Walker, former Senator from Mississippi and the first to be appointed by President Buchanan, had promised the constitution would be submitted for popular vote before being sent to Washington. But instead of allowing a simple "yes" or "no," the vote was only "for" the constitution "with" or "without" slavery. But the Free Staters didn't want or believe these to be their only options, and their now exonerated executive, Charles Robinson, told them so from a podium in Grasshopper Falls.

"What do you propose, Robinson?" yet another man raised his arms in the air, his sleeves tumbling down his forearms.

"That we refuse false choices. That we refuse to vote in the referendum on the Lecompton Constitution. That we declare we are doing so in the press. That we de-legitimize the document. That we allow the Bogus Legislature to attempt to force a bastard document on the Congress, thereby undermining every decision that body has ever made with respect to this territory. Every member of Congress who voted for the Kansas-Nebraska Act of 1854 cannot—simply cannot!—also vote to admit Kansas as a state under the Lecompton Constitution." His features took on a resolve Roger had not seen before. Even his kind, blue eyes became hard and impressionable. "And they will not, gentlemen. They will not."

A silence fell over the crowd as a slow moving thunderstorm slipped overhead, darkening the hall and the brows of the men considering the risky proposal Robinson had just laid before them. If it didn't work—if the Lecompton Constitution were submitted to Congress as "with" slavery (as it surely would if the territory's Free State Party boycotted it), and approved, and Kansas were admitted to the Union under it—all was lost. All. But it if worked, why, it would be political genius.

Robinson smiled broadly again, his eyes shining as white as his strangely perfect teeth, giving the darkened room a hint of illumination. "And now, I believe General Lane has something he would like to say."

Lane strode to the podium in the same manner he had in Big Springs, but he struck an altogether different tone. All his fiery oration of the past years, both within the territory and on her behalf in the established states, preceded him, but the stillness Robinson had achieved enveloped even General James Henry Lane.

"I ain't much for politickin', but Mr. Robinson is right. Last summer we showed the world we would defend our rights, our property and our lives. We demonstrated our ability to strike back, to organize an armed resistance to an invasion. And now the bankers and investors are seeing that if our enemies carry the day, all kinds of money will be lost. But more importantly," now, as the sun began to find its way through the thunderclouds outside, the buoyancy of Lane's characteristic speaking voice returned, and his body became more animated, "we showed the world we are here to stay. No false voting, drunken mobs, disease or famine or pestilence or cyclone can push justice out of Kansas!" His voice cracked as it rose to a crescendo on the final syllable. So quiet and enthralled was the audience, his catching of breath could be heard. "If we lay down our weapons this fall, boycott the constitutional referendum and win the territorial elections, we will carry Kansas in the Union as she should be—Free."

Some members of the meeting stirred in anticipation of the usual thundering applause after a Lane speech, but looked around, realizing they were in the minority. The hall remained silent until a clap of thunder broke the summer sky above. Roger smiled and a tear came to his eye. This was where life was. This was where he felt most alive. The collective thought of dedicated citizens, the resolve of the pioneering strength, and utter belief in the justice of their cause: clearly, something was happening here. Patrick was not only wrong about the world ending in Kansas. The world was beginning anew. This new America, this West, would change the world forever. He stepped up on a bench and took a deep breath.

"I will boycott this referendum." The entire convention turned and stared at him. He nearly fell from the bench, so surreal was the feeling. "If it doesn't work, we can always go back to fighting!" He could see Lane smiling from the stage. "I will die if I must," he said in a low tone.

"I agree," said one man, followed by others. Some nodded, others whispered to the men standing next to them. Thunder and lightning quickened outside, and the smell of rain flooded in.

Robinson stepped back to the lectern, and from somewhere inside of him Roger could feel there were still eyes staring at him from the crowd. He didn't need to look to see to whom one pair belonged—it was the steely glare of John Brown. But knowing that, he intuited another pair. He glanced around and saw, in the back corner of the room, by the windows and in the iridescent glow of the passing storm, the slightly crooked eyes and square jaw of a young lady several years his senior. She was smiling in a way that was restrained, as if she smiled so often she frequently had to restrain herself. Smiling at him. And she didn't seem the sort of girl who smiled often, and the sun emerged from the clouds only so he could see her better.

XVIII

Maria could tell J.P. couldn't get back to the farm quickly enough. He'd ridden Paddy's horse to froth in just those three miles. Mud and leaves were splattered all over his underside as if J.P. had ridden straight through the woods and ignored the trail. The old man seemed cloaked in shadows, his wiry, half-grey beard as wild as his blue eyes that were once attractive, but were beginning to appear deranged.

"Maria," he said, spittle showing itself on his beard (almost frothing himself), "where's Paddy?"

She paused a moment, not out of hesitation, but purposely. "In the fields."

Her father in-law turned to go but she accosted him by the arm. "No. Tell me first."

"Why?" he was incredulous. He needed to shave his ears. Badly.

"I want to know. If you haven't realized it yet, Patrick often prefers to hear bad news from me."

J.P. hesitated. "Very well, so. May I have a cup of tea?"

"Of course."

"You might make it a strong one, my dear."

They went inside and Maria poured two small glasses of whiskey and set them on the table. "Let's not bother with the tea, so."

J.P. downed his, wiped his mouth with the back of one hand, and poured another. "There are financial troubles, Maria. Serious ones."

"For whom?" She sipped her whiskey.

"All of us. The world over, I'm afraid."

"Is that so?"

"Yes."

"Can you be more specific?" She smiled. It was the first time she'd seen where Patrick inherited his penchant for something like hysterical exaggeration.

So far most of this conversation had been nothing surprising. Something about this man rushing in was predictable, and she was also prepared for such a man crying so suddenly. This too seemed to be the source of her husband's predisposition toward tears when excited, and she felt a pang of yearning to know her mother in-law. But she was surprised by the reason.

"I've ruined us, Maria!" His head sunk into his hands. "Stringfellow is a boob! The Kansas Valley Bank is bankrupt! Land is worthless here! I've nothing left! You've nothing left! And your claim goes to public auction next June! You'll not be able to purchase it!" He sobbed in his hands.

All too familiar with the panicked feeling of the earth falling away, Maria looked out the window to steady herself, searching for the horizon. But she found only wilting trees against a sky of uninspired grey-blue. She reached across the table and slapped her father in-law in the head. "No! No, no, no, no, no! You silly old stupid goat!" She stood, slapped him again and threw her whiskey at him. "Why must you men ruin everything!?" She turned to the stove, retrieved her shovel, and stamped it on the floor, thinking it may cover the well from which the tears were rising. "Look at me!" He did not. She stomped again and slammed the shovel into the floorboards. "Look at me, damnit!"

He looked up, his tears soaked into his beard. "I'm so sorry, Maria."

She felt a wave of pity for him, seeing her husband in his eyes, and rested the shovel at the table. "Go and get Patrick," she said. But as he turned to go, she stopped him again. "Wait. Not yet." She turned around and calmly replaced the shovel, standing a moment and studying her house, her lovely stove, regretting the chink in the floorboards her shovel had just made. Something steadied within her, and the trees no longer seemed wilted—only hunkered against a long life. "Let's let him enjoy his land one last time. I shall tell him later." She turned back around. J.P. was breathing heavily, his frame centered in the doorframe. "I shall tell him. When I feel the timing is right. Not a word from you. Understand me?"

"But Maria…"

"Not a word!" She jabbed a finger at him, took a deep breath, and sat back down. "Now, tell me what happened, J.P.. Banks don't suspend overnight."

"Well," he sighed. "It's all very complicated."

She leaned across the table, her jaw set, an ivory feeling taking shape within her, and said flatly. "Try me."

He smiled wetly and sniffled. "Very well, so. It seems that the English have fallen on hard times and no longer have the money for western goods—grain and the like—and have decided their word is as good as gold, so gold shall no longer back their currency. A silver-tongued demon if I ever did see one…"

"So our land is less valuable." She was impatient.

"Yes," he had a feinted look of surprise about him. "And that means railroads are less valuable."

"Yes, yes, of course."

"And that means a lot of Americans are losing a lot of money. It means people are going to banks to get their money back. But the dollar is still tied to gold."

"And?"

He sighed, and she knew he was finally going to say something unpredictable. "And so the vaults in San Francisco loaded a giant ship with tens-of-thousands of tons of it and sailed for the east (because there are yet no railroads!), and it was just sunk of the coast of California. God Himself, Maria," he stood and rubbed his beard, choking a little. "God Himself sent a hurricane," he looked to the heavens in near supplication, raising his hands, which his eyes then followed back to his waist. "The banks don't have the money. Our money. Your land will go to someone who has money."

Maria sat back in her chair. "It's gone," she said. "Just like that."

"At the bottom of the sea," he sniffled. "Just like that." He sat back down again. "Gold, land and the goddamn English," he said. "The story of my life." He paused for effect.

Falling away, the earth still seemed to right itself somehow, like a hawk diving and tumbling and then finally spreading its wings, leveling. "Stop sniveling," she snapped, swatting the table and forcing him to raise his head again. "Are you quite sure Stringfellow's money is gone?"

"He claims it is not. He claims they are solvent. But it's all in railroads and without any gold—" he sighed again, letting his forehead fall to the table with a solid thud. "But—"

"But what!?"

"He won't give me the money back," his muffled voice came from below the table.

Maria paused. A group of swallows drew erratic lines across the bright canvass of the window, and she smiled. "You aren't certain if the bank is ruined, are you?"

He was still. "No."

She shook her head. "Men," she said under her voice and stood. "You let me handle this, Mr. Dugan. You 'professional gentlemen' are nothing but a bunch of langers. Complete idiots," she muttered, leaving the room.

***

It wasn't as if slaves were hard to find or treated well in Missouri in the winter of 1857, so it was surprising to Roger that he had such trouble finding one who trusted him more than their master. He offered freedom to at least two dozen—to escort them safely through Kansas to Nebraska, north along Lane's Trail—before finding an old man who finally agreed, but only reluctantly. He was to meet this man at midnight on the road outside the tobacco plantation west of Weston where he'd lived his life in servitude. But he, Elias, wasn't there.

Roger knew John Brown and the others would be waiting just across the river, at the ferry near Quindaro, until dawn if they had to. But the old man's patience had worn even thinner since Roger had last encountered him, on the eve of the Battle of Osawatomie last summer. John Brown had lost one son that morning, shot dead in his skivvies, and John Brown Jr. had been taken prisoner and was reported to be going slowly insane inside his cell. This was even more personal a battle now, and for a man like Brown—who had ordered the murder of five defenseless men in the Pottawatomie Massacre, having lost patience with the cautious approach of the Free Staters after the siege of Lawrence—to wear even thinner on patience, could only mean one thing: Kansas had more blood to spill.

But that wasn't what he had proposed to Roger after the convention in Grasshopper Falls. Not at all. "These men are as interested in investment as they are in freedom," he had said in the eerie moonlight of September, "they do not care about our poor suffering black brothers and black sisters." He reminded Roger about the "Negro exclusionary clause" written into the Free State Party's platform back in 1855. Slaves would not be allowed in Kansas, it amounted to, but neither would free blacks at all. At the time it had bothered Roger but he hadn't made much of it. Stopping slavery's spread westwards was the goal. But now Roger saw what Brown suggested—it may be a worth fighting for, but perhaps not one worth dying for. And so when John Brown proposed Roger Dugan help him and others with an "underground railroad" through Kansas, that would smuggle slaves out of Missouri, he knew he must accept. That was something worth dying for. Not the greed and caution of men like his father.

Not to mention the fact that the girl from the convention, the one in back with the eyes and jaw of a hero, who was illuminated by the sun as if it were the only sort of light worthy of her face, lived in Quindaro, where the slaves' Kansas journey usually began. Yes, the Underground Railroad was the road to love for Roger Dugan; both the love of God and of man.

Crouched now in the elderberry bush beside this decrepit plantation house, Roger began to doubt himself. Elias was old and calm, his face sunken and wrinkled, and his eyes were grey-blue, and despite obvious suspicion, finally accepted Roger's offer with the nonchalance of an invitation to tea. Something seemed awry, something Roger should have noticed, he thought. John Brown or a young J.P. Dugan would have done this better. Roger felt young and naïve and in some danger. He gripped his rifle and snuck toward the porch.

The entire porch area was crawling with spiders and there was no light on. Perhaps the master had discovered Elias's ruse and had killed him. Perhaps Elias had lied to Roger and this house was not even occupied at all. It sure didn't look as if it were. Roger decided to creep around back to look for a slave cabin or back door, but just as he turned from the porch he was startled by a voice, that of a white man with a pure Missourian accent.

"You here ta steal my nigger?"

Roger wheeled and began to raise his rifle, the back of his neck tingling as it had at Osawatomie, as he'd imagined Patrick's did at Hickory Point, flanking Hawkins to the left.

"Ah, ah, ah, ah . . . I'd a-put that down, son," the voice in the shadows said again. It was coming from a corner of the porch and Roger could now see the barrel of a very old Sheridan rifle pointing at him. "You don't want to wind up like me."

The man stood now, his rocking chair and the discolored floorboards of the porch creaking like cottonwoods in the wind, and stepped into the moonlight. Half his face was scarred and had been mangled many years ago. Roger lowered, but did not drop, his weapon. He felt sick.

"Who are you?" Roger asked in the steadiest voice possible, when the rifle rested at about a forty-five degree angle, half-way between the man and his own feet.

"The man who's nigger you's about to steal."

He felt sick again. "How do you know?"

"He done tol' me."

"What!?" The bile rose into his throat and his heart pounded. He tried to breathe slowly through his nose.

"Elias," the man called across the porch, "You's leavin' me tonight, is that right?"

"Yessir." The old man stood and came into the moonlight alongside the other.

"I ain't a-treated you well 'nough all these years?"

"No, sir."

Roger stammered and looked at both of them. "I—you— he's going to let you leave? You're going to let him just go? Isn't he a slave?" Disappointed at the disappointment that crept through in his voice, Roger felt he may cry.

The man with the missing eye laughed heartily. "Yes, son, he shore is. But I done given up a long time ago on a-keepin' slaves. On everything. Funny what life is like when you can only see half of it." He spat. "A man needs the whole thing."

"So..." Roger hesitated, glancing around, "I can just take him?"

The man laughed again. "If he wants to go with you! You can both burn in hell for all I care."

A breeze blew through. It was cold and their breath rose into the trees and illuminated the hanging threads of silk worms. "Well, Elias, shall we go then? Our party is waiting for us at Quindaro."

Elias hesitated. "How do I know yer actually a-takin' me north, young man?"

"You'll have to trust me."

The white man laughed again. "You want a nigger from Weston to trust a white man?"

Breath came more easily now, as his heart made one leap and settled in like a rider mounting, then soothing, his horse. "It's the only way. He can trust me, you, or his own ability to get north."

"I'd a-go with him, Elias. If you run away alone I'll put a bounty on your head as big as your nose."

There was a moment of silence. An owl called in the distance. "Why would you do that?" asked Roger. "He can come with me but if he—"

"Somebody's a-dyin' tonight, Irishman." Little Dan Baumgartner cocked his Sheridan and smiled. "I just ain't figgered out who yet." He was slurring now, wavering in his boots like tall grass in August.

His rifle held steady, the stock at his waist, angled down toward the steps in front of the other two men, Roger was steady as an oak. He would have to raise the barrel and fire very quickly, probably while dropping to his knees, if he were to out-draw a man above him with his gun pointed now directly at him, no matter how drunk the man was. Somehow he felt he held the higher ground anyway.

"It doesn't have to be that way," Roger said, bending over cautiously and setting his rifle on the ground. "I'm not going to shoot anyone."

"I know you ain't," Baumgartner replied, grinning madly. "I am." He looked over at his slave. Elias stared back at his master without a drop of fear in his eyes. Something told Roger this wasn't the first time Elias had faced death at the hands of his master. He was unmoved.

"Do it, then," Elias said in a low voice. "You and I both knows how long you's wanted to. Just get it over with. You's the biggest coward I ever did see, Mr. Baumgartner. Not like yo' daddy."

"You know, Elias," said Dan Baumgartner, smiling. "You're right."

He moved the shotgun quickly and Roger went for his rifle. But there was no need. Baumgartner placed the shotgun under his own chin and pulled the trigger. His almost headless body thudded on the planks of the porch, his head scattered on the door and front window.

Again, an owl called in the distance. "C'mon, son," said Elias, picking up his satchel, "Let's go."

***

Sarah Sally heard the hooves before anyone. They were hurried and hushed, but friendly. She knew the sound of men on horseback coming as enemies as well as she knew the sound of her own breathing at night.

She woke Del first, surprised her daughter in-law hadn't woken already.

"Del, there's someone out there. Del! Delilah!" Del reached over and woke Joseph James immediately, before she even opened her eyes, it seemed.

"Sonofa—" he stammered, jumping out of bed, in his boots and hat and coat in seconds.

Winter came in the door as Joseph opened it. Sarah Sally counted four horsemen immediately, maybe five.

"Hawkins!" one called in a hushed tone. "Is that you?"

Her son looked comical in his disheveledness but so trustworthy in his posture. She smiled. "Wh—well, why should you know?"

"We're friends," the same made replied as he dismounted and his horse snorted. "It's Micah Cook, Jimmy."

Sarah Sally could see this assuaged all fears in her son, but she didn't trust the man for some reason. Then again, she probably wouldn't trust anyone arriving on horseback in the middle of the night.

"Jimmy," the man said, extending his hand. "Good to see you."

"Why do I not think I'm about to say the same?" Jimmy replied, shaking the man's hand.

"Jimmy," Cook removed his hat. "Little Dan's dead. We're a-huntin' his murderer right through here."

XIX

Maria had known about Patrick's secret all along. She knew part of the reason he came to Kansas was not the optimism of a new beginning, but fear of the end of the world. They didn't speak of it often—perhaps they never even had very explicitly—but she knew it in the way he held his body stiffly in bed at night, as if the dark were a wild animal perched atop him, waiting for him to move. She knew it in the stare he had when he looked out across the land in the morning, as if he were watching a monstrous army march over the top of a ridge and into view. There was a fear about her husband that at times roused a heart-breaking sympathy and yearning to be closer to him; at other times, it irritated her endlessly.

He was so peaceful reading in bed next to her this wintry night, she knew the apocalypse was far from his thoughts. Certainly, he was worried. He was always worried, and there wasn't much wonder as to what about just now. His father had returned from the grave suddenly, had acted rashly and brazenly and compromised all they had worked for; not only had he put all their earthly possessions in danger, he had put a neighbor's property in the same predicament, thereby threatening to upset a delicate truce between them that was forever teetering between friendship and violence. Patrick had to be worried about it.

But still, he looked peaceful. As peaceful as his son, sleeping in a homemade bassinet beside the bed. Patrick had crafted it lovingly from the timber of one of the "three sisters," an odd trio of elms on the property adjacent to their original shack. Lawrence made little grunting noises as he slept, grunts that were very close in tone to those he made while waking and in preparation for screaming. He kept his mother in a perpetual state of half-consciousness all night by doing it, but not his father, and not now. Snow was falling outside, the cabin was warm. All was well.

And then, with all the roar of a wildfire, a thought came to her. This wasn't going to last, it said to her. Not even a minute longer. She tried to shoo it away, even made a hand gesture about her ear like it was a mosquito. Patrick looked over from reading his paper.

"A mosquito? This time of year?"

She smiled. "I don't think so, love. A feather from a pillow maybe. I'll check them for holes tomorrow."

Patrick grunted and returned to his reading. It occurred to Maria that it was the same grunt that little Lawrence made all night long every night. But that thought was very rudely and loudly interrupted by the previous one: It's not going to last, it said again. She slapped herself a little on the side of the head.

"Maria? Are you all right, girl?"

"Yes, I'm fine." She rolled over and put her head on his chest. He stroked her hair as he often did. And then his hand stopped.

She could almost hear his eyes darting about in their sockets and he read manically. She lifted her head. She knew now, and before she could squelch it, she acted on it.

"It'll be alright, boy," she said. "'Tis but a rumor."

"A rumor? That the lands will be up for auction next June? It says it right here." He tapped on the paper with his forefinger.

She lifted her head some more and acted as if she had already read it. Next to the notice of public auction was a statement folded up in the paper from the Board of Directors of the Kansas Valley Bank. They were responding to rumors that the bank was out of money, crashed in the Panic along with so many territorial speculations. It listed their assets, being some several thousand dollars more than their debts, and decried rumors from a town called Sumner that had started a run on their office in Atchison.

"No, that." She plunked her finger on it. "The bank. It's just a rumor."

He paused a moment, and in his face she saw a stupidity that often irritated her. But today it was soft and sad. "But where is Sumner?" he asked blandly.

"What?"

"It says a rumor started in Sumner," he said, poking the paper. "I've not heard of it."

Maria Dugan sat up in bed, felt a chill down her nightgown, and gathered the quilt in front of her. She chuckled. "It's a town just downriver from Atchison. On the other side of the white bluffs, just a few short miles." She scanned his face for recognition. "How can you not know about it?"

"I've been farming."

"So have I!" She shook her head. She was irritated now. "It's rivaling Atchison for business, Patrick. It's our Free State sister city. They call it the 'lower landing.' Atchison is the 'upper.'" Lawrence grunted. She sighed and lay down heavily on her side of the bed.

"Another circle to hell, so?" He put down his paper, smiling. "I thought it was just a ghostly town."

She looked over at him again. "Patrick, aren't you the least bit worried that perhaps the rumor is true?" Nearly standing now, she snatched the paper out of his hands and poked both articles with both hands. "Do you not see the significance of these two notices?" Her conversation with J.P. was on the tip of her tongue now. But no. No. If Patrick was going to hide in the furrows of his farm, it was just as bad as hiding in a bottle of whiskey. She would have to leave him if he were that stupid. But he would come through, a voice came through from the place of knowing. He would come through. You must be patient with men like Patrick. There is strength in their gentleness and patience.

"Well," he picked up the paper again. "It says here their assets are twenty—"

"Who do you think wrote that?" she asked flatly, knowing this was a tone Lawrence would one day come to know well, and hate, only to love it as a man.

"Well—" he stammered stupidly.

"Stringfellow! It's his bank! It's his paper! And he owns half of Atchison!"

He had the stupid look again. "Well—" This time it enraged her.

"Oh, Mother of God!" she snapped, rolled over, and blew out her candle.

***

The following night Elias found himself almost as far away from home as he'd ever been in his life, with men in whom he had no faith. He knew it was John Brown the moment his form was distinguishable among the shadows of the shoreline on the other side of the river. This was the form of a man who was of his age, but not its place. As if the water stood up in the form of a man, he seemed inserted unnaturally into the backdrop of trees and levee behind him, dropped there by the hand of God Himself, if God were a false god. A man who did things men cannot do. The form of a man out of a bible or a dream, but not one you'd want to read or have. At that moment Elias knew he had a real chance of making his way north, to Nebraska, to Iowa, to freedom; but he also realized he was in more danger now than he ever had been.

Brown had a route, he'd said, straight up through the territory and into the North, with Free State settlements, small fortified cabins ("forts," he'd called them) and cairns along the way to mark a safe passage. The old man had held his hands up and made a parting gesture with them as he'd told Elias all this, as if he were Moses parting the Red Sea. "Lane's Trail" was to be the path to the Holy Land, it seemed.

It seemed unreasonable that a man like Brown would ever harm him, or be so thick as to allow a Missourian spy of some kind infiltrate such a small entourage who would, but Elias still knew that the company of a man like Brown was dangerous company. This odd-eyed white man with his stiff accent and posture and Lutheran ways sought danger, the fight, confrontation. Everything about him told you so. Someone would come for them. For John Brown, and the fools who worshipped him.

So when Brown told him one night where to sleep as if he were a dog and Elias refused, and when they all heard the hooves coming in danger and the ridiculous cry of what sounded like a giant bird shattering the night, he knew to run. He'd never had to really run, it occurred to him. Not in all those years that Dan Baumgartner ruined the Baumgartner House, letting all the help go, abusing them until they left with nowhere better to go but the brothels and labor markets of Weston. Not once had Elias run from a white man, but now he did. He bounded away from the fire and into the branches stiffened with frost, his wool blanket still clung around his shoulders.

He was suddenly seized by the arm, and could feel that it was John Brown's wiry fingers that had sprung from behind a tree and were now holding him. "Hush now, Elias," he said. "We knew they were coming."

Elias could see now back at the fire a small group of men dismount and investigate. He could tell immediately they were Missourians, and almost as immediately that they were neighbors of his former master's. They must have found Little Dan dead on the porch. They must have realized Elias was missing. They must be looking for him.

"I know them," he said, catching his breath.

"No matter." Brown let him go, stepping forward into the moonlight, his rifle raised, while from all the trees around the fire came the rest of his men.

"You are surrounded!" Brown called into the night. "Surrender your weapons!" The Missourians hesitated. It looked like panic. Brown fired and shot in the air and all the men dropped their weapons. The Free Staters moved in and made them kneel.

"Brown, I believe it is?" one man said. "You are a wanted man, John Brown."

"You are a kneeling man, Mr.—?"

"Porter."

"And you are my enemy. You are an enemy of God."

Another man spat suddenly and stammered, "Go to hell you murderer!"

Brown aimed his rifle at the man. Both knew it had been discharged and not reloaded. Brown turned it around and wielded it like a club. "Who is in a position to decide the other's eternal fate, Mr.—?" he said.

"Hawkins. Joseph James Hawkins." The man spat as he spoke.

"You have stolen goods, Mr. Brown," said the first man, Porter. At this point Roger Dugan, the boy who'd brought him here, stepped forward and slapped the second man, Hawkins, in the back of the head.

"Stolen goods!?" he screamed. On the other side of the fire he looked orange and flickering as if he were a ghost. And he spoke to the man named Hawkins as if he had used the term "stolen goods" and not Porter. "This man's name is Elias you sonofabitch."

"Why, Roger Dugan," Hawkins turned around and looked at him. "I should a-known."

"As should have I, Jimmy," the young Irishman replied.

"Enough," snapped Brown. "You are our prisoners now," he said.

Later that night, after they had cleaned the Missourians of everything that could be used as a weapon, tied their hands behind their backs, marched another few miles north and west off Lane's Trail so as to escape potential reinforcements, Brown made them all pray. Before they began Brown eyed the first Missourian who had spoke and asked his name again.

"Thomas," he said, glancing over at Elias. "Thomas Porter."

Brown looked as if he were chewing something. "I believe you are lying. I believe your name is Cook and if I was certain of it I would kill you," he said. "You—if you were Cook—killed my son last year at Osawatomie. If I were you, I would get on your knees and pray." Brown stood over him. Cook muttered a Lord's Prayer under his breath. The man next to him quivered.

"What is your name?" Brown asked him, standing over his prostrate body now.

"Jim," he replied. "Jim Herford."

"Why are you so frightened of me, Jim Herford?"

"I can't pray," he said.

"Didn't your mother teach you to pray?"

"She taught me to say, 'Now I lay me down to sleep,' and that was all."

"All right, get down on your knees and say, 'Now I lay me down to sleep.'" Herford did as he was told, Brown stepped behind him and went toward Hawkins.

"I ain't a-prayin' around the likes a you," Hawkins said, standing.

Brown eyed him calmly. For a moment, Elias thought Brown would shoot him for refusing to pray. In another moment, he knew he would not, would never, could never. "Very well, Mr. Hawkins. It is your soul you spurn."

"To hell with you, John Brown! Yer a damned murderer!" He clenched his jaw as Brown held his stolid glare on him. "Goddamnit!" the Missourian stomped and spat, turning to Roger. "How the hell did you know we were a-comin' Dugan!?"

The boy named Roger grinned now. Elias could see his teeth in the firelight. Even they were delighting in the moment.

"Mah daddy done tole me," he said.

Elias looked around at the men, two on their knees praying, three staring one another down, the sickly glow of the sputtering fire making them seem even paler than they were; and he noticed a long, snake-like shadow move its way across then around the ring of trees marked by the fire. He didn't need to look up. Elias knew what it was, and saw that it cast no shadow on Brown, whose grey eyes seemed to turn golden as he smiled.

Let these white men fight over slavery, thought Elias, I shall escape it. He slipped away into the night, found the North Star, and started walking.

XX

The following March J.P. Dugan received a notice from the Land Office in Kickapoo that his claim to the property east and south of his son's was in dispute by a "Joseph James Hawkins of Missouri." He'd spent much of the cold days of winter lying in a cot in a shack, hidden in the timbers along Deer Creek. Some mornings he woke with a start and could hear Joseph James lurking in the woods on the hunt and thought perhaps what he was doing was wrong. For all his evil beliefs this man was still a friend to one son. And he did belong on this land; you could hear it in his footsteps and how they caressed the very land they trod. But now was not the time to be realizing it.

The soles of his feet may not be as familiar with these woods as this man's, but J.P. decided he would be as unmovable in Kansas as he was in Ireland. Everything he had worked for in nearly ten years on three continents was in danger, and all he had left—to give to his sons and atone for the mark he had left on their lives—was this little cottonwood hovel, and he would protect it like a castle. Some nights J.P. stayed awake reading the notice he'd received from the Land Office, removed from Doniphan to the more Southern-friendly hamlet of Kickapoo in one of the last acts of the Pro Slavery legislature. Some nights he read the *Sovereign*, now as rabidly Free State under its new editors as it was Pro Slave under Stringfellow and Kelly. But mostly he stared at the warped planks and yellowed canvas that passed for a ceiling and plotted his next move, waiting for Roger.

It had been a cold, dry winter. Colder than he ever imagined, but less snow than he expected. J.P. Dugan knew what was happening to him; or, rather, what he was doing. He was doing what he'd done aboard the ship from Liverpool to Tasmania; what he did in the labor camps and the mining shacks of the South Pacific. And whether it was in the tarred oak of the old British ships, the eucalyptus of the island continent or the cottonwood of Kansas, it was all the same creaky cocoon. He was reinventing himself; or, rather, the world was reforming him. Yet again. And somehow J.P. Dugan knew that he was in the exact right place to do so. A metamorphosis in Kansas is worth ten anyplace else.

Patrick was half-right that the world ended in Kansas. And Roger half-right that began there. Only the Kanza had it right—it was both, because they are indistinguishable. And they all understood now that Atchison did things to a man. J.P. had begun to learn about the Kanza from an old man that ran a ferry boat in town. Million, he called himself. Or, was he the man that operated the saloon? No matter. This man took your money and took you somewhere in exchange. Someplace else. Sometimes with booze, sometimes with a boat, and mostly, with a story.

"They coulda called me 'Million' 'cause-a what I done got for this here land," he once said, kicking a stone with his worn boot toe. "Stringfellow and all his friends wanted this land so badly, I coulda asked for a million! Instead I said a thousand."

"Why would they want it so?"

"Some foolish notion about it bein' the great bend to the west. A few miles closer to the Pacific than the rest of the river," Million tapped his toe and puffed his pipe, looking at the muddy curls of the river as it tumbled down the continent to the sea.

"Makes sense to me. I would say my son chose it for that reason, too, but I know it isn't so. He would have chosen it for the soil." They were standing on the bluffs just south of the ferry landing, the Missouri tumbling along beneath their feet.

"Ha! What's the difference, Mr. Dugan?"

"He's a farmer. He's not interested in speculating on overland routes and future railroad lines. Patrick sees only what is just in front of him, not like his brother."

"What else is there to see? That river there," Million then pointed just upstream where the giant river had cut a forty-foot bank into the sandstone, "it has been bending to the west that way for thousands of years. But look across her," he pointed now to the Missouri bottoms, a great expanse of Clay County that stretched several miles to bluffs in the distance. "All that will flood one day. Has a hundred times since that bank was cut out. I've a-seen it, creepin' up until there ain't no more 'up' to creep. I been here twenty years, Mr. Dugan, when all that was just reeds."

"But if the river floods, it will flood that way." J.P. pointed out across to Missouri.

George Million shook his head, almost disappointedly. "Don't you see, Mr. Dugan? What is a great bend to the west may not always be. The river changes this land, the land changes this river. Don't you see? Speculating on the best route to the gold of California or the finest crop for next year's market ain't the point."

"What is the point, Mr. Million?"

The old man had smiled a strange smile. "The Kaw buried their dead in these bluffs, Mr. Dugan." He stood and looked back at the outcroppings of stone. "This great bend to the west, a yearning for tomorrow." He turned and looked at J.P. now. "Which never comes!" he laughed and took another swig from the bottle they were sharing, turning back toward the east. "Tomorrow comes from over there," he said, pointing to the Missouri side of the river.

George Million was right. J.P. knew it this fine spring morning, listening once again to his neighbors footsteps near his shanty. It was amazing Joseph James still hadn't found him. J.P. had stolen his livestock, jumped his claim, and nearly had him killed by Roger on John Brown's underground railroad. And he liked him. Sweet Mother of Heaven, J.P. couldn't help but like Joseph James Hawkins. He was a good man. He really was. Unfortunate that they should have to compete for land, he and this honorable man.

And so when the pathetic door to the shanty was kicked in and Joseph James stood over him and cocked his weapon, J.P. knew he wouldn't pull the trigger.

***

Sometimes it occurred to Patrick that it often happened in life that after thinking about a long-lost friend or family member, that person wrote you a letter. Or, they emerged from the memory somehow, manifesting themselves on your front stoop like mushroom after a spring rain. It was almost as if the world of elves and fairies, the world of the jayhawk and moaning hanged slaves and French fur trappers that appeared near eternal springs in the moonlight, was a world that threaded people together across time and space. And so he was not surprised when a letter from Harry Clegg arrived at Atchison, because he had been thinking of him lately. The only surprise was how the letter had found its way to Atchison at all, given there were as yet no mail contracts between the territories. But it had.

Clegg had been Patrick's first and probably only true friend in Kansas. He'd met him in the first growing season, trading with his Mormon Grove community, and had later begun to work with him on the levee, back in the summer of 1855. Clegg and his son Joseph had also lived at the Dugan cabin the following winter, having lost their mother and sisters to cholera and their land to Missourians. They had also spent far too much time in the Pioneer Saloon together, gotten sober together, and decided that each was on his own path to a Zion, a land of family and freedom. Patrick's would be Kansas and Clegg's would be Utah, but each had to face a holy war in order to obtain it. Patrick's family had survived "Bleeding Kansas" in 1856, and now, apparently, it was Clegg's turn. For in 1857, the "Utah War" had begun.

My dear friend, began Clegg.

> *It has oft occurred to me in this life that everything—every person, event, place—is indelibly related to everything else. During some of my longest, darkest, most sleepless nights I have beheld this truth as a great tapestry. Anyone I have met, place I have been, or occurrence in my life is a thread in this tapestry. Some are brilliantly colored; others, dull. Some are strong as a well-spun length of hemp rope, others as worn and delicate as a strand of an old woman's hair. I can see them all, all at once. And, during some of my most illuminated moments, I catch glimpses of the culminating image of the tapestry. It is the face of God Himself.*

Patrick set the letter down on the table and proceeded to make himself a cup of tea. This was the most competent piece of sentimental writing (which he liked best) he had read in quite some time and he was going to enjoy it. He flipped the two pages with one hand on the table to examine the letter's length, disappointed to find only a sentence or two on the fourth page. Yes, he would have to savor this moment.

> *However, I must admit that these moments are few. The image on the tapestry generally escapes my feeble eyes. In discovering Mormonism I found that the image was sharper in contrast and beheld more frequently than in my previous life. After I converted the individual threads tortured me less often and with a somewhat palliated pain. The Mormons gave me God.*

> *But I must confess in total confidence that the image has begun to fade. And that is why I am writing. I am having a crisis of faith, Patrick, and can think of no one else on this earth to consult but yourself. I have seen my Elders, have even found some English friends. But with some irony I know with certainty that you, Patrick—an Irishman, a Catholic, a Kansan—are uniquely positioned to understand me.*

Patrick set down the letter and rose again. The tea was ready now, and he sipped it as he stared out the window at his farm. Maria had taken her letters into the bedroom to read them while she fed Lawrence, who had fallen asleep, and the quiet in the house was mirrored by the stillness in the trees and grasses painted with a late frost outside. There was a hint of spring in the activity of the birds and on the trees. Patrick thought of Clegg in a faraway land and wondered what it looked like, if the soil was good, what it felt like in your hands. He returned to reading.

> *You may have read of the so-called "Utah War." The President fancies that perhaps we shall rebel along with the South—that the barbarians of polygamy and slavery shall destroy the Union—and has sent troops to quell us (from Leavenworth, in fact—another thread between us). At first I thought he was irrational, provoking a God-loving people intent only on what all*

> *Americans covet: freedom and equality. But Patrick, I'm afraid that is not so.*

Lawrence began crying in the next room and distracted his father. Patrick quickly gathered his hat and scarf and went outside to finish the letter. For a moment he was surprised at his own impatience. For all his faults, J.P. had always been quite patient with him as far back as he could remember.

A terrible thing has happened here, wrote his friend in what had become a shaky hand. *A thing that makes Utah no better than Kansas.*

The letter was a bit difficult to read in the soft, dull light of an overcast day, but the returning quiet was all he needed. Poor Clegg, he thought to himself. Patrick could see his friend writing this letter. Again, he could not imagine Utah, knowing only that it was unlike any place on earth, but he could see Clegg in some small, candle-lit room, agony on his face. At least he was sober. Patrick told himself that any reply must include that reminder.

This is not my god. This is not my Eden.

Patrick sat on a stump and lit his pipe. The sound of his son's crying carried out into the March wind and irritated him again. He wondered where little Little Joe was while his father wrote this letter, what Little Joe thought of Utah, what Little Joe knew or didn't know about god, about slavery, about polygamy or any of the nameless things that man did unto man, and unto woman.

God help me, the letter concluded. *But I must return to Kansas, and I must ask that my son and I be allowed to impose upon your family yet again.*

When Clegg left Atchison a year ago, Maria had fled Patrick's drinking and was living with her mother in Boston. He would have to reply that Maria had returned, had given birth to their first son, that the veins of Kansas held their blood in a bit better these days, and that of course, Harry and Joseph Clegg were welcome on the Dugan farm should they need a few months to stake a claim somewhere in Kansas. Of course.

And of course Patrick knew, having been married long enough to know, to tell Maria about the letter. He went inside, found her suckling Lawrence and reading a letter of her own with a somewhat distraught look on her face.

"Clegg may return to Kansas," he said, waving the letter a little.

"Oh?" she answered without lifting her eyes. "That's nice."

"No, it isn't nice, I'm afraid. The Mormons are more of a problem to the President than Kansans, it appears. He's lost his god, Maria." Maria looked up from her letter and stared blankly at her husband. "Did you hear me?" he asked. "Maria, Clegg is coming back to Kansas. Godless." At moments like these Patrick noticed his penchant for being dramatic when he wanted wife's attention.

She blinked, and a wave of recognition came across her face. "Oh!" she said. "Forgive me, Paddy. I'm a bit distracted. You see," she held out the letter to him, "it appears that everyone is coming to Kansas."

Paddy took the letter. It was from Maria's little sister in Boston, and it simply read, "Maria, We are coming to Kansas. All of us. Mother and I, then Uncle Ed, Aunt Chloe, Sean and Ed Jr., sometime next year. Love, Kathy."

It seemed Edens were collapsing all over the continent. Patrick dropped the letter on the bed in disbelief. "Does this mean your mother will be living with us, so?"

***

Joseph James smiled as he saw the fear in the eyes of J.P. Dugan. Then he frowned when he saw it dissipate. Then he smiled again as he realized he liked the old Irishman. He really did. After all he'd done, there was something about the old man that made sense to Joseph James.

"Get up, old man. And put some pants on for Chris'sake."

"I didn't hear you coming," J.P. said as he pulled on his wool pants and hoisted his suspenders over his shoulders, both with the left hand due to a bad right shoulder.

"They never do."

"But how—"

"You think someone could squat on my land all winter and I wouldn't know it, Dugan? Where do you think the smoke from your fires goes, anyway? You are stupid. You are as stupid as your youngest son."

"Leave Roger out of it." He put his hands up for some reason and Joseph James glared at him. He dropped them.

"Leave—" he spat, not from nervousness this time but incredulousness. "Leave Roger out of this? You think I don't know he's behind all this? Him and you?"

"Behind what, Jimmy?"

"Don't call me that. And put your damned hands in the air a-fore I shoot you!"

"Honestly, Joseph—"

"Shutup! I know you told Roger about us coming for Brown."

"Yes, he told me—"

"Aha! And only a Yankee like that Roger would set you up here."

"What do you mean?"

"Here!" he kicked the remnants of J.P.'s front door. "This is my hunting blind you idiot!"

There was a pause and J.P. began to laugh. Joseph James choked back his laugh. At first he did find it funny, and honestly liked J.P., but then he realized he also hated him, very much. "Shutup!" He fired his rifle at the old man's feet. He seemed shocked. "I will shoot you, old man. Goddamnit, I like you, you Irish sonofabitch, else I woulda come here and killed you months ago." He grunted in frustration. "Just get out of here! Git offa my land Dugan, for the last damned time!"

J.P. seemed to calm suddenly. "No," he said calmly.

"What!?" Joseph James bore his teeth. "What did you just say!?"

"I said 'no,' Joseph. I intend to dispute your dispute. I shall hire counsel."

"This!" he screamed, kicking the shanty harder now, "don't mean you improved the land! You ain't broke a single clod of dirt!"

"You!" the older man raised his voice as far as was prudent, "aren't even living on this plot, Joseph! You have no claim to stake!"

"I have a record," he stammered. "I have witnesses! I have proof that I built a cabin, raised a family, voted, and farmed! Proof!"

"Witnesses to what, Joseph?" J.P. smiled and began to sit down. "You mean my son Patrick or my son Roger are witnesses to your history on this land? You mean Patrick *Dugan*? Roger *Dugan*? My *sons*? Which of them do you think would vouch for me, and which for you?" The old man grinned in a way he hadn't in a long time. His teeth were more yellow than usual.

Joseph James felt the rage boiling inside him again, the rage he hadn't felt since Hickory Point, El Brazito, or the Battle of the Sacramento River. He hated this feeling. He raised his rifle. "You don't have the money. I'll wait you out until it's up for auction."

"You can't shoot me, Joseph," J.P. completed his slow sitting motion. "You can't trust the law in Atchison is as friendly to you as it once was. You know that. You can't risk losing your family. And, someone else will bid more than you ever could. Patrick won't vouch for you."

Lowering the rifle, he took a deep breath and thought of Patrick. "We'll see, Mr. Dugan," and he even managed a smile. "We'll see what kinda son you raised after all."

He stomped off and turned around, remembering he had one last thing to say. "And J.P., you tell Roger if I find out he pulled the trigger that killed Daniel J. Baumgartner, I will kill him. So help me God, I will not hesitate this time!"

XXI

Everything young Roger Dugan had fought for in Kansas over the last three years was succeeding in May of 1858, and yet he had the sense there was more left to do than had already been done. Kansas, he began to imagine, was a turning point, an island in a great water sought by seamen as they navigated their way to its middle, and the rest of the ocean lay ahead, rife with storms and monsters; the future was so infinitely deep and vast one could fall into it and be lost forever. Still in his second decade, he began to understand his journey had only begun.

The political victories of the Free State party had been resounding that winter and spring. They had defeated the Pro Slavery Lecompton Constitution, won the territorial elections, and seated their own legislature. Governor Walker had resigned, even he believing the referenda on the Lecompton Constitution to be patently unfair; his successor, James W. Denver, quelled Pro Slavery demonstrations, including a riot in Leavenworth, where the new legislature decided to hold its own constitutional convention. Though it would ultimately be rejected by the Congress, their document was ratified by the voters of Kansas on the 18th, and it not only outlawed slavery, it allowed free blacks and didn't even explicitly refuse them the right to vote.

But if slavery was wrong in Kansas, wasn't it wrong in South Carolina, Kentucky, and Louisiana, and shouldn't he work equally there to oppose it? The next step was to abolish slavery altogether. It was God's plan. John Brown was right, and he had invited Roger to leave Kansas with him and start an uprising in the South. But Roger delighted in being one of the few trusted agents in a fledgling Underground Railroad that snuck slaves over the river to Quindaro and moved up the trail Lane had blazed with his Army of the North two summers earlier. He'd personally helped deliver three Missourian slaves to the North and freedom. His dedication to that, and to his family, led him to declining Brown's offer. Or so he told himself.

What really kept Roger in Kansas was one thing, and one thing only; and it was the only thing that could ever keep a young man of his age so awake on so many a night, and also keep him from dreaming about Big, Important Things: a girl.

Birsha from Quindaro.

The first time he'd seen her, she was in the back of the crowd at the Free Staters' convention last fall. Only noticing her as the meeting drew to its close, he told himself afterward that it was only because he was somewhat surprised to see a woman there. It was only because the sun had lit her face through the window, drawing his eyes there. It was only because young people notice other young people, and of course, it was only because he had never been with a woman. It was only because he'd happened to file out of the filled room and brushed alongside her, made eye contact, and asked who she was and where she was from. It wasn't because she'd said, "Birsha" in such a way that no other person ever could, and "I am a school mistress in Quindaro," in a way that made the town seem like the city of Heaven itself. It wasn't because he'd fallen in love with her at first sight, and working in Quindaro was as much about himself as it was the cause.

But now, finally catching a glimpse of her as she led her small class, of both free black children and whites, into her mother's house, which served as her schoolhouse, it became clear to him that all this was wrong. He'd stayed in Kansas just for the chance to see her again. She had a chiseled look to her cheeks that was classical. She had a shape through her mid-section that could only be described as reminiscent of a stringed instrument of some kind, resting so comfortably on its musician's lap it didn't weigh an ounce. Her dark, slightly crooked eyes were like those of a prized calf, and when she smiled at him this fine spring afternoon (obviously because she recognized him from the convention), the sunlight flickering through the leaves of the cottonwood, almost as angled as this odd town resting on its precarious perch above the river, he had the sensation he'd had ducking cannon shot at Osawatomie, or while assaulting the blacksmith's shop at Hickory Point. If love, he thought, was as exciting as battle, perhaps it would sting just as much in the end. But no matter.

Any wound was worth that smile.

***

Maria wasn't totally sure why she didn't want to go the circus until she saw the clowns. They turned out not to be the primary reason she shouldn't have come, but they frightened little Lawrence so badly she wondered if they shouldn't suggest children under five years of age not attend the circus at all. She should have known then and there, while the parade slogged its way down the terribly-graded streets of Atchison, to turn back and go home. Just go home. They weren't here on business, which they should be, asking for their money back with only a month left before the auction, so what was the point? She should just turn back and go home. But she didn't listen to herself.

Instead, Maria agreed to accompany her brother, husband, and father in-law all the way to the clearing just south of town where a great tent had been erected by the circus so she could witness one of the two shows put on that afternoon. It all had an air of ridicule about it—from the deformed and grotesque to the flaunting of Indians as if they were the same by their very nature—and it gave her a sense of unease, of a déjà vu too eerie to ignore. The acrobats were lovely, but the rest reminded her of listening to her grandmother and mother chatting, telling stories of strange creatures in the woods of County Offaly. Stop! she would scream at them, tears in her eyes. But they carried on, just as the clowns had after nearly frightening Lawrence to death.

Kansas was getting scary again, too. The continuous fistfights and middle-of-the night threats had spilled over into executions once again. Word has just come that a Georgian, Charles Hamilton, had led thirty guerilla fighters over the Missouri border into the southern part of the territory, rounded up eleven unarmed Free Staters, ordered them to their knees, and shot them in the back. The Marais des Cygnes Massacre, as it would come to be known, would surely be avenged. And it was clear the Pro Slavery party would not give up the politics of Kansas without further fighting, however hopeless their cause.

So when Shi-na-poh-mah took the stage, Maria rose to leave, but Patrick held her in her seat, saying she'd disturb the people around them if she tried to file out of the isle now. Poor Patrick, always so worried about what others would think. "Let's go to the bank," she nudged him. "Let's get our money," and he shushed her. He should have listened and left too, because as they watched the "Winged Bird" trounce about the half-circle, he also became quite uneasy. It was nothing but a young, talented Sac Indian rider on a horse with a feathered bridle and saddle-blanket and artificial wings tied to it so as to appear Pegasus-like, but it was somehow quite frightening. Maria understood its attraction—this was one amazing horseman, and at times it leaped over barrels and fences as if it could indeed fly, but there was something not right about anything winged in Kansas.

"Okay so, let's go," Patrick finally said, pushing his way through the knees of his fellow gawkers so rudely she knew he too was disturbed. "From one circus to another," he said. "Let's go get our money back."

To Maria's surprise, both J.P. and Roger followed. She thought they would have stayed and watched the performance, but they had come along and they all now stood in the soft sunlight. She felt safer now, as inside the giant tent it was dark and insidious. Even Lawrence was happy, and Maria realized (and in seeing her husband's smile, saw that he realized the same) it was the little boy's first real experience with the sun. March and April had been a bit too chilly, he a bit young, to really uncover him. But now the light shone through his fine hair and showed just how much red there was in the blonde, and he smiled, gasping when a breeze came upon his face. Perhaps, Maria thought, everything was going to be okay. Perhaps the "Winged Bird" of the circus meant nothing.

Then she heard the gruff voice of an angry Joseph James Hawkins behind her. She turned and saw Del and Sarah Sally a few yards behind him, Del swaddling her new baby and shuffling Missy behind her legs, looking very displeased with her husband. Joseph James had Roger by the scruff of the neck, and he spat.

"I said, did you kill Daniel J. Baumgartner!?" Joseph James was scowling, his lips twitching in anger.

"What!? No! I didn't." Roger appeared almost afraid, unlike himself. He was clearly caught by surprise and he tried to step away, but Joseph James would not unhand him.

"That was his slave you were sneaking out of the territory!"

"I know."

"You *know*!? So you killed him!"

"No, Jimm—Joseph. He killed himself." Roger appeared almost regretful, also unlike him.

"You 'spect me to believe that!? And you!" he pointed menacingly at Patrick and moved toward him. "Do you know your dad thinks—"

"You're on the wrong section, Joseph," replied J.P. "You know that."

Joseph James continued. "—thinks you won't vouch for me!? What kind of man does he think you are!?" His voiced softened. "I know you are a decent man, Patrick Dugan. You and I has our differences, that's fer sure, but I know you won't lie and a-put me 'n mine out in the th' cold just so this man can make a little Ireland in Kansas." He paused. "I know you won't do it." But Patrick stood there like a statue. If he was aware of what his father was up to, he didn't show it. And if he was aware of what his brother was up to, he didn't show that either. So Joseph James raised his voice again. "I don't know which of you white niggers to fight first!" He turned his attention back to Roger, who looked concerned. Usually he smiled in this sort of situation, but he looked unsure of himself. Joseph James grabbed him by the scruff again. "Yes, I do," he smiled. "Oh, yes I do."

"Jimmy!" Del called from behind him. "Enough!"

"Joseph," Maria interjected, glancing at her son, whose hair seemed to deflate now, like the feathers of a chicken settling after ruffling them. "Think about what you are doing."

He appeared to think a moment. And then he wheeled Roger around like a doll and punched him in the face, sending him to the ground.

***

Birsha Carpenter and her mother emerged from the circus tent after the equestrian show was over and found it was too bright to see very well. They never should have come. Imagining a display of human athleticism and prowess, they thought a circus would be rather boorish, but had no inkling that it could possibly be so heretical. An Indian on a winged horse? To what golden calf, false idol, pagan sorcery did that display allude? Brisha didn't want to know. And the drinking. Oh my, the poison that was Atchison. What could be next, she couldn't possibly know.

But the sounds of a fight made it obvious. She became separated from her mother in the crowd and the blinding sunlight and clenched her jaw. Yes, of course there would be fighting. What ungodly barbarians did she expect to see now rolling in the dust. They probably contended over a few drams of rum. She would see the fight so as to circumnavigate it, find her mother, and be off to Quindaro.

But she soon saw that the young man from the convention, who smiled at her and her children in Quindaro in the springtime, was on the ground being attacked by another man, and quite viciously so. She almost cried out for them to stop, but soon saw others were trying to stop it. She pulled and twisted and knotted her handkerchief, her teeth grinding and the muscles in her jaw rippling alongside her face. She nearly shouted again, and tried to relax; a clenched jaw was unattractive, or so her mother told her.

Two other men jumped on the man attacking the boy she liked, and the fight balanced some, its combatants tired, and they all stood with blood in their noses arguing. But she didn't hear a word they said. She could only stare at the boy from the convention, and soon realized he didn't seem to care about anything but her presence as well, once he noticed it. She gleaned from the screaming that his name was Roger Dugan. Dugan, she thought. Birsha Dugan, she thought. Birsha Dugan, she turned over in her head several times.

Two women now joined the crowd, and one of the women who had been trying to stop the fight—a short, Irish woman with strong legs and red hair—looked shocked to see them. "Mamma!?" she blurted out, beginning to cry. "Kathy!?" she said to the girl beside her mother. The tears began to flow and she embraced them. "Why," she chuckled, "welcome to Kansas!"

And then two men joined the crowed, one an older man with sad eyes, the other a boy that wasn't yet ten. One of the men involved in the fight—a tall man with skinny legs—seemed shocked to see them. "Clegg!?" he blurted out. "Little Joe!?" And he now joined them in a conversation a few yards away, shaking their hands vigorously, enough so that his bleeding lips dribbled blood onto the cringing man unfortunate enough to have remade his acquaintance. "Welcome back to Kansas!"

And then another man joined the crowd. He was well-dressed. The man who had been attacking Roger—her Roger—seemed shocked to see him. "Colonel Doniphan!?" And she heard the colonel say "I'm sorry to see you are still fighting."

Just like that, they were alone, she and her Roger. All these barbarians were interrupted by the others, and their arrivals stopped them all from their horrid behavior, only so she could have her moment. Roger tried to wipe blood from his nose but only succeeded in rubbing dirt on his face. She chuckled and took out her handkerchief. She felt woozy.

"Here, let me get that for you," she said and dabbed the blood from his upper lip.

"Birsha," he smiled. "From Quindaro."

She smiled back. "Roger. Roger Dugan."

She kept dabbing until the blood was gone, then licked her handkerchief and rubbed the dirt from his face.

"I don't know why all those people are still inside the tent," she said. "The real circus appears to be out here."

***

Once again, she was the most interesting thing in an otherwise electric environment. Nothing—not thunder and lightning, not applauding and hollering men, and now, not a broken nose or an entire circus—was more interesting than she was. Here he was, in the middle of a town bustling with all the families in the territory, exotic creatures, aberrations of nature, and the most intriguing illusions, and he only saw one thing. Her. Birsha from Quindaro.

Her prim collar, perfect posture, hair as black as the night of a new moon pulled tightly into a bun, and her beatific mouth, seemed to rise above the mud of Kansas. She was the essence of righteousness, a perfect Beatrice, the movement embodied in Yankeedom. And though a bit of Cork County recoiled, the rest of Roger kneeled, offering his life and sword in some chivalric thought that played in his eyes so obviously even she could see it. The slightest, most discreet hint of approval came to her face, and it was the most beautiful thing he had ever seen, as if it descended from heaven.

An older woman with similar eyes and jaw came and took her arm. Roger stood dumbfounded, his nose bleeding onto his breast. He found himself now with all the living women he knew or had ever cared about, and those they cared for in turn. While the men sorted out land tracts and grudges a few feet away, Maria and her mother and sister; Del and little Missy on one hip and her infant at her breast; and now Birsha, his Birsha, all introduced one another and met Birsha's mother.

"Clarina," she said in a way that was both refined and personable, offering her hand to each in turn. "Mrs. Clarina I. H. Nichols."

There was a pause, and Birsha's sweet lips parted a little when Del was the first to recognize her. "Now, ain't you the Mrs. Nichols who edited that paper down in Quindaro?"

Clarina's face beamed in the same understated way her daughter's had. "I am a former associate editor of the *Chindowan*, yes. I must admit," she said with a refined chuckle, "I am surprised you are acquainted with that publication."

Maria seemed to hold back her own surprise, the slightest hint of an eyebrow raising and an askance look at her friend.

"Well now," said Del, looking back over her shoulder to ensure her husband was minding his manners, "I'm sorry to hear that. I enjoyed your writing."

"Aren't you the widest read woman in Atchison, Delilah?" Maria patted her friend's shoulder.

"You know I'm a-teachin' myself to read, Maria. We don't have the money," her eyes shuffled momentarily back to Joseph James again as he raised his voice but she did not look back and continued, raising her own voice, "to subscribe ourselves but I get the papers I can find when I'm in town."

Birsha and Roger had barely taken their eyes off other, and Roger's heart leapt and she said, to the other women but while looking at him, "You ladies should visit us in Quindaro. We have a literary society there where women of such intelligence might discuss matters of the day."

"Come, Birsha," Clarina interrupted. "These ladies would tire quickly of our endless talking, and it's so far from Atchison to Quindaro." She paused. "We really must be getting back. A circus in Atchison?" She regarded the pyramidal tent sloping into the dull blue sky, and her face included a wry smile when it pivoted back to Birsha's. "'Tis an inverted Malebolge and only the meanest of beasts can take us there."

XXII

Maria had to admit, it did seem at times the world was coming to an end. Just when your son's hair is feeling its first breeze, its first ray of sun, utter chaos emerges from the mud. Her father in-law was almost single-handedly restarting Bleeding Kansas and had turned her only friend back into a sworn enemy. Her brother in-law was deliberately trying to provoke a nationwide civil war with one of the world's most infamous fugitives. All their money—and their land, their future—were still tied up in a failing bank managed by a man who had once threatened her husband's life and laughed at her as she clung to life after she lost her first baby. Patrick's best friend was retreating from his Zion and the Utah War, preferring Kansas (of all places) to the land his prophet led him. Her son wouldn't shutup at night for a single second, and now, just to top it all off, her mother's voice just kept going and going, talking about something she'd already talked about before.

At least she had Lawrence. If men are born vessels into which the world pours life, Lawrence Dugan was already, not even an entire year on this earth, fuller than any man Maria had ever met. He reminded his mother of the few Madonnas she had seen, a replica here or there in County Offaly's revived churches; deeply inlaid into her childhood memories; and others in books at the library in Boston. He seemed born unto the world with a certain wisdom.

His hair was light and downy, his face broad, open; his cheeks so large they pulled his mouth and pushed his eyes so he seemed to smile at all times. And not just his cheeks; all of him had a springy, spongy, pregnant feel to him, as if he burst with the fullness of his short life, an udder of a boy, aching to be set into motion among men.

Always willing to rise in the hands of his mother, he would throw himself with full confidence toward her, arms outstretched. It was not just confidence in her, that she'd catch him; but a fearless belief that no matter what befell him, he'd adapt. Maria often studied him as if he were a fine piece of art, watching him crawl about the cabin or in the yard. Rooster or tree, frog or rock, it didn't matter—he wanted it. Once she watched him observe a mosquito biting his arm, and as the proboscis pricked his skin his face lit up not with pain but with wonder, amazement at the ingeniousness of this little grey miracle come to survive. And then he smashed it, shrugged, and went about his life.

You felt it. You knowed it. He had more to offer the world than most, so unafraid of it was he. So unlike his father, she had to admit.

Patrick had decided to continue keeping his secret from Maria. Sometimes it seemed he knew that she knew anyway, but by pretending he wasn't concerned about their money in the Kansas Valley Bank he must have thought perhaps he had her fooled, which was maddening. She knew he worried. She knew he prayed. She knew he rarely drank anymore. She knew all the things he did well, and she knew he'd learned over the years that when one of those things he did well hurt, to try and replace it with another thing that didn't. He must be worrying, else he wouldn't be walking and praying so much.

"Mother," she interrupted her own thoughts and turned around, having finished the dishes, and was drying her hands on a towel. "I think I will go for a walk."

"Lovely day for it! I shall join you, girl."

"No, I'd rather go alone. Would you watch the baby for me?"

Her mother looked hurt. "I see." But then she smiled and gave her daughter a peck on the cheek. "I shall try to stay out of your way more, Maria. This is your house, after all."

She walked to town, infuriated the whole way that her husband had known about the Panic and the notice of public auction since the winter, yet he had done nothing. They had only one month left to purchase the claim or forfeit it to auction. She was even more infuriated to see the offices of the bank closed with no indication of return posted. She continued walking, muttering to herself, to the southern reaches of the town. She remembered that almost two years ago, while she was in Boston, Patrick had come this way along the river, climbing the bluffs.

Before she could stop him Patrick told about meeting the Ferryman and seeing the oddly-lit, non-existing town over the great white bluffs. He'd heard the moans of the drowned slave, Molly, atop the bluff and ran back to the farm. So much had changed since then. Atchison was bigger now, despite its growth being halted by the Panic. The ferries were more frequent, the streets so heavily used they were scarred by wagon ruts two feet deep. But that bluff looked the same, and she meant to avoid it.

There was a wagon trail heading out of town toward the south where the circus had been. Perhaps this was the road to Sumner, and perhaps Sumner was the ghostly town Patrick had claimed to see that haunted night in 1856. Nonsense, she thought. "Nonsense," she said aloud, stopping in the clearing where the great circus tent had flattened all the grasses. "You mustn't start thinking that way," she said aloud again. Just because mother is here, she thought, doesn't mean it's time to start believing in leprechauns all over again.

She continued down the road as it wound its way through the rolling hills. She came to one that looked different from the rest. It was uniform and small, as if made by man, and she flinched as a wave of panic hit her when she saw there was a man standing atop it. He was wearing skins, though it was warm out, and he motioned to her. She stood frozen. Was it? Yes, it was the man who'd untied her from the chair last fall, the Frenchman named Pascal. But she didn't follow him.

"Maria Dugan!" he called, descending the mound. "I've been waiting for you."

She waited until he was close enough that she wouldn't have to shout. "Waiting for me?"

"Of course!" he chuckled. "Who else would I wait for at this point in the story?"

"I don't know what you mean."

"Good!" he laughed heartily. "May I join you?"

She thought a moment. "Pascal, I'm grateful to you for your assistance last year, but—"

"But you don't need any now?" He didn't smile. It seemed odd.

"Well, I'm not sure—"

"I'm the man for the job." His face was as expressionless as possible. It irritated her.

"I don't mean to be ungrateful. It's just that."

"You want to be alone." Paschal took a deep pull on his ever-present pipe and leaned toward Maria. His skin was so sallow he seemed only half there, his teeth so yellow they looked like corn stored for seed, but oddly, he didn't smell. It was only his smile that was nauseating. "You want to be alone, Maria Dugan. Who's to say you aren't?" He laughed again, and handed her a pipe. "Here," he said, "come have a smoke with me atop this mound."

Soon she was very comfortable. This man was not threatening at all, and the more he smiled, the less it bothered her. He lounged the way she'd seen Patrick lounge at times, as if the earth and sticks and rocks conformed to his contour out of deference or respect. The earth made a bed of herself for this man, and now she was doing the same for Maria.

"Do you know what this hill is?" he asked after a pause.

"Yes." She heard the word come out of her mouth, almost as if of someone else's volition.

"Hmph?" Paschal grunted in question.

"A burial mound." She was surprised at herself. "The Kaw are buried here."

"And how do you know that, Maria Dugan of County Offaly?"

She thought a moment, sitting up, and the feeling left her. Reclining again, taking a puff from her pipe, it returned. "I can feel them," she answered.

Paschal smiled, and all at once she was nauseated again. She stood quickly. "I—I have to go," she said. "I shouldn't be here. I have supper to cook."

Paschal didn't rise, and his smile left him. "If you must."

"I must," her hair betrayed the twitching in her forehead. "I do apologize Paschal, but I—we are not to speak of these things!" She stopped twitching, fidgeting to go, and stood still now, waiting his reply.

He stood, slowly, and with a languor she envied, the steadiness of the sun's course across a long summer's day, he came to her, took her hand. "You cannot slay this beast, Maria." The smile was friendly now. "It will follow you to the ends of the earth, into hell itself."

She dropped his hand and turned to go, then hesitated. "That town, Sumner," she said. "Is it there?"

Paschal laughed. "For now it is!" He turned again and noticed a broadside tacked to a tree that she could have sworn was not there before. The oddest place for a broadside, she thought. "My, my," he said, puffing his pipe. "Ain't that interestin'? I'd a-read this if I were you."

She walked over to it. It was a posting from the Land Office Superintendent in Washington. The auction was being postponed until further notice. A wave of relief came over her, washing the discomfort of the last several moments away like cold water over a burn. But just as her neck and shoulders began to relax, they sprung back to life again, rippling like a burn in the sun. She heard a moaning from atop the bluff.

Paschal began laughing. He laughed and laughed until she looked at him, and then, at last, to the top of the bluff, where she saw a black woman struggling against a noose that was hanging from the branch of an aged oak. Maria looked back at Paschal, a flash of anger in her eyes, and took a harried step toward the bluff, thinking she would run and help this poor woman. But suddenly, Molly was gone. And so were her moans.

Paschal's laughter subsided and he took a deep breath. What had been hysterical and non-human about his laugh now was familiar and amused, and very, very human. He tipped his cap. "Evenin' Mrs. Dugan."

And Maria ran home. Home to Lawrence, who was nothing if not human.

***

It didn't feel too good mounting the horse and sitting in the saddle, so Del was pleased when the thought came to her that she didn't need to go see Maria—Maria was already on her way. The dragon curled itself like the tail of a muskrat around the top of an evergreen tree in the west, and she smiled at it. Appearing almost tamed, its grotesque human-like face licked its feline-like paws just like a housecat cleaning itself. Maria was coming, the land on her mind. Del went back inside.

"I don't think we have the money," Maria began, sipping the tea she'd taught Del how to make, swiveling Lawrence away from the hot cup with a swing of her knee. "My, girl! The tea is lovely! You'd make a proper Irish wife any day of the year."

"But what happened to—?" Del sipped hers. It *was* good!

"We put all our savings in the bank." She looked up at her friend. "I know—you warned me not to. Not to go to town that day." She sighed and looked into her cup. Even in the height of summer she appeared to thoroughly enjoy the steam rising and condensing on her chin and nose. Del felt a wave of pain, the sort only love can conjure. This, the only friend she had ever really had other than her husband (and now, perhaps, her mother in-law), was alone.

"Pomeroy's bank?" she asked.

"Yes. Pomeroy's and Stringfellow's. Imagine the curse of the child born to such an unholy union. The townspeople have even elected Pomeroy their mayor! Imagine that. A Free State man the mayor of a town named for Senator Atchison. The very man who's taken all their money, lost it, and deals with the devil." She sighed again and sipped her tea. "Lawrence stop that!" Her son seemed to be trying to hit her friend's daughter with a stick. "My, how things have changed, Delilah," she turned back to Del with another sigh. "I don't know what is worse— the blood of '56 or the blind greed of '58."

Del rose and topped of both cups of tea, wincing again as her newborn rooted feverishly. "So that is why your father in-law wants our land," she said, turning to the wash basin, wondering if she'd said so with kindness in her heart.

Maria looked confused. "He what? Doesn't he have a claim to the north of you?"

Turning back, she glanced at Maria, but her soft eyes were too lovely to hold. "Ain't no more sections to claim, Maria." Instead, she looked to the front door as if she could see through it to the sloping land. "At least not right 'round here there ain't."

Forcing herself to look at those eyes again, she changed the subject. "Hasn't your mamma found that out already?"

Maria chuckled to herself. "Mother hasn't quite seen her way to looking for a claim just yet. She's still . . . adjusting . . . to Kansas."

Del chuckled aloud. "I can only figure how that might be." George began crying in the bassinet next to her. She rolled her eyes and picked him up.

Maria looked over at Lawrence, who was following Missy around, two rocks and a stick in his hand. "Do you think they'll be friends, Del? I mean, will Kansas do to them as it's done to us? Not in the sense of Pomeroy and Stringfellow, I don't mean that."

Del winced a little as her son began feeding, but it soon eased. Every time it worked without pain she said a little prayer of thanksgiving. "I think that depends on us, Maria. Don't you?"

"Yes, I suppose so."

"Maria," Del was comfortable again and sipped her tea. She had an overwhelming urge to make it right, to ensure the Dugan and Hawkins farms would stand side by side for a hundred generations. Whatever the men had done to one another would not matter one day. "What makes you think you don't have your money? I thought that's what banks are for—to protect your money."

"It's a long story," Maria just looked so darned sad, Del could barely bear it. "The short of it is 'gold and the goddamned English,' as J.P. says. But I think it's men. Stupid men—Irish, Catholic, Protestant, Southerner, Northerner, even Mormon— they're all stupid." She was always short, but she seemed caved in upon herself now, an old barn ready to be reclaimed by the earth. "Especially my father in-law. How in the world does he think he'll have your land?"

"He's squatted on it."

"Has he now? Well, that's rather useless, I should think. But then, he's familiar with being useless."

"I don't think so, Maria." She stroked George's dark, thick hair. "You see," she sighed, tired of the position the world had put her and her friend, "we are on your land. Technically, at least. So J.P. submitted a pre-emption claim to the land we thought we owned. We aren't really on it, so—"

"But you can't be more than a stone's throw off it! And how were you to know where the property line would fall before it was surveyed!?"

"Well, so we'll have to explain it all and make a case that we were here first, made the improvements, and the property lines should be adjusted or . . . something. It's just that—" she hesitated, sipping her tea, and raised one of her rather thick eyebrows. "Has Jimmy not come to see Paddy?"

Maria rubbed the backs of her arms. Del could feel them. They were weary from hoeing in the garden all day. "Not that I know of. But Patrick seems unworried about all this. Which can't be true. That man worries like a priest in a brothel."

Del smiled. "It's just that we'll need testimonies, Maria. Witnesses." Maria didn't seem to react. She continued to massage her arms, grimacing. "We don't have any, Maria. Not any . . . neutral ones."

Maria seemed distracted, but soon came back to the table. "Do you mean you're worried Patrick—we—won't vouch for you because—" she seemed less hurt and more incredulous.

"It's a hard thing to ask, Maria. For a man to testify against his own father."

The oddest smile came across Maria's face. She seemed delighted, as if this conflict made their conflicts resolvable. "Patrick will do what is right," she stood and finished her tea. "If there's anything I know about that man, it's that he's an honest one."

"It's a hard thing to ask, Maria. I mean, for all the hell Jimmy's father put him through, he still named his first son after him."

"Patrick will do what is right," she repeated and smiled the same sardonic sort of smile that seemed almost a little sinister. "Or he'll find himself alone." And she laughed. "Again!"

"Oh Maria," Del lurched forward and clasped her friend's hands. "Do you remember that woman we met at the circus, Clarina Nichols?"

"I do."

"She is giving a lecture downriver on women's responsibilities next week. Our right to vote."

"Yes?"

"Let us go, you and I, together!"

"Oh, Delilah—"

"Don't you a-turn away, Maria. Look at the mess these professional gentlemen," she said this in a way that made Maria laugh, "have put us in. Why," she leaned back and slapped the table, "I sometimes think we should be the ones running the towns and the men should be home with the babes!"

"Oh, Delilah—"

"Maria," she said flatly. "You are coming with me."

"Oh, Delila—"

"Good," said she, standing, her son unlatching from her breast with a smack, her nipple swaying unashamedly. "It's settled then. Next Wednesday in Quindaro. Be here after breakfast and chores and we'll make a day of it." Maria left to go, smiling. Del began to clear the table and ran to the door. "Maria!" she called after her, "Invite Kathy! And don't forget to tell Paddy where you're a-headin'!"

XXIII

Elias Freeman, as he'd renamed himself, wondered why he couldn't just get on with his life. Omaha was not the safest place to be for a freed . . . runaway? . . . ex-? . . . slave, but there seemed to be little reason for him to fear his past more than be exhilarated by the future. It seemed unlikely anyone was coming to take him back to Weston. And few in Nebraska cared if he was a slave or not. Finally, at sixty-two years old, he had a future.

Which may explain why, he thought (as the men in the bunks about him snored and the moon cast a grotesquely oblong triangle on the booted foot of a man below him), the past seemed more prominent in his life than it ever had before. Perhaps he didn't know what to do with a future, having never had one before. Perhaps, worse yet, he was frightened of it. Definitely, the present was of little note. Living in boarding houses with other poor men, white and black alike, and doing odd jobs for a bit of beans and cornbread, just wasn't terribly interesting. The future, well, it was both totally new and somewhat frightening; the present, just boring. So the past came to prominence in his mind at night.

He was probably wanted for murder in Missouri. Not only that, he was probably considered a runaway. Property taking the life of its possessor was likely the most unacceptable possibility in Weston. Elias knew he would be lucky to be hanged. Mutilated was more likely. Yes, if he ever returned to Missouri he'd be butchered.

Suppose, however, that in some alternative universe the authorities saw the clear evidence that Dan had killed himself; that his slave simply took the opportunity to walk away. Just walk away. Where would that past leave him now? He wasn't freed. He wasn't a runaway. That would give a lawyer a real knot to chew on and pull at, a real problem for a professional gentleman to solve. An academic one, certainly, as it seemed easier for everyone involved simply to want him for murder in Missouri.

On his mind went, especially at night, the sounds and smells of Omaha clopping this way and wafting that. Elias had spent many nights in the last decade thinking about killing Little Dan, and still did, despite the fact he'd finally done it himself. He used to tell himself that nobody would know because nobody cared about Dan, and he could slip over into Kansas, maybe head for California or Oregon. And do what exactly? Do what? This thought kept him on the Baumgartner place near Weston. He spent ten years waiting for the next furrow of his life to be seeded.

Something inside him always told him that a moment would come. It seemed it finally had the moment Little Dan's brains spread across the front porch. And yet, the waiting seemed to continue. Perhaps that moment had yet to arrive.

Suddenly he realized he'd finally fallen asleep but that'd he'd started awake almost just as soon. The moon had peeked around the corner of the window pane and was spilling onto his bunk now, catching him full in one eye. He rolled over and tried to ignore it, but the sounds of other men in the room came to him again, breathing and swallowing and chewing their mouths and any number of sounds he hadn't heard in a very long time, and which were both comforting and irritating at the same time. There was no sense in fighting his mind any longer. He rolled out of bed, into his boots, and carefully snuck out the room.

Outside the boarding house the moon shone over Main Street. Omaha reminded Elias of what he saw in Quindaro: a town perched on the future as much as it was on the west bank of the river, as if either great prosperity or drowning may be its destiny. Scantily settled yet teeming with freighting activity, it seemed to offer any number of opportunities to the savvy, the weary, the liars and the preachers, the drunk and the sober alike. He thought he would walk awhile, the way he had since he was a little boy; sometimes into town if he felt the sounds of people would do him well, or into the fields if the sky would, or the river bottoms if it was trees and water he needed most. Omaha was strange, and he found himself staring at the moon from a street corner. Just staring at it, noticing it had the slightest hint of a shadow on the left, a prism of a halo around her. She would be full tomorrow.

Someone, a drunken someone, tried to speak with him, but he was transfixed by this Nebraskan moon, and somewhat suddenly, but gently like a flower blooming one day, he began to think of Roger. This boy had, for some reason he considered grandiose, decided to free slaves and follow John Brown. Yes, Brown struck a sinister silhouette across the river that night, standing like some sort of colossus on the stone shelf of Quindaro; and as he threatened the Missourians just short of the Nebraska border a few nights later, Elias saw that while there was enough righteousness in him to, say, name oneself after if one never had a last name, there was also something else, that the sinister under-glow to him remained. He may be a god, but one that believed in a higher, vengeful God, if anything. But with Roger, it seemed a bit different. Arrogant, maybe, but different in a positive way. Especially when considering it in the light of this moon, which Elias came to believe was the brightest he'd ever seen.

Though it had all ended darkly and comically, the way most things did with Dan Baumgartner, the fact this little Irish boy from across the river would risk so much when he didn't have to was, well, touching. Why would he do such a thing? Was his opinion of himself that high? Was he, potentially, simply that good a young man? That well raised? There was a moment during his standoff with Dan on the porch back in Missouri, in fact, that had stuck in him like a burr and had finally, it seemed, managed to find a nerve under the fur to bother. This moon did it, maybe.

It was the moment Roger had to choose. Dan was clearly trying to provoke Roger into killing him; just the way had had so many times with Elias during the last couple years. He wanted someone else to burn for eternity for ending his life, the coward. Or, Roger could have chosen to simply walk away and leave Dan and Elias to their private little hell east of Weston. These were the choices Dan gave him. But Roger chose something else. There, this moment, and Elias saw him make that choice, was quite sure he'd made that choice himself at some point. And the boy said something, too. What was it that he said? It was about his choice.

A small group of young men and women passed Elias now on the street, harassing him some, and he worried they would continue and it would get ugly, but they kept walking. He looked up at the moon again, and it all fell away. Weston and the Baumgartners, Dan and spiders, John Brown and their capturing the Missourians from Atchison, the road north, Omaha and everything about. Tears came to his eyes, obscuring the moon, and all that was left in his mind was that moment. Not Roger, even, but just that moment. What was it that Roger said, rejecting the false choices of the men of violence, of greed and avarice? Oh yes.

"It doesn't have to be that way," said he.

***

Maria was lost in thought until she saw them behind the barn. Perhaps Del was right—the men had indeed made a mess of things. It seemed that Patrick must know about the brewing battle between his father and the Hawkinses. Joseph had referenced it at the circus as if no explanation were needed. If Joseph James hadn't come to tell him what moral dilemma befell him this year, it seemed J.P. must have. He had to know, she thought, and was lost in the revelry of relaying all their conversations over the last couple weeks, wondering if he'd hinted at all. But she could find very little evidence of it in everything he'd said in two weeks—more animated about corn height than anything, which was impressive this year, she had to admit—and it was all lost once she saw Roger kissing Birsha Carpenter in the pen that used to hold the calf.

"You didn't tell me we had a visitor, Roger," she called out from a safe distance. "My, nor a pretty one at that! You must forgive my brother in-law," she extended her hand when she came close enough. "We've a lot to civilize in Kansas, our men being the more difficult, wouldn't you say, Ms.—?"

The girl not only hesitated; she stammered. "Carpenter," she finally replied, "Ms. Brisha Carpenter. We met at the circus in May. And I am just passing through."

"Oh?" Maria smiled sweetly. "Interested in circuses are you, so?" She plunked Roger on the arm. "This one's a bit of an act, he is."

"No, I cannot say I am." Birsha recoiled and Roger now looked younger than he ever had in Kansas.

"Birsha and I—Miss Carpenter, excuse me—were talking about women's rights, Maria. You would be interested to know her mother—"

"I have met her mother," she interrupted, suddenly realizing she liked this young woman. Something in Birsha's jaw was strong. And yet, she couldn't be that smart if she were kissing Roger in a barn. "Can we expect you again with your mother, so?"

"As I said, Mrs. Dugan, I was just passing through. I would reiterate my invitation to you and your mother, however, to visit us in Quindaro."

Maria stared at her. "Perhaps. I should be glad to invite you in for some tea just now."

"I really must be going." She glanced at Roger, who looked away.

"Very well, so." Maria stayed close by as Roger unhitched Brisha's horse from around the barn, the girl mounted, and seemed to barely hang onto the pommel as the horse rode down the now well-worn path toward Atchison. "My, now that's a Yankee girl if I ever saw one." Maria said as Roger tried to walk away. "A pretty one, like."

"Yes, I suppose. I—I wouldn't know. Particularly." He was only half-facing his sister in-law, who suddenly wanted to slap him. She settled for boxing his ears.

"What in the name of the Mother of God are you doing, Roger Dugan!? Are you determined to cause trouble everywhere you go?" She grabbed Roger by the ear and pulled him toward the barn.

Roger dragged his feet. "Where are you taking me? I'm not going into the barn with the likes of you. There are shovels in there!"

"You're sleeping here tonight like the animal you are!"

"No!"

"Yes!"

Maria stopped dragging him and let go his ear. He rubbed it in an exaggerated way. She sighed. "Very well, so. I've more important things to do with my time, Roger Dugan. But if you keep snogging that prim Yank her father will shoot you and there's nothing your brother or I can do about it." But he kept rubbing his ear. "Now," she sighed and rubbed her forehead. "Go do something useful."

XXIV

The following week Maria and Delilah left the children with their respective grandmothers, took Kathy, and rode south, through Atchison and Sumner, through Kickapoo and Leavenworth, to Quindaro. The roads were hard and dry, the ride rough, but the wind generously light and the sun bright. Patrick had bid Maria goodbye with a befuddled and somewhat disinterested grunt as he read the paper, and Kathy was as annoying as a child at Christmas, so excited was she to meet a refined woman of letters in Kansas.

But Maria was suspect. The Clarina Nichols she met at the circus seemed aloof. Her back was too straight to be strong, and Maria was as suspicious of words as her sister was trustful of them. And of protestant, New Englander ladies, for that matter, whose daughters seemed to find the eroticism of taboo in young Irish lads and barns far flung from their mothers' watchful eyes. Yes, poor Roger, thought she—for Birsha would inevitably break his heart, and a bigger, more feeling heart never was in this wild land.

That Del wanted her to go, however, meant the world to Maria. For her, this was as much about getting off the farm with her friend as it was anything. Quindaro and Mrs. Nichols could be Timbuktoo and the Queen of England for all she cared. Girls teasing boys, snobbish comments at circuses, the politics of religion and region meant nothing when compared to a true friend in trying times.

They finally arrived, hitched the team, found the small wood-sided building that would host them this evening, and took their seats. Anxiety billowed through her like a curtain of rain for a moment, remembering the only other time she'd been in an audience in the last few years—the strange, unnatural circus. There were perhaps two dozen in attendance, mostly women, but there were a few men. Mostly Yankees of the sort she remembered as a girl in Boston, which rather surprised her. Wealthy Protestants.

She wondered if she, a poor Catholic, would be included in their sentiments. Kathy seemed to think so; she sat and reviewed the evening's bill, something of a summary of the speech to come, as if she'd done so a hundred times before. But Maria felt like a chick newly introduced to the henhouse, soon to be turned away a few feathers lighter.

As Mrs. Nichols took the front of the small room and began speaking, however, Maria felt a certain charm in this woman's approachable manner. It was as if she spoke directly to her. Every time Clarina looked her in the eyes she looked away, afraid she'd be called to the stage, somehow. So conversational was this speech Maria felt she would soon be required to say something. But the audience didn't seem to think so. Most sat still with an encouraging grin, a nod here and there, Kathy and Del included, probably taking their cues from the crowd.

Clarina Nichols began by sharing something of her own story—a drunken louse of a husband, who not only failed to provide for her and her children, forcing her to work as she could, but who took whatever he wanted of her earnings. She briefly told the humiliating story of petitioning for divorce, having to explain all this in front of a room full of men, Vermont legislators; then living as a disgrace in her father's house until her current husband restored her respectability. That first man was the "H" in "Clarina I. H. Nichols," and it had driven her permanently into a world she was taught to forever inhabit.

"I commenced life with the most refined notions of woman's sphere," she continued after a pause that allowed the story of her divorce settle into the minds of those whose bowed heads showed their sympathy for the speaker's shameful past.

> *My pride of womanhood lay within this nice sphere. I know not how it was, perhaps because I am of mountain growth, but I could, even then, see over the barriers of that sphere.*

In the corner of her eye, Maria saw her sister sit up even straighter, as if she were reaching her head to the heavens to see over this barrier herself. Maria chuckled to herself. Kathy would soon learn that in Kansas these barriers were as flat as her great prairies.

> *And I could see that, however easy it might be for me to keep within it, as a daughter, a great majority of women were outside its boundaries; driven thither by their own, or invited by the necessities and interests of those they loved. I saw our farmers' wives, women esteemed for every womanly virtue, impelled by emergencies, helping their husbands in labors excluded from the modern woman's sphere. I was witness, on one occasion, to a wife's helping her husband who was ill and of feeble strength, and too poor to hire to pile the logs, preparatory to clearing the ground that was to grow their daily bread.*

Aha! See, thought Maria, you didn't need to come hear this prim puritan to understand this, Kathy. You could have stayed on the farm and helped Paddy weed the winter wheat. Or better yet, help me with the bankers and lawyers and doctors while my husband hid among those rows of our daily bread.

> *And my sympathies, which recognized in her act the self-sacrificing love of woman, forbade that I should judge her out of her sphere.*

How long had this woman been in Kansas? How had she possibly survived the winter thus far if she had only seen such a thing once? It was a bit sad, really. Looking around, Maria saw, however, in the faces of those present, that this was not as obvious to them as it seemed to be to her. She sighed and studied this woman. There was not only something approachable about her, there was definitely in her eyes something special. Maria could see this from about fifteen feet away, Clarina's irises so round and centered like stars in sockets that turned downward, like little moons.

> *But, friends, it is only since I have met the varied responsibilities of life, that I have comprehended woman's sphere; and I have come to regard it as lying within the whole circumference*

> *of humanity. If, as is claimed by the most ultra-opponents of the wife's legal individuality, claimed as a conclusive argument in favor of her legal nonentity, the interests of the parties are identical then I claim, as a legitimate conclusion, that their spheres are also identical. For interests determine duties, and duties are the landmarks of spheres. Wherever a man may rightfully go, it is proper that woman should go, and share his responsibilities.*

And now, Maria realized, rather suddenly, as a cold wind pushed on the walls of the little room and a groan came into the still drying wooden planks, that this woman's brilliance was not in observing the obvious, but in expressing and summarizing it so plainly that it the only way one could disagree was by admitting their own ignorance. She felt suddenly at home.

But just as suddenly, she thought of her husband and another wash of discomfort came to her. She shuffled in her seat and cleared her throat, had to breathe deeply in order to swallow. It was because, really, she began to see her husband in terms of these spheres. Emergencies were not exactly why Maria had to join him in the duties of manhood in Kansas. It was just when something didn't go his way and he, like a boy, a child, walked and drank and prayed and ate his way away from it.

> *Wherever my husband goes, thither would I follow him, if to the battle-field. No, I would not follow him there; I would hold him back by his coat-skirts, and say, "Husband, this is wrong. What will you gain by war?" This is the way I would follow my husband where he cannot rightfully go.*

Once upon a time, Maria had sent her husband something she had read in Boston while away from him, refusing to return to Kansas until he quit drinking. It was about civil disobedience, and it reminded her of Patrick. His gentleness. His unwillingness to become involved in the troubles that it seemed the whole rest of the world wished to contest. And from that distance of trains and steamships and carriages, she saw it as strength, not cowardice. But only a few months later she had handed him a gun and urged him to war, so filled she was with the causes of

Kansas, so swept away in the feeling that it had to be that way in this world.

But Mrs. Nichols continued:

> *But the pen is not always mightier than the sword, and I must lift up my voice against the crying wrongs of the people of Kansas—my adopted home. If I had needed mementoes to inspire me for the duty, this is such an one—a bullet taken from the shoulder of my son, A. O. Carpenter, and shot thither from the rifle of Capt. Pate, at the battle of Black Jack, on the 2d of June, during that terrible summer of '56.*

She held it aloft and many in the audience gasped.

> *It entered near the arm pit just below the collar bone and carried pieces of his clothing to where it lodged just under the shoulder blade. My son has sufficiently recovered from his wound, and I thank a kind Providence that without having "run away" he lives to fight "another day" in the hand to hand struggle against the most monstrous oppression, that the civilized world has ever seen. I thank Heaven, that I have sons ready to live or die for the rights, for which their great Grandfathers fought and sacrificed treasure.*

Maria thought back to that day now—the day she handed her husband his weapon and urged him forward, to join his brother in arms. It was the day they learned Southerners were marching north of the Kaw—far too close to home. He blanched not, but with steely-eyed determination met his oppressors in pitched battle. He stood eye-to-eye with his neighbor, and shot him. To protect her, himself, and their rights. She was proud of this, and yet—

Joseph James. It was Jimmy he shot that day at Osawatomie. A man she loved. His olive skin and reddish hair, his silliness while drinking, and his banter. Like a willow he was hard in the bark but soft inside, and lovable when nervous, so obvious while he spit.

And—

Oliver John, poor Ollie. Sweet little Ollie buried between her and her Delilah J. Poor Del. Perhaps it didn't have to be this way.

> *I think Kansas is fortunate in having so many able and firm men to represent her interests in a home Legislature, and if there should be any scrambling for offices in such trying times as are upon her, Kansas may well glory in her aspirants for martyrdom. Her "strong minded" women were content to run bullets, transfer ammunition, and inspire their husbands and sons with hope, faith and courage, until public offices of honor and trust are redolent of domestic peace and quiet before they ask a share in their responsibilities.*

She thought now of Governor Geary, his youthful beard, bumbling lieutenant, carefully political manner. What is it he had said to her after she persuaded him to take her to her imprisoned men? Oh yes, it was good to be back in the West. Where women arrive at governors' offices unannounced, with shotguns, thirsty for coffee.

> *I stand before you, a wife, a mother, a sister, a daughter; filling every relation that it is given to woman to fill. And by the token that I have a husband, a father and brothers, whom I revere for their manliness, and love for their tenderness, I may speak to you with confidence, and say, I respect manhood. I love it when it aspires to the high destiny which God has opened to it. And it is because I have confidence in manhood, that I am here to press upon it the claims of womanhood.*

Maria looked over at Kathy and Del. Both were smitten, proud, tears in their eyes, and Maria realized her eyes, too, were swelling. She was proud they resisted the fight, but that they fought. Proud that now Kansas was governed by men who actually won the right to govern.

But it occurred to her now that perhaps if women governed, that need to fight would not exist.

Clarina continued, speaking now of woman as having a mission from God to raise children under His direction. She argued this responsibility was so great it demanded education, the right to vote, to hold office, one day, even. It was right. This was right, and she was glad she had come, and she ached to attend Mass, to kneel before the Mother and feel her Sacred Heart grow and encompass hers; to smell incense and hear Latin, the silence of the congregation that followed the bell, ringing in the magic of transformation, the ineffable, the Divine hiding in the recesses of existence. Maria decided she loved this woman, Clarina I. H. Nichols, and would kneel before her, too, this Saint Patrick of Kansas.

Perhaps Roger snogging this woman's daughter would turn out to be acceptable. She chuckled, drawing an askance glare or two, thinking that perhaps Roger Dugan would marry Mrs. Nichols's daughter one day, and that a poor, hot-tempered Irish lad would run for governor. Jesus help us all.

Del talked the whole way home. Kathy had her moments, but Del seemed to hardly take a moment to breathe. Maria sat and listened. Del announced she would someday invite all the women of Atchison over for supper. They would read and discuss their rights and responsibilities, and number of other things, on and on, while Maria's thought went back to Patrick. Gentle, kind, strong, peaceful; but also, at times, so cowardly. Hiding in his fields and his corn he was allowing this dog-pack of professional gentlemen to steal their future. She ached, feeling so much love for him, but knowing she also often wondered if she loved him at all sometimes.

"Don't you think that would be wonderful, Maria?" Del asked. "Maria? Don't you?"

"I'm sorry Delilah," she said, "I wasn't listening."

"You women," Del said, "Always so distracted."

And they laughed.

XXV

George Marshall Hawkins had been born on what would be the coldest day of 1857, Christmas Eve. It was the most uneventful birth any white settler had experienced thus far in Kansas Territory. Lasting only three or four hours, Delilah J. Hawkins felt she was in a sort of trance through that December morning. Sarah Sally and Joseph James attended to her with the skill of experienced midwives, and though the pain was worse than it had been with little Missy, its brevity made it a preferable labor to that of her first child. George Marshall, thought his mother as she drifted to sleep during his first feeding, was a sweet angel who would never distress his mother.

But the next few months proved otherwise. Colicky, squirmy, shrieking like a banshee both when frustrated and when content, Georgy was a monstrous infant. He did sleep well, which was a blessing, because the worst part was his feeding. Del's nipples, particularly her left, had become cavernous sores that rarely had time to heal between feeding the ravenous beast, and she often wept while feeding him. It felt like he had teeth, and he'd struggle to latch on, over and over again, snorting and gnawing, making the proceeding look like he was trying to eat his mother's breasts. With only a visit from Maria and the trip to Quindaro as her sole respites, Del spent the winter in the cabin this way—miserable—and decided she'd take two days of labor and an easy infant over an easy delivery and a demon child any day. Any damn day.

"You gotta plunk him on the nose when he bites ya like that," her mother in-law said.

"He's not a dog, mother," Del replied.

"You sure about that?"

Her husband was particularly useless in all this. He did spend time with Missy, who was learning her first words and was old enough now to chase chickens in the barn while her father fed all the animals, not irritating him too much. That got her out of the house, at least, which helped. But with Georgy, Joseph James was perfectly helpless. He avoided being within ten feet of his wife while feeding his son, and couldn't bear to look at her ravaged breasts. Squeamish at the sight of them, he'd only said once that perhaps she should see a doctor.

She pounced on him. "I don't need a damn doctor! I'm a good mother!"

"I—it's only that—Del, please."

"Shutup and go find something outside to do," the old Sarah Sally said.

By June it had started to get better. Georgy looked more like a baby now than some sort of primordial creature, and he was gentler while feeding, happier. He still shrieked, but more when content than frustrated now. He did seem to grow his fingernails quickly, and scratched his face with them often, which lead to him wearing bits of cloth tied to his hands. One day, his father came in, saw a pleasant Del and a cooing Georgy, and said, "Ain't that a perty sight? My wife and my little rag boy. How ya doing, Rags?" They all laughed, and it stuck. "Rags" it was. George "Rags" Hawkins.

As the zenith of summer approached and her baby boy became a little less demanding, Del was able to pay more attention to the world outside the cabin. Her husband had said very little about their odd Irish squatter, his dealings with the Land Office to try and remove him, and the death of his childhood friend, Danny; the man who had saved their farm, or at least given them a chance to purchase another one if the decision went the way of J.P. Dugan and they were forced to move. At least now they had more time. The postponement of the public lands sale meant they could sort out their legal dispute with J.P. and know what land to buy, even if it wasn't where their precious Oliver John was buried. It all came out after the circus—her first outing since the Nichols lecture—and he told her everything.

"I outa shoot 'im," he said one night with a mouthful of bread.

"Which one?" she asked, dabbing the sweat from her brow.

"Both of 'em."

"Jimmy," she took a bite of bread herself, "what d'ya think Colonel Doniphan would have to say about that?" This appeared to hurt him, so she changed course. "Let me talk to Maria. We women have a better way of working these things out."

"I dunno, Del. She's liable to shoot you for all you know."

"Jimmy, don't be ridiculous."

"You know how many folks are a-dyin' in this territory over boundary disputes, Del? Why, more 'n those who died in '56 over the politickin'."

"Jimmy—"

"Why, James Henry Lane shot his neighbor just a few days ago. If that man were a Missourian you could be sure there'd be another war on our hands."

It was true. Lane—the Free State Leader and its presumptive candidate for the House, its general during the bloody summer of 1856, and now the official general of its territorial militia (despite the objections of Governor Denver)—had shot his first man earlier in the month. For all his valor and talent during the Mexican War in the '40s and reputation as the leader of all Free State Forces during the battles of Franklin, Ft. Titus, and his feigned campaigns north of the Kaw, James Henry Lane had never actually shot a man. And now, he'd killed a fellow Free Stater over a property dispute. It often seemed that the two had become indistinguishable, in fact. In many ways, Kansas bled as much over imaginary property lines as it did over the high, moral considerations of slavery and the equality of men.

But Del was still unimpressed. "Men," she said, getting up from the table while un-swaddling her sweaty son. "You'll never learn that biting ain't the only way to eat."

***

The last sky of June, 1858 held no moon whatsoever. Nor cloud, and the stars were brilliant, floating atop the waves of night, pinnacles of light amid troughs of darkness. Still, to Harry Clegg, they were obscured ever so slightly, much as the waves of an ocean appear from below the surface. He was glad to be back in Kansas, but the heavens in Utah were something to be missed. In both light and in blackness, it seemed the farther West one went, the veil of the world thinned and the face of God emerged in the nothingness. For a time, anyway; until man brought the veil along, holding it aloft like an ark.

Many memories had been made on this farm. When he had first arrived he was drunk, holding his son back from the edge of a wagon in the middle of a storm, a dying boy writhing in agony next to him. Oliver John had recovered from that accident, but of course it was Oliver John. It had to be Oliver John, the most innocent, loving, and kind of all. He had to be the one to die, and it seemed to Clegg that prophets, if anything, understood that simple fact: that the language of God is irony. He rested his body against the elms they called the "three sisters," near where his first shack once stood, and remembered Oliver John sitting up in bed for the first time, smiling with color in his face, while Little Joe bounced on the bed beside him and they all realized—Irish, English, Catholic, Mormon, Northerner and Southerner—they had common heroes. Not the prophets, but those who refused to slaughter them.

The cabin door opened slowly, creaking behind him, and the weak yellow light of a lantern emerged. It was Patrick, of course, sneaking out into the muggy night while his poor cabin burgeoned with in-laws and guests, struggling to breath like a pregnant woman.

"I thought I might find you here," they both said to the other simultaneously, and smiled.

Patrick sat next to his friend and they both lit their pipes. "Too bad we cannot share a little whiskey," the younger man said.

"Yes," Clegg chuckled, "we hold our liquor about as well as our belief in mankind, you and I."

Patrick sighed and shifted, nestling into the outcropping of stone that had once been their dining room table. "Right," he replied, yawning. "I figure Utah was no better than Kansas, so?"

Clegg smiled. During his absence Patrick had begun to sound even more American, more Kansan, though the Irish accent still made him feel at home in Britain. "It's the same sky there, you know," he began, not knowing where this first sentence would lead him. "The same stars, the same moon, the same sun. But Utah is different. More of a desert. A few hundred miles from here," he sat up and looked to the west, "it stops raining. The grasses shorten, the rivers are dry, and the mountains stand like gates to the house of the sun." He smiled and shook his head, watching his hands, amused at his own attempts at being poetic. "Listen to me, an old man full of words and nothing more."

"No, go on," Patrick said, exhaling his smoke. "I like it."

Clegg smiled, encouraged, despite knowing he'd sought and that encouragement would be granted. "Well, on the other side of the gates there is almost no grass at all. Scrub bushes, rocks, rocks of the most amazing shapes and colors you can possibly imagine. I think the desert in Utah may be the crucible of the world, Paddy. Time there is old. Very old." He sighed heavily and said heavily, "you would think it could be an Eden, you really would." He groaned heavily and stood heavily, feeling huge and old and immobile. "But men are like the sky. They are no different in Zion than they are in Kansas, or in England for that matter. No different than anywhere." He turned and looked at his friend. "They are beasts, Patrick." He groaned. "You once told me that man is all hind legs, Paddy. Do you remember that?"

"Don't mind anything I say, Clegg," came the reply. "For me, the world appears to be ending one day and a paradise the next." Patrick looked to be paying even more attention than Clegg thought he might. "What happened out there, my friend?" His face, furled in concern, was full of angled shadows behind the orange glow of the pipe. Clegg sat again, nearer Patrick, his back against the earth, his hands between his knees turning a rock over between his fingers.

"At first I thought it was the same as Kansas," he began. "Instead of marauding Missourians, the South sent the army to Utah, and the North was with them this time. I am no polygamist, Patrick, you know that—but I found it odd that a people divided over slavery should find a common enemy in polygamy. Marriage may be its own form of servitude, but—"

he didn't finish his joke, smiling half-heartedly. "I thought the government had enough to do containing criminal Kansas that it had no business in peace-loving Utah. But—" he sighed clasping the stone he had been fiddling with in one hand, and shook his fist a little, "I thought that because I was told to think that, Paddy." He looked over at his friend, who was still frowning into the glow of his pipe. "I was told they were coming for us again, just as they had in New York, Iowa, Missouri, Illinois, Kansas . . . I was told the Americans are the enemy of God," he said very heavily. "Being a Mormon, and having lived in Kansas, perhaps it is understandable."

"It is," came a definite reply in the darkness.

"Thank you, my friend, I do appreciate that. But you know, it wasn't true, mate." He looked over, shaking his head and rubbing his eyes with his fist. "It was not the truth, and my faith led me astray. Can you imagine that?" Clegg chuckled, shifting his boots in the dust. "Faith led me from the truth. What an irony."

He paused a moment, and Patrick said through teeth clenched around his pipe, "I did read about that some, Clegg. The 'Utah War,' they were calling it. They made it sound like you had seceded from the Union." And now Patrick sighed, plucking his pipe from his teeth. "I—I am sorry I did not write you, Clegg. I—"

"Please don't apologize, Patrick. I know you are busy here, in Kansas, the other circle to our hell." Clegg realized that Patrick had never seen him this despondent. Even in the grief and drunkenness during 1855 - 1856, he had always had some scrap of faith in him. "I'm sorry, Paddy. I don't mean that..."

"That Kansas is a hell? You should mean it."

"It is your Eden, Patrick."

Patrick puffed his pipe poignantly. "Not yet it ain't."

Clegg laughed. "Well, they done a-prepared us fer war, Paddy, them Mormon Fathers of mine." He paused, wondering if he should say it. Looking over at his young friend, seeing the shadows of his eyes shaped in sadness and contemplation, he decided he must. "Yes, my fathers led me into war, Paddy, just as yours led you."

Patrick looked at him, quickly and sharply, and an owl called in the distance, rustling far too many tree branches for a bird its size.

***

The only part of Clegg's face that Patrick could see was the shape of it, bulbous beneath the flat brim of his straw hat. Even in the utter darkness he could see the round cheeks were pinched in trepidation. Clegg had said what he said because he believed he must, and Patrick knew he should inquire into the older, wiser man's intent.

"What do you mean, 'my father'"?

"Why did you go to war that summer, Patrick?" He could imagine the Englishman's face as it turned to him, so kind and gentle and faithful.

"My family, my home, were threatened."

"So you were told."

"So it was." Hearing no reply as he expected, Patrick continued. "You weren't here, Clegg. You do not understand what it was like that summer, so."

"No, I do not." A slight breeze wound its way through the upper reaches of the trees, then fell gently upon the grass like a sheet. "But the following summer in Utah was the same story, Paddy."

"But what 'fathers' do you mean, Clegg? For me?"

"Oh Paddy, I'm afraid I mean your father, J.P. And your Yankee fathers. And—" he sighed, "your brother. They all told you these demons were stomping across the land, and you followed them into war."

The breeze peaked quickly into a gust of wind, then fell suddenly silent. Patrick could feel the round, cold earth supporting his body, its delicate glaze of stars hardened and encasing him, and Clegg, and everyone. Warmth welled up from his heart, and tears came to his eyes. Clegg was right. Even if going to war in 1856 was the right thing to do, he had been led into it, following in blind rage and fear. Like a giant bird on the attack.

"You may be right," he said with a sigh. "I don't even know if I shall keep this land, Clegg." He stood, rubbing a sore knee.

"Why not?"

Patrick picked up a long stick and poked the ground with it as he spoke, as if testing its firmness under his feet. Sometimes he thought it may fall away into nothingness, and all mankind would tumble into space. "Because I've followed my father, as you say." He looked up and waved the stick as if it were a fishing rod, only to return it to the ground again. "I've invested all our money, Clegg." He shook his head. The disgust he'd felt when he'd learned about the Panic had subsided some, but he still couldn't laugh at himself. "What was left, anyway, after our cow was stolen."

"Stolen?"

"Yes, by jayhawkers. But . . ." he turned now and knew it would be harder to hear him, but still he mumbled. "My father paid them to do it." He faced Clegg again, knowing the severity of the disappointment that shone through his eyes, and that he could never (and wouldn't need to, though it was still embarrassing) hide it from the older man. "And then he convinced me to invest my money in a bank that may be bankrupt. I just—" his voice stammered along with the stick he tapped on the ground, "—I just may not have the money before the auction."

Clegg paused, clearly regretting what he'd just said. "I'm sorry Paddy." Another pause and he added, "But you said 'may be bankrupt.' When will you know for sure?"

Patrick laughed, his friend smiling in delight at it, and tossed the stick into the woods. "When I decide I want to know. I haven't asked yet." He sat back down with a sigh, and Clegg patted his back.

"I understand. And I know you will face the world again, Paddy, when you are ready." He appeared to consider something, then asked, "But where has your father gone?"

Patrick shook his head. "I don't know. He says he's squatted the farm up and over, toward the river. But I'm sure he's up to something."

"And you haven't asked him, either?"

Patrick laughed awkwardly. "No! I'm hiding completely, Clegg. Afraid." He stretched out and leaned back, wanting to change the subject. He knew, deep down, that he wasn't as afraid as he too readily admitted. "You still haven't told me what happened out there, Clegg," he finally offered.

Clegg was immobile as a statue as he spoke, sitting cross-legged now against the dirt. "The same," he said. "The same as what happened at Pottawatomie, to Sam Collins or Thomas Barber." He took a breath but his body did not move or heave. It appeared cold and almost lifeless. "Innocent people were murdered."

"And the Church—?"

"I believe they ordered it, Patrick. Over one-hundred human beings—women and children, husbands and fathers— were tricked and butchered by the Navoo Legion." He still did not move, and had little inflection in his voice, staring off into the distant darkness. "They were on their way to California. We were told they had insulted the prophet, threatened to kill Brigham Young, and that some of them were Missourians who had been there when the prophet was killed in Illinois. We were told this because it was supposed to justify their deaths. We were told this so we would see them as animals. And Patrick—" his revelry broke and he turned to Patrick once again. "—I believed it. God help me, I believed it." Clegg began to breathe heavily, very quietly so, and Patrick sat up and patted him on the shoulder.

"You didn't murder anyone, Clegg. You are a good man and all you want is what is best for you and your son." But Clegg let his face fall into his hands, un-consoled. "And you're here now, in Kansas, Clegg. You stopped believing it, obviously. God will forgive you. God will forgive both of us."

Clegg looked up now, and the light of the stars was enough to illuminate his face, now wet with tears, and Patrick could see that he was much older now than he was when he left for Utah. "But do you forgive me, Patrick?"

He hesitated, surprised by the question. "Why, of course I do, like."

"Thank you, my friend." Clegg leaned over and put his arms around the bony shoulders of the younger, wiry man, who reciprocated, but with as much confusion and hesitancy in his arms as there was in his heart. Why his forgiveness of Clegg's victimless (deedless, even) crime would be so meaningful made little sense to him.

Strangely, Clegg crossed his legs once more and resumed his posture of utter detachment, staring into the darkness as if he were speaking with someone else, someone from the past, or perhaps a ghost.

"I read a speech in the *Sovereign*, Patrick, delivered by a man opposing the 'Little Giant,' for the senate in Illinois. You know Douglas—the man who architected Kansas and gave us both our sovereignty as squatters—" Patrick nodded, though he did not need to, "—well, this man opposing Douglas gave us a prophecy. Now, I am soured on prophets, rest assured." He looked away and said, almost as if there were another person to his right, "(I still believe, I think, that Joseph Smith spoke to the Angel Gabriel, but my soul aches with doubting everything else.)" He returned to Patrick. "But this man, this . . . politician, said something very wise. He said that he believed we must become all one thing, or all the other. That we cannot endure as half-slave, half-free. He spoke of slavery, but I must also take this to mean many other things—Mormonism included. Mormons cannot endure half citizens of the United States, half citizens of the Kingdom of Deseret. A house divided against itself, he said, cannot stand."

Clegg broke from his trance. His head moved again like the head of a man and not a portrait or sculpture of some figure from the East, and it turned its eyes on Patrick.

"But what is to be done when a man is divided against himself? What is to become of a man whose soul is half one thing, and half another?" The anguish in his eyes was almost intolerable, and Patrick looked away as he would from a dying man.

But he replied with firmness and without the slightest hint of doubt, "One side of his soul must be purged," said he.

XXVI

Maria "Maggie" Kenny didn't so much care for Harry Clegg, or his son. She didn't like that her son in-law hadn't the sense to keep his distance from the Mormons. Or the English. She particularly didn't like Kathy consorting with Little Joe. She'd come all the way across the ocean to escape the Perfidioius Albinon, all the way across the continent to the wilderness of Kansas, only to find they lived with her daughter. She'd have to stay until they left. She'd have to make sure that before her brother arrived Atchison County was purged of the damned English. At least she had an ally in her daughter's father in-law. Yes, the elder Dugan understood, which was somewhat surprising for a County Cork man.

"They keep to themselves back there, don't they?" she asked Maria, her arthritic hands sore from kneading dough, referring to the Cleggs' spending so much time in the back room.

"They don't want to intrude, mum," she replied without even looking up.

"There's intruding and there's being aloof."

She did look up this time. "Ask them to join us, so."

The elder Maria looked away from her daughter. "You sound like a westerner, love."

"I am a westerner."

"I don't mean an American westerner. An Irish one."

"Mum," she wetted her hands in the basin and dried them. Apparently the potatoes were peeled enough for her taste. "I've lived with Paddy and Roger for five years now."

"My point exactly."

But it wasn't her point, and she now regretted her tangent. Her focus was on the Cleggs, not the Dugans. She'd long since let that go, ever since Maria had shown she would leave Paddy if he didn't take good care of her. His impulsivity in moving to Kansas—all because of a damned book!—had irked her to no end, but she could see Maria was in love with him. And when she returned to Boston because he'd been drinking, only taking him back when he quit, she'd shown she'd be just fine in the wilderness with a man raised in one. No, it didn't matter that her daughter now sounded like a mutt of some kind—a little Offaly here, Cork there, American otherwise—it only mattered that she had two English Mormons in her house. A more heretical mix of breeds Maggie Kenny could not imagine.

"I'm sorry, love," she said, wetting and drying her own hands before putting more flour on the dough. "Listen to me, an old nagging woman, just like my mother." She laughed. "It's only that I am uncomfortable with the English here, Maria." She gave her daughter the most pitiable smile she could muster.

"I know, mother. But this is America. You must let that go."

"Right, so." They both smiled now. "But—" she glanced around furtively, "—don't you find Mormonism heretical?"

Maria sighed, but it seemed there was as much pensiveness as irritation in it. "I don't know, mum. I'm not sure it matters here. People are free to worship as they see fit. Americans of every persuasion seek God in one way or another. I don't think the word 'heretic' belongs in this land. It is sort of the whole point, isn't it?" She handed her mother a rolling pin.

"But they're . . ." the old woman looked about again, and whispered, "*polygamists.*"

"Clegg's not," was Maria's simple reply. "In fact, he's not even Mormon. Not anymore. He's here because he lost faith."

"But . . ." she looked about again, "he once was. A man who once believed that some second Jesus—an American Jesus!— walked the earth, can't be a stable man."

"Let he who is without sin, mum."

"You may be right, love." She sighed and began wrapping the dough in a pie tin, her daughter ready with the pork. "But . . ." not looking back this time, "he's English, to boot!"

Maria smiled now, and it eased her mother. "Mum, he's not the enemy. Harry Clegg is not a rich man bent on exploiting us. If there's one thing I've learned about America, mum, it's that we must learn to live with all sorts." She filled the pie with the meat and began adding carrots and potatoes, glancing into her mother's eyes. "If there's something else I've learned, it's that doing so will be very difficult. Very hard indeed."

The elder Maria smiled at her daughter. "Right, so." She wrapped the edges of dough atop the pie. "I will do my best. But . . ." she looked about again. "I still think it's best I stay here until they're gone. We can't have you alone with all these men. No," she turned back to the pie, shaking her head. "Kathy and I will stay until they've gone."

Looking back at her daughter, Maggie Kenny saw the crestfallen, pouting look that had so often visited her daughter's face as a little girl.

Living with "all sorts" included one's mother, her smile offered in return. Yes dear, the turn of her mouth and sag of her brow said, before you are rid of me, the Mormons will simply have to go.

***

Despite what her mother would think, Birsha often met Roger privately before or after literary society meetings. Their rendezvous place was under a cottonwood tree beside the river below the town, just about where Roger had helped escort Elias to the Underground Railroad. Quindaro was perched above, atop a steep bank, and the muddy river rolled along at their feet as if carrying them forth through an involuntary parade. Sometimes they would talk of the Free State movement and its successes, and sometimes Birsha would share with Roger her views on women's rights—or, rather, her mother's views, which she tended to share but didn't feel were just quite hers just yet. He would pet her and talk of life aboard the *Colonist* on the wintry Atlantic, the ship that sent his mother to her grave, and what he could remember of his life in Ireland. Life before Kansas. Before politics and causes and justice. Life. Just life.

Roger told Birsha of his father's plot to build an Irish Kingdom in Kansas, and Birsha told Roger of her family's shame—that her mother divorced her father. That he was a louse, a good for nothing failure in several industries, and often left his family half-starved and half-clothed and wholly shamed. Sharing all, they would chatter away the hours along with the birds in the tress above and about them, but as time wore on she would silence him, poor boy, with her finger upon his lips as he became excited, and kiss him on the cheek.

Sometimes they would kiss on the mouth, the way they had when Roger's sister in-law caught them in his brother's barn. It was electric, feeling his lips on hers, these lips that had said so many things hers had not, could not, in ways she found not only erotic but exotic. And also wrong. Birsha found herself caught in the vicious cycle of glee and guilt on those late summer's eves beneath the cottonwood leaves, and she lay awake at night both dreading and delighting in the thought of the next rendezvous with her Irish lad. And in this way, one perfect evening as the cotton spilled off the tree in a cloud of oncoming summer, their secret love was discovered yet again.

Just as they leaned in to kiss and Birsha removed her stern finger from Roger's twitching lips, a couple emerged from the trees. "Now, now! Quindaro's first love affair, I do suspect!" bellowed the man. Birsha spun and stood in one deft movement, Roger doing so slowly and nonchalantly as he could. Both knew the man by his voice, though Roger had only met him once. Neither were surprised to find the big red beard of Abelard Guthrie and quiet certainty of his wife Nancy behind them.

Abelard began to bellow again, but a subtle look from his wife stopped him, and he smiled gently. "I didn't mean to frighten you, Ms. Carpenter," he said, offering his hand. "Please excuse me. I'm embarrassed." His wife looked pleased.

"I was only startled, Mr. Guthrie," she hesitated. "This is Roger Dugan," she turned to him, "a friend I met in the Free State movement. Roger, Mr. and Mrs. Abelard Guthrie. They are town founders."

Guthrie moved to speak but Nancy stopped him short yet again. "Pleased to meet you, Mr. Dugan," she said, stepping toward him and offering her hand.

"And you, Mrs. Guthrie," Roger replied, wiping his hand on his trousers first.

"Tell me," Nancy continued, "how do the two of you like Quindaro? I am interested to know what the town is like for those still blessed with such youth."

"Yes," Abelard looked enthusiastic, the topic being his favorite. "For Quindaro to prosper it must attract youth!"

"You have no reason to sell the virtues of this town to me," Birsha said. "My mother and I are quite happy here."

They all looked at Roger now. "Well," he began, looking at the river and back again at his company, "Quindaro seems to have everything a young man like me could possibly want. The only town in Kansas. It is an abolitionist stronghold."

"Now, now," interjected Guthrie. "All are welcome. In fact, some of the Wyandotte, my wife's people, keep slaves."

Roger looked stupefied, but quickly resumed. "Yes, but I can't imagine that can last long in Quindaro. In Kansas, for that matter."

"Whatever is good for business," said Mr. Guthrie.

"I suppose," Roger smiled, "though my list of Quindaro's virtues is that it has freedom loving people. People who believe in equality." He smiled again. "But most of all, Quindaro has Birsha."

Nancy nearly gasped and her mouth opened into a wide grin, and Abelard laughed knowingly. Birsha blushed and stiffened, and Roger felt the steep banks of the Missouri sinking into the silent waters below.

***

Clegg sat in the rocking chair he'd dragged all the way to Zion and back, his mouth agape in disbelief. Too odd for words.

"What an odd place is Atchison," Clegg said without looking up from his paper. "Tell me, Kathy, how do you like Kansas?"

Kathy reminded Clegg of his deceased wife—or, what she may have been like at thirteen. Her brown hair, long eyelashes, sharp nose and cheeks, pouting eyes, tall and slender frame, she was something of a counterpart to her older sister Maria.

He could see her move a little in the periphery of his vision, just to the side of the edge of the newspaper where a terrible poem had been published. (He was glad to see the new editor, John Martin, had continued the tradition of printing bad poems, which he loved to read almost as good ones.) She was lying on her stomach on the floor, reading as well, and he wondered if she were cold. It was drafty on the floor of the Dugan cabin, and a thunderstorm was moving in, promising to make a mess of an otherwise pleasant July day.

"A bit boring at the moment," she finally replied. "But in Kansas we are deciding the future of mankind. Of all humanity." She said this so nonchalantly, it was as if was simply obvious.

Clegg laughed, folded the *Champion*, and handed it to her. "I believe you may be right. Though I have been in a few places that claimed such." She looked at him and took the paper, looked at the paper, set it aside, and said, "Read it already, thank you Mr. Clegg."

He smiled. "But Kathy, isn't it odd reading about a Pro Slavery crime in the Atchison newspaper and seeing it condemned? A town founded by Senator Atchison? The town that nearly hanged a preacher just for being a Free Stater?

"So much has changed since I was last in Atchison, it is almost unrecognizable. The mayor the town, Sam Pomeroy, is an agent of the New England Emigrant Aid Society, of all most unthinkable things! Not only have the town-folk voted not to *hang* him, they've voted him their leader! By the toss of a coin, even, they have decided the Free Staters would hold the mayor's office and three town council seats, the Pro Slavery party four council seats. Pomeroy has even purchased the *Sovereign* and gone into business with Stringfellow, banking and railroad stock." Kathy looked, either perplexed or as if this too, were quite obvious. "But it is unbelievable. Just as unbelievable as reading about the Marais Des Cygnes Massacre in what is now not the *Sovereign* but the *Freedom's Champion*."

Kathy took the paper again, as if he'd referenced something she missed. She unfolded and perused it. Clegg made note of how deftly she unfolded and handled the paper. It was clear she had read newspapers before, and would likely one day be as bright as beautiful. She reminded again him of his wife, who also had Irish blood and adorable cheeks and eyelashes.

It was also very odd being alone in the house with Kathy. He knew Maggie Kenny was suspicious of him, and couldn't blame her, really. He was both English and Mormon. For an Irish-Catholic woman seeking what she seemed to be seeking—land ownership, social legitimacy in America—either one of those attributes alone would justify mistrust. But she seemed to have to decided that young Kathy was strong-willed enough to be left alone with such a man. Clegg smiled, hoping that one day he would have such faith in Little Joe.

When she was done she set it back down again and said, "There are economic considerations to this whole affair." He raised his eyebrows, and she rolled her eyes. "Mr. Clegg, you know I'm smart!"

"Yes Kathy," he chuckled, "I do know that."

"Well," she sat up now, cross-legged, and tossed him the paper. "Isn't it obvious to you why Atchison has changed?" She didn't wait for an answer. "There's no use in spreading slavery if you're losing money doing it." She paused, rolled her eyes again, a bit playfully, and said, "Ideology always seems to take a back-seat to money, doesn't it?"

Clegg leaned back and rubbed his chin. "You know, they even let the Mormons work for them. After trying to execute our prophet not fifteen years before."

She smiled. "Yes, even you are tolerated," she winked.

"My!" he said, standing. "It is good to be back in Kansas!"

***

"Yes," Abelard jested, intending to break again the awkwardness of passion with the cold, egalitarian comfort of professionalism. "Quindaro has cause and Birsha," he smiled, "but it also has wonderful investment opportunities."

Birsha breathed now. "Yes, tell them about your father, Roger."

Suddenly very exhausted, Roger proceeded to tell Abelard and Nancy about J.P.'s failing investments in Atchison. Abelard, of course, encouraged him to encourage his father to invest in what was surely the future railroad hub of Kansas, etc. & etc., until Nancy tugged his coat sleeve, staring at his beard as if it were next, and they excused themselves to "allow the future of Quindaro to rekindle."

A breeze blew through the cottonwood as they left, and Roger and Birsha turned back to the river, watching it tumble and swirl calmly on, ever on, both unhurried and unrelenting.

"I meant it, you know," said he, sitting down.

"I know you did," said she, sitting next to him.

He leaned in to kiss her, and she kissed him back. For a brief, sad moment.

"No," she said, pulling away from his lips with an indecorous smack that made her want to continue. But then: "It is wrong."

"Wrong?" His tone was one she had not heard before. "What do you mean, 'wrong,'?"

"Unmarried, with other lives to live; what could be right about you and me?" She pitied him.

"Love is never wrong," said he, leaning toward her for more.

Her finger on his lips silenced now his talk of love, not politics or cause or justice. "This sort of love is the cause of all wrongs, my dear," said she.

XXVII

On a gentle slope beside Deer Creek the Dugans gathered around the wood from J.P.'s shack, swatting mosquitoes from their arms.

"How could you put your son in such a predicament, J.P.?" Maria began. Lawrence struggled to free himself from her hip, she rolling him through her arms as if he were a caterpillar crawling through her fingers and hands.

"You have put yourself in this predicament," J.P. paused. "By befriending them."

"Our *neighbors*?" she snapped with a distorted face.

"Someone other than your family. Strangers," he replied.

"The Hawkinses are not strangers to us," Patrick explained. "For two years they were the only family we had in Kansas, Pappa."

"We are at the edge of the world," Maria said almost as an aside. Her long red hair tumbled over her shoulder. It looked cleaner than the hair of most Kansas women.

"Paddy," J.P. turned and sat on a stump. "You must be rational about this. That man has tried to kill you. More than once." He shook his head in a frustration that seemed a little contrived, as if the expression didn't belong to him and he was borrowing it. "You had to shoot him!"

"You sound like Roger," he said, covering the sun with his hand and looking into the sky. "When you first arrived you told us the Hawkinses are not our enemy, Pappa. Do you remember that?"

"Of course, and it's true. You must do all you can to ally yourselves with your neighbors here. But they are *not* your family." He paused. "You never know when the next political tumult will turn them against you."

"All that is over!" Paddy shouted, but his voice flickered not in exasperation; in doubt, as if it were a flame and a door opened. "Kansas is clearly going to be a Free State, Pappa. Don't let Roger tell you otherwise. Joseph and Delilah have resigned themselves to this inevitability. It is over." And then, "they are not our enemies."

J.P. stood, frustrated. "You think this is *over*!? You think those little spats settled the Americans' differences? You can't believe that Paddy. No Dugan could be so naïve."

There was a moment of silence, and the wind shifted.

Patrick sighed. "I can't do it, Pappa." He looked at the ground. "I cannot lie. I cannot because you raised me to be an honest man." Maria smiled, her eyes swimming as she looked up at her husband's silhouette against the bright sky.

J.P. stood now, approached his son, and placed a hand on his shoulder. "You won't be lying, son." He spoke softly. "He's moved his cabin twice, and he's still farming the wrong land."

But Paddy backed away, shaking his head. "No, Pappa. I cannot betray Joseph James Hawkins and his family, no matter what's passed between us." He paused. "I cannot lie to the government that gave me my freedom."

J.P. chuckled. "You *won* your freedom, Patrick Dugan. You *earned* your land. *Your* land. *Our* land."

Paddy backed away again. "No, Pappa. It's not your land." He turned to Maria and looked around at the trees and the prairie and the furrows of corn. "It's not even my land. I am its caretaker."

J.P. sat again, clearly incredulous. "Very well, so." He put his head in his hands.

"You'll come back, then?" Maria asked. "Back to our house, and let the Hawkinses have their claim?"

The old Irishman looked up. "No," he said. "This is my claim, Paddy's testimony or not, this is *my* land. *Our* land." He stood, angry now. "This is Dugan land!" he shouted. "Look around you, my son and daughter. One day you will own all of this! All of it!" Stomping, frothing, a horse in a snake pit.

To the north, where the woods were wild, a line of trees began to arch into the sky, the long spine of a beast stretching from horizon to horizon. It rolled across the land like a blanket hung to dry in the wind, and they all watched it.

"Ah, the Fairy of Kansas," said the older Irishman. "From the grass he rises."

***

Birsha had explicitly told him never—ever—to arrive at her mother's home uninvited. And he had even promised he would not, on the condition she meet with him at the river again. Yet here he was, standing grey and frumpy in the doorframe, a wet linen of a man. A young man. Younger now than ever, and flashes of red and white stunned Birsha.

Mrs. Nichols answered and with a perplexed look asked him who he was. Being a friend of Birsha's did not seem to quell the expression, and Birsha became aware of her dress swishing as she paced about the room, wondering just exactly what she should do now. Mrs. Nichols asked why he had come and he said he did not know, and this answer was just curious enough to gain him entry.

"I believe I understand," said she. "Please, do come in, Mr.—?"

"Dugan. R—Roger Dugan."

Birsha stood quickly. Approached him quickly. Offered her hand quickly. Greeted, offered him a seat, took her seat, stood again, offered him a glass of water, and sat again, all quickly. Her dress swished. Her mother stood and watched, her arms folded over her breast.

"Remind me, Roger," Mrs. Nichols began, "Have we met before?"

Both Roger and Birsha began answering at once, and Mrs. Nichols snapped a look at her daughter. "Briefly," he said. "At the circus in Atchison."

The same glimmer came to the mother's face, and Birsha felt pale. She tried to slink back into the shadowy corner of the cabin.

"Of course," she said, sitting on the front edge of a chair with perfect posture. "Of course."

After a moment's pause he said, "Come to think of it, I may like a glass of water after all, Birsha."

Birsha stood quickly and went outside to the cistern. But she did not return quickly. She fumbled with the wooden lid and tin cup, the rickety gate to the garden; she brushed soil from her skirt only to find that muddied it, and returned to the cistern to wash it out; she left her lover and her mother inside to have the conversation she was too confused to have. She waited as long as she could, but eventually returned.

"I agree, Clarina," said Roger (they were on given names terms already!?), taking the cup of water from Birsha with a wink, "I have spent much of my life under the roof of my sister in-law. And I do mean to say it is her roof, all due respect to my brother."

"Very good, then, Roger," Clarina smiled. "And, I believe I may have met her?"

"Yes, also at the circus."

"Of course," she said again. "Of course." Now, after a pause where she regarded Roger as he awkwardly sipped his water, she turned to Birsha. "I believe your friend desperately needs this water, Brisha, don't you?"

Birsha twitched. Suddenly she smelled a hint of whiskey and knew her mother had also detected it. Poor Roger. "Mr. Dugan appears thirsty, Mother."

"Yes, yes he does." She turned back to Roger. "Would you like some more water, Roger?"

"Why yes, yes I would."

Birsha rose again, went to the cistern again, and returned more quickly now. But it mattered not—it was all over, her love for him was falling apart like tissue in the rain. Poor silly boy.

"I adore Quindaro," Roger was saying as she handed him his second full cup and he gulped it down. "And not just for your daughter." This hung in the air redly for a moment, but Roger seemed not to notice it. Notice any of it. As stupid as he was silly. "It's Free State sentiments are more of my kind— abolitionist, above all—and, it has you, Mrs. Nichols. As prominent an advocate for women's rights as there is in the country. The world."

"Why thank you, Mr. Dugan."

"Not to mention it is owned in part by Indians."

This also hung in the air in the room, and Roger did notice it. He pursed his lips, set down his cup, and glanced at both women.

"Yes," Clarina replied. "The Wyandotte nation sold the land to the Town Company at a generous rate. The Wyandotte are very civilized."

Roger stumbled a moment. "Yes," he said. "I—" he hesitated, "I certainly feel the struggle over the black man in America will be followed by a struggle over the rights of red men. And women, of course." He glanced again. Birsha felt sick. Sick for Roger, sick for herself.

Clarina sat upright, unmoving, and said nothing for a moment. Then, "Mr. Dugan, have you been drinking?"

Roger slumped, and Birsha suddenly noticed how small this cabin was. How small Kansas. How small her life. "Mother, I'm sure Mr. Dugan must be going," said she.

"No, no," she waved her hand as if a queen. "I'm sure he would like to answer a question or two. Wouldn't you, Roger?"

"O—of course."

Another horrible pause later. "And?"

"I would not say I have been drinking, Mrs. Nichols. I had a dram of whiskey before I came here, yes. To build the courage, as we say in Ireland."

"Whiskey? Why, a devil in every dram, wouldn't you say?"

Roger looked stunned. He looked at Birsha. He looked up, to the window, the wall, his feet, and finally looked back at Mrs. Clarina Irene Howard Nichols. "No, Mrs. Nichols. I do not agree with that. Devils are in men." He clenched his jaw. "And women."

Clarina smiled and stood, strolling over to the window. "Mr. Dugan, have you ever met a Kaw?"

Roger looked confused a moment. "Yes, I have."

"The Kaw are different than the Wyandotte, Roger." She turned back to Roger. "You agreed with me when I said that women have, in their domestic powers, the ability to cultivate civilization, yes?"

"Absolutely."

"From where do you believe we women derive such power?" Roger only shook his head. "From God, Mr. Dugan. From God Himself. Directly, with no intermediary. It is our duty to teach our children of His Word. His Will. To teach them classics, language, the arts and science. To teach them a Christian nation is a civilized nation. That a Christian is a citizen."

Roger looked strong again. Flat. "I see, so."

"So? So what?" Clarina chuckled and shook her head. "Oh, an Irish expression, I suppose."

Roger thought of Pat Laughlin's comparing Free Staters to the English now, wondering if perhaps he had been right "Yes, Mrs. Nichols, it is an Irish expression. Particular to Cork, in fact. You may even say it is an Irish Catholic expression."

Clarina turned, almost on him. Birsha stood to leave, thinking she could cry, but her mother's waving hand sat her down. "I may not agree with meditators between myself and the Father, Roger; nor in the Transubstantiation of the Eucharist. But I am no enemy of a Catholic man than a Lutheran or an Orthodox." She paused. Birsha knew this pause, the ones before it, and her intonations. She was orating. "Certainly not an enemy of a temperant Irish Catholic. One uncorrupted by his Church."

Then something happened. Birsha would only understand it years later, but she did notice it in the moment. Roger sat upright, his shoulders dropped. And she fell back in love with him as he said, "If you are accusing me of intemperance, Mrs. Nichols, I readily plead guilty. You see, your caution and self-righteousness can legislate and invest all it wishes, but true change only comes when those of us bold enough rashly and without regard for our own lives jump into the things with all that we have. Those of us who drink life to its lees."

"An appropriate analogy."

"Of course."

Mrs. Nichols sighed and looked down. It wasn't clear to her daughter if it was pity or surprise at being challenged by the mere boy who'd suddenly become a man in her sitting room. "Roger, I do not wish you any ill will." She sighed again. "When I was new to this land, I came upon a group of Kaws. They were burying one of their party beside the road, and do you know what they did? They—"

"—buried him with his food."

"They shot his pony. So he would have it in the afterlife."

"I have seen the same."

"And they were thin, Roger, their collars and ribs showed as if there were nothing else to them but their red skin. They were hungry, and their religion, if one were to elevate it to such a status, compelled them to do irrational—"

"—I should have thought you would admire their faith."

"In what Roger!?" She raised her voice at this, something Birsha had almost never seen before. Clarina Nichols had suffered the stupidity of men all her life, and rarely had she ever lost her temper. She glanced over at her daughter, who did her best to suppress the smile that forced itself through her through and into her mouth. "Their faith in an afterlife God could never grant them?"

And now Roger paused, with all the deft clarity of his debater. "And what did you do, Clarina, after you met these Kaw?"

Mrs. Nichols looked as if she did not anticipate this question, something also very unusual for her in any debate. "What do you mean? I moved on, of course, thoroughly disgusted."

Roger smiled, seeming to be pleased with himself. "Do you know what I did, Mrs. Nichols?"

"Baptized them I hope."

He stood and donned his cap. "No," he chuckled. "I gave them my horse." He paused and glanced at Birsha. "My reading of the gospels is why I did that. I think you should ask yourself if your disgust was inspired by the same."

Birsha's mother stood, stiffly, but her anger well within her control again. "Do not speak to me of the gospels, as your priests had you interpret them, with the same mouth that just drank liquor. My son was wounded in this affair, drinking life to its 'lees,' as you say. I stand for the rights of women, and negroes—of all intelligent beings. You are not my minister, Roger Dugan."

Roger's smile was wide now, full of teeth. "It isn't pleasant being judged, is it, Mrs. Nichols?"

"There is but one judge of mankind," said she.

"And on that point, we will agree," said he.

And as Roger stood and left, Clarina did not bid him goodbye, or look at him. Neither did Birsha, hanging her head, her fingers interlaced before her.

***

They met at the river one last time, Brisha and Roger. Roger traipsed into their spot with all the swagger of a conquering king and sat beside her. Once she saw this, Birsha knew he didn't understand. He didn't see. Their love was impossible, selfish and greedy. She could never, would never marry a man like him, and this wrongness and impossibility was exactly what made it love, which was exactly what made it impossible. Her mother may have been wrong, but she was not only a good woman and mother—she was a truly amazing person in every way, and Birsha could never reject her. Never.

Good, thought she, Roger seemed to sense her stiffness as he sat, kicking a rock off the ledge with his boot. They watched it tumble into the river below.

"I'm sorry, Birsha."

But she looked at him now, she became aware, with her real face. A face bereft of any other thought but one—love. A full face, a conduit to her soul, not a deviation between. "No," said she. "Do not apologize, Roger Dugan. You are the last person on this earth who deserves any sort of shame or regret whatsoever."

"Aha!" he smiled in his usual unbridled way. "I was afraid you were not pleased with me."

The river below seemed farther away than usual, as if it had dug just a bit farther down into the earth. "Roger, you are . . ." she hesitated. "You are an incredible man, do you realize that?" She looked back at him, again, with her full face, then reigned in the muscles slowly, gradually, one by one.

Still smiling, he said, "Incredible enough to marry?"

She felt the obduracy return to her face, but within her an ache took root that reminded her of being a child, watching her mother suffer. It was the ache of love, the pain of separateness. "Oh, Roger."

"I'm sorry. That was too forward of me."

"Don't apologize!" she said in frustration, losing control of her face again, a solitary tear slipping through, which she deftly and immediately wiped away. But he still looked confused. "Oh, Roger," she shook her head and breathed deeply. "Don't you see? I am not incredible."

The passion this stirred within him was palpable to her, as if an animal had sat down between them, and she stayed it with her hand, amazed she had such power over it, as if it were domesticated by her and her alone, the first woman. "Oh yes you are!" he leaned toward her.

"No," she said, in a manner only that single word can justly accommodate. "No, Roger. I am not." She stood, her legs coming apart in a way she would usually never allow, but a fire was within her. "Don't you see, Roger? Don't you see?"

He stood too and clasped her by the elbows, looking her fully in the eyes, again, so purely, so earnestly, so genuinely. She would miss it. "See what? Look at me!" he gently turned her face by her chin with two fingers only. "See what, Birsha?"

"Oh Roger." She let her face tell the story now. She was almost uncertain if she were even capable of it, so trained was she. I am not brave enough to love you, it said. I want what is wanted of me too much. My shackles are my blankets.

"What!?" He stepped back. "No," said he, in a way only that word can accommodate. "No," again, a third time in a third way, this syllable as whole and self-contained as a planet. "Your mother? You're going to let her puritanical snobbery keep you from love!?" She let her eyes answer. Don't speak of Mrs. Clarina I. H. Nichols in such a manner, said they. He took a step back. "Don't do this, Birsha. You are better than that."

A deep breath now, a tear in her eye she did not wipe away and a distant look to them like a baby drifting to sleep, she began to see an older Roger, both hardened and softened by life and its fortunes; always remembering his first kiss beside a barn in

Kansas, and the impossibility of young, lustful love beside the river.

She knew, coming back to his face, that it would be a long time before he understood what she was telling him. There was only pain in his expression, only self-pity and confusion and shock that would soon become rage. He was still so young, so bathed in the light, that he couldn't see across the river of time.

One day, though, he would. She closed her eyes and could see that distant, older Roger once again, children about his knees, books in dark oak cases and a beautiful stained-glass window inlaid into a stone wall beside him, a patient smile on his face, and understanding emanating from his person like a dandelion shedding its seeds into a breeze. And she chuckled inside, feeling she could no longer do so for anyone else. Stupid, useless men and their ridiculous ways of destroying one another. It was a wonder the world survived the adolescence of males.

She left him alone wailing like a toddler beside the river, thinking, Silly, silly boy. My silly, silly boy.

XXVIII

Roger staggered West, along the old military roads, through hamlet and village and town, day and evening and night and morning again; clear to the Great American Desert. He didn't know what happened beside the river after he left, if Birsha wept for him, returned to her mother, or found another lover. He didn't know it was day or night, or even that he was staggering. He only knew which way was West.

At length he vomited. He must have walked thirty miles before doing so, emptying his brother's flask, then kneeling suddenly over in the grass, clutching it like the hair of a giant demon, crawling west and clutching a handful at every step of his hands as if he were climbing the earth upward, dragging his legs through his vomit. And he rose quickly, like a man in a hurry, a man with a destination, a man short on time. And he kept walking.

Roger walked west into the night as quickly as he could. He wanted to run away from the sun and stay in the shadows for the rest of his life, flee from the light, round and round the world, forever in darkness. But Orion hunted him down, the dipper turned over and spilled all her milk, and as the sun rose Roger found himself vomiting again, clutching the strong, short grasses of the prairies, the very pelt of the earth, unable to rip them from their deep roots, tensing his muscles in the hopes they would tear his bones apart. He decided he had finally—after losing loved ones, seeing murder and warfare, monsters and childbirth and slavery—experienced the most painful part of this life; the torture of unrequited love in youth. He screamed into the brightening day with rage.

As all cries must, this too faltered and died away, leaving only the living sway of the land under the gentle hand of the sky.

***

Elias knew from an early age that one day he would be called upon to do something great. It was a knowledge that existed alongside the moon. Alongside the feeling that a moment would come to him one day, and a choice would be called for. At first it seemed it was the moment Little Dan died. But he realized in Omaha that it wasn't. His freedom was not the reason. For a mean man to die so he could have a future, well, it only mattered if that future meant something. So Elias decided to come back to Kansas.

Only in Kansas could he find this moment. There still existed a cause in Kansas, a fight, a noble one that Roger Dugan understood. He must find this boy that said "it doesn't have to be that way," this boy who risked so much. This Roger Dugan, this Irishman who was called a "white nigger" (as if anyone but a nigger could be a nigger). And yet, this boy who had suffered. Who found grace. Who had his moment on a porch near Weston, Missouri, where he decided it didn't have to be this way, this life. Yes, he would find Roger, Elias would, and help him forge a new path for the earth.

He made his way back along Lane's Trail, back along the Independence to the Missouri, and fished. He'd jigged for catfish most of his life and considered himself quite good at it. There were times since Little Dan returned from Mexico that catfish were all there was to eat. Dan would be drinking, refusing Elias any penny needed for the pantry; so this strange, wealthy household relied on slave-caught catfish for sustenance. No matter. Elias enjoyed the hours in the boat on the water, the rhythm of drainage, the smell of primordial mud. And so it was tonight, the familiar pang of hunger in his bones, and his strange ability to see the fish in their holes beneath the swirling Missouri.

An irresistible urge for the water came over him. It was warm enough, so he slipped out of his clothes and into the river, slipping slowly down, the silt finding its way between his toes. Leeches awaited him. Snapping turtles, beavers and muskrats, poisonous serpents. But he knew where each one was, and he inched his way along the riverbank, hanging onto roots and brush and rocks to avoid being pulled out into the main channels where only death awaited any man. He knew where the fish was.

It was a monster, some two-hundred pounds, and it wedged itself in a hole in the bank, face-out, waiting for prey. Elias reached in, felt its mouth, lips, eye, and whiskers. He smiled, said hello, and finally the fish struck, taking in his arm almost up to its elbow. A brief moment of panic came to him as he realized the old catfish was as able a hunter as he; that, despite his hand finding its way out the gill from inside, giving him an advantage (probably a somewhat painful one at that), he was no more than even with this monster. It too had a firm hold of him, its little nubs of cartilaginous teeth scratching his forearm, and the fight could go either way. Fish would drown man in water, or man would drown fish in air.

Elias felt suddenly thirsty. The fish pulled his face down to the water, and he decided to drink. For some weird reason it seemed more important now to drink the river than fight the fish, and he drank. Ravenously. Greedily. And then he was sick, barely able to find enough space between his lips and the water to breath in between wretches.

When it passed he felt all his muscles relax. His abdomen, neck, mouth, and arm, all the way down to the hand that was still wedged in the giant fish's mouth and clinging to its gills. And further yet, into the fish itself, who was little more than muscle upon muscle. The old catfish relaxed as if an extension of Elias. And he came out smooth, like a calf from the cow who has calved many times over, a brown weed in the damp autumn. He almost helped Elias to the bank, and died slowly at his feet, without the slightest hint of a flop, just the calm gulping of air that gave no life.

At this moment Elias credited the river with his safe passage, and all those to come.

***

Harry Clegg could tell that man was a lawyer from a mile away. A lawyer not long since arrived from the east, a man still uncomfortable in Kansas. He held Little Joe and Kathy close, looking around for Maggie. As usual, she was in some corner of the house making plans of some sort or another. She'd made bigger plans and taken possession of larger areas of the house of late, and Clegg could not for the life of him decide how this woman could possibly be so daft that she didn't realize this was driving her daughter mad. Or, possibly she did realize it. Yes, she probably did.

Never the matter. On hand was a man approaching, the children under his supervision alone and in grave danger of meeting their first lawyer.

"Mr. Clegg," Kathy tugged at his sleeve, "look there."

But he did not look, only said through a stiff jaw, "Yes, I see him, love."

"No," she said impatiently. "Look there, in the trees!"

Harry Clegg did look, but he did not see the dragon draped about the tree-tops like a valence. He did not need to see it.

"If that man could swing from the trees he would Kathy. Now go inside and tell your mother to keep you busy for a while."

But Kathy Kenny merely rolled her eyes at him, and he smiled. She reminded him of his wife, and he wished Little Joe had a little Kathy Kenny in him. One day Joseph Clegg would need to know how to talk to professional gentlemen such as this.

"How can I help you?" he asked shortly as the skinny, wide-eyed man approached.

The man was short of breath and did not answer at first. "My goodness! One does perspire here!" he replied. He had a deeper voice than his body foretold, and though he still seemed a lawyer, he was suddenly more likable. "Even in autumn," he removed his hat and fanned himself.

"Yes, indeed. Though it could snow tomorrow."

The man looked honestly surprised. "You don't mean that."

Clegg laughed. "Yes! I think two of the three Octobers I've been here have seen snow. Cold temperatures certainly. How long have you been here, Mr...?"

"Forgive me," said the man, who in removing his gloves revealed the hands of a very young man. "Long enough to forget my manners, apparently. My name is Ingalls. John J. Ingalls." He stepped forward, offering his hand, and Clegg delighted in feeling the smooth, white skin of the lawyer's hand. He really hadn't felt a hand that smooth—nor the English language being spoken so smoothly—since leaving England.

"Pleased to meet you, Mr. Ingalls. And I don't mean to be rude myself, but I should probably ask what in the hell you are doing here."

Ingalls sighed and blinked, almost hurt. "Yes, I understand. It's not the most congenial place, Kansas. I'm afraid I've been taken in by dishonest advertisement. I came to Sumner just a few short weeks ago and expected something—different. I thought I would have an office for my practice, for one."

"Legal?"

"Why yes," he chuckled good-naturedly. "Too apparent, it seems. Well, I am here to discuss a legal matter with Patrick Dugan. I would assume you are he if not for your accent?"

"Why no, I am not." Clegg wondered how he could still get information from this man. "I'm living here, temporarily—leaving next week in fact, for my own claim west of here near Ft. Riley. I'm afraid Patrick is in town and is not expected to return for a few hours. I can relay your business to him, however."

Ingalls looked around and took a deep breath. Clegg knew he was contemplating whether or not to give him the message, weighing confidentiality against the logistics of Kansas. "Well, I'd rather speak with him directly, of course, and simply must at some point. But—" he looked back down the road toward Atchison, "I'd rather not make such trips unnecessarily."

"You'll need a horse, Mr. Ingalls."

"Yes, but first I'll need some money for one," he smiled again. "As I said, I'm afraid Sumner—nor Atchison for that matter—are not as, shall we say 'refined'—as the circulars suggest." He shook his head. "But never mind that. My message for Mr. Dugan, Mr...?"

Clegg paused just for effect. "Clegg. Harry Clegg."

"Yes, thank you. Mr. Clegg, if you will relay to Mr. Dugan that Mr. Hawkins, a Mr...uh.." he rifled through his bag and removed a small piece of paper, "One Mr. Joseph James Hawkins of Atchison County has retained my services for their property dispute. Mr. Hawkins believes he is the rightful owner

of—" he referred to his paper again, "Township 5, Range 20—
"

"Mr. Ingalls, I don't mean to interrupt you," Clegg spoke more loudly now, remembering that this man was indeed a lawyer, "but I believe your services were retained unnecessarily. I don't believe there is a property dispute. Your client is concerned Patrick's father will lay claim to his section, and that Patrick will not bear witness for Joseph due to this, but I can assure you he will. Patrick Dugan is as honest as any man I have ever met—a rarity in Kansas, I can assure you—and he knows Mr. Hawkins is the rightful claimant to that section."

John J. Ingalls blinked, and in that blink Harry Clegg remembered why he distained lawyers. "I'm afraid you don't understand, Mr. Clegg. Mr. Hawkins is laying claim to this section. The one upon which you stand."

And then, suddenly, Harry Clegg noticed the silhouette of the trees lying between him and Atchison change. They were . . . thinner.

***

Maria decided it was time. It seemed Patrick, the coward, was either going to assume their money was gone rather than risk the shock of knowing it was so, or he was so intent on seeing the world as an inevitable series of misfortune and struggle, he would wait forever before confronting Stringfellow and Pomeroy. Not even this legal threat from Joseph would spur him. Starvation was probably the only thing that would drive him to Atchison anymore, so hiding from the world was he. Sometimes she could see the little boy in her husband—at times she wanted to cuddle this boy, swaddle and rock and nurture and nest—but just now she hated him. She left Lawrence with his grandmother and started for Atchison herself, then turned back, deciding she'd bring her son with her.

The colors of October seemed to calm both the horse and the boy as she rode it side-saddled all the way, so pregnant now it was impossibly uncomfortable to ride at all, much less straddled. Once upon a time she may have worried about riding these miles on horseback with a baby ready to come; now, she knew these were the least of her worries. Should he live at all, he may not eat if she didn't make such a trip. And once upon a time she would have worried about Lawrence riding with her side-saddled, not firmly tucked between her legs, but it was good to learn, often and early in this life, to hold on tight.

As she made her way down the sloping streets toward the river, she saw a commotion developing. Riders and runners moved in the same direction, and when she finally reached Commercial Street she saw the epicenter of the tumult. A crowd of men had gathered just a few streets down the street from her objective—the offices of the Kansas Valley Bank and the St. Joseph Railway Company. The crowd jostled a little, like a colony of ants, and she soon saw its epicenter. It was a single man with a pistol raised at another, but the rest of the entire crowd had pistols raised against him.

"Don't shoot yet, Judge!" one man yelled and grabbed the shoulder of the lone man. And about six men around this "judge" raised theirs at the rest of the crowd. "Now, Judge," the man continued, "whenever you're ready."

But the judge didn't shoot. As Maria (breathing as steadily as she could, not wanting her son to notice the commotion) stood apart about thirty yards atop her horse, clutching the back of her son's wool vest and he slapped at the mane with cold, purple hands, she saw that this man was smiling. "Mark my words. Mr. Lane will speak in Atchison," he said steadily. Oh wonderful, she thought. Lane.

"Judge Adams," said a man in the crowed with simple self-assuredness, "He will not."

"He will," the judge smiled even broader. "Or you will be forced to murder a justice of the peace."

Guns were slowly lowered, and all the men split into their camps and withdrew. They did this as if they had done it a thousand times before, thought Maria, rolling her eyes and kissing Lawrence's downy hair. Stupid men, she thought, they are forever boys, especially James Henry Lane. She smiled, thinking of the wild-haired man in a dress she'd help sneak into Kansas two years ago. They were all so very stupid. Perhaps all this mess over slavery wasn't over, even though these gentlemen had finally realized they could make more money in cooperation than opposition.

To her dismay, many of the men who'd opposed the judge ambled up Commercial Street toward the bank. Stringfellow was not among them, nor Pomeroy, and she decided she'd call upon the doctor at his house instead and not risk interacting with these armed, red-faced children with fire in their eyes. Perhaps he kept the money there, anyway, she thought. Like a boy would. Under his mattress. Lawrence babbled on.

But Maria found only Mrs. Stringfellow at home in the brick house. She too was with child, another one (a boy) running about like a wild beast. To Maria's surprise, the woman invited her in. It was an enviable house if ever there was one in Kansas. Solid brick with stone floors; an oven that could roast a ham, bake bread, and fry flapjacks all at once; a cellar, and windows that opened! Mrs. Stringfellow chattered uselessly about why her husband was in Missouri and how he wouldn't return for several days while drying her hands.

"I see you are expecting as well, Mrs...?" she asked.

"Dugan," Maria said lightly, pulling herself away from admiring the kitchen, setting Lawrence down on the floor so the wild Stringfellow boy would discover him.

"My, an Irish name. I expect you are a —" the woman noticed something out the window, "Free Stater," she finished in a weak, distracted voice. Her hands had ceased their business and she held the drying towel like sand. "Look there," she pointed out the window. "Don't that woman a-look mighty familiar?"

Maria looked out the window, first noticing that it was screened, with perfect hinges and well-painted trim, and only then seeing what it framed. First, she thought the other woman must be remarking on the jayhawk, which stood off behind a tree, kicking dirt and pecking the earth, but she knew somehow that Mrs. John Stringfellow could not see the bird. Instead, it must be the very familiar dress with a very familiar figure in it. It was Lane, climbing into a covered wagon, wearing the dress she'd made him in Nebraska back in '56. Atchison must still be dangerous. Money may now trump ideals in Kansas, but hatred still reigned supreme.

"My, that woman sure does a-look like Jim Lane, don't she?" Mrs. Stringfellow said slowly.

"I don't think so," Maria replied, turning to go, smiling toward the wall opposite the other woman. "I must get back to my farm, Mrs. Stringfellow. Will you please let your husband know that the Dugans would like to withdraw their deposit from the bank?"

The other woman hesitated a moment. "Why yes." She glanced down at her hands. "I'd a-hoped you were here to see about your baby," she pointed feebly at Maria's abdomen, and sighed. Her eyes were older than the rest of her. "But I s'pose you are as concerned about your land, that which feeds your family." She smiled (her mouth was younger than the rest of her, and her teeth), and shook her head. "But never mind. I shall tell him." Looking out the window again, her eyes and mouth aligned themselves with the rest of her now, all in one place at one time. "Why do you suppose a man like Lane would do something like that?" she wondered, looking back at Maria.

There was a moment now that Maria realized was one she'd come to Atchison to have. She thought somehow Lawrence would see and hear all this, or imbibe it in some way, let it come into his soul through osmosis. Men pointing guns at other men because they disagreed on whether or not a man could speak to other men in their town. That man dressed as woman so those other men wouldn't recognize him. Again.

So she turned to her son, picked him up, and said to him in answer to this woman, "Men are never as brave or as wise or as pious as they claim to be," said she. "In each of them there is a boy, lonely and afraid, and most of their bravery and wisdom and piety is really just this loneliness, this fear." She turned to Mrs. John Stringfellow now, and began to ask if she thought this were true, but the woman was smiling so broadly Maria knew she agreed. Vehement, spartan agreement.

***

She woke when she heard his first gasp. It was a horrendous sound, something between a horse frothing and a cat hissing, and she knew it wasn't right. In her dream she'd heard it, and dreamt of pulling something—someone or some thing she loved—out of a viscous pool of black. It pulled back on her, and she woke with the sense of being dragged into the pool, suffocation and enclosure, and expected to have a man's hand on her nose and mouth. But it was her Lawrence, her hope, her promise, her proof that this life was worth enduring. And he was gasping for breath. She felt him in a breathless panic.

He was even hotter, almost hard to keep one's hand upon, as much from sheer heat as from the alarming unnatural sense it gave the hand, to touch another human's skin in such a condition. So hot he felt like a black cow baking in the sun. She gasped herself, threw the quilt from her baby, rose to run into the next room, froze, remiss to leave him alone, then ran back to wake her husband. And Patrick woke as he almost never did—immediately.

It was impossible to keep it a secret from the guests of the house, strewn about the room, Kennys keeping as much distance from Cleggs as possible while still being near the stove, and soon the young parents lit lanterns and enlisted their help. Patrick and Clegg rushed to the well and back with cool water. They held Lawrence near the open door, shushed the old meddling Maggie and shot fleeting glances at the terrified Kathy and silent Little Joe Clegg, arguing as to whether or not Patrick should ride for Atchison and a doctor.

"Maria, love, it will be more than an hour at least," he protested. "Let me stay and help here." He was suddenly furious with his brother for having gone missing, yet again, in some futile quest to save the world, when he could be here helping save his nephew. "Let me be with my son."

But Maria looked at her husband with a desperation uncharacteristic of her. Whether he went or not didn't matter anymore. That he hesitated was all that was in the world. "You," said she through clenched teeth. "You would let your fear of the world kill your son." Rage rose within her, and she needed no shovel. She threw herself at her husband and struck him and his silly hat. "My son! My boy!"

He stood there dumbly.

"Go!" Her voice broke as she screamed this, but it was more than her voice breaking. It was all of her. "Go goddamnit! Just go!"

And he went.

***

"You know, Patrick Dugan," Clegg said, leaning back onto the rock after taking the whiskey from his friend's limp hand, and scratching his head, "you have never told me much about God." Earlier in the day they buried Lawrence Dugan next to where they had buried the unnamed, stillborn Dugan child not even thirty months gone from the earth, on a little mound beyond the garden, near were the sun set over the horizon in early autumn. They had yet to erect a tombstone for the first, so put in both today, small wooden crosses that that made the little hill a little Calvary in Kansas. "Not surprising for a Catholic," he continued, smiling, letting the half-formed joke fall flat on the cold autumn ground. "We have spoken often of heaven on earth, you and I, and of religion, but I do not know your views on God. On Heaven. On the Everlasting."

Patrick's entire head was numb, but his mind still screamed in pain. "Does it matter?" The picture of his limp, lifeless child in the lap of his mother. He attempted to take the whiskey back from Clegg, who hid it behind a rock on the other side of his body.

"I don't know that it matters, no," Clegg replied, fending off Patrick's feeble lunge as if it were a small, flightless bird. "Not to anyone but yourself." He sighed. "But I am still curious." He looked over his shoulder at the graves, not ten yards away.

"I am Catholic, Clegg, and it was my undoing. Robbed of our land, forbidden from practicing our religion for centuries, forced into a form of slavery by—"

Clegg sighed. "You can say it."

"By the English. But not by you. In fact, Clegg, we were the Mormons of Britain, you might say."

The older man smiled. "Yes, yes you were."

"I s'pose that's why I could never fault a Mormon for . . . for whatever. They are doing to you what they did to us."

Clegg paused. It was still and silent. "But we are speaking of religion, Paddy. But what of God? What of heaven? What of death?" He motioned to the Dugan graves. "What do you think became of those boys over there?"

Still, there was only the dead son in Maria's lap in Patrick's mind. And Maria's soft face gazing at his body.

"Patrick?" Clegg said gently, touching him on the shoulder as if he were sleeping. "Patrick, are you with me, my friend?" He sighed again and looked away. "My wife and girls," he said. "Where are they? Where are your boys?"

The word came to Patrick from some place inside him, a place he realized had always been there, and it rose from that place along with all his bile and whiskey, and emerged from his mouth along with all of it.

"Purgatory," said he.

***

On Christmas Day, 1858, the Dugans and Kennys attended a proper mass together for the first time in years. Maria had been during her visit to Boston, and J.P. had been in Australia. And yes, Patrick had taken the Eucharist several times at the house of a man named Charles Burnes in Atchison, who hosted priests from Doniphan once a month over the last year or so. But now the Benedictines had arrived.

The monks erected a wooden frame parish on the northeast edge of town, on a hill just below the apex of the river bluff, and a quarter-mile north of where the old Kanza paths converged. No structures had been built this far from Commercial Street, and the tract was donated to the Benedictines by Stringfellow's older brother Benjamin. It was a small clearing at the end of a scrub-riddled, ancient path, one Patrick had walked many a time.

And on this holy day they consecrated the church with its first mass.

Everyone walked somberly the three miles or so to mass as if it were a funeral procession. The church was something of a large cabin, perhaps the length of ten to twelve men and width of five or six. A wooden stove in its center warmed it, and a simple altar was complimented by a gold-plated tabernacle. A dozen or so families were in attendance, and the Dugans felt pained that most were far more celebratory than they. Little Lawrence was on everyone's mind.

The procession and liturgy of the word were completed with little enthusiasm by the family, though the phrasings of Latin comforted them all. But as the monk held aloft the bread, in his simple vestments, and the bell rang as the bread became the Body of Christ, Patrick began to cry. Softly at first. But as he struggled to breathe steadily, his wife noticed; then his father; and his wife's family, until they were all in various states of wet anguish. Patrick tried to comfort his wife, but she shrugged him away horribly. So noticeable was this—a crying family of eight Irish immigrants—the priest improvised his sermon and spoke of grace through suffering, the light in the darkness that is the Christ, and the promise of the everlasting life through the crucifixion. It was a homily more for Easter than Christmas.

But it wasn't Easter, and the Dugans and Kennys were not redeemed. They were in the depths of the shadows on the holiest day not only of that year, but of all the years they had spent in their wild home. Their God's church had finally come to Kansas, but on this marking of His Word made Flesh, they were suffering as only flesh can.

XXIX

At last, John J. Ingalls, Esq. found the Atchison men he was looking for all this time. The lands his client contested in Range 20 had been withheld from public auction, and there was time yet to win the case and collect his fees. Still, finding J.P. and Patrick Dugan had proven next to impossible, and he found them at the last place he tried, and the first place he should have considered, given their surname—the Pioneer Saloon.

"Wh—what do you mean, he is claiming my land?" the younger Irishman said from atop his whiskey, the curl of his lip forming a perfect parabola with the rim of his oily glass. "Jimm—Joseph never had any right to my land."

"He claimed it before you did, Mr. Dugan, way back in 1854." He paused, knowing there was no need to repeat the story. "Haven't you wondered why your land wasn't put on auction last November, Mr. Dugan, as was scheduled and publicly posted?" The lawyer's face showed an incredulity that only study of the law can inculcate.

"I—" he was so drunk he nearly hiccupped, "I am afraid I allowed that deadline to pass unnoticed," he blinked so long he seemed to nod off mid-sentence. "I have other griefs to which . . . to attend . . . to." His attempt at good English was annoying and ridiculous. "I've lost my son, Mr. Ingalls." Both Dugans bowed their heads now, the brown of their hair on the tops of their skulls matching the stain in the wooden table.

"Yes, well, perhaps you may have had the money to buy that claim in November, but good Mr. Million has it now."

That seemed to sober him some, and his language improved. "Are you suggesting I threw my claim money away on whiskey?"

"Exactly so," he smiled, a wave of pity washing over him like the warmth of the whiskey he'd just taken (when in Rome, he thought). "But never the matter. What does matter is that you've been subpoenaed." He placed the documents on the table between them, glancing over at the elder Dugan, who sat stolidly behind his beard, holding his immense amount of liquor immensely well. "You have six months to prove and purchase your claim, or else the court will order you quit it entirely and immediately." He took his other subpoena from his coat, smiling now, pleased at what a good lawyer he'd become in Kansas. "As have you, Mr. J.P. Dugan. You, in fact, are ordered to quit Mr. Hawkins's property immediately, or I shall have you arrested." He stomped his finger on one of the papers between them.

The older man pretended to look over the documents, smiled, and slid them back across the table with a sad look in his sad eyes. "No need for that, Mr. Ingalls, sir. I withdraw my claim. I have no money to pay for it anyway." And, much to Ingalls's surprise, the man stood and left, not with pride as much as with utter surrender.

"Pappa, wait," said Patrick, now suddenly completely sober. But the older man did not wait, his youthful frame, for a man his age, disappearing into the summer light beyond the door.

"Jimm—Mr. Hawkins, cannot pre-empt two sections. Mr. Ingalls." Mr. Dugan stared back across the table with a resilience, and cleverness, the lawyer had not expected. "Suppose both your cases were successful. You'd be breaking the law." True, but this was a technicality, a bridge to be crossed once met. And now that the elder Dugan had quit his claim, there was little need for it.

And yet it chilled him when Patrick Dugan gave a wry smile, stared him in the eye, and in the thick, sad air of the saloon hovering above the dusty wooden table said, "What kind of lawyer are you, anyway?"

***

Maria had seen her husband ready to fight once before— when he left for war two autumns ago. And she'd seen him this sadly drunk once before—when she left him, for Boston, three summers ago. But she'd never seen him this drunk and this violent and this desperate. It didn't scare her. She stood in the doorway barring his way, shovel in hand, her pregnancy filling the doorframe.

"No," she said. It was the first word she'd spoken to him since Lawrence died.

"Maria," he said calmly and impersonally, almost soberly. "Get out of the way, girl," with a force he had never used with her, and she stepped aside.

"You will regret this," she said.

"We shall all regret it if I do not do this," he said in the doorframe.

"We all regret it all," her mother said from the corner of the cabin.

"Oh, shutup, mother!" they both said.

***

The girl had never seen a man approach the farm this way. He was dangerous and she didn't need any more than two years' experience to see it. Staggering and stomping all at once, he looked like a deranged, rabid thing from her nightmares. Limbs longer than his body, knees and elbows swollen out, he looked like one of them white trees by the creek, done ripped itself outa the soil and a-learnin' how ta walk. And he had a gun.

"Daddy!" she yelled into the house. "Daddy!" she yelled, playing in the cold dirt in front of the door, wondering where her mother and grandmother were and why she had been left alone with her father, his scratchy face and pointed eyebrows.

Joseph James came out into the dull, cold afternoon, drying blood from his hands. And at once he swept her up in his arms, she felt his rough, red-brown cheek, and he took her inside, closed and locked the door, shuttered the windows. It grew dark, and she could feel his muscles were rigid and shaky. She began to cry.

"Hawkins!" she heard the white-tree man scream in a voice that was like cold. "Come outside!"

Daddy stepped forward into the tilted rectangle of light coming in from the door. The dust danced in the air above it.

"You git yerself outa here, Paddy!" her father boomed. It scared her when he yelled like that, most often at the dog, Clay, when he ate something he wasn't supposed to, and his big boot thudded into Clay's ribcage. "Or you lay that gun down on the ground good 'n far away and come to the door and we'll talk."

"You come outside right now," the man hissed from a distance that had shrunk disproportionate to time, just like her nightmares.

She imagined this man again, hissing outside the door, and he looked less like a tree now and more like an animal. Scaly and writhing, clawed and hairy, a grotesque face, tilted and unnatural. "Daddy?" she asked, unaware of her own sniveling. "Devil man?"

"No baby, it's the neighbor," he father smiled and glanced over at her. "He's just drunk."

"I'm giving you ten seconds." He was closer now, she heard the lever of the rifle cock, and she began to scream.

"You're gonna kill me, Paddy? Me 'n my little baby daughter?" There was more than a hint of desperation in his voice, and Missy cried harder. "You ain't that kinda man."

A loud bang, dirt sprinkling the window. "How's that for an answer?" the monster hissed from just outside the door.

"Paddy," Daddy's voice sounded like water now, and was more scared than she had ever heard a person be. "Listen Paddy, I'll come out there and talk. Like we shoulda done months ago. But—"

"Now, Jimmy."

"I can't just a-leave Missy in here alone." She screamed again.

"Bring her with you."

"Put the gun down."

"I'm not shooting an unarmed man and a baby."

"How do I know that?"

"You just said it yourself."

"Alright, we're coming." Daddy turned to her and held her tight. "Hush now, Missy, we're gonna go see the neighbor." He swept her up and they went to the door. He opened it and a small shaft of light spilled in, a long triangle. It reached exactly to the table.

"Hands first!" the Treeman ordered. Daddy put her down, then put his hands out the door. "Alright, the rest of you, so."

They stepped out into the light. The Treeman was a deranged shadow at first, the sun directly behind him. He held the gun at Daddy. "Put Missy down and come here." Daddy did. "You tried to kill my wife, you sonofabitch." He struck Daddy in the face with the gun. "And now you're trying to take my land, through a lawyer, you coward."

"You're daddy's a-tryin' ta take mine. You and your daddy and all them white niggers you got runnin' 'round the place."

"Call off the lawyer and I'll vouch for you."

"I can't trust you, Patrick."

They both stood still, and Missy felt the air buzz around her, like the light had come to life like fire and ran across the sky like fire did grass.

"Then I'll shoot you."

"And spend the rest of your life in prison."

"Last chance, Hawkins." He held the gun up again. "Call off the lawyer and I'll vouch for you."

The air was on fire again. "I can't, Patrick. I gotta see to mine. You go tend to yours."

The Treeman shook, like the wind were in his leaves something terrible. But then he wilted. "That laywer is corrupt, Jimmy. I'll win and you'll be out of a farm."

"We'll just have to see 'bout that."

"I s'pose we will, so."

And the tree, more of a man now, sauntered off into the setting sun. But Daddy suddenly ran forward and grabbed him, spun him around and ripped the gun out of his hands.

"Next time you threaten me, Paddy, you better be sober. Think I'll keep this for a while."

It was over, and Melissa Carrie Hawkins cried into the crook of her father's elbow.

***

Irish folk sure did find themselves in a mess, thought Elias Freeman as he watched Roger's family sort out their problems. They had gathered in counsel around the table with food and drink, as many families do in times of crisis, welcome, or when one of their numbers has done something asinine. In this case, it seemed to be a bit of it all.

They had already heard about the Farrells' steamer ride from St. Louis now, and were discussing a letter they'd received earlier in the day, delivered via the brand new mail contract granted to the Pike Peak Express. It was from Roger, from a new place far off: Denver City, Kansas Territory. It had everything to do with death, mountains, and gold. They couldn't tell if it meant he was going mining, becoming a mountain man, or worse. Whatever it was, it was a goodbye. It seemed Roger may just kill himself in Denver, and his family was in crisis because of it. Elias felt only he understood it, even admired it in a form. For only at the foot of a mountain is suicide a noble thing, a sign of deference, respect, and deep understanding of the puniness of mankind.

"You can't go chasing Roger and Clegg to the edge of the earth in the middle of planting, across Indian land, with no money and not even a gun to protect yourself." Elias saw something of Roger in this woman. Maria was direct, pragmatic, strong.

Finding them was easy enough. Little Dan had an uncle he trusted, Dutch Dan, and his wife had once told him where they were settling near Atchison; a few questions around town, only one or two suspicious, "what you a-doin' here, boy?" and it turned out Dutch Dan's was just a farm northeast of the Dugans'. And now here he was in this little cabin, with a bunch of Irish folk. Strange how life worked that way—so slow for so long, then quick.

"It's over, and—" Patrick hesitated, either upset or simply trying to control his rage, "—and, I was drunk. Jimmy knows we need grouse and duck for the winter. He'll give me back the rifle." There was something in his eyes that was hardened, almost lying as he said this, and Elias saw something of Roger in this man.

There was a pause, so the old woman spoke. She seemed to be one of them women that always spoke when there was a pause. "How many times do you have to try and kill that man, Paddy, before you suppose he won't forgive you anymore?" But they seemed to ignore her.

"Getting the gun back doesn't solve everything," said Maria, and again, as they had after she last spoke, they all fell silent. "Are you going to walk all the way to Denver City?" Again, silence, and she sighed. "We have no money, Paddy. We need whatever we have to buy this land, even if we win the pre-emption, or we may as well all pack our things and head West all together."

A long silence ensured, a boy of perhaps nine or ten filling it with nonsensical babbling.

"Shutup, Sean," a young girl whispered harshly.

"Kathy!" admonished the older woman.

"You can live with us," said Edward, the newly arrived man from the east. "We will save the money and buy an owned claim. Prices are still low."

Maria sighed at her uncle's offer and looked at Patrick. "Not low enough."

Then Patrick stood, and they all watched. He stood in a way he didn't often stand, it seemed, an old cottonwood beside a river, unmoving, the way Roger had at the porch in Weston. "I will go to the bank," he said. "If our money is gone perhaps Stringfellow and Pomeroy will give us a loan." He tried to push a smile to the front of his face from some place deep inside him. "Edward, with your blessings we may ask your help with the planting. And then I will go to Denver and get my brother back." He blinked. "Bring him back from Denver."

He turned for the door, but then Elias realized this was his moment. A moment for him to stand, declare he had blankets and shoes and the will of God behind him. A moment to stand and say he would save the savior; he would go to Denver, where he could of his own freedom make something meaningful. He did so.

But it was also a moment for J.P. Dugan to smile and say, "Why, Elias Freeman, I can't think of anything more appropriate than for the two of us to find my son. I've ruined us all," J.P. said with not a hint of apology, "and now I will go and seek my fortune yet again, in Denver, at Pike's Peak." He smiled for effect now. "First I will find this Englishman for you, and then I will find a whole lot of gold and we will rebuild our Irish

Kingdom in Kansas." He looked around at the members of the family, spread across the little cabin, and an odd shadow snaked itself across the rectangle of light that framed the men and women. "God has chosen me for this mission, boys and girls." J.P. spread out his arms, palms up, a preacher with a beast in the window behind him, ready to sweep him up and take him across the land.

"Gold and the goddamned English," said he.

A moment, yes. The Moment? Elias smiled, downed his whiskey, and thought that perhaps not. Perhaps it had yet to come. But moment led to moment. He only wished, somehow, he was going to Denver City alone.

***

Late that night, with the house full of her in-laws, her mother, sister, aunt and uncle and nephews and a freed slave, Maria Dugan gave birth in near silence to her third child. She woke during the first contraction, rose her husband upon the ninth, and said, "He's coming." She stilled the rising man with her hand. "Hush." She winced through another contraction and said, "We will call him Thomas."

Patrick sat up through the force of his wife's hand and held it tightly. "Why Thomas, love?"

She looked at him, tears in her eyes, thinking of little Lawrence and the baby whom preceded him into death, all the prayers they had for them both, only for naught; knowing now, without hoping, knowing from somewhere deep inside that Thomas would survive, as they all, in some way, always have and always would. "Because I have finally been blessed with doubt," said she.

XXX

Thomas Roger Dugan was a white baby. Everyone remarked on it. As soon as the purple and red of childbirth faded away, the whitest of skin emerged like the moon after a passing storm. It was as if the trauma surrounding his birth was a bruise that only appeared in the shade of old trees. His mother was, by Easter—and she couldn't explain why—a reasonably happy woman. Maybe it was because her mother was finally moving out, now going to live with her brother Ed and family a few farms over, just north of the spring that Paddy came to call the "Eternal Spring." Maybe it was because she finally had a son that she knew would survive. Or, maybe it was because she had in Delilah a friend she knew would last no matter what, because that "what" couldn't be much worse than their husbands trying to kill each other over and over like mongrels of the same litter with a scrap of carcass that just wouldn't split in two no matter how they pulled, yanked, or whipped.

She'd grieved for Lawrence that winter more than she thought possible—so dark, so cold—and coddled and cooed to herself as much as her unborn baby, ignoring her husband all the while. And as the grass rose from the earth she still felt the wrench of loss, sometimes bitterly in the night, particularly that of Good Friday; and she felt guilty for it, but she could no longer deny she was happy by that Easter. The thaw of the ice told her the world wasn't really coming to an end, any more than it did every day, every season, and with every generation. Her happiness was old and understated, a stone whose edges have been rounded by a thousand years of being battered by the river. The Great River, that never ceased, never yielded, and rolled along forever.

She knew this was not due to her husband being happy, because he wasn't. She began to feel for him. For him the apocalypse was once again at hand. Both his brother and his father—all he had left from his childhood—were to flee to Denver, a land that while was still called "Kansas" was the journey of a lifetime away. Clegg was gone too, resigned to the purgatory of Kansas for his Zion had been hell, and Patrick's only remaining friend had once again, perhaps finally this time, become his sworn enemy. His wife wouldn't speak to him, and she rarely let him hold his son. As a man, Patrick Dugan was alone. The last in Kansas, the last on earth.

She didn't even have to tell him to stop drinking again, and he spent every night inside the cabin, every day on the farm. He did everything she needed without being asked, doing so much of the work that Maria was able to spend a month in bed with Thomas, while she bid goodbye to one boy and welcomed another. Perhaps that, she thought, was why she felt like a weathered stone. By Easter she was as strong and healthy as she had ever been, and her little white baby, "Moon Dugan" as she came to call him, basked in her light.

Then, on Eastern night, as an overcast day gave way to a dark, still, starry night, and after a simple supper that Patrick clearly prepared with no enthusiasm whatsoever, she decided to speak to him, the first words in months.

"I miss Roger," she began, swaddling Moon in the firelight as her husband put on his hat and coat, pipe in hand, heading out to close the chicken coop. She didn't turn to him at first, not until she heard him pause.

"Sorry love?"

"I miss Roger," she repeated, then looked at him. He was subduing a look of shock and hope on his face. "Paddy, come sit next to me."

He did so, removing his hat and coat, placing his pipe carefully in a pocket (not on her stove, which he'd been asked to never do again, and he hadn't). She gave him Thomas. A wide grin spread across his face, just like a crescent moon rising in the east.

"My, he is beautiful," the father whispered to himself.

Maria touched his face and turned it to hers. "We have our Thomas now, our little Moon." She smiled, a well inside her rising to her eyes. "Whatever becomes of the farm, we have our family."

He grinned and nodded, making brief eye-contact with her, then did genuinely smile as he gazed back at his son. "I know."

"Patrick," she sat back and wrapped her shawl closer about her, "I think I owe you an apology."

He seemed genuinely surprised, and she smiled, even laughing a little. "Why, so, girl?"

"I miss Lawrence," said she, beginning to cry.

"Oh, love, so do I," and he began to cry too.

She reached for him. He embraced her. Their son tucked between them.

"It wasn't your fault," said she.

"Perhaps if I had gone—"

"No." She began to cry harder now, and one image came to her: it was of Patrick walking into the door that night. Clegg had been sent to retrieve him after the boy passed, sending the doctor back to Atchison, where they'd just barely left. He walked in and found his son dead on his mother's lap. The look on his face was pure anguish. What hers looked like to him, she did not want to know, for within her was a hatred reserved only for those we love; a hate borne of the disappointment only faith can bring, only the faith of love.

He staggered over, arms reached out to her, and she, shaking with life and anger and fear, sat the still lifeless body on the chair and stepped away, screaming, "It's your fault you goat! You stupid, useless, coward of a man! You are so afraid of men you let your boy die! I hate you Patrick Dugan! I hate you!" But looking back, as she fled, she watched as her husband bent over his son and touched him. Everything in the world was in that motion, in that face. Kindness, suffering, anger, fear, love, hate, all of it. For months she had only felt the screaming. But now, this expression of his rose like an August sun. Something about it embodied a strength reserved only for men such as Patrick Dugan.

"I'm so sorry, Paddy," said she.

And he embraced her again, holding her while she cried, and as the pain began to fade he held her at arm's length and looked into her eyes, saying, "I'm just happy you didn't have your shovel that night."

There was a pause. At first she was hurt. But in his eyes she saw what she loved most about him, and she began to laugh.

Gently at first, then harder, and soon Maria Dugan was laughing so hard she was crying again. "We have our family," said she, taking Moon back from him. "We have our family. We have our farm."

"Yes," he smiled, picking up her cup, rubbing his thumb over its lip. "I should be happy." He stood and turned back to the window again and sighed heavily. After a moment he turned back to her, and with the saddest of eyes, said, "But something is wrong."

She swaddled Thomas closer to her, encouraging him to sleep with warmth and tightness, and thought about this. Deep within, as if rising from an ancient well that had run dry, she felt as she did in August of 1855 when she told her husband it was time to leave, that Kansas was no place to rear a child, that it was a godforsaken wilderness. She knew what he meant, and yet, she wondered again if she really loved him.

"I fear this land is cursed, Maria," Patrick finally said, in a weak, distant voice, as the fire popped and gurgled and Thomas squirmed in its orange light.

***

The previous summer, over a thousand men and nearly eight-thousand oxen pulled over seven-hundred wagons out of the rutted streets of Atchison, bound for the gold fields of the West. One train alone, destined for Denver City in July, consisted of over one-hundred wagons, two-hundred men, a thousand oxen, two-hundred mules, fifty horses and over two tons of merchandise. Rattling harnesses, chains and the stomping hooves of impatient beasts; blacksmith hammers and their fires coughing orange embers into the streets; and rustling papers changing hands between professional gentlemen everywhere: the sounds and smells of migrating and prospecting lined Commercial Street from river to prairie. And these were but a fraction of the numbers preparing to leave the imminent summer, man and animal and machine sinking into the ruts and mud, tipping the earth into the mighty river astern while the men toppled over the grassy bow pointing West, ever west.

But J.P. Dugan's train was not one of these. Leaving town as soon as possible in May it consisted entirely of one ornery mare by the name of "Chance," an old horse without a name, a dog, "Erin," two pounds of salted, dried beef, five pounds of flour, a wool blanket and a Bowie knife, a slave who was neither freed nor escaped, and an Irishman who had been on three continents and two oceans, and was entirely too old for such things. Most of the stage lines operating out of Atchison—of which there were suddenly a great many—charged as much as the value of sixty acres of land just to be escorted across the grass, as J.P. saw it. And they took weeks, some with six oxen pulling ridiculously huge wagons, women and children, furniture and butter churns, provisions to last two months. No, they wouldn't do. Roger could be dead any day now, and every dime mattered. They had to get to Denver as quickly and cheaply as humanly possible.

In the Massasoit House, the town's newest and largest building, host to boarders and businesses nearly as temporary, they'd found only untrustworthy red-nosed mountain men with flimsy hats and skins hanging from them like they were molting, purporting to be able to guide him to Denver for less. Two steamers were anchored at the levee, and the town seemed as if it would drown under the weight of oxen and mules. J.P. had no patience for this. His son needed him, and one man provided answers.

"You don't need no train," he said. The man smiled numbly and did his best to fix J.P. in his glassy eyes. "Get to Ft. Riley," he said. "And take the Smoky Hill from there." He glanced around. "You got a good horse?"

"Yes I have."

"Your nigger got a horse?"

"My traveling companion here, Elias, has a horse, yes."

He glanced around again. "Just keep 'em headed west until you see the mountains."

J.P. had read passingly about this "central" route to the gold. This new route, the *Champion* wrote, saved over one-hundred miles, striking directly west from Ft. Riley along the Smoky Hill Branch of the Kaw, and was laden with wood, grass, and water—though admittedly, the fact established stations and provisions were as yet scarce on the new trail made it more dangerous. Anxious to find his grieving son before he did something unthinkable, J.P. decided, as they neared the farm of Harry Clegg well before lunchtime on the fourth day, that come hell or high water he would take the Smoky Hill. Having come some eighty miles thus far, after all, in perfect weather on a pleasant road that followed the colorful undulations of the Flint Hills as their northerly reaches dipped back down into the earth like a whale returning to the sea in breach, he and Chance were enjoying themselves. Why, he was almost one-fifth of the way there, according to what he had read in the papers.

Chance was light of foot and almost restless as they crossed the Blue River, Erin nipping at her heels and barking at her master, who was forced to drape the wet shivering yellow dog over the pommel of the saddle as the river deepened, perhaps more than he'd expected. Clegg's farm lay just north of the road, two miles from the crossing, he was told, a small footpath with a stone marker leading to it. But he couldn't find it, and spent the greater part of the afternoon trying not to eat too much of his beef while he went up and down the road looking for any indication of a path—hoof or foot prints, gravel strewn out onto the road, the tiniest bit of grass laying down, anything. The only thing he had seen since the last settlement were the tops of the Kaw lodges on a ridge to the south, the horizon striking its bold profile behind the waving grasses and blocky formations atop the hills, and a dull sky aching with the last grasps winter. At last he dismounted, kicked and cursed the impatient Erin, let Chance graze while he smoked his pipe, doubled-back across the Blue with his wet yellow rag of a dog, and headed for the Indian village.

The lodges were either round or oblong, framed with timber and sealed with hides. There were many of them, set up atop a ridge across an expanse of flatness beside the river, which was strewn with evidence of a previous, older village. But as he approached, J.P. saw the village must have been abandoned some years ago, tattered buffalo hides falling in between the bending wood. Not a soul was in sight, until quite suddenly a man appeared. It was as if J.P. happened upon him, stepping out from behind a tree, but there were none. He appeared to be Indian on first sight, clad neither in the traditional garb of the Kanza nor as a white man, but a smattering of deerskin, wool, and leather, wearing a flat-brimmed hat. He sat on a flat rock halfway up the hill that led to the village, his right sleeve dangling as if he had no arm.

"Afternoon," he said in the oddest of accents, raising his left hand and standing.

"Hello," replied the old Irishman, halting Chance. "I didn't see you there. You appear as lost as me."

The man smiled, briefly and faintly, revealing through his rotten teeth that he was older than his face foretold. "No, I ain't lost," he said.

"Perhaps you can help me, then. My name is Dugan, J.P. Dugan, and this is Elias Freeman. We are looking for a farm near here."

"There are many farms," he said. "Many graves, too."

"Yes," J.P. grunted as he dismounted, noticing now that Erin and Chance seemed not to notice the man. "It seems this village is no more, Mr...?"

"Joejim," the man nodded, taking a few steps down the slope to flatter ground, closer to J.P. "Just Joejim."

"Was this your village?" J.P. was reminded now of an aboriginal village he had seen while hunting gold in Australia. It was, in fact, an extremely odd coincidence that he had had this experience on two continents now, and an intense feeling of deja vu overcame him. The dull winter grass and still creeks of the Kansas plains could be that of Victoria, this man much like the aboriginal interpreters he had so briefly met. This was not new to him, he decided. "I do not see any graves."

"You are standing on one," said the man. "Indian graves, white men's farms." He held up his left arm. "I farm with this one," he pointed to his right shoulder, "and buried this one."

"You are a half-breed?"

Joejim blinked. "Yes," he said, then smiled. "And the government gave me land for being half-breed." His smile faded, tired of itself. "Give land to white," he held up his left arm, "then take from Indian," lowering it. "And yes, this was a Kaw village."

"Yours?"

Joejim's expression showed that he would not answer this question. It was not an expression of unwillingness, but one of patience, almost pity. There was no answer to this question, his face seemed to say. J.P. decided to ask another one. "What grave is this?"

"Many," Joejim sighed, looking around. "The river took them in sleep." He nodded toward the Big Blue, which shimmered slightly in the grey light in the distance.

J.P. looked back at the river in the distance. "They drowned in that river?"

"This river," Joejim pointed to the ground. "That river," he pointed to the Blue.

"Ah yes, a flood?"

"Yes. Many years ago."

"And you moved to the hill. But what became of the village then?"

Again Joejim had an expression of patience, almost a restrained bewilderment. He seemed to ask why such a question would be asked, as if it was not only answered, but known to all men of all times. He held up his left arm, his right arm moving under the sleeve like a lamb in hay, and a smile broadened his face.

"White man farm, Indian grave," he said.

J.P. paused and smiled back. "I suppose we have seen the Indian grave, so. Now can we see the white man's farm? Harry Clegg's the name."

Joejim was still apparently pleased with his own wit. "The Mormon with no wives."

"Yes—well, he isn't a Mor—yes, Clegg, and his son Little Joe. Do you know where they live?" He moved abreast Chance and saw Erin in the distance, ready to call her and go, but Joejim's answer was unexpected.

"No," he laughed. "But I have seen him here before."

"Here? Why would he have come here?"

"He lost his way."

"To his own farm?" J.P. was incredulous that man could lose his own farm. It didn't occur to him that this land of grass and hill and river enjoyed itself so much it spent a lot of time in its own reflection, and that even the most seasoned of travelers could become lost.

"Yes." Joejim wasn't laughing now, but J.P. wished he was. He didn't like the stern, serious look on this strange man's face. "There are many things to lead him astray here," he said, looking straight into the Irishman's eyes without blinking, without changing his expression, a portrait of a general, a rebel, some brooding philosopher or a poet.

"Like what, so?"

"Birds," came the odd reply. "Snakes and otters, buffalo and beavers. Women," he did smile now, but it disappeared as quickly as it arrived, like a storm catching its breath. "Men. Of course, and always, men. Men with the faces of men and bodies like ghosts."

J.P. knew this sort of talk well, and didn't need an explanation. The land was haunted, like all lands are, and the beasts and ghosts of Kansas led one astray, apparently, into the lost and into loss, a wilderness. "I see," he chewed his lip and felt his scratchy beard with his tongue. "But you can take me there, can't you?"

Joejim didn't smile, and barely moved his mouth. "Yes," he said, "follow me."

XXXI

One bright morning Delilah realized over a year had passed since she attended Clarina I. H. Nichols's lecture in Quindaro, and she'd yet to organize her discussion on the Rights and Responsibilities of Women. The township was full of them now, women; why, even a German one just north of her, from what she understood. Most were Irish, and many were just like she was—just from another state. Poor white women with hard calloused hands and strong backs. And Clarina was right—no better place on earth to get women their rights than in Kansas, where a constitution as blank as a Monday afternoon sheet was being written. And she knew her husband would not only let her do this now, if she was sweet with him he may just let her butcher a turkey for it.

For one thing, Delilah J. knew that for a Hawkins man to engage a lawyer—and one from New England at that—instead of simply using big boots, wide knuckles, or an old gun, meant something deep inside was different.

But more importantly, she could feel it in his touch, at night; in the way he held himself, or, rather, didn't while he slept, more of a length of fabric than a plank; and in the softness of his eyes even while he strained with tools and earth and animals. A hardness that had been with him long before she met him had subsided into the subsurface of his soul. It was still there, which comforted her because she knew Kansas was still Kansas and he may need to steel himself again someday, but it wasn't a bit and bridle that led him through his life the way it had all those years. It was a weapon in a scabbard, hidden away but readily available only when needed.

And in this way Joseph James reminded Del of her father in-law, and she realized it was really the only time she had ever noticed that George Sherman actually had fathered this man. That man walked through his life leaving sons and women in his wake, all of whom still loved him, because when George was with you, he was with you. He wasn't thinking of anyone else (but that meant when he was with someone else, he wasn't thinking of you). He was gentle and good-natured, like Oliver John, but because he was no father at all he had left Joseph James a principled, even pious man, a soldier in domesticity and war alike. Only now, after all he had been through, had her husband let go, unclenched his teeth, and let himself become buoyant upon the undulations of this life.

Still, she said it to him. He was just starting to remove stumps and rocks from the back 40, pretty near the house.

"I know it," he replied. "I'm a-gittin' soft, Del. Old maybe. A-hirin' lawyers to do my dirty work for me."

"I figgered I might just go see Ingalls for you, Jimmy," she replied, her eyes soft. "Might be nice to get Missy off the farm and have her see the town."

He smiled, like he rarely had but now often did. "Yep."

"I'll ask mamma to watch Rags."

"Mm," was her husband's only response.

"And Jimmy, I'd sure like to have the women of the township over for supper soon."

This seemed to get his attention. He stood up from his work. "Jus' the women?"

"Yeah, we got some things ta talk about, Jimmy. The constitution is a-bein'—"

"I don't like politics, Del."

"You don't have to be there." She smiled. "I just think women need to know one another in Kansas. We need a voice."

He smiled again in that way. "Wouldn't that be the way, Del? You get to vote and I don't. Hell, maybe niggers'll vote before I do."

"Jimmy," she came to him, placed her hand on his back. "The way I see it, you're as white or as Indian as you want to be on any day."

He chuckled. "Hell if I care 'bout that." He winked at her. "But ya know, if a man can live his whole life a-thinkin' he's one thing and he ain't, well, maybe we all are a-thinkin' we's one thing and we ain't." He stood and stretched his back, looking across his land. "Maybe none of this is what it seems."

Delilah touched him again. She could feel the knowing growing inside of him. "It isn't," said she.

He winked her again. "You can have anyone over for supper you like, Del. Butcher that ol' Tom turkey if you like. I'm a-sick of that old sonofabitch anyway." He laughed. "Just promise me you'll give a half-breed a break one day if he needs it."

"Joseph James Hawkins, you ain't never gonna need a break from me." She turned him toward her, kissed him. "You could grow a tail and I'd still love you."

He smiled. Then, "S'pose I'll head up to the claim just north while you're in Sumner. Might like to bring something special up to the new neighbors. See how they're a-gettin' along."

"Take them the cake your mother made." He paused, clearly considering whether welcoming his neighbor was more important than eating his mother's cake—the only thing of his childhood he associated with her fondly. "Or take him some eggs, Jimmy, if yer so keen on that cake." She paused, picked up her daughter and mounted the mare, whose sloppy clopping they'd all come to love. "Do you think I should invite Maria?"

He looked perplexed. "Dugan?"

"Of course Dugan, you idiot."

He smiled but didn't seem too happy about the idea. "Not sure what the lawyers'd a-think of that."

"Maybe you're right. I'll invite her sister, though, if I can. Kathy was all a-talk on the way home from Clarina's lecture."

"Hell if I care."

Del turned her attention to the new mare. "She's a good one, Jimmy," she smiled and patted the soft brown neck. "Maybe we should name her." Since Ninny died on New Year's, 1856, Jimmy hadn't named an animal. Perhaps it was time.

He looked back to his work, not having to squint into the sun to see his wife, and replied simply. "She's got a name."

"Oh? What is it?"

"Becky," he replied, resting his hand on the stump as if to ask it kindly to leave its nest.

Del smiled. "You named your horse after your mother?"

"The mother I never knowed."

"Well I think it's lovely. C'mon Becky," she gently clicked her cheeks and began leading her back to the barn. "Let's get Missy and go see the town." And as Becky's overgrown hooves found their way in the mud, Del called back over her shoulder to her husband, "And give the German woman my invitation when you get there!"

"You already made 'em out!?"

"They're on the table!" she called out. "Ask your mother!"

"Aw, hell," said he.

***

"The Mormon man and his boy are this way," Joejim told J.P., pointing not in the distance but to the ground beneath him. He didn't see.

J.P. dismounted Chance, nudged the anxious Erin away from his legs, and turned around. "What do you mean? Which way? You don't mean they are buried here, do you?"

Joejim was amused, but Elias was not. "No, Indian grave, not white man's. This is the path to the white man's farm."

Again J.P. turned around, and Elias watched him warily. They were standing on the north side of the Parallel Road, across but still within hearing distance of the Blue, whose tinkling melody joined the breeze rustling the grass in a choir of prairie song. There was nothing that indicated a path. Nothing at all. "I don't see the path," he said. Elias was surprised at his patience with Joejim, despite all his ignorance. "I don't see it at all, Joejim."

"You must take the first step," he said.

And J.P. Dugan did just that. He stepped off the road into the grass, and a path appeared before him. It eased a crooked way up a small hill and disappeared over a windswept ridge. "Thank you," he said, and again Elias was surprised. Perhaps J.P. was not so ignorant.

But as J.P. gathered Chance's reigns and began to walk the path, Joejim stopped him. "You must remember this when you seek him," he said.

"Seek who?" J.P. looked back over his shoulder, suddenly grasping his hat as it was nearly blown from his head. "I'm already seeking Clegg, and you have shown me the way."

Joejim smiled again, but in a piteous way this time. Poor J.P., thought Elias. Poor me, to travel with him.

"No," Joejim replied, "not Clegg. Your son." He glanced toward the west and nodded. "The boy who sought the Land of Death with a boulder upon his back."

***

"Of course I will provide a written testimony," said Clegg. Then, pensively, "I should have thought of that before I left Atchison." Then, with worry and regret, that made Elias's heart sink just a little, "I must say, it's very sad to hear it should have come to this for both families."

"You know," he continued as he sat at the table with pen and paper. "I can't help but wonder why Joseph engaged that Ingalls man, the lawyer." He bit his lip in feigned rumination, the way Elias's grandmother used to when she was trying to teach something. "Patrick would never try and jump the Hawkins claim." He tapped his pen on his lips. "Why a simple arrangement could not have been brokered I do not know."

J.P. smiled at him wryly. "Clegg, you and I are, shall we say," he clicked his tongue against his teeth, "wizened men." He laughed in feigned consideration, too, as if he were the teacher now and Clegg the pupil. "It's good to know someone our age in Kansas. Men of experience." Clegg set down the pen and interlaced his fingers. An invitation to continue. "I have great respect for Joseph James Hawkins," said J.P., glancing over at Elias then at the carafe of coffee, and motioned to it. "May I?"

Clegg nodded and tipped his fingers in approval. Elias's back straightened, his chest tight. He wondered how Roger, the Roger who came to Weston, could have been born of this man.

"And I have a great empathy for the Hawkins family. Del is a good woman. Sarah Sally is not without charm, and," he smiled as he dropped a cube of sugar into his coffee, "Missy is a gift from God, is she not?" Clegg nodded very slightly in agreement. "And Clegg, I want you to know that I not only respect and like the Hawkinses, I don't even see them as threats to my sons." He took a sip of coffee and set the cup back down again, but before he could continue, Clegg interrupted.

"You did it," he said, straightening his back.

J.P. smiled. "Why yes, yes I did."

"How?"

"I simply jumped the Hawkins claim."

Clegg's expression waited for an explanation, so he turned now, uncrossing his legs and aligning himself with his interlocutor, mirroring the interlacing of his hands. "Clegg, I think you can understand me. At least, I hope you can. My son Patrick," he glanced over at Little Joe, who averted his eyes, then at Elias, who kept still, "though he has suffered and struggled greatly, has failed to learn something very important in life thus far."

Clegg's wry smile slackened a little and his eyebrows arched in anticipation. At least he didn't trust J.P. either, thought Elias. "Oh? And what is that?"

J.P. grunted to himself with a smile. "Paddy has yet to learn that the Reckoning is not yet upon us." He sipped his coffee and guffawed. "Not even close. It's a long way off, and until that day, God reserves all judgment."

"And?"

"And, that means the wicked do as they please." J.P. Dugan's moustache dropped now, sagging under the weight of what was obviously his disappointment, and folly. Elias still held himself. There was no use in disagreeing with such a fanatic. Perhaps he would find his own way to Denver. "The meek may inherit the earth, Clegg, one day," he glanced one last time at Elias, "but until then, dragons have run of the place."

XXXII

At first, Missy didn't seem to want to sit atop the heavy-breathing, twitching, steaming Becky. But once she did, she didn't want to dismount ever again. Her mother had labored with some difficulty to keep the young, impatient mare to something short of a cantor the whole way, but the occasional bounce in an otherwise undulating trip to Atchison excited Missy. She laughed and giggled, bouncing in the crammed saddle with her hands in the air, until Del would clasp her little arms and place them on the pommel again, saying, "Don't you let go, now, my little star." But Missy seemed to know it didn't matter. Mamma would catch her.

Something was transfixing for Missy about the way Becky's mane, long neck, and head showed the way. She gazed at it like her reflection in a pool. Then she glanced at the river and said, "Mommy?"

"Yes, baby?"

"Horse water?"

Pause. "Do you think Becky is thirsty?"

Pause. "No," she pointed to the river, which they had begun to leave behind row of trees. "Horse. Water."

Pause. "Missy baby, we can't take her to the river now. We have to go to Sumner to see a professional gentleman. A lawyer."

"No!" Missy bounced. "Horse water!" Missy turned, nearly spinning herself out of the saddle, so she could see her mother's face.

"Baby, hold on tight! We'll get Becky some water in town. She's not so thirsty it's—"

"No! No! No!" she shrieked, bouncing (and finding that her mother was right about holding onto the pommel as she slipped off a little). "Horse water! Horse water! Horse water!"

"Melissa!" her mother retorted, holding her in the saddle after she slipped. "We can't go to the river now!"

"Mommy!" she said in her reddest voice. "Horse! Water!"

Pause. "Melissa, I don't know what you're trying to say, baby."

Del wasn't listening to her place of knowing. Missy saw the river in the mane of the mare, and realized horses come from water. She wanted to know if her mother saw how the water gave birth to the land. To everything.

***

Oddly enough, the Rocky Mountains reminded Roger of his mother. Not only had she never seen them, she had never seen anything like them. Not only that, she had never laid eyes on the continent to which these mountains served as a spine, a roof, center pillars that held up the fire-fretted blue. Yet, Roger could not help but think of her every time he looked west from Denver City, and saw the jagged horizon that towered indifferently above the puniness of man.

Just as oddly, the mountains also reminded Roger of the ocean. The night she died, his mother lay in her bunk in one of the deepest, darkest parts of the hold in a ship completely overladen with the desperate Irish. It was now also overridden with the sick and the dying, and rough seas meant the brothers either had to keep an arm pressed upon their mother's chest so she wouldn't roll off the plank like a restless child, or she herself had to clutch its frame with whatever strength she had left. Mountains, it seemed, were like that night on the ocean— impossibly humbling. Demanding of utter capitulation to their volition-less, uneven will.

Denver City was every bit as dangerous as Atchison, and even more void of morality. At least in Atchison the villainy often had at least the pretense of a higher cause. In Denver all that mattered was gold. Money, land, and gold. Even the good people who came to this tent city at the confluence of two small rivers—an altar at the feet of the blue and white knave—soon forgot their better natures. Cold, hungry, lonely, scared, they lied, cheated, stole, and fought over dust. To Roger Dugan, this meant they were nothing more than just that—dust. And so was he.

If anyone was ever more than dust (and he had come to wonder if anyone was), it was his mother. Mary Dugan was more than a woman, a mother, wife, or sister; she was more, even than her own, tear-ridden laughter; more than her slow way of moving; and more than her ability to feed starving sons with nothing more than water, salt, a bit of buttermilk, and a half-rotten potato while still somehow, someway, having them concentrate on what they were learning to read. She was more than her patient way of supporting, yet somehow still challenging, her activist husband, and certainly more than a victim who died needlessly. And it was because she had faith. Not in God, but in man. It was a faith as awesome and immovable as the mountains. And Roger knew he was losing that faith. Perhaps he never had it.

No better way to discover a lack of faith than in those days following Birsha's rejection. She'd broken his heart on the eleventh of September 1858, and it seemed to Roger that he somehow simply found himself in Denver City on the twenty-first of October. He remembered that he wandered into the wild prairies somewhere to the west. He knew that by day he could see herds of buffalo, thousands of them, and by night, no longer able to walk and huddling in the grass, he could feel, hear, smell, and sense their strange, hulking, misshapenness standing sentinel in the darkness. Grass, of course, grass that waved and chafed his lower legs raw; and sky. Pain, then emptiness, then nothing but dust.

At one point he had found a bit of a cliff, and considered jumping to his death into the flint and sandstone below. It wasn't the sort of mountain he knew now, here, but it was tall enough to precipitate his death, probably. He remembered licking a stone, thinking it was a loaf of bread. And yet another time he met a goat. A goat, of all things, in a place like that, and he remembered lunging for it, thinking he'd simply break its neck and eat it. But he missed. The goat didn't even move. Roger fell asleep and when he woke it was gone.

And he remembered the Kanza village emerging from the waves of prairie like billowing sails over the sea. Both the arched roofs of traditional log houses, covered in hide and bark, and the triangular roof of a large, stone, two-story building stood against the morning haze of the west, the smoke rising from them only in wisps, the tenders of the fires still sleeping. Roger simply happened upon the village in the dead of night, half-starved and delirious with grief, collapsed and fell asleep. Rising, he staggered across the river, up its steep bank with great difficulty and went to the stone house. He knocked, not sure if he would ask to be killed or beg for food and shelter. But there was no answer.

All was quiet. Horses were tethered between trees, patiently waiting for the day to begin. A dog chewed on a bone near one lodge, eyeing Roger with some suspicion but far more interested in the last shreds of flesh on the bone than any stranger. He decided he would announce himself at one of the lodge houses, wondering just what the etiquette for doing so might be. He decided he'd simply call out "hello, I am here."

Just as he prepared to do so, a man emerged from the flap of hide at the front of the lodge. He had been asleep, clearly, but there was more weariness than recent slumber in his face—it was a face he knew too well. The face of starvation and imminent death, the face of the men he remembered as a child marching to Cork City, clinging to each breath. It was how he felt.

And the man laughed. He took one look at this boy and laughed, and turned and in his native tongue to the women inside: "Come see the hunger of the white man, who so misunderstands love," said he.

And just then another man rode into the quiet village, one sleeve of his coat folded at the elbow and pinned to his shoulder flopping with the gait of his horse. He sat the horse and smiled oddly.

"You must choose," he grinned. His teeth were impeccable.

But it didn't seem to Roger he had much choice. This land would not let him starve, nor leap from a cliff, nor have the fortune of being trampled by bison. This wilderness would not kill him. It would only give him the choice of how to save himself. So he chose the one-armed Indian named Joejim. He'd have to find a different land if he was to die.

And now here he was in Denver, waiting, for what he did not know. For death, for birth, for love. Waiting at the foot of the cathedral of Earth.

***

Much like Quindaro, Sumner was built on an impossibly steep bank. A graded street rose from the river and lay upon the sandstone and soil as if the water and the earth were playing upon a see-saw together. And the water, bigger and older and ornery, sat heavily at the bottom, leaving the earth dangling its legs in the air like an idiot, crying for its mother.

This town was clearly built to rival Atchison, a Free State alternative on the Great Bend to the West in the river. Its founders had forced its existence into the woods on this bank, intent on leveling and clearing until the land bent to their will. Del sometimes could not help but think towns like these must have been built by young men without wives, so foolhardy were their settings.

"Mrs. Hawkins, do come in," said Mr. Ingalls. Missy laughed, as if this man's stiff wool suit and slick hair amused her. "I must tell you that you are the very first visitor to this office!" He led them in and they sat at a wooden table in wooden chairs that creaked.

"Missy, sit still," said her mother.

"It seems clients in Kansas prefer house visits."

"We are hard-workin' folk," said Del.

"Yes!" Ingalls had laughed twice already though nothing was funny. Perhaps this is what professional gentlemen did. They wore silly suits and laughed, all to entertain toddlers and their mothers. "Now," he set down a cup of coffee in front of Del without asking if she wanted one. Missy reached for it and Del pushed it away. "How can I help you?"

"I thought I'd a-come down here and see about our claim."

The man's eyes sparkled as if a candle sat between he and Del. "Yes," he began, blinking the sparkles into nothingness, "quite the complicated case, you see."

"I know." It occurred to Del that Missy had never seen her mother this way. Stiff, erect, hands in her lap. It didn't seem Missy liked it. Jumping down from the chair, she wandered over to a side table and picked up whatever it was that was on it.

"Oh no, please," said the man.

"Missy, sit down and a-keep quiet," said her mother, in the tone she'd only used a few times, the tone that was the end. Missy sat and slumped her head into her hand, feet dangling. "Please," said her now-stiff-backed mother, "continue, Mr. Ingalls."

"Well, I spoke with Mr. Patrick Dugan a while back, Mrs. Hawkins."

"Paddy."

He looked surprised. "Yes, uh, Mr. Paddy Dugan. And his father, Mr.—"

"J.P."

"Yes. Well, as you know, our strategy has been to file two claims, one against . . . J.P., as you call him, ordering him to quit the quarter-section upon which your cabin currently rests, and another contesting . . . Paddy's, claim, to that quarter-section."

"We only need one."

He looked surprised again. Even disappointed. "Yes. And this strategy was to ensure that would happen, one way or another, as it were."

"Yes," Del noticed she was mimicking his language, "and that is why I am here. What did Paddy and J.P. say?"

"It was interesting," Ingalls rose, his thumbs in his belt loops and boots on the floorboards looking unnatural, the way a bat does when crawling on the roof of the barn. "It seems Mr. . . . J.P., has decided to remove himself from the equation."

"Good!" Del rose in her seat even more, and her eyes sparkled. "I was a-hopin' so, as we ain't seen him. It's all settled then." She reached down beside her chair to pick up her things and Missy hopped down, ready to see the town again.

But Mr. Ingalls turned. His eyes sparkled now in a different way, swimming in themselves, almost as if an eddy moved across them, or a snake. "It doesn't have to be."

"What do you mean?"

"I mean," he said, turning again, "there are ways we can delay the claim upon which Mr. Paddy Dugan's cabin currently rests." He turned again, his eyes solid now. "It means that perhaps you can have both, Mrs. Hawkins."

Delilah J. Hawkins did not move, a raccoon caught by the coop at night. "We only need one."

Mr. Ingalls sat heavily in his chair now. "Mrs. Hawkins, perhaps I may speak with your husband about this matter? Gentlemen have a way of understanding such things in a different light."

And Deliliah J. stood now, smiling. "Of course," she said, turning to go. "But I reckon you'll find he's another sort of man, Mr. Ingalls."

***

Between Sumner and Atchison lay a bluff, white cliffs towering above the water. Deliliah J. and Missy decided to follow Becky up it; the mare was fairly adamant about it once the road curved around toward the west, making an arc between the towns. Becky seemed tired of things that slithered across the ground and preferred a direct route, and this just happened to lay up, then down. So be it, thought Del. Becky will get us home.

But she stopped at the top. The wind played in the leaves of the scrub oak and elm, and in the silence among and between the signing leaves something else could be heard. A moan. Missy began to cry.

Del held her tightly but gently and soothed the horse, speaking to both in hushed tones and in a language older than one she knew, one she didn't speak and had no meaning. Both calmed and sighed.

Delilah J. Hawkins sat erect again in the saddle, peering into the trees that fell into the shadows as the bluff fell toward the river and the east. She was listening now.

"Hello Molly," she said. "We hear you." She took a deep breath, closed her eyes, and opened them again. "We hear you, girl." The moaning stopped, and all, everything—mother and daughter, horse and trees and river and earth and sky; all the world atop this little hill in Kansas—began to breath together.

"I'm so, so sorry," said she.

XXXIII

Joseph James and Delilah J. buried Sarah Sally next to her son in the grove. Just after noon, the last shovelful of earth being laid upon her, a wind ripped through the land and a thunderclap sent them running inside, barely able to breath. Just over the trees to the northwest, too, the Dugans covered their Doubting Moon, their Thomas, in blanket after blanket, and they all knew the dragon was in this storm, scattering himself over the land in a hundred million droplets of water.

Sarah Sally had passed in the mid-morning, the only warning being that she said that it was time to die. Joseph James didn't believe his now-not-mother at first, as she had said this a hundred millions times before, but then realized she had turned green, and that Hawkinses turned green just before they die.

Del stroked her mother in-law's hair and she slipped away. It was a beautiful morning, a breeze moving through the cabin, carrying with it the dawn chorus. Sarah Sally seemed to want to speak with her now-not-son, but he sat apart, awkward and uneasy. Looking at the ceiling and the floor, the walls, the bible upon the table, anything but her, this woman who had taken him in with love but spent decades withholding it.

Finally, Sarah Sally found the strength to say with enough force that he could hear, "Go to her." The Hawkinses sat, silently, not knowing what the dying woman meant. "Go to your mother," said she, "go to Rebecca." But Joseph James fidgeted, spat, and busied himself.

After some time she slipped away some more, and enough morning had passed that Rags and Missy were hungry, not to mention the next Hawkins, who grew alarmingly quickly inside her mother, and Del decided she must feed the family.

The cabin filled with sounds and smells now, of dishes and bacon and eggs, of children and sticks and rocks, of a married couple discussing adult things that involved land surveys and lawyers and money and crops. They opened the door and a window to try and move the air, and the songs of cardinals and finches filled the room. Even a frog's voice could be heard as he passed the front door, reminding them all again of sweet little Ollie.

And Sarah Sally passed peacefully, alone, in the corner of the Hawkins house, listening.

***

Sunday evening, the night of Del's party, it began to rain. Yes, it had rained hard the last couple days, but that evening it rained so hard it was as if the water wanted the land back; that, as Missy observed in the mane of Becky the mare, the mother wished to resume gestating her child. Perhaps the earth wasn't ready yet to sustain the myriad things, the Kanza and Wyandotte, Germans and Irishmen, Northerners and Southerners, the slaves and freemen, the women and men with their livestock and cabins, reservations and treaties, trails and surveyor's chains that marked off the land eight feet by eight feet by eight feet until the curvature of the globe made them pause, and correct. Perhaps if it rained enough another earth could emerge from the great waters, and the pause, the correction, would last forever.

Most were safe enough, the women having arrived at Delilah's cabin before the creeks began swelling. The men, all insisting they escort their wives, saw the storm coming and huddled beside the Hawkins barn. And the children all had bigger children to watch them. Loving cousins and sisters and brothers, as well as the occasional grandmother who didn't care about Del's party.

Only J.P. Dugan was in peril.

Joejim and Elias had both warned him, yet J.P. woke in the middle of the night as the river licked his toes. So gentle, so horribly and duplicitously kind was this prairie stream, a predator toying with its prey. J.P. should never be fooled by water, having seen what it could do in Australia. And yet he'd not heeded Joejim's warning, thinking it was about Indians. The river took them in sleep, he'd said. White man farm, Indian grave, he'd said. J.P. took it as a warning that lying in wait beneath the waving crests of the grasses were the wronged, that at any moment an Indian who had lost his cousin, say, or squaw, may rise up and strike down the lonely traveler and take his scalp. But Joejim was speaking of another vengeance cut deep into the soils of Kansas. The wrath of the flood, of God Himself. Elias had understood all this, halting his old horse beside the creek, suggesting they camp out in the open land above. But J.P. had followed that cut straight down, deep into the earth, into Hell Itself. Elias refused, said they would meet again in Denver.

The Smoky Hill branch of the Kaw had been at least four body-lengths from him as he fell asleep, but as the current now pulled his entire foot out from his blanket, he realized that could only have been a quarter hour ago. By the time he stood, it was already around his ankles, filling the ravine from bank to bank, tearing both apart, large chunks of mud falling into the onslaught. The crossing, the only hope for scrambling out, was upstream a good quarter-mile. So wise, he thought of himself at the time, leading Chance and Erin downstream into the snug hug of the earth, where an Indian would almost have to step on him to see him. But now he was trapped. As the water came now to his knees, and the rumbling of the approaching flood became louder than the rain itself, he saw his blanket and boots wash away. He heard Erin bellow above the scream of the water.

She had scrambled up the muddy bank and was trying to climb atop Chance, who was also sidling up beside the mud, a large root system exposed in the cut of the bank. Her hooves sank and slipped in the water as both tore the dirt at the foot of the earth. But she pulled them out and seemed to be moving up, toward the grasses still swaying happily in the wind. Erin jumped for the saddle blanket, pulling it halfway off and falling into the water below the mare.

J.P. lunged and caught the dog, hauling her by the scruff toward himself just before she was swept away. He scrambled up the bank with great effort, almost losing Erin twice and himself once, tossed the wet rag of a dog up and mounted behind her. The water was now just inches below Chance's breast, but she clung stubbornly to the slope and J.P. reached up, tangling his arms in the roots as best he could, as the roar of the flood reached an ungodly tone and volume. It sounded like a million-billion people dying, as if all the wronged and the guilty alike cried out from eternity.

For a moment he thought perhaps they should let go, allow the river to take them downstream to another flat section. Chance was a pretty good swimmer. But with a man and dog on her back, in the roiling, twisted debris, she didn't seem sure of her abilities either. She seemed to prefer clinging to earth. So this was it. He would have to sit atop this horse and hang onto this branch and pray. Pray the water would not rise any further. Pray the horse had the strength to stand in the rapids for as long as it took for the rain to ease, drain, make its way to the sea.

*****

Delilah J. Hawkins knew she knew better. Just before the knock came at the door, something told her Maria would arrive unannounced, uninvited, hurt. But she was too busy preparing for her new friends to hear it. How could she be so cold? Her hands busied themselves in an arachnidan way as this thought paled her face, and she glanced over at the women with their tea and newspapers.

"Come in," she called out, then stopped, went to the door and opened it.

"Del?" Maria looked in and saw them. The women. And she began to walk away.

"Maria, wait!" But Maria didn't wait. She stormed past the barn with her basket swaying on her arm thudding into her hip. "Maria! Maria, wait!"

Delilah J. ran after Maria Dugan, and as the wind swirled the rain began to fall and she clasped her friend with her hard hands softly. "I'm sorry Maria," she began. "I shoulda invited you."

Maria smiled, her small freckled mouth quivering. "I would not expect that of you, Del." She looked up, so sadly Del felt her heart quiver like her friend's lips. "Not two months ago my husband came here with a gun and threatened yours. Perhaps we have finally had enough, you and I."

Above them and to the west the storm began to gather its legs under itself. It paused, purple and black curls swirling as if a snake around a tree. And the rain began to louden the world, one curtain blown across the window at first, but then suddenly in a torrent. Del's response was interrupted by this, but also by the shouts of men, which could be heard even over the roar of the oncoming storm.

Lightning streaked across the sky and she saw by the barn, her husband shouting at Maria's; other men gathering around. They looked like a pack of wild dogs hiding in the shadows. Yes, Del should have known. She watched it all unfold, crescendo into the raging wind. Once, as a girl, she'd seen the very birth of a Platte River flood. Sure, it grew gradually as each little droplet from miles away added to each little droplet, and rose slowly from the depths, but there was most certainly a single moment when the river topped its banks and the tipping point began. One bird can start an entire flock into panic. One drop begins a flood. One warm day begins the spring tornados, and one fight rekindles a war.

And Del felt from within a rage, a wild desire to chase the stupid men from her home where inside her friends were breaking bread together. And so she did.

Picking up a stick she ran at them screaming, "Just stop it! Stop it! Stop it!" In another flash of lightning she saw all their eyes. Utterly useless was their expression. She beat each one once with the stick—her Joseph James, Paddy, Ingalls the Lawyer, two or three other men she did not know. Each took their caning like a child.

Yes, Del might have known. She only wanted the women, but the men took them to the Hawkins place and thought they might—what?—stand stupidly beside the barn all evening a-waitin'? This full mooned flood in the middle of May, 1859, thrust it all to this spot on Deer Creek, this place they called home. All the mud of Kansas was at her feet now.

This small mob of useless men now appeared to be a single creature and looked at her. They had heard her voice, but with it they felt the wind from the wings of the beast as it alighted on the earth next to her. It lay beside her, its tail quivering in the woods behind, and its benign face fell into a tamed sadness.

But Del's did not. She glanced at the dragon, smiled and chuckled at the shocked faces of the men; her housedress fit her the way only a homemade and recently patched and newly hemmed garment can.

Then, quietly, "Just stop," said she.

***

Some one hundred miles to the west J.P. Dugan still clutched root with hands and horse with legs with all his might. The rain began to subside, and he was finally able to look up. The storm lifted itself off the earth and lay flat above her, lidding the plains and impossibly closing what just that evening was an endless sky. That endlessness now lay east and west, the tail and nose of thunderous clouds arched moonward as it bucked and wound its way over the land. The moon began to fall in behind the storm with the stars to the west, which she dulled unintentionally as she peered from behind the veil of the flat swimming fins of the cloud, embarrassed by her own brilliance. And J.P., for a moment, thought he was safe.

To his right lay the muddy bank, and it occurred to him that perhaps he must do the unthinkable and leave Erin and Chance to their fate; jump from atop the saddle and pull himself up by the grass, the whiskers of the earth. But in glancing upward to gauge how high he must jump, a nose peered from over the ledge of the bank. It was an odd nose, not dog, not human, not cat or horse or even kangaroo. And yet, it was all those things. And he knew what it must be. The dragon. The devil. The slithering beast he'd unleashed into the world, he himself; the one that peered from above him in Ireland and Tasmania and now Kansas. He was peering down at himself, watching himself drown. No, he would not be permitted to abandon his animals again. They would share their fate now.

Hearing the subsiding in the rush of the water after another fifteen minutes or so of pain, of aching in forearms and thighs as he and Erin and Chance clung to one another, he realized, almost as if a voice deep inside were telling him that the beast—who still sat peeking over the edge—would allow only one option. To swim. To let the flood decide his fate. To share his fate not only with beast, but with water.

He prodded Chance into the steady stream. She resisted, her haunches quivering in exhaustion, and clung to the bank with a snort. Erin shivered now, again, and looked at him imploringly.

"Don't worry, my dear," said he. "In the end, the water takes us all." He petted her lovingly on the head, leaned over and stroked Chance on the neck, whispering to her in Gaelic and Aborigine, English and Kanza, in tongues unknown to any tongue. And he said, "Come my dears, we mustn't resist, for that is insanity. We are one."

And so horse, and man, and dog, all one three-headed, ten-legged, two-armed creature, eased with great grace into the deepest part of the channel, turning serenely as if made for swimming, and began to float downstream. It was all too easy. They came to the clearing, fought some in scrambling to the rocky, hoof-packed dirt, and collapsed in the grass.

And along the sky swam the beast.

***

But Maria had gotten away. Del ran for her again, into the violence of the west, where a clearing in the storm revealed a funnel falling to the ground, as if God wished to wipe out this corner of Kansas and rid the puny humans of their suffering.

Maria turned on her now before she could clasp her arm.

"It's done!" she cried, the quivering in her face taking hold and tears streaming down her red cheeks. "We can't be friends, Del. God has cursed us." She looked over at the approaching tornado, with irritation at first, and then a beatific sigh came to her. She raised her hand to silence the sky, and an eerie pause came to the evening. The swish of the distant funnel could be heard as if a giant hand were washing linens in the clouds, but the wind and rain immediately around them stopped, and the hand in the heavens began to draw the funnel back, pulling the sheets out of the washtub and leaving a turbid but calming basin of life. With a wave of her hand she bid the storm north.

"No, but no!" Del lurched forward and grasped Maria's hands. They were cold and pasty. "Kansas is a-drownin' us all, Maria, you know that. If it ain't a-squabblin' over slavery it's over these little lines and the squares in them. But," she looked at the black sky, then back to Maria, waiting for eyes to be met, "you and I, we's like water, Maria. Let the rest be stones. You and I, we find our way around them. We a find our way to each other."

Maria smiled through a large, final tear.

"Oh honey, don't cry," said Del, but she also began to cry. "Don't you go and a-make me cry too!"

Maria chuckled and sniffled. "You invited my mother and not me."

And they laughed, both of them. "No I didn't! I invited the rest. Your mother invited herself."

And they laughed some more. "Delilah J.," Maria said, "I believe God gave you to me."

"Aw now, it's just like I said. We's like water, you and I."

"We always find each other."

"Yes honey, we sure do."

And they turned back to the east, to her cabin and her farm and the warmth inside, the returning light of spring dawning again that day; while the rest watched the storm gather again in the north, above the patient earth.

Glossary of Principal Historical Characters

Paschal Pensoneau. Considered the first permanent white settler in Atchison County, Pensoneau was a French fur-trapper, trader, and interpreter who had long lived with the Kickapoo Indians. He fought in the Mexican-American and Blackhawk Wars, for which he was awarded land in Kansas Territory near the present site of Potter. His house served as the county's first polling place, though he later moved west with the Kickapoo when their reservation was diminished.

Charles Robinson. An agent of the New England Emigrant Aid Society, Robinson helped found the Free State Party, write its constitution, and was elected territorial governor by that party. He organized the defense of Lawrence during the Wakarusa War of 1855 and negotiated the truce that ended it. The next May he fled, following the shooting of Sheriff Jones, was arrested in Missouri, and held for several months by the Pro Slavery legislature under charges of treason. Upon his release, he resumed being active in Free State politics and helped found the town of Quindaro.

James Henry Lane. Former Lieutenant Governor of Indiana, Lane also served as a member of the United States Congress and as a Colonel in the Mexican-American War before moving to Kansas in 1856. A renowned orator who was very active in territorial politics, he helped form the Free State Party, write its version of the state constitution, and was elected to the House of Representatives under it, only to be denied the seat once arriving in Washington. He subsequently went on a speaking and fund-raising tour and returned to Kansas with armed men from Iowa and Illinois, "Lane's Army of the North." Their route into the territory was known as "Lane's Trail" and approximates the current path of Highway 59 from Topeka to the Nebraska border. He remained an active leader in Free State organizations and his army sought to police constitutional referenda.

Patrick Laughlin. Laughlin was an Irish immigrant involved in the organization of the Kansas Legion in the northeast part of the territory, a secret military arm unofficially supporting the Free State Party. During one of its meetings he was accused of treachery to the Legion by a man named Sam Collins, who also threatened him repeatedly. Laughlin may have been acting in self-defense when he shot Collins. He later moved into Atchison where he became a tinsmith and was widely known to have killed Collins, but was never prosecuted.

John H. Stringfellow. A Virginian by birth, Stringfellow was a doctor from Missouri who helped found Atchison in 1854. He was active in Pro Slavery militias and the territorial government, serving as its Speaker of the House. His Atchison-based newspaper, the *Squatter Sovereign*, was as vehement a Pro Slavery publication as any in the Territory, often associated with the motto "Death to all Yankees and Traitors in Kansas!" He later became a subscription agent for a bank owned in part by Free Staters and sold the *Sovereign* to Free State interests.

Mrs. Stringfellow. Wife of Dr. John H. Stringfellow, Mrs. Stringfellow reportedly saw James H. Lane dressed as a woman one fall afternoon, and also entertained him in a separate incident.

Judge Lecompte. Samuel Dexter Lecompte was appointed by President Pierce as Chief Justice of the Kansas Territorial Supreme Court. His decisions were frequently heavily biased toward Pro Slavery interests.

George Million. Million owned one of the first two tracts of land in the future site of the town of Atchison and sold his land to the Town Company, joining it in the process. He operated a ferry across the river for many years as well as several businesses in town, including the Pioneer Saloon.

Samuel Jones. Appointed in the summer of 1855 by Acting Governor Woodson, Sam Jones was the first Sheriff of Douglas County. A Virginian with staunch Pro Slavery views, Jones assisted in destroying ballot boxes during the elections of 1855 and used his office to promote the views of Southerners and repress those of Free Staters. He was personally involved in both the Wakarusa War and the May, 1856 sack of Lawrence, which largely started as a result of Jones's being shot by a Free State sniper while sitting in his tent one night. It was widely reported that he had been killed and his death became a rallying cry for Missourians intent on destroying Lawrence.

John Brown. One of the most prominent figures in American history, Old John Brown was a zealous abolitionist from New York and saw himself as a key figure in God's plan to purge the Union of slavery. He followed his sons to Kansas in 1856 and orchestrated the shocking murder of five unarmed Pro Slavery men in the "Pottawatomie Massacre" as a reprisal for the siege of Lawrence. He is credited with winning the first battle of "Bleeding Kansas" at Black Jack Springs, an engagement some believe to be the first battle of the Civil War. He then helped organize small defense companies and became a Captain in the Free State Militia. His son was the first casualty of the Battle of Osawatomie and he became known nationally as "Osawatomie Brown." He was a fugitive for many months afterwards, operating an underground railroad that smuggled slave from Missouri to Nebraska, following Lane's Trail. He left Kansas to lead an uprising of slaves in the South.

Alexander W. Doniphan. A lawyer and western-Missouri politician, Doniphan was colonel of the 1st Missouri Dragoons in the Mexican-American War. From 1846-1848 he led his men west from Ft. Leavenworth, Kansas to New Mexico, south to the Sacramento River, and east to the Gulf of Mexico in one of the longest marches undertaken by any army since Alexander the Great. His command won the Battles of El Brazito, Monterrey, and Sacramento despite being a volunteer force that was largely distrusted by the rest of the army. In the Battle of the Sacramento River, a Mexican cannon was captured by his men, labeled "Old Sacramento," and hauled back to Missouri where it stood silent in the armory at Columbia for nearly ten years, until it was stolen and pressed into service by Atchison's Kickapoo Rangers in the May, 1856 siege of Lawrence. It was then captured by Free Staters at the First Battle of Franklin and used against the Missourians in the Battle of Hickory Point. Doniphan is also well known in Mormon history for his refusal to execute Mormon prisoners in 1838, including the prophet Joseph Smith, despite being ordered by Missouri Governor Lilburn Boggs to do so. He remained neutral in the battles over Kansas.

Samuel C. Pomeroy. An agent of the New England Emigrant Aid Society, Pomeroy was involved in the founding of Osawatomie and served as a Captain in the Free State militia and Secretary of the Lawrence Security Committee during the absence of Lane and Robinson in May of 1856. He later became active in Atchison businesses and owned shares in other settlements, including Quindaro.

John W. Geary. The third Governor of Kansas Territory, Geary was the last to be appointed by President Pierce. When he arrived in Kansas in September of 1856, he inherited a region on the brink of civil war. He acted quickly to disarm the militia his predecessor, Acting Governor Woodson, had mustered and stopped yet another attack on Lawrence. Nearly a hundred prisoners were taken shortly after the Battle of Hickory Point and held for trial near Lecompton under his authority. His administration strengthened more objective federal responses but he was soon run out of the territory by Pro Slavery forces.

Clarina Irene Howard Nichols. Perhaps the most unsung heroine of the women's rights movement in the 1850s, Clarina Nichols moved to Kansas to support abolitionism and to advocate for suffrage for women in the state constitution. She was a gifted and courageous leader, politician, writer, and orator.

Birsha Howard. Birsha was Clarina's daughter from her first marriage. She lived with Clarina for many years in Kansas and was a school mistress for both white and black children in Quindaro.

Robert J. Walker. Walker served as governor of Kansas Territory for much of 1857. A former senator from Mississippi and a staunch defender of slavery, he was nonetheless unsupportive of the Pro Slavery Lecompton Constitution and resigned, citing voter fraud. He was replaced by James W. Denver.

John James Ingalls. Ingalls was a young and skillful lawyer and writer from Massachusetts. He was attracted to Sumner as a Free State port on the river, and his letters home to his father provide wonderful glimpses into life in Territorial Kansas.

Joejim. Joseph James Jr. was an interpreter for the Kaw and U.S. government. Of Osage, Kaw, and French descent, he is credited with naming Topeka, Kansas. His arm was amputated in his 30s.

Principal Locales in the First Two Songs

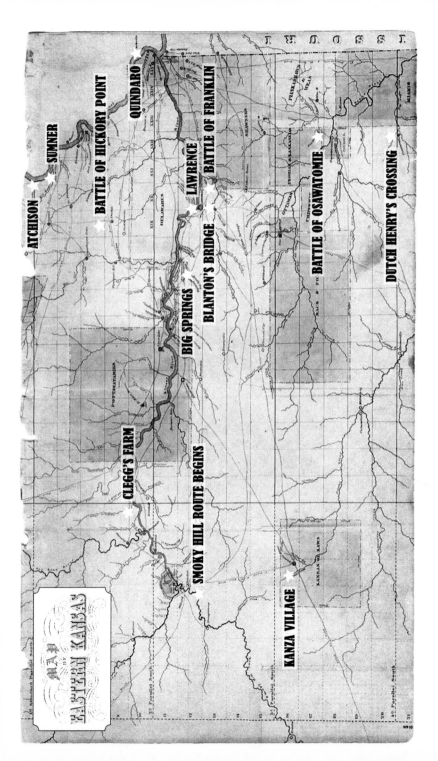

MAP OF EASTERN KANSAS

ATCHISON
SUMNER
BATTLE OF HICKORY POINT
QUINDARO
LAWRENCE
BATTLE OF FRANKLIN
BLANTON'S BRIDGE
BIG SPRINGS
CLEGG'S FARM
SMOKY HILL ROUTE BEGINS
KANZA VILLAGE
BATTLE OF OSAWATOMIE
DUTCH HENRY'S CROSSING

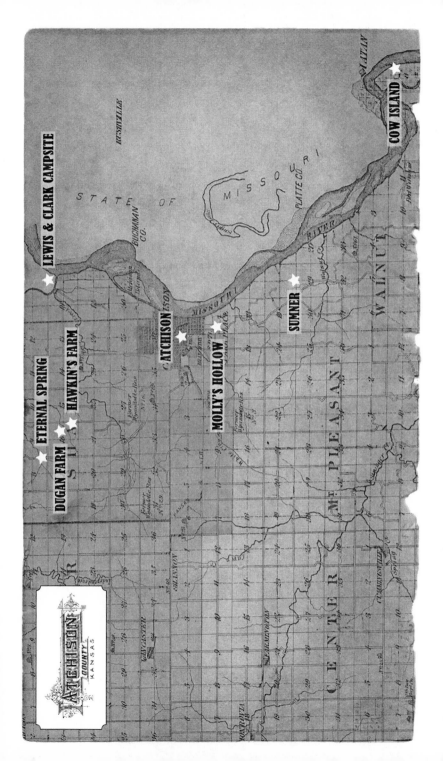

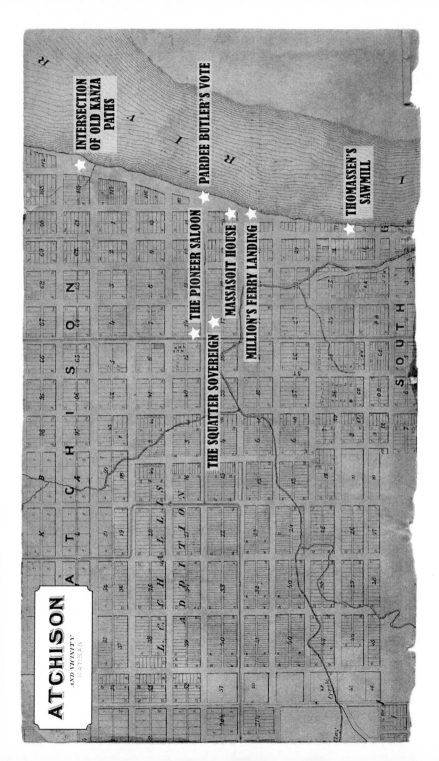

ATCHISON
AND VICINITY
KANSAS

INTERSECTION OF OLD KANZA PATHS

PARDEE BUTLER'S VOTE

THE PIONEER SALOON

MASSASOIT HOUSE

MILLION'S FERRY LANDING

THOMASSEN'S SAWMILL

THE SQUATTER SOVEREIGN

Acknowledgements

Again, I am indebted to my family and all the people at Wooden Stake for their support, advice, and kindness. Joan the Ruthless, who is more than an editor, guided my hand a second time. Lindsey, an old friend and talented artist. My son, of whom I am proud, but who I also deeply admire. With this second novel I am also grateful for the readers of the first, particularly those who attended readings and book talks, sharing their family stories with me. They influenced my writing and my life more than they realize.

Most of all, I am thankful to my wife Laurie. In her I find a convergence of love and strength I could never express in words.

Bonus Material:
www.jackmarshallmaness.com

CPSIA information can be obtained
at www.ICGtesting.com
Printed in the USA
LVOW12s0120150416

483699LV00004BA/147/P